Holiday by the Sea

Annie's Holiday by the Sea

bookouture

Published by Bookouture
An imprint of StoryFire Ltd.
23 Sussex Road, Ickenham, UB10 8PN
United Kingdom
www.bookouture.com

ISBN: 978-1-78681-297-1
ISBN: 978-1-78681-063-2
eBook ISBN: 978-1-78681-062-5

For Tim, my very own handsome hero

Chapter One

There's a hand on my arse – and it isn't mine. Some pervert in this sauna-hot Tube carriage has clamped his sweaty fingers to my left buttock, like a climber clinging on to a rock face. And as the three men squished up against me in this London transport hellhole are all looking shifty, it's hard to tell which one of them is the groper.

Fortunately I'm wearing comfortable big pants today which means that, as well as my jersey skirt, there's a substantial layer of easy-wash polyester between me and skin-on-skin contact.

As luck would have it, I'm also wearing my best shoes. Black, shiny shoes with two inch spiky heels, just perfect for my last day at the charitable trust where I've been working as a PA to the chief exec – and ideal for spearing the fleshy upper part of a man's foot.

The sour-smelling businessman behind me, whose breath is warming my neck, gives a high-pitched yelp as my heel hits home, and the hand slides off my backside. Result! And lucky first time, too. Years of living in London have sharpened my instincts when it comes to identifying the dodgy bastards, from crack addicts and lairy teenagers to middle-aged, married businessmen who get a thrill from touching up strangers.

'Nice one, love,' whispers the large perspiring woman crushed against my boobs, giving the buttock-clamper a glare. 'They should all be thrown off the train, preferably while it's moving.'

We grin at one another while I slip my hand into my bag and feel around for my lip salve. Chilly January winds are drying out my skin. But I pull my fingers out quickly when they brush against the edges of an envelope. I'm not sure why I'm still carrying the letter around with me, especially as it's been in the dustbin twice, so the thick cream-coloured paper is stained with tomato sauce and grease.

'I promise that I'll throw the damned letter away properly when I get home,' I mutter under my breath. And I won't almost upend myself in the dustbin trying to get it back out again.

Once I'm rid of the letter I can get back to my lovely, carefree life in the thriving, beating heart of the nation – where we pile into tin tubes and whizz round the city's arterial system, deep underground with the rats and the gropers. London might be dirty and noisy and a ridiculously expensive place to live, but it's been my home since I was born in Ealing twenty-nine years ago and I love it.

There's plenty of city centre dirt and rush-hour noise when I emerge, blinking, from the Tube station at King's Cross. A police siren is wailing in the distance and a fug of car fumes drifts like mist around the people hurrying along the packed pavements. The small bouquet of hothouse roses presented to me by staff at the Trust is looking decidedly droopy but the flowers might revive if I shove them into water at Maura's flat. I'll probably let Maura keep them because she could do with a treat.

Three months ago, when Harry was born, Maura's tiny flat was filled with flowers. But since then the heady scent of fresh blooms has been replaced by a faint aroma of last night's tea, dirty nappies and rubber. The rubber whiff comes from the cycle shop underneath whose clientele is made up of whippet-thin women in neon-striped Lycra. Or 'lucky cows without kids who still have a life', as Maura refers to them. Though I know she loves Harry to pieces, even when he's projectile puking like something from *The Exorcist*.

'Come in,' says Maura, yanking open her front door and tucking a strand of blonde hair behind her ear. 'Don't worry about taking off your shoes. The place is a total tip so I'm not worried about mud on the carpet.'

I slip my shoes off anyway and follow her through an obstacle course of baby paraphernalia piled up in the narrow, dark hallway. The lounge is equally cluttered, with a pushchair in the corner and a boxed travel cot. Maura has to move a mountain of cloth nappies onto the floor so I can sit down. There's so much stuff everywhere I feel claustrophobic, especially when a pile of baby clothes falls into my lap.

'So how was your leaving do, then?' asks Maura, rubbing her eyes. Without waiting for my answer, she gives the nappies a kick. 'Sodding things! It's all very well saving the planet by not using disposable nappies but where are the eco-PC brigade at 3 a.m. when I'm scraping shit off terry towelling with my eyes shut?'

She stifles a yawn and grimaces when Harry starts squealing in the small bedroom next door.

'Paul!' she yells, putting her head round the door and shouting towards the galley kitchen. 'Harry's crying and it's your turn.'

'Bloody useless,' she mutters under her breath when Paul drops pans into the sink with a passive-aggressive clatter and stomps into the bedroom. 'I was up all night doing feeds so the least he can do is pull his weight during the day.' She closes her eyes and takes a deep breath. 'Anyway, enough about my domestic bliss. How did it go with the big goodbye? Did you cry?'

'Hardly! I've only been there a year and it was time to move on.' I think back to my low-key leaving do with tea and cake and people giving me awkward hugs. 'I'll miss them but I don't feel sad about it.'

'No, you really don't,' says Maura with a puzzled look. 'Personally, I'd hate all the chopping and changing you do with your jobs but I guess you're just brilliant at goodbyes.'

She's right. If there was a degree in saying goodbye and moving on, I'd have a double first. Moving on is underrated by people who opt to put down roots and – shudder – settle down. Mortgage, marriage, babies, lunch with the parents. It's fine if that's what you want but keeping on the move when it comes to jobs and relationships makes life far less complicated. Particularly if, like me, you have no family ties at all.

Maura squeezes in beside me on the sofa and puts her hand on mine. 'But will you be OK without a job? I know you like these short-term work contracts but they seem stressful to me.'

She looks so concerned, my heart suddenly feels fluttery with panic. But I quickly get a grip on myself.

'Of course, I'll be fine,' I reassure her with a smile. 'I always knew the Trust job was a maternity cover contract. It's nothing to worry about, and certainly nothing to spoil our evening out. I'm planning on celebrating the end of my contract and the start of my freedom. Who knows what's next? That's part of the fun.'

'Ah yes, our evening out.' Maura stands quickly and kicks shut the door of an overflowing cupboard. 'I'm really sorry, Annie. I know we were supposed to be going out but Paul has suddenly remembered that he's got a works do this evening –' she moves closer to the door and raises her voice '– which is really inconvenient and inconsiderate and unfair when I so rarely get out of the flat these days.'

'Oh, do give it a rest, Maura,' shouts Paul from the bedroom, which starts Harry wailing all over again.

'Sorry, Annie,' says Maura, seeing my face fall. 'I'd love to go out, but you're welcome to stay here and we can get a takeaway and watch telly instead.' She stifles a yawn. 'Though I won't be vibrant company, what with Harry not sleeping through. My mum thinks he's teething which is terrifying if one tooth causes so much chaos. He's got another nineteen of the little buggers waiting to carve their way through his gums between midnight and dawn. I kick Paul to get up and do his bit but he lies there and pretends he's dead.' She lowers her voice and leans towards me. 'I so miss what I had.'

'Before you had Harry?'

'No, before I got feckin' married,' says Maura darkly, picking up one of Paul's socks from the floor and twisting it viciously into a tight knot. 'You are so lucky, Annie.'

I nod sympathetically and try not to look smug because I know I'm lucky. I've got my own life. OK, so I don't have a job at the moment but something will come up, it always does. But I'm mortgage-free with a lovely, handsome boyfriend who doesn't cramp my style, and no family to tie me down. An image of the grease-spattered letter nestling in my handbag floats into my mind but I bat it away.

'Here!' Maura waves a takeaway menu for the Terrific Thai Palace in my face. 'Pick what you fancy and I'll give them a call. Order as much as you like because Paul's paying.'

In the end I stay for the takeaway and a cuddle with Harry, who smells of milk as he dribbles onto my shoulder. But I give Maura a hug and leave when she starts nodding off into her pad thai. What Maura needs is an early night and my change of plan means I can pay a surprise visit to Stuart.

Normally, Stuart and I never see one another on Fridays because we go out with our own friends instead – it's become a kind of rule. But he told me he was having an evening in tonight, and rules are there to be broken. Plus I'd really like to see him. We've been going out for more than six months now, which is a bit of a record for me, and I'm getting used to having him around.

It's dark and chilly when I hobble down Pentonville Road to the station, with my earphones in and my favourite Ed Sheeran tracks playing. My weapon-grade shoes are pinching my toes and all I can think of is sinking my throbbing feet into a hot bath. Maybe I'll have one at Stuart's, in his gleaming tub with its jacuzzi jets, and he can join me. I smile at the thought and a young man lolloping towards me with his jeans at half-mast smiles back and winks.

The traffic is still crazy busy at King's Cross and I ferret through my handbag for my Oyster card while waiting at the crossing for the green man to appear. It never ceases to amaze me how much crap can fit into a small bag – a half-eaten tube of Polos, hand cream, a tatty notebook, a ton of tissues, the lip salve I couldn't find earlier.

My fingers close round the letter again, and this time I give in and pull out the thick envelope which has 'Miss Annabella Trebarwith' in black type above the address of my Stratford flat. It arrived almost a week ago and, after I'd quickly scanned through the letter inside, it's been in my handbag ever since – apart from a couple of forays into the bin. Out of sight, out of mind, though that doesn't seem to be working too well. I'm usually great at ignoring things that upset me but the letter keeps niggling at the edges of my brain, like a panther waiting to pounce.

'Why can't people leave me alone?' I murmur, shoving the letter back into my bag as the green man beeps and I'm swept across the road by a surge of impatient commuters.

Chapter Two

There's no one in the foyer of the mansion block near Earl's Court station, where Stuart lives. Ageing concierge Peter is usually at the front desk but he's nowhere to be seen, though curls of steam are wafting from his coffee cup so he can't have gone far. Taking advantage of his absence, I run my fingers across his desk and stand for a moment absorbing the atmosphere. I love this glorious 1930s building; the cherry wood panelling on the walls, twisting banisters and thick smell of furniture polish. Visiting Stuart is like stepping back in time into a bubble of art deco elegance, while people with heads buried in their iPhones hurry by outside.

I usually take the stairs – especially now I'm approaching thirty and determined to get fit – but my feet are killing me. So I wait for the creaky lift instead and take it to the fourth floor. If the weather's nice tomorrow, I'll slap on some blister plasters, put on my comfy trainers and go for a run round the Olympic Park to make up for it.

The burgundy carpet outside Stuart's flat is worn but his door is a freshly painted navy blue with a gleaming gold letter box. I turn my key in the lock and creep inside, keen to surprise him with the jumbo bar of his favourite chocolate that I bought at the station.

The TV's on so I tiptoe through the hall, past the art deco floor lamp with its black and white dragonflies picked out in glass across the shade. The hall walls are a delicate shade of duck-egg blue which contrasts beautifully with the snow-white coving and cornicing. Stuart has the most amazing taste – particularly when it comes to women, he reckons, and I'm hardly going to argue with that.

The front room door is closed but I fling it open and jump inside with the chocolate held out ahead of me like a magic wand.

'Behold, I come bearing Toblerone!'

'Oh fuck!' Stuart's head bobs up over the back of his black, corduroy sofa which is facing away from me towards the flat-screen TV. His white shirt is unbuttoned, his face is sweaty and there's a lipstick-red rash on his neck.

'Stuart?' I stride round the side of the sofa and there's Melinda, the woman who works in his office at Base and Harwood Financial Accountancy. I met her at Christmas in the pub, where she was looking beautifully turned out in a taupe trouser suit and perfect make-up with a Chanel bag. She intimidated the hell out of me.

She's not looking as self-possessed right now. Her white-blonde hair is mussed up and her cashmere jumper, scarlet to match her lips, is on the floor along with her skirt and red-soled shoes.

Though I feel like someone's punched me in the chest, I'm still with it enough to notice that the bra and tiny pants she's wearing are matching. They're probably Myla, damn her. She's undoubtedly the type of woman who never wears big pants, even on days when she doesn't expect to be shagged by her boyfriend. Or rather, my boyfriend.

'Look, Annie, I can explain,' blusters Stuart, rubbing a hand across the faint stubble on his chin and smearing the lipstick marks on his neck. 'It's not how it looks.' He winces. 'Well, I suppose it is but I was going to tell you.'

Melinda is cowering in the corner of the sofa, hands across her breasts and genitals which are inadequately covered by scraps of exquisite lace.

She doesn't meet my eye when I pick up her clothes and shoes and shove them towards her.

'Um, thanks,' she mutters, grabbing them, leaping off the sofa and running into the hall. I follow her and watch as she wrenches open the front door, clothing still draped over her arm, and slams it shut behind her. She'll be getting dressed in the communal hallway then, which will liven up Peter's day no end when he reviews the CCTV footage later.

Stuart's not in the front room when I stomp back in and sink onto the sofa. I still feel as if someone's sitting on my chest so I let off steam by punching one of his beige Habitat cushions. I was with Stuart when he bought them, so I give it another hard whack with the Toblerone and clasp the cushion across my stomach as Stuart comes into the room.

He's wearing blue tracksuit bottoms, the white T-shirt I bought him from Gap, and a sheepish expression. The marks on his neck are gone apart from faint red outlines.

'I'm really sorry you saw that, Annie,' he says, pushing a hand through his short, fair hair which is standing up in spikes.

'Sorry I saw it or sorry you've been shagging Melinda behind my back?'

'Don't start twisting my words. This is difficult enough as it is.' He pulls an unopened bottle of whisky from the cupboard underneath the TV and twists off the cap. 'I need a drink. Do you want one?'

'You know I don't like whisky.'

'I forgot.' Stuart pours a triple into a crystal glass, perches on the edge of the cupboard and takes a large swig. 'Look, this is really awkward.'

'You think?' The panicky fluttering I felt at Maura's is back, though this time my heart is being jumped on.

'Don't be snippy, Annie,' says Stuart sharply.

'How should I be? We've been going out for months and I've just found out you're cheating on me. I think I have every right to be snippy.'

In more ways than one: a vision of large kitchen scissors poised around Stuart's testicles springs into my mind.

'Look, I'm really sorry, Annie.' Stuart puts down his glass, sits beside me on the sofa and stares at his knees. 'I've behaved like a shit and I should have told you sooner but, be honest, our relationship was never going anywhere, was it? It was just a bit of fun for both of us. You've made it very clear that you like being independent and doing your own thing. We spent most of Christmas apart and there was no way you were ever going to move in or do the marriage thing.'

The back of my neck starts prickling because I hate these heavy conversations.

'You seemed happy enough with the way things were going,' I say bitterly.

'I was and you're a great girl, Annie.' Stuart touches my cheek and drops his hand when I flinch. 'But I've started to feel differently now I'm in my thirties and Melinda wants the same things I do.'

'What kind of things?'

'More long-term stuff: commitment, maybe a family one day. And I know you don't do family.'

'You should have told me.'

'I tried,' says Stuart in a whiney voice. 'I mentioned I'd like kids one day, just in passing, and you couldn't get out of here fast enough. Remember?'

I do have vague memories of a conversation getting more intense than usual, finding it difficult to breathe properly and making some excuse about having to go.

'And when I suggested that we visit my family at Christmas you said you couldn't go to Dartmoor because you're allergic to the countryside.'

'I am,' I protest. 'I get sneezy and my eyes run if there's too much grass.' I snap the Toblerone in two and watch chocolate shavings cascade onto the beige carpet, unsettled that Stuart has me pegged as family-phobic. He might be right, of course, though I do want to have children and a family one day. Well, probably. But not for ages.

Stuart gives a heavy sigh.

'Face it, Annie, you're allergic to commitment and you prefer being on your own. So I'm doing you a favour by ending things now before they get too serious.'

'That's rich. You're getting off with Melinda behind my back and you're doing me a favour? And it's not true that I prefer being alone.'

'Really? You only want to meet up on set days each week, and you've got hardly any of your stuff here even though you often stay over.'

'It's normal for couples to want to spend time on their own.' Isn't it?

He grabs my hands and holds on fast when I try to pull away.

'You're a free spirit, Annie, and that's great. I admire how you're making your own way in life and you don't need anyone, but I want something different. We can still be friends though, can't we?'

And he kisses me on the cheek while I try to remember where he keeps his scissors.

Chapter Three

It's three o'clock on Saturday afternoon and, rather than spending the day with Stuart, I'm eating my own weight in pretzels while watching a box set of *The Bridge*.

There are three reasons why life traumas trigger a Scandi-noir box set binge:

1 - concentrating on subtitles clears the mind;
2 - I bloody love Saga, *The Bridge*'s autistic heroine who gets by on her own; and
3 - though this probably sounds nuts, I reckon one of the more mature male actors might just be my dad.

I'm convinced my dad is Scandinavian, so who's to say that he didn't go on to find fame and fortune in Denmark as a TV actor after knocking up my mother at a music festival in the mid-eighties?

I'm not daft. I know there are like a million men in Scandinavia and my dad is more likely to be working in an office than on TV. But I'm still fascinated by Scandi dramas which feed an alternate fantasy life that runs through my head; a life filled with bleached wood and snow and uncluttered homes straight out of the IKEA catalogue.

Mum never confirmed that the man who impregnated her was Nordic but she once referred to him as a Viking and often told me I was the only one in the family with bright blue eyes. So I've constructed a story about my heritage based on that. The rest of me is pretty nondescript: thick shoulder-length brown hair that goes frizzy in wet weather, pale complexion, not terribly tall, size twelve in jeans. But people have always remarked on the vibrant colour of my eyes.

I've had to take it on trust that I'm the only blue-eyed Trebarwith because I've never met another member of my family. Not one, apart from Mum, and I like it that way because it means there are no stressful Christmases spent with warring relatives, and no trying to find the perfect birthday present for a stroppy sibling.

Now Mum's gone, there's just me which suits me fine except on days like today when being alone feels a bit sad.

'Not out with Stuart, then?' My flatmate Amber plonks down next to me on the sofa. She's ten years younger than me and at university doing media studies.

'No, we split up.'

'OMG!' exclaims Amber, searching through her pockets for her mobile that's just dinged with a text. 'That's a bummer 'cos he was hot. Are you OK about it then?'

'Not really, I—'

'OMFG!' squeals Amber, her eyes fixed on her mobile screen. 'Siobhan has got tickets for us to see Beyoncé at the O2 and she's like my favourite person of all time. That's totally sick! Lauren will go mental 'cos her dad's getting married to some random woman the same day so she can't come.' She glances across at me. 'What did you say about Stuart? Are you all right about it?'

'Yes, fine,' I lie, while Amber does her Happy Dance round the room, totally blocking Saga who's kicking some bloke's arse.

By the time Amber leaves to meet up with Siobhan, I've heard more than I ever wanted to know about Beyoncé's general awesomeness, and Lauren's stepmum-to-be who's a right bitch, apparently. But the flat's too quiet without Amber so I listen to my break-up playlist on Spotify. Yep, I'm such a loser I've created my very own playlist for occasions such as this because the magical power of music can soothe a broken heart. But today even Sinatra and Streisand aren't cutting it and I try another episode of *The Bridge* instead.

Being without a job and boyfriend has never really bothered me before but this time it's hitting home. Maybe it's because there's a significant birthday looming or because I got closer to Stuart than was sensible. I'm upset about what happened and I'll miss him when I stop feeling so angry with him. But I also feel relieved, as if I've escaped from something scary, so maybe Stuart was right when he said I don't need anyone.

'Yay, girl power!' I say to the empty room, pumping my fist and feeling rather pathetic.

I wish I could talk to someone about how I'm feeling but, when I scroll through the contacts list on my phone, there's no one I can call. I've got friends from my various jobs over the years, people like Maura. But they're all busy these days with partners or kids and they can't drop everything to suit me.

Putting the TV on pause, I sit in silence for ages as the penny drops that I'm heading for thirty and I'm not the most important person in the world to anyone. Now that Mum has gone and my friends are drowning in responsibilities, I'm completely on my own, although… reaching across to my handbag, I pull out the envelope and smooth out the letter inside. It's on headed paper from a solicitors' practice called Jasper and Heel in Penzance.

Globules of grease have made the paper transparent in places, and the writer's surname has been obliterated by a smear of something that looks disgusting. But I can still make out what the letter says:

Dear Miss Trebarwith,

I am contacting you on behalf of Mrs Alice Gowan, your maternal great-aunt. Mrs Gowan is keen to have urgent contact with you and requests that you visit her to make her acquaintance. I have enclosed a cheque to cover the cost of your journey.

Mrs Gowan lives at Tregavara House in Salt Bay, Cornwall. She understands that you may be surprised to hear from her which is why she has asked me to act as an intermediary. If you are able to visit Mrs Gowan, please call me on the phone number above as soon as possible and I will liaise with her to arrange a convenient date and time.

Yours sincerely,

My maternal great-aunt Mrs Alice Gowan – a woman I never knew existed until her solicitor's letter dropped onto my doormat. Mum never mentioned her and wouldn't speak about her family. They were shadowy figures when I was growing up; ghosts who inhabited a place far away. All Mum did say, after having a few too many, was that her parents had thrown her out after discovering she was pregnant so she'd travelled from Cornwall to London to make a new life. And it was a good life mostly, except on the days when Mum would sit and cry for hours until I got scared.

Her family have never had anything to do with us, so why now? I rub my fingers across the Jasper and Heel cheque and wonder what I should do. Visiting Mrs Gowan would feel disloyal to Mum but I can't help being curious. The letter has opened a hidden doorway and I'm tempted to step through it. And I'm lonely. There, I've finally admitted it. Being independent is all very well but it's a bugger when you can't find a friend in your hour of need.

I glance at the blonde woman frozen on my TV screen. What would Saga do, if she could step out of the telly in her leather trousers and advise me? She'd tell me to call Elliott whatever-his-name-is and find out what's going on, though of course she would say it in Swedish so I wouldn't understand a word.

I'm about to make a life-altering decision based on imaginary advice from someone who doesn't really exist. But I pick up my mobile, dial the number for Jasper and Heel and leave a message before I can change my mind.

Chapter Four

A dank mist is hanging over the village below me. Gulls are wheeling overhead calling mournfully to one another and the sea looks like a sheet of cold, grey steel. Welcome to Cornwall, also known as the Cornish Riviera apparently. People are really taking the piss!

The main thing I've noticed about Cornwall is that it's wet. I'm used to London rain that washes the streets clean and freshens the air. But this is something else; a curtain of endless drizzle that seeps through coat seams and soaks you to the bone.

Even my socks are soggy, and I'm seriously regretting my choice of footwear. Ankle boots are ideal for the flat streets of Stratford but they're not so great when trying to keep upright on a potholed road which is almost vertical, as if it's been carved out of a frigging cliff. It's so steep the taxi driver refused to take me down into the village, saying he valued his gearbox. So he abandoned me here in the middle of nowhere, stumbling towards houses huddled around a harbour far below.

There's a tang of salt on the breeze and a faint boom from the waves which are crashing into the grey harbour wall, sending plumes of sea-spray high into the air. On the more sheltered side of the harbour, the water is churning about and brightly coloured fishing boats are lurching violently. I'm so busy watching the boats sway back and forth, I don't notice a pothole which catches the back of my foot, snapping off my heel with a sharp crack and sending it skidding across the road into a hedge. Fantastic! Now I'm dripping wet and hobbling.

I stumble on down the mountain, cursing myself for coming to this godforsaken place and vowing to head home once I've discovered why Mrs Gowan sent for me. Her solicitor Elliott gave nothing away when we spoke on the phone. All he kept saying in a husky voice – obviously thinking he was being sexily mysterious rather than knobbishly annoying – was that everything would be explained when Mrs Gowan and I met. If I had a job and a boyfriend, I'd have told him and Mrs Alice Gowan to bugger off. But I'm fancy-free and, though I hate to admit it, curious about this stranger who shares my DNA. Even if she is part of the family that turned its back on my mum.

The houses are getting closer when I hear the growl of a car coming up fast behind me on the narrow road – *really* fast. Just in time, I flatten myself against the hedgerow as a battered black Mini hurtles past. It misses me but its front wheel bumps into a rain-filled pothole and a wall of dirty water arcs over the rusty roof and splats onto my head. Like Taylor Swift doing the charity ice bucket challenge, except she looked drenched but gorgeous and I look like a cat that's been thrown into a bath head-first.

'You idiot!' I yell, picking up a stone and hurling it. There's a clunk as the stone hits metal – oops, my aim is usually rubbish – and the car screeches to a halt and reverses at speed. It stops next to me and the driver leans across and winds down the passenger window. He's about my age and wearing a Clash sweatshirt, which reminds me of Stuart.

'Did you just throw a stone at my car?' Raindrops are splattering onto the passenger seat and the dark-haired man winds the window up halfway. 'What are you, a complete moron?'

I swipe aside my fringe which is plastered to my forehead and dripping into my eyes.

'I'm sorry, I didn't mean to hit your car but didn't you see me? You almost knocked me over and you drenched me when you went past.'

'You shouldn't have been walking on the road.'

'Don't be ridiculous. Since when has it been a crime to walk on the road?' I say those words confidently though maybe it is against the law here. The whole place is weird enough. And it's obviously against Cornish law to be polite to strangers and offer them a lift when it's peeing down.

The driver gesticulates wildly over my shoulder. 'There's a footpath over there – just over the hedgerow. You should be using it! Any idiot can tell that the road isn't safe.'

'How am I supposed to know about the footpath when there aren't any signs telling me it's there? I'm from London where we know how to put up signposts and motorists don't drive like dickheads.'

Which isn't strictly true because I've had several near-death experiences courtesy of dickhead drivers racing through red lights. But right now I don't care about the truth. I'm tired and hungry, it's taken me hours to get here, and what I want more than anything is to go home. Back to cliff-free, drizzle-free, wanker-driver-free civilisation.

'Ah, I get it,' smirks the man. 'I thought you weren't from around here. You emmets are all the same, acting like you own the place!'

'Don't call me an emmet,' I shout through the endless rain. I'm not quite sure what an emmet is but it can't be good. 'You almost knocked me over and soaked me in the process. I wish I'd never come to Cornwall.'

'I suggest you bugger off back to precious London then,' yells the man, crunching his car into gear and screeching off into the distance.

The Mini disappears round a bend while I send up a quick prayer to the gods: please don't let him be related to me.

I hobble on down into the valley, keeping my spirits up by singing show tunes and thinking of new marketing posters for the county. 'Visit Cornwall: the Ratsarse Riviera in the Back of Beyond.' The local tourist board wouldn't like it, but at least they wouldn't get visitors here under false pretences.

When I eventually reach the village, yellow lamplight is glowing from cottage windows and piercing the gloom. The cottages are brown granite or painted white with rough, bumpy walls. They look like doll's houses, with tiled roofs and climbing plants trailed around their front doors. Some are grouped together around a small green and there's a narrow river meandering past the houses toward the sea.

It's chocolate-box pretty but the place is like a ghost town so I poke my head round the door of a small shop selling newspapers, fruit and… plastic sunglasses. The shop owner must have a good sense of humour.

'Excuse me, I'm looking for Tregavara House.'

'What will you be wanting there, then?' asks the middle-aged woman behind the counter, looking up from her copy of *OK!* magazine.

'I'm looking for Mrs Alice Gowan.'

'Is that right?'

'She's expecting me.'

The woman raises her eyebrows and points along the road. 'You'd better carry on the way you're going, then. Her house is set back near the cliffs. It's the last one in the village so you can't miss it. If you end up in the sea, you've gone too far.' She chuckles at her own joke and crosses her arms under her huge chest. 'Tell her Jennifer says hello and I'll have her magazine in tomorrow if she feels well enough to call in for it.'

She comes to the door and watches me hobble on, past a church for the smallest congregation in the world. The ancient building is so dinky it must be a squeeze if more than fifty people turn up at the same time, and the churchyard is equally small and packed with weathered stones, pock-marked with green lichen. Maybe my ancestors are buried here, but most of the stones I can see have been scoured blank by decades of wind and rain so it's impossible to tell.

Beyond the churchyard is a house with white-framed windows and a porch overhanging the black front door, held up by two thin stone pillars. The house is larger than the cottages in the village and behind it the land slopes up steeply towards towering cliffs which drop into the sea. This must be Tregavara House. It looks weathered and neglected – the garden is untidy and window frames are peeling – but it's a handsome house, made of grey stone which mirrors the sky.

All of a sudden I'm nervous and it takes all my courage to open the rusted iron gate and walk through the garden. A large shrub near the front door has been blown flat by the wind and the metal bell-pull crunches with salt when my fingers close round it.

A bell clangs deep inside the house and, just as I'm starting to think no one is in, the door swings open.

'Hello. Mrs Gowan?'

Much to my surprise, the woman nods. Mrs Gowan is not what I was expecting. 'Great-aunt' to me says small, round and cuddly with a tragic grey perm, but the woman in front of me is tall and slim with a shock of straight, white hair falling to her shoulders. She looks like a stern headmistress who's just discovered me snogging behind the bike sheds.

'You must be Annabella. You'd better come in.' The scary woman pulls the door wide and, with a gulp, I step past her into a narrow, flagstoned hallway. 'My, you are wet, aren't you? Stay there.' She disappears through a doorway at the end of the hall and returns with a fluffy blue hand towel. 'Here! You'd better hang your coat up and come and sit by the fire. Try not to drip everywhere.'

I hang my coat on a wooden coat stand and it drips onto the floor while I pull off my boots and put my socks across a huge iron radiator which is only lukewarm. Mrs Gowan watches me without a word and then beckons for me to follow her across the cold stones into a sitting room where a fire is blazing. She gestures for me to take a seat on one side of the tiled fireplace and she sits opposite, with her back to a large stone-framed window. Behind her I can just make out the sea roiling against the dark harbour wall and I shiver.

'Do you need a blanket?'

'No thank you, Mrs Gowan. I'll be fine when the fire warms me up.'

'You'd better call me Alice.' The flames cast shadows on her wrinkled skin as she picks up a silver bell from a side table and rings it. 'I'll get you a hot drink.'

A plump, teenaged girl in jeans and an apron comes bursting into the room.

'You rang,' she says wearily. 'Again.'

'I did, Serena. Could you make us a pot of tea, please.'

'Not really in my job description,' mutters the girl, stalking out of the room. But she returns a few minutes later with a flowered china teapot, two matching cups and saucers and an open carton of milk on a tray. I'm beginning to think I've wandered into a scaled-down version of *Downton Abbey*.

'Thank you, Serena, though next time could you put the milk into a jug,' instructs Alice, ignoring the eye-roll and heavy sarcasm as Serena assures her that next time she will be delighted to decant the milk.

The girl gives me a hostile stare and rushes out of the room, almost knocking over a large ornament of a cat as she goes.

'Serena lives nearby and comes in some days after school to do a few jobs for me.' Alice picks up the teapot and stares into my face. 'You look very like your mother, apart from your blue eyes. Your mother's were brown.'

'I know,' I say sharply, searching for some resemblance between my mother and the stern old woman opposite me. There's something about the crease between Alice's eyebrows that looks similar but that's all. Nothing about Mrs Gowan or this place feels familiar and if I came here hoping to find an echo of my mum I'm going to be disappointed.

'Tell me about your mother,' demands Alice, handing me a cup of tea. 'I want to know what happened to her after she left Salt Bay.'

She really doesn't. I could tell her the truth about our constant moves between small flats across London because Mum got bored, the 'uncles' who came and went, her crazy schemes when she would encourage me to play truant so we could ride the Underground all day, and her low moods that would strike out of a blue sky and smother her for weeks.

But I don't think the family that abandoned my mum deserves the truth so I give great-aunt Alice the sanitised version, where the sun shone every day until Mum died three years ago of breast cancer she had ignored for too long.

When I've finished, Alice gives me a hard stare and takes a sip of tea. 'And what about you, Annabella?'

'It's Annie, and there's nothing much to tell. I'll be thirty just before next Christmas, I work as a PA – a personal assistant – and I share a flat with a girl in Stratford.'

'No boyfriend?'

'Nope, I'm a free spirit.' This sounds a bit pathetic even to me as I sit steaming in front of the fire in Alice's old-fashioned sitting room. 'I don't mean to be rude but why did you ask me to come here?'

Alice gives a faint smile.

'I'm afraid I'm not up to travelling to London these days and I was curious to see what my great-niece was like. I also have a business proposal to put to you. I was going to wait a while before speaking about it but it seems you'd prefer me to be direct.' There's a tremor in her hand when she puts down her tea cup. 'I need someone to help me around the house for a while, someone to live in, and I thought you might be interested, especially as Elliott tells me you're between jobs at the moment. I can't pay much but you'd have bed and board and time to explore Cornwall. Think of it as a working holiday.'

I look past her at the rain lashing down outside. 'Why are you asking me?'

'I'd like to get to know you and I'd rather it was someone who's family than a total stranger.'

'We've only just met so I am a total stranger. I could be an axe murderer for all you know.'

'Elliott made a few discreet enquiries about you before sending my letter and there was no hint of homicide. They say that blood is thicker than water, Annabella. Wouldn't you like to find out? Aren't you curious at all about your family?' She stops abruptly and gazes into the distance as though she's seen a ghost, which freaks me out. 'Anyway.' She suddenly looks weary. 'Please think about it and we can talk more in the morning. There's some food ready for you in the kitchen and I'll show you where you'll be sleeping, because I'm sure the travelling has made you tired. Serena has prepared a bedroom for you.'

On cue, Serena pokes her head round the door.

'I'm heading off now Mrs Gowan 'cos it's almost six o'clock. Josh has come to collect me seeing as it's still pissing – sorry, pouring – down.' She nods towards the window through which I can see a tall, dark-haired man unfolding himself from a battered black Mini, the same Mini that almost took me out an hour earlier.

'Who exactly is Josh?'

Serena gives me a surprised look. 'He's just my brother.'

'Josh works as a teacher in Trecaldwith which is a town a few miles away. I expect your taxi went through it,' says Alice, pouring more tea. 'He teaches English and he's about your age so you might have a few things in common. Could you ask him to come in for a minute, Serena.'

Before I can protest, Serena grunts 'S'pose', disappears into the hall and there's a murmur of voices before she and Josh come into the room. He's at least six foot tall and fills the low doorway.

'Hello Mrs Gowan.' When he's not yelling, his voice is deep and he has the same soft-burr accent as Alice. Though he doesn't sound particularly pleased to see my great-aunt.

'Good evening, Josh. This is Annabella, my great-niece, who's visiting me for a while from London.'

Josh looks at me and starts to smile until the penny drops that we've met before. He shoves his hands into the pockets of his jeans and pulls his shoulders back.

'From London, you say. Fancy that.'

'Annabella works as a PA,' says Alice.

'Really?' Josh sizes me up and down and rubs a hand over the faint stubble on his chin. 'Isn't that just a fancy title for a secretary?'

Ignoring his question, I smile at him sweetly.

'Alice tells me you're a teacher. It must be lovely only working for nine months of the year.'

Serena smirks at her brother and picks up her bag from the floor while he glares at me but says nothing.

'See you on Friday then, Mrs Gowan.' Serena puts her purple rucksack over her shoulder and glances at me with a slight smile. 'Bye Annabella. I might see you on Friday too, then.' She looks round for her brother but he's already swept out of the room.

As Josh and Serena pile into the Mini, I take another sip of my tea which is lukewarm and tastes vaguely of aftershave. I don't know why I said that about teachers. Some of my friends are teachers and they work their socks off, but the man's an idiot and he started it with his snarky comment about secretaries. He brings out the worst in me and I'll do my best to avoid him during my brief stay in Salt Bay.

Chapter Five

The rain has finally stopped when I wake the next morning but thick clouds are still scudding across a grey sky. The house is chilly and after pulling back the brocade curtains I rush back to my bed with its old-fashioned sheets, blankets and patchwork counterpane. Maybe duvets haven't made it as far as Cornwall. The weight of the blankets felt suffocating when I first slipped under the covers but I was so tired I soon fell into a deep sleep, only roused occasionally by the creaking of a strange house.

None of this feels familiar. I thought it might – like some sort of inherited memory from my mum – but everything just feels strange and awkward. And Alice's proposal out of the blue is bizarre. I'll stay for a couple of days because she shelled out loads for my train fare and it would be rude not to. She's also quite scary. But then I'll head back to my proper life because I was right, I don't need family. Keeping in touch with Alice might be appropriate – Christmas cards and perhaps a postcard when I go on holiday – but I doubt I'll ever visit her here again. Why on earth would I?

Alice is moving around downstairs so, after a while, I throw back the covers and head for the wooden-floored bathroom next to my room. The bathtub has a rolled top and claw feet and looks amazing but everything else is slightly shabby. A cold draught is snaking in through the closed window, there are cracks in the cream walls and paint is flaking from the blistered ceiling. But at least the water is steaming hot and I feel revived after soaking in the tub for ten minutes.

Alice is polishing a brass coal scuttle when I go into the kitchen, which is warmed by a vast black Aga. She's laid a cloth over the table and is scrubbing at the brass with scrunched-up newspaper.

'There you are.' She stops polishing and brushes a strand of snow-white hair from her forehead. 'There's tea in the pot and cornflakes in that cupboard. Milk's in the fridge.'

She goes back to her scuttle but watches me while I pour myself tea and a bowl of cereal.

'Did you sleep well, Annabella?'

'Yes, thank you. The bed was really comfy and I love your beautiful old bath.'

'That was my mother's pride and joy and it still serves its purpose so there's no point in changing it.'

'How long have you lived here?' I ask, wondering if I've poured myself too many cornflakes. At home I don't usually bother with breakfast.

'I was born in this house. This is the Trebarwith family home and has been for generations. My great-great grandfather bought it after making a lucrative investment in local tin mines, and it's been passed down to me through the Trebarwith line.'

She scrubs at a mark on the scuttle while I wonder what it must be like to have long-standing roots in one place. There isn't one part of London that feels like home because Mum and I moved around so much. Even Stratford, where I've lived for two years, is just a pit-stop on my way to somewhere else.

'What do you think of the house?' demands Alice.

'It's… it's very handsome.'

Alice scrunches up another sheet of the *Telegraph* and rubs it across the brass.

'Handsome. Yes, I suppose it is. Though I don't suppose it has all the mod cons you young people in London are used to.'

'Do you have Wi-Fi?' I ask hopefully but Alice looks puzzled. 'So I can get onto the Internet?'

'Ah, I'm afraid not. I'm not sure the Wi-Fi can reach us here. And if you've got a mobile phone, that won't work in the house either. Too many cliffs, apparently.'

Great, I really am in the huge black hole that time forgot.

Alice looks up and gestures towards the window.

'I thought you might want to explore the village this morning. Your coat has dried off overnight. It's too windy to take an umbrella so you might want to be back by lunchtime because it's going to rain later.'

Of course it is.

Chapter Six

Salt Bay is small. It takes me only half an hour to wander along the valley from one end of the village to the other, and you could fit the whole place into a floor or two of the Westfield shopping centre in Stratford. It's prettier than Westfield, if you like teeny tiny cottages and views of cliffs and boats and endless seagulls. But it's a lot less vibrant. The only people out and about are an elderly couple walking their dog who, when I look back, are standing still as statues, staring at me. It's like the start of a horror film where a new girl arrives in the remote hamlet of Satan's Den, little knowing what fate awaits her – even though the name is a bit of a clue.

Salt Bay is also nothing like a retail mecca. Apart from the newsagent's and a closed ice-cream kiosk, there's a tiny grocery store and Maureen's Cornish Tea Shop which has brightly coloured cloths on its tables. And I'm not surprised to see that the village has a pub, The Whistling Wave. I bet the people who live here drink loads. I would.

Giving the pub a miss, I queue up in the tea shop behind an old man in a thick fisherman's sweater who orders cheese on toast.

'Can I have a soy caffè latte with extra foam please,' I say to the girl behind the counter when it's my turn. She wrinkles her nose and shrugs her shoulders. 'What kind of coffees do you do then?'

'Instant, with or without milk.' She scoops a pile of mugs off the counter and drops them into the sink behind her.

'Soya milk?'

'Nope.'

'Cappuccino?'

'We had a machine but it's on the blink. So we've got instant, black or white.'

A loud Australian voice booms out, 'Personally I'd kill my own grandmother for a honey macchiato.'

A red-haired girl behind me in a purple fleece winks when I turn round.

'If I were you, I'd go for the hot chocolate. They put Cornish cream on top. It'll give you a heart attack but you'll die happy.' When she smiles, her green eyes crinkle at the edges.

'Thanks. That's good to know.' I order hot chocolate and the girl does the same before sitting opposite me at a table near the window.

She puts out her hand. 'I'm Kayla. Nice to meet you.'

'You too. I'm Annie.' I shake her hand and spoon the yellow cream floating on thick liquid chocolate into my mouth. It tastes like heaven.

Kayla laughs at my expression and cups her hands round her mug. 'It's good isn't it, though I've put on half a stone in the last three months. Have you been here long, Annie?'

'Only since yesterday. I'm visiting Alice Gowan. She, um, she knew my mother.'

'I know Alice. Mind you, I know just about everyone and I didn't think I'd seen you around. Your first visit?'

'Yes, and you're obviously not from round here.'

'Well spotted, Sherlock!' Kayla gulps down a mouthful of chocolate and wipes a cream moustache from her upper lip. 'I'm from Sydney on a gap year, though my gap year has lasted eighteen months so far.'

'Why would you leave the golden beaches of sunny Australia for Salt Bay?'

'Hey, have you seen my colouring?' Kayla picks up a strand of her long, auburn hair and shakes it. 'Australian weather is a nightmare for people like me. The climate here is bloody great. I only have to wear suncream in July and August and there are plenty of fantastic golden beaches round here too if you know where to look.' She taps the side of her freckled nose. 'I can show you.'

'Where are your family from originally?'

'My grandmother was Irish and my grandfather was English but they decided the best place to emigrate to, with their pale complexions, was one of the hottest countries in the world. Madness! Both of them looked like wrinkled prunes by the time they were sixty. That was in the days before slip-slop-slap.'

'Slip, slop, what?'

'Haven't you heard of "slip on a shirt, slop on sunscreen and slap on a hat"?'

'No, though "slip on your anorak and slop on your wellies" might be more appropriate round here.'

'Nah, the weather can be good sometimes and, when it is, there's nowhere more beautiful than Cornwall in the whole world.'

When I raise my eyebrows in disbelief, Kayla gulps down the last of her hot chocolate.

'Drink up, I'm going to show you the local sights.' She stands up and pats her flat-as-a-board stomach. 'Look at that! Too much clotted cream and not enough striding over cliffs. I work in the local pub, too, with all those bags of peanuts and pork scratchings around. I bloody love pork scratchings. If we don't have them in Australia, we should. Maybe I could set up an import business.'

She leads me away from the tea shop towards the village green where a child with tumbling golden curls is hurling bread at two seagulls. A crust bounces off one gull's head and the girl giggles.

'That's seven-year-old Celine who's bunking off school again with some imaginary ailment. She lives in that cottage over there,' says Kayla out of the corner of her mouth. 'Face of an angel but the personality of a freaking psychopath. I caught her pulling the wings off flies a while ago. Mark my words' – she taps the side of her head – 'psychopath. And the woman who lives in that house by the tree is having an affair with a fisherman from Perrigan Bay. I hear all sorts of stuff working in the pub. Do you know anyone around here apart from Alice?'

'I met Serena, and I had a few words with her brother Josh.'

'Josh Pasco?'

'I don't know his surname.'

'Tall, dark, brooding? Looks a bit like Poldark off the telly?' Kayla bends her arms as though she's weightlifting. 'Nice pecs.'

'Possibly. I wouldn't know.'

'Not gay, are you?' asks Kayla, zipping up her thick purple fleece.

'Blimey, that's direct! No, I go for blokes.'

'That's a shame. You could have been the only gay in the village. What?' laughs Kayla. 'We like *Little Britain* in Australia too. And we're renowned for being direct. It's a national trait.' She points over my shoulder. 'See the church over there? That was built like a gazillion years ago and it's hardly used these days but it's worth a look inside. Are you religious?'

'Not really. My mum was into alternative stuff, like Gaia and sun worship.'

'Cool,' says Kayla, pushing open the churchyard gate and letting me go through first.

The church is built of large, granite blocks scored by centuries of full-on Cornish weather. In the full-to-bursting churchyard, gravestones are crammed up close to one another, with some tilting at crazy angles.

Kayla runs her hand along the top of a stone that's about to fall over.

'There's another cemetery on the cliffs, to take the overspill. They seem to have a lot of dead people round here. Would you like to see inside the church? The door's usually unlocked during the daytime.'

She pushes open the heavy wooden door and a musty smell of dust and damp hits my nose. The church smells like an old library full of secrets. It's very simple inside. There are a few dark pews with embroidered kneelers in reds and greens, a tall vase of lilies near the stone pulpit and, on the altar under a stained-glass window, there's a chunky wooden cross that has been bolted down.

Kayla spots me looking at the bolts and giggles.

'They had to put the silver stuff in storage after one tourist was nabbed trying to walk out with a huge silver crucifix stuffed up his jumper. What an idiot! You can't trust emmets.'

'What exactly are emmets?'

'That's what the locals call tourists. I think it means "ants" or something. You can't move round here in mid-summer for emmets in shorts shouting at their kids and stuffing their faces with ice cream, but there's none about at this time of year.'

Perhaps Mum used to call tourists "emmets". Maybe she once stood in the spot where I'm standing now. A wave of longing to see her just one more time sweeps over me and my eyes begin to water. I was wrong to think there were no echoes of her here in this isolated village that's shackled to the past.

To be honest, I can't imagine my new-age mum in a church but I light a candle near the altar just in case and put a pound in the donations box. *This one's for you, Mum.* The flickering flame dances and reflects in a brass plaque above it.

The plaque is polished to a gleaming shine and reads: *In loving memory of the members of Salt Bay Choral Society who drowned in the great storm of April 15th 2002. Still singing in Heaven.* Beneath are listed the names of seven men, including 'Samuel Trebarwith, aged 70'.

A shiver goes down my back as I wonder if Samuel Trebarwith was a relative. I've no idea how common the surname is round here, and I don't remember the storm, which might not have reached London. But it must have been devastating for this small community to lose so many men on one day.

'Sad, isn't it,' whispers Kayla, who's crept up behind me. 'I don't think the village has ever fully recovered. No one talks about it, like it's unlucky to even bring it up. I mentioned it in the pub once and everyone went quiet as though I'd brought up my kinky sexual practices.'

'What is the Salt Bay Choral Society?'

Kayla peers more closely at the plaque. 'I dunno. What it says on the tin, I guess. It's not still going so I guess the storm finished that off, too. I don't s'pose there's too much call for singing when you've had a tragedy like that.'

The mood has lowered and Kayla suddenly grabs hold of my arm. 'Come on, I'm supposed to be showing you the wonders of Cornwall, not burying you in its tragedies. Let's go up onto the cliffs so you can get a good view. They're a bit steep, mind.'

Kayla wasn't kidding. I've borrowed a pair of Alice's flat shoes but, by the time I reach the top of the cliffs overlooking Salt Bay, I'm out of breath and incredibly hot. I peel off my scarf and stand full on into the wind to cool my glowing cheeks.

I'm used to stale, hot air gusting out of Tube tunnels but the cold air gusting around me here smells clean and fresh. The late-January sky is still heavy with clouds but there's a sudden gap between them and a shaft of golden sunlight falls onto the churning sea. It lights a glimmering path across the waves which are beating hell out of the rocks below us.

'Look over there,' shouts Kayla, above the wind and the screeching seagulls. 'Can you see it?'

Gingerly, I move closer to the edge of the cliff and peer over the top. Far below there's a perfect curve of washed, golden sand littered with huge dark boulders. Each boulder is circled by a rock pool edged with crinkled, brown seaweed.

'That's the real Salt Bay,' shouts Kayla, turning her back to the wind. 'Most tourists think Salt Bay is the village and harbour and don't even know about the beach. We keep it a secret so emmets don't spoil it with ice-cream wrappers and empty suncream bottles. A couple of tourist guidebooks have given the game away but you have to go down a tricky cliff path to get there so that puts lots of people off.'

She catches her hair which is being whipped into her face and tucks it into the neck of her fleece.

'The beach is defo worth a visit, but make sure you check the tide timetables or you'll get cut off. A couple of tourists got stuck there a few months ago and they had to launch the lifeboat to rescue them. Some of the lifeboat crew came into the pub afterwards. Very nice!' Kayla grins. 'But then I've always had a thing for men in oilskins.' She pulls me back from the edge of the cliff. 'Come and look at this, too.'

She leads me over a small mound to a more sheltered area encircled by a low wooden fence. Inside the fence are tidy rows of dark-grey marble gravestones.

'This is the overspill cemetery above the beach. It's a lovely idea, though the stones will all fall into the sea one day when the cliff erodes far enough. Maybe that's what they want, because the sea is God around here.'

I leave Kayla sitting on the grass and wander for a while among the stones. They're newer than those in the churchyard so it's easier to make out the names and I soon spy the one I'm looking for. The stone is a simple marble oblong with black lettering: **Samuel Trebarwith – February 24th 1932 to April 15th 2002 – husband of Sheila and father of Joanna. Loved and missed.**

I touch the top of the gravestone, which is cold and slippery, and trace my mother's name with my fingertips. So Samuel Trebarwith was my grandfather. It doesn't seem right that her name is here, next to the man who threw her out when she most needed help. How could Samuel Trebarwith abandon his child? How could he abandon me?

The wind has picked up even more and catches an empty chocolate wrapper which dances between the gravestones.

'Hey, don't be too long,' yells Kayla, standing up and brushing grass from her damp backside. 'I'm working in the pub soon so I'd better get back, though you can stay up here longer if you like.'

'No, that's fine, I'll come with you,' I shout back, keen not to be alone in this wild, spooky place where the past and present collide and the wind seems to whisper with the secrets of the dead.

Chapter Seven

Tregavara House smells like the bakery counter at Tesco when I let myself in using the key Alice lent me. Mmmm. There's a definite whiff of freshly baked bread and something delicious mingling with it – possibly bacon, streaky bacon, fried until it curls into a crispy sliver. My mouth is watering though I can't possibly be hungry, not after the calorie-rammed hot chocolate I shoved into my face an hour ago. Not when I can go the whole day in London on a medium salad and a can of Red Bull. My stomach rumbles traitorously and I realise that appetite-boosting sea air could be seriously damaging to my waistline. It's a good job I won't be here for long.

The gorgeous smells lead me to the kitchen where Alice is standing with her back to me, huddled over and gripping the table so hard her knuckles are white bumps beneath her thin skin.

'Are you OK, Alice?' I ask gently, standing in the doorway.

She straightens quickly and turns around.

'Don't fuss, I'm fine, just having a little rest and I didn't hear you come in. Are you hungry?' She pulls her shoulders back, picks up a wooden spoon and starts stirring a steaming pan on the hob. 'I've made some bacon and pea soup and there's bread in the oven; just part-baked baguettes from the shop, not home-made.'

'That sounds wonderful. I'll find some bowls.'

I root around in the crockery cupboard, touched that Alice has cooked for me. No one has made me soup from scratch since – well, since ever. Stuart always ate out, even though he has a top-of-the-range kitchen, and Mum used to open a tin of Heinz tomato soup, which was as far as her culinary skills went. Most of the time I ended up cooking for her, even as a child, especially when she was feeling low and food didn't register on her radar.

Alice ladles thick, green soup into the china bowls I've found and puts steaming bread onto a wooden board in the middle of the table.

'Sit and eat before it gets cold, and you can tell me what you think of Salt Bay,' she orders, turning off the hob and sitting at the head of the table.

'The village is great,' I lie, burning my fingertips when I break a baguette in half. 'I met someone called Kayla, an Australian girl who showed me round. She was really nice.'

'Kayla, the girl who works in the pub? That was kind of her.' Alice blows on her soup and sips a mouthful, grimacing because it's still too hot. Her hand wobbles, tilting the spoon, and some of the green liquid splashes onto the tablecloth. 'I hope you like the soup. It's an old family recipe.'

'It's delicious.' And this time there's no need to lie because the soup is bursting with flavour and beats shop-bought hands down. I slurp down a whole bowlful while we chat about Maureen's tea shop and the girl behind the counter who's called Nettie, and budding psychopath Celine, and Jennifer who's run the newsagent's forever. Everything's going well until I bring up my visit to the church.

'There's a plaque on the wall to the men from the Salt Bay Choral Society who died in the storm,' I say, pouring more soup from the saucepan into my bowl. 'That must have been terribly sad for the village.'

Alice pauses with her spoon between the bowl and her mouth.

'This soup could do with a little more salt. I never add any when cooking with bacon but this is rather under-seasoned, don't you think?' She puts down her spoon, grabs the salt cellar and sprinkles it so liberally that white specks scatter across the table. Then she looks up, her chocolate-brown eyes staring straight through me. 'Yes, it was sad. Did you notice the name of my brother Samuel, your grandfather?'

'Yes, although I didn't realise he was my grandfather until I saw his gravestone up on the cliffs.'

'Kayla really did show you round,' murmurs Alice, using a crust of bread to wipe soup from the rim of her bowl. 'My sister-in-law Sheila, your grandmother, went downhill after Samuel's tragic death. She couldn't get used to being on her own so suddenly after over forty years of marriage.'

'Then she should have made sure she had more family around her.' That came out rather bluntly and Alice looks taken aback. 'What I mean is, my mum could have been a comfort to her.'

'She could have been if she'd been here.' The space between us suddenly feels fizzy with tension.

'Did they have any other children?'

'No, Joanna was their only child.' Alice places her bread back on the breadboard and pushes away her bowl. 'I think I've had enough for now. My appetite isn't what it was and I'm feeling tired.' She stands up slowly and steadies herself against the table. 'I'm going upstairs to have a nap but do help yourself to more soup.'

Alice walks slowly upstairs while I sit at the table feeling guilty for bringing up the tragedy and being so abrupt about Mum. I'm totally within my rights to be angry about how Mum was treated, but all I managed to do was upset an old lady. Nice one, Annie.

After pouring leftover soup into a china jug, I do the washing up and dry my hands on a tea towel before going in search of a phone. Kayla is right that scars still run deep in this close-knit community and, although Alice has offered to tell me more about my family, perhaps that's all best left buried. It's time to go home.

The sitting room is chilly, with no fire in the grate and dark shadows lurking in corners untouched by daylight. There's an old-fashioned Bakelite phone with a silver dial on the sideboard, and I switch on the fringed lamp next to it. Mustard-yellow light pools across the rug while I find National Rail's number in the phone book and make a call.

It's picked up by a cheerful man with a broad Brummie accent who tells me there's a train from Penzance at ten o'clock on Friday morning that gets into Paddington almost five and a half hours later – a long journey back to my uncomplicated life. Relief washes over me as I replace the receiver, though I also feel sneaky for sorting out train times without telling Alice. But she hasn't mentioned her business proposal again and I'm more convinced than ever that leaving Salt Bay is the right decision. Alice will find someone else to help her, and witnessing how she's still affected by the village tragedy has cemented my view that having family only leads to hurt and pain.

I'm leaving the room when a large painting on the wall catches my eye. Framed with ornate gilt, the painting is of a woman dressed in a long dark skirt and white high-necked blouse, with a delicate cameo brooch at her throat. She's standing outside, with a blue-grey sea behind her, and the artist has captured the exact moment something has amused her and she's started to laugh. Sunshine is glinting on her brown hair which is piled up into a bun and her dark eyes are full of warmth.

It's a magnificent painting in rich oils and the woman makes me catch my breath. She seems so alive, frozen by a spell that might break at any moment, and she looks familiar. I've never seen her before, I'm sure of that, but there's something about the shape of her mouth and the way she's tilting her head back as she laughs that strikes a chord. She looks a little like my mum. Actually – I peer more closely at the delicate brush strokes – she looks a lot like me. Ooh, that's spooky; it's like coming face-to-face with your own ghost. In an old house. With a moaning wind outside whipping off a cold sea. A shiver goes down my spine and I can't get out of the room fast enough.

My heartbeat is thumping in my ears so I sit on the bottom stair for a while and give myself a good talking to. I'm almost thirty years old, for goodness' sake, and spooked by a painting! Gradually, the thump-thump fades while I focus on dust motes caught in a shaft of light from the landing window.

The house is deathly quiet apart from the steady ticking of a grandfather clock and, as my bum goes numb on the step, I realise I have no plans for this afternoon. In London there would be deadlines to meet and food to buy and rush-hour crowds to battle through but here there's absolutely nothing to do – apart from outdoorsy things which I'd never choose to do, obviously. So instead I do something I never would at home; I follow Alice's example and take to my bed.

There's something deliciously indulgent about sleeping in the afternoon when you're not full of cold or crippled with period pain. I open my bedroom window a little before slipping under the sheets and the dull, rhythmic boom of the waves lulls me to sleep while a breeze blows across my face.

When I wake up, the room is dark and freezing cold and I'm amazed to see that it's almost six o'clock. Sea air appears to knock you out as well as make you fat.

I run a brush through my hair and go downstairs. Alice is up and in the sitting room. She's lit the fire and is sitting close to it, mending what looks like a 1940s tea dress made of emerald-green silk.

'I'm so sorry, Alice. I fell asleep.'

Alice glances up from the fabric on her lap. 'I peeped in but you looked so peaceful I didn't want to wake you. You young girls must get worn out rushing round London. I used to burn the candle at both ends once but it catches up with you in the end.' She sighs as she pushes her needle through the soft fabric and pulls on the green thread.

'Can I get you something to eat, Alice? I can cook for you since you cooked for me at lunchtime, and I'm not bad in the kitchen. I used to cook for Mum all the time.'

'Thank you but I've already had a sandwich and finished off the soup. There's food in the fridge if you'd like to cook yourself something. There are chicken breasts and some green beans or pork chops in the freezer.'

'That's kind but I thought I might go to the pub this evening and have a meal there.' It's hard to tell how well off Alice is and – bearing in mind the effect of the sea air – I don't want to eat her out of house and home. I'm also trying to be extra nice after what happened at lunch-time.

'Would you like to come too? My treat?' I ask, perching on the arm of the Chesterfield-style sofa.

Alice shakes her head. 'No I don't think so. I'll finish my mending and watch TV and get off to bed before long. But you go out and enjoy yourself.' She sees me glance at the painting which freaked me out earlier, and smiles. The painting is in shadow, with its rich colours muted and the laughing woman less defined. 'It's quite a picture, isn't it. That woman is an ancestor of ours. My father used to refer to her as "The Lady". Ouch!' She puts her hand to her mouth and sucks her finger.

'Are you all right?'

'No harm done,' says Alice, taking a tissue from her pocket and soaking up a bubble of blood from her fingertip. 'My hands aren't as steady these days so I keep slipping with the needle, but there's no staining on the silk, thank goodness.' She's about to say something else, but thinks better of it and bends her head over the soft material that's draping to the floor. Her white hair glows in the firelight while she concentrates on keeping her fingers away from the sharp needle-tip. After a while she looks up. 'You get off to the pub, Annabella, and we can talk about things tomorrow.'

'Things' meaning me giving up my perfectly good life to move to a dead-end village. That is so not going to happen but putting off telling Alice until tomorrow sounds good to me. Procrastination is severely underrated, especially when it comes to disappointing an old lady with crackpot ideas about mending a fractured family.

Chapter Eight

Do waves whistle? The sign outside The Whistling Wave shows an unfeasibly turquoise crest of water forever poised to break onto acid-yellow sand. I'm all for alliteration but surely it should make some kind of sense. A wave might crash or even roar but it's hardly likely to start playing a tune, is it.

'Are you coming in, love?' A stout man in a beige anorak looks back at me over his shoulder while he holds open the pub door. Light spills out from the whitewashed building, along with a hum of conversation and the clink of glasses.

'Gazing at the sign won't get you a drink,' he laughs. 'There's no way Roger will walk outside to take an order.'

'That's true enough,' mutters the woman with him who lets me go into the pub ahead of her.

Inside there's a heavy smell of polish and beer, and shiny horse brasses on walls that must be at least half a metre thick. The window ledges are so deep, some have been fitted with colourful cushions and are being used as seats. They look comfy enough but the small, single-glazed windows are ancient and must be dead draughty. I make a mental note to sit near the flames blazing in the blackened stone fireplace, though maybe not too close. A woman at a table next to the fireplace, who's perspiring heavily, gets up and moves to a window seat.

'What can I get you me 'andsome? The barrel-shaped man behind the bar puts down the pint glass he's polishing and squints at me over the top of his heavy-framed glasses. This must be Roger. He nods towards a row of gleaming optics festooned with fairy lights.

'There's plenty to choose from.'

'I'll have an orange and lemonade, please.'

'Make that a gin and tonic, Roger,' says a familiar Aussie voice. Kayla has appeared from a door behind the bar in a rust-red dress that matches her hair. 'You do like gin, don't you? It's good local Cornish stuff,' she says, tipping a pile of pound coins into the till drawer. 'My treat.'

'I love gin but I'd better not roll in drunk tonight.'

'Woah, I'm only buying you one,' snorts Kayla. 'You'll be fine with that unless you're a real lightweight or an alcoholic.'

'I'm neither,' I laugh, gratefully accepting the drink and taking a sip. I think Roger's gone light on the tonic. The alcohol burns all the way down.

'I was hoping you'd come in,' whispers Kayla as Roger lumbers from behind the bar and starts collecting glasses from tables. 'Some nights the average age in here is about seventy, though that's better than summer Saturdays when we're besieged by teenaged tourists and have to work out who's under age. Nightmare!' She smiles at a plump woman in tight black leggings who's come up to the bar. 'Same again, Laura?'

'Yeah, fill it up please.' She looks at me and then at Kayla and raises her eyebrows.

'Annie, this is Laura, who lives near Celine,' says Kayla, giving me a wink so I realise that Laura is the woman who's having it away with the fisherman from Perrigan Bay. 'And Laura, this is Annie, who's staying with Alice.'

Laura's heavily made-up eyes fill with concern. 'How is Alice? Poor woman, it's such a shame.'

'What's a shame?' I ask but, before Laura can answer, the door is flung open and a group of men bundle into the pub. They head for the bar and my heart sinks because one of them – with his wallet in his hand and about to order a round – is tall, dark and glowering. My luck really is rubbish these days. Grabbing my drink, I nab the only free table in the pub which happens to be the 'sauna table' near the fireplace, but sweating buckets is worth it if it means I avoid another awkward run-in with Josh Pasco. He's a knob and I don't feel much better myself. Throwing that stone at his car was a ridiculous thing to do. What was I thinking?

Sitting huddled over the table, I notice a small sign tacked above the bar, next to the cheesy Wotsits. Hallelujah! The Whistling Wave has free Wi-Fi; my gateway back to civilisation. I find my phone in my bag, put in the password – 'Whistling Wave', who'd have thought it – and suddenly I'm connected once more to the outside world.

Feverishly scrolling through social media, it's obvious that I haven't missed much over the last couple of days. Facebook is full of friends telling me what amazing thing they had for lunch/what their amazing child has just done/what an amazing person their partner is/what amazing place they've booked for their holiday, interspersed with a few political rants and wacky 'cures' for cancer. I deliberate over updating my status to say I'm in Cornwall, but no one would be interested so I don't bother.

My inbox has twenty-three new emails but most are marketing and can be deleted straight away. There's a brief message from Maura, checking how I am following my split from Stuart and informing me that Harry has a new tooth, and one from an agency saying there are no available temporary contracts that match my skills. I fire off a quick reply to Maura and delete the email in ungrammatical English promising me £50,000 in return for my bank details.

There's loud laughter at the bar and, when I glance across, Josh Pasco is staring straight at me. The moment he catches my eye, he looks away and turns round to talk to a friend so his back's facing me. His black jeans are just the right side of tight and he's wearing a short-sleeved green polo shirt which shows off his muscular arms.

'Told you, nice pecs!' says Kayla, suddenly popping up with a cloth and making a show of wiping my table. She glances up at him. 'Mmm, and a bonzer backside. He's quite a hit with the ladies, apparently, and I can see why.'

'Kayla, you are terrible! You're not interested in him, are you?'

'Nah.' She rubs at a beer stain on the wood. 'He's too dark and brooding for me. I go for totally oblivious blondes.'

I follow her gaze to a man among Josh Pasco's group of friends who's built like a rugby player and has hair the colour of straw.

'Him?'

Kayla flushes slightly and shoves the cloth into her dress pocket. 'That's Ollie Simpson, who lives in the next valley. Looks like a Greek god but doesn't know I exist. Oh, the things I could teach that man!' she sighs and winks at me. 'I'd better get back to the bar, Roger's struggling. Crikey.' She wipes beads of sweat from her upper lip. 'It's bloody hot here by the fire. Reminds me of summer in Sydney.'

When Kayla's gone, I take advantage of the Internet and try to find out more about the tragedy that's still affecting this small community. There's scattered information on various websites but the most comprehensive account is from the local paper, the *Cornish Coast Gazette*.

The story starts:

> Seven men from the Salt Bay area have died after their fishing boats capsized in the severe storm that hit Cornwall on Monday night.
>
> The lifeboat from Newlyn rescued six men from the huge waves but the bodies of seven fishermen, ranging in age from twenty-four to seventy, were later found washed up on local beaches.
>
> The storm – one of the worst in Cornwall for a decade – took weather forecasters and fishermen by surprise.

How appalling! There's a list of the poor men who drowned, including Samuel Trebarwith, and the story includes a head-and-shoulders photo of him. For the first time I'm face-to-face with my grandfather, who looks stern like Alice, with grey hair and wire-rimmed glasses perched above a long nose. The piece says he shouldn't have been at sea that night at all; he was retired but doing a favour for a friend who was too unwell to work. Samuel is described as a married father of one daughter, though it doesn't mention that he'd chosen not to see his daughter for almost fifteen years.

Whatever my feelings towards Samuel, I'm terribly sad for all those men – ordinary men like these in the pub – who set out from Salt Bay and never returned to their families. Swallowed by the sea and their bodies spat out onto the sand. I wonder if any of the men were found on the beautiful beach at Salt Bay. I wonder if that's where Samuel ended up. He might have been a bastard but he didn't deserve that.

'Oops, sorry.' Kayla, stumbling past with two plates of spaghetti bolognese, trips on the worn rug covering the flagstones and almost throws them into my lap. 'That was close.' She rebalances the steaming plates and grins. 'Let me know if you want anything to eat and I promise not to throw it at you. There's a menu on the bar and the food's not totally shite, though I'd avoid the pasta.' She plonks the plates down in front of the couple at the next table who eye their spaghetti nervously.

'Could you bring the menu over?' I call after Kayla, but she's already talking to other customers and doesn't hear me. Bugger! I'm going to have to brave the bar myself but at least Josh Pasco still has his back to me.

'The fish is good round here,' says a voice in my ear while I'm scanning the menu. Greek god Ollie has broken away from the group and is standing beside me, trying to attract the attention of Roger, who's ringing up at the till. He gives me a smile that lights up his grey eyes, which have almost invisible pale lashes. 'You're new around here, aren't you?'

'Yes, I'm Annie.'

'She's from London,' says Josh Pasco drily, sidling up to us. He runs his fingers through his unruly hair, pushing it back from his forehead.

'London! Very cosmopolitan!' Ollie waves a tenner at Kayla, who almost leapfrogs Roger so she can serve him. 'Can I have a pint of Betty's and a pint of Scilly Stout, please.'

'Coming right up,' simpers Kayla.

Ollie grins and puts the ten-pound note on the bar. 'Thanks, Carrie.' Kayla shakes her head sadly and starts pulling pints with more force than is necessary. 'So what brings you to Salt Bay, Annie?'

'I'm here visiting Alice, Alice Gowan who lives at Tregavara House.'

'She's Alice's great-niece,' interjects Josh. 'She's a PA.'

'Interesting. I didn't realise that Alice had family outside Cornwall. How long are you here for?'

'Just until the day after tomorrow.' It's annoying how easily that trips off the tongue right now but how nervous I feel about saying it to Alice in the morning.

Ollie nods and folds his arms. 'I bet Alice is enjoying having you to stay, even for a few days.'

'Here's your beer, Wally,' says Kayla, slapping the drinks down on the bar.

'It's Ollie.'

'Yeah, whatever.' Kayla grabs the ten-pound note, flounces to the till and hits the keys with a thwack that makes the till drawer fly open.

Ollie shrugs his shoulders and uses a beer mat to soak up the spilled liquid before picking up the brimming glasses and walking carefully towards his friends. Now's my chance to make amends.

'Look, Josh.' I take a deep breath. 'About throwing a stone at your car – I'm not the sort of person who usually does that kind of thing. I don't know what came over me and I apologise.'

'Yeah, well, I didn't mean to almost run you over.' Josh gives a wide, white smile and rests his half-drunk pint against his chest. He looks much nicer when he smiles, much more… bonzer. No wonder the girls like him. 'I don't usually drive that fast when it's raining but I was late and had to get home to Mum.'

Oh no, he surely doesn't live with his mother. He must be about thirty.

'Do you still live with your mum, then?'

Josh's face clouds over. 'Yeah, we can't all have fancy-schmancy places in London to go back to.'

'Fancy-schmancy? You've obviously never been to Stratford.'

'I've hardly ever been to London because I can't stand the place. Too noisy, too much dirt and too many idiots.'

'That's funny. I can't stand Cornwall – too boring, too much rain and too many bad drivers.' Oh dear, my mouth appears to be running away with me, thanks to Josh Stupid Pasco who's scowling at me over his pint.

'Children, children!' Ollie has come back to collect his change that Kayla has dumped on the bar. 'What are you two like?' He swigs a huge gulp of his beer and wipes his mouth with the back of his hand.

Josh flushes and glances at his friends, who are peering at a mobile phone and laughing loudly.

'I'd better get back to my friends. Goodbye, Annie. Have a safe journey back to lovely Stratford. Come on, Ollie.' He grabs Ollie's arm and pulls him away, as Ollie shouts, 'Bye Annie' and tries unsuccessfully to stop beer slopping over his jeans.

For the first time since arriving in Salt Bay, I'm not hungry. But I order fish and chips anyway and sit gently perspiring at my table until it's ready. I don't even glance at Josh and his friends, preferring to keep my head buried in my mobile phone instead. Who knew there were so many videos of cats doing somersaults on YouTube?

'Here you go. Enjoy!' Kayla bangs down a plate piled high with fried cod and chunky golden chips.

'Thanks, that looks great. And, um, Ollie seems nice.'

'Huh, Ollie who? Months I've worked here and he still doesn't know my name. That man is dead to me,' she says darkly, drawing her finger across her throat. 'There are plenty more fish in the sea. More handsome fish. Fish who might actually get my name right.'

She wanders off, still grumbling, while I bite into a chip and then try the cod. Ollie is right. The fish is very good here. In fact it tastes incredible; fantastically fresh and nothing like the plastic-wrapped cod I buy from the supermarket. And the chips are crisp on the outside but fluffy on the inside. It seems a shame to smother them in vinegar and ketchup but I reach for the bottles that Kayla left with me. Mum and I always went heavy on the condiments when we visited the chippie and old habits die hard.

I manage to polish off the lot and, though it's only just gone nine o'clock, decide to call it a night. Kayla is busy at the bar and everyone else in the pub is either part of a couple or a group. People seem friendly enough and have been smiling at me but no one has made conversation. Josh is as far away as he can possibly be without sitting in the pub garden.

At the door, I wave at Kayla who lifts a hand and mouths 'Bye' from behind the bar. It's a shame that she lives here, surrounded by fish and seagulls, when she could be living it up in London. Especially as I think we could be good friends if we weren't three hundred miles apart. I'll have to nab her tomorrow and convince her that the big city has more to offer.

Outside, it's quiet after the buzz of the pub and the cliffs are dark shadows looming over the houses. The whole place seems sombre and sad and it strikes me that there's no music. There was no music in Maureen's tea shop, no jukebox or piped music in the pub, and I haven't noticed a CD player or even a radio at Alice's. It's as though the whole place is still in mourning.

Feeling like a rebel, I plug my earphones into my phone and whack the B-52s on loudly all the way back to Alice's. There's nothing like 'Love Shack' to shake off the blues. It was music that kept me going over the years while we were moving from flat to flat and Mum was ill. I'd stick the radio on loud or plug in my iPod and listen to disco, jazz, classical, hip-hop – anything to block out the difficult stuff. And music still almost always manages to lift my mood. I'd have gone crazy with grief after Mum died if it wasn't for Jackson Browne and Elvis Costello. Will Young's 'Leave Right Now' still turns me into a blubbering mess.

Alice has left the porch light on at Tregavara House and its beams reach the edge of the dark harbour where boats are resting on wet sand. The tide is so far out it's invisible in the blackness but, when I switch off my music, there's a faint, repetitive whoosh as the waves are sucked back out into deep water.

I stand and listen to it for a while before letting myself into the house as quietly as possible, trying not to disturb Alice, who's far too trusting. For all she knows, I could be ransacking the place while she snoozes, shoving cat ornaments up my jumper like the emmet who stole from the church. The stairs creak with every step but Alice doesn't stir then or while I'm brushing my teeth and getting ready for bed.

Lying under the covers, I decide I'm glad that I came to Cornwall because I'd have always wondered 'what if' had I given Alice the brush-off. But tomorrow I'll tell her I'm leaving because I don't need family and Salt Bay is boring. Though maybe I won't say it in quite those words.

There's something soothing about the rhythmic whoosh of the waves carried by a breeze through my open bedroom window. But it's only as I'm sinking into sleep that I realise why – it sounds a lot like music.

Chapter Nine

I'm in the middle of a lovely dream about Bradley Cooper when I wake with a sickening jolt. A strip of pale light has sneaked under the thick brocade curtains and across the floorboards but the rest of the room is still gloomy. It must be too early to get up. Stretching out across the bed, I remember when I worked in Putney and had to get up really early and catch three different Tube trains to get there. Sixty minutes of urban, rush-hour hell before my working day even began, with the prospect of doing it all over again a few hours later. That's one thing I certainly don't miss.

I turn over and snuggle gratefully under the blankets, keen to slip back into sleep and Bradley's manly arms. He was only wearing a towel and I'm sure he was about to snog me. My thoughts are becoming nicely jumbled when I hear a small sound, like a kitten mewling. There it is again. I'm suddenly wide awake and holding my breath. It seems to be coming from inside the house but Alice doesn't have a cat. If she did, I'd be sneezing my head off by now and shovelling down antihistamines like Smarties.

Groping across the bottom of the bed, I find last night's jumper and put it on over my pyjamas before creeping onto the landing. I'm feeling spooked after being jolted awake and the stained-glass window on the landing doesn't help. Dawn light is streaming through the thick glass and throwing red streaks like blood stains across my bare feet. Damn my overactive imagination, and Stuart's love of horror films!

There's that sound again, coming from downstairs. There's nothing to see when I look over the banisters so I creep down the carpeted steps. The elegant staircase folds at its middle into a perfect right angle and I gasp when I reach the bend. Alice is lying on the floor in the hallway with her dressing gown tangled around her.

'Oh my God, Alice.' I fly down the rest of the stairs and kneel by her. She's huddled in a foetal position and her eyes look huge in her pale, faded face.

'Thank goodness you heard me calling at last,' she croaks, trying to lift her head. 'I'm all right. I just felt a little dizzy.'

'Did you fall down the stairs?' I ask, feeling for her thready pulse under the thin skin on her wrist. She seems so fragile.

'No, I went down like a sack of potatoes in the hall, like a stupid old woman.' She starts shifting about until I put my hand on her shoulder.

'Just stay there and don't move. I'll call for an ambulance.'

'Don't you dare!' Alice is almost shouting. 'No ambulances and no hospitals!'

'But you're hurt.'

'I'll be right as rain if I can sit quietly in my chair for a while.' Her mouth sets into a thin line – and the stern headmistress is back. 'Call Doctor Rivers. He lives in the village so he'll come over. His number is next to the phone. Annie, I insist,' she adds firmly when I look doubtful. 'Do what I ask.'

If we were in London I'd ignore Alice and call 999 but who knows how long it would take an ambulance to navigate the steep, winding lanes to Salt Bay? Especially without sat nav, which probably doesn't work around here. Maybe a local doctor is the better option.

I run upstairs, grab my counterpane and drape it over Alice to keep her warm before ringing Dr Rivers. He sounds bleary-eyed when he eventually answers the phone but, as soon as he hears about Alice, he barks, 'I'll be there at once' and abruptly ends the call.

Five minutes later, Dr Rivers is at the front door with a heavy grey overcoat on top of his striped pyjamas and carrying an old-fashioned doctor's bag straight out of the 1930s.

'Where's the patient?' he demands, ignoring any social niceties and pushing past me to kneel by Alice, who has more colour in her face, thank goodness.

'Now then, what have you been up to?' he asks gently, lifting off the counterpane and handing it to me. 'Do you think you could make us all a nice cup of tea while I check that Alice is OK?'

Glad to have something to do, I fold the counterpane into a pile on the kitchen table, put on the kettle and drop teabags into three mugs. My hands are shaking, partly from the shock of finding Alice but also because it's taken me right back to when Mum was so poorly with cancer. She was too stubborn to stay in bed and I once found her collapsed on the floor with her blonde, post-chemo wig fanned out round her head like a halo. We called it her 'angel look', I remember, furiously scrubbing away a tear that's rolling down my cheek. *Get a grip, Annie; this is about Alice, not you.* But it's hard not to think about Mum when I'm standing in the house where she grew up. The past has a horrible habit of leaching into the present.

When I carry the steaming mugs back into the hall, Alice is sitting with her back propped up against the wall. She gives me a faint smile and then frowns.

'Mugs, Annabella? There are proper tea cups in the bottom cupboard.'

'Don't worry about that now, Alice,' says Dr Rivers, stashing his stethoscope in his bag and clipping it shut. 'There don't appear to be any bones broken but I'd rather you went to hospital for an X-ray to check.'

'Please don't fuss, Stephen. I hate hospitals and I'm not leaving my home. I felt dizzy for a moment and went down. But it was all rather graceful, like a building collapsing from the foundations up, and I didn't hit anything.' She gives a wobbly laugh. 'If you could help me into my chair, I can sit quietly for a while. That's all I need.'

Dr Rivers sighs and his bushy, grey moustache quivers. 'All right, you're lucky that your great-niece is here to look after you or I'd be insisting that you go to hospital. Come on, then.' He puts an arm under Alice's arms and beckons for me to help him.

I slip my arm around Alice's waist and, between us, we slowly pull her to her feet. She weighs almost nothing and the bones at the bottom of her ribs feel hard through the piled fabric of her dressing gown. With our support, she walks slowly into the sitting room and sinks onto the sofa.

'Oof, that's better.' Alice settles herself back while I plump up the cushions and make sure her dressing gown is covering her legs.

'Oh, do stop fussing, both of you.' She puts her head back against the antimacassar, embroidered in blue and gold cross-stitch to match the cushions. 'Where's that tea?'

I hand round the mugs and Dr Rivers has a few sips before picking up his bag.

'I've got surgery this morning so must go, but call if you need me. And if you feel worse, Alice, make sure you call an ambulance if necessary.' He glances at me and I nod.

'Thank you, Stephen, for coming round,' says Alice, lightly touching his arm. 'You've always been good to me and to the Trebarwith family.'

'You're very welcome.' Dr Rivers places his mug on a side table and walks into the hall with me scurrying after him. When we're out of Alice's earshot, he says quietly, 'I'll call round when I get back from surgery but keep an eye on her for a while and make sure she has a peaceful day with no stress.'

'Will she be OK?'

'For the moment. She's a tough old girl; she's had to be. But she shouldn't be left alone at all for a few hours.'

'Of course. I can look after her today.' It's the least I can do before heading back to London, just so long as she doesn't start depending on me.

Dr Rivers pauses on the doorstep. 'It's worrying that these falls are becoming more frequent.'

'Have there been others?'

'A few. But you'd better ask Alice about those, doctor-patient confidentiality and all that.' He pulls the overcoat more tightly round him and glances up at the sky which is streaked with pink and gold. 'It's going to be a nice day now those clouds have shifted. I'll see you later Annabella, and call if you need me.'

'What did Stephen say to you?' asks Alice sharply when I hurry back into the sitting room to check on her.

'Nothing. Just that I need to keep an eye on you because you've fallen before.'

'Hardly! There have been a few little trips, that's all. Stephen does tend to be overdramatic at times.' She puts down her tea and closes her eyes.

'Would you like me to help you into bed?'

'No, thank you,' murmurs Alice, with her eyes shut. 'I'll sit here for a while and catch my breath.'

Within a few minutes she's fast asleep, or I presume she is. It's hard to tell because her skin has a greyish tinge and you never know how old people will react to a shock. So, copying something I've seen Maura do with Harry, I put my face close to Alice's to make sure she's still breathing. At first there's nothing but, as I'm about to panic and start doing chest compressions, she gently exhales and her breath warms my cheek. That's a relief!

Suddenly she opens one beady eye and stares straight at me. 'I'm not dead yet, Annabella.'

'Oops, just checking.' Alice might have the body of an old woman, but her mind is still sharp as a tack.

Chapter Ten

Alice dozes on the sofa for an hour while I throw on some clothes and do a few jobs around the house. It's good to be helpful and it also gives me the chance to have a good look round. I'm not really nosy, I tell myself, peeping round doors. I'm just curious about this house and its history. And the family who've lived here for generations? Maybe.

Tregavara House isn't huge but there are five bedrooms, a dusty dining room that looks unused, a small scullery as well as a kitchen, and a cellar behind a scuffed, black door. There's nothing in the cellar, when I carefully navigate the wooden steps, except for a few bottles of wine and some boxes of books which smell of mould. I don't linger there because drops of water are hanging from the low ceiling and the stone walls feel cold and wet, which is alarming with the sea only a few metres away, especially as some of the stones are loose where the mortar has powdered with age.

The cellar, and the whole house in fact, could do with updating and renovating – sympathetically, so it doesn't lose its coving and cornicing and lovely old-fashioned windows. But sympathetically usually means expensively and Alice doesn't look like she can afford it. Which is a shame because the house oozes faded splendour and could be magnificent if a shedload of dosh was spent on it. With some TLC it might even make a fab B&B, though I can't imagine Alice sharing the Trebarwith ancestral home with emmets.

After a while, Alice wants to get dressed so I follow her up the stairs to her bedroom, arms poised in case she topples backwards. So far I've resisted the temptation to peek into Alice's bedroom because her door was shut and it didn't feel right but I'm itching to see inside because, let's be honest, I am dead nosy.

Alice's bedroom doesn't disappoint. It's like the cover of a Regency romance novel. Her bed is magnificent – a mini four-poster with a dark wooden canopy, plumped-up pillows and a rose-coloured satin counterpane. There's a dark pink upholstered chair with stout, wooden legs against one wall and a huge wardrobe covered in carvings that must have been a nightmare to get through the door. Her stone-framed window looks out over the sea and the cliffs which are dotted with seagulls.

'This is David,' says Alice, picking up a black and white photo in a silver frame from her bedside table. She rubs her thumb gently across the face of a stocky man in a dark suit who's standing next to a young woman in a long, full-skirted dress. 'It was taken the day we got married in Salt Bay Church. The suit belonged to my father and David hated wearing it. He was a fisherman who ran a boat out of Perrigan Bay so he was more used to wearing oilskins and Guernseys.'

'How long were you married?'

'Forty-three years.' Alice sits down heavily on the bed. 'He passed away thirteen years ago from a heart attack, soon after we moved back here to look after Sheila following the storm. This is Sheila with Samuel.' She picks up a photograph of a middle-aged woman on a sofa beside a man I recognise from the newspaper cutting. The woman is wearing a frumpy beige dress with a brown cardigan and has sad eyes. 'It must be strange seeing the grandparents you've never met.'

She hands the picture to me but I put it straight back on the bedside table, as if the silver frame is burning my skin. There are too many ghosts in this house and the threads of my uncomplicated life are beginning to unravel and entangle with this family I've never known. A family who never wanted to know me until now, when I might be useful.

'I'm going back to London tomorrow, Alice.'

Alice looks up in surprise from the wedding photo she's still holding. 'For good?'

'Yes, I'm sorry. Thank you for inviting me here and for having me to stay but my life is back in London.'

'Of course, but I thought you might be curious about your roots and your mother's early life. This used to be her bedroom, you know. I could tell you about what happened between your mother and her parents, and the difficult years after she left Cornwall.'

'I know all about those,' I say bitterly. 'We went from flat to flat with no money and no support. I loved my mum, even though she wasn't always easy to live with and she obviously didn't live up to what her parents expected of her. But how could anyone abandon their own child and grandchild? That was a monstrous thing to do.'

Alice opens her mouth and then snaps it shut. 'So your mind is made up?' She puts her wedding photo on the bed with shaky hands and steadies them in her lap.

'It is. I'm sorry, Alice. I'm sure you can make other arrangements for the help you need.'

'I'm sure I can, and you're probably right that it's best not to rake up the past. What's done is done and it's all too late anyway.' She swings her legs onto the bed and lies on top of the covers, her arms across her chest as though she's in her coffin. 'I think I need another little rest before I get dressed. Perhaps you could walk to the newsagent's to pick up my magazine.'

'Dr Rivers said you weren't to be left on your own.'

He also said she should avoid stress, I suddenly remember, wishing I could take back what I've just said. I'm leaving tomorrow and it would have been kinder to leave Alice with the Disney version of my life with Mum; the version that I've been peddling to my friends because explaining the chaotic reality is too unsettling. And what's the point, anyway?

'Stephen is a good doctor but he worries too much. I'll be perfectly fine here on my own,' snaps Alice without opening her eyes. And she doesn't move while I go out of the room and quietly close the door behind me.

It's still early but a pale sun is throwing shadows across the garden and the sea looks like a heaving vat of molten green glass. Its constant motion is soothing and I stand at the harbour for a while, looking across the water to boats that are specks on the horizon.

One small boat has come into harbour and two men in oilskin trousers are unloading their catch. One of the men breaks off from his tuneless whistling and nods at me. 'Good morning. Nice day for it.'

'Morning. It looks as if you've caught quite a few.' A large plastic tub near my feet is piled high with flapping fish and I feel faintly uneasy about watching them in their death throes.

'We've only been out for a while and had a good catch today. There's more than we need but Roger might take some of the mackerel off our hands.' The man gives the tub a shake and the fish inside it move in a silver wave.

'You're staying at Alice Gowan's, aren't you?' He stares at my face, trying to work out who I am. 'It's good Alice has some company. That's a big place for an old lady to be rattling round in on her own.'

'I'm just here for a few days. I'm leaving tomorrow.'

'That's a shame.' He peers more closely at me before picking up a fish that's slithered onto the stones and throwing it back onto the pile. 'I'm Peter, by the way. What did you say your name was?'

'It's Annie.'

'Annie what?'

'Annie Trebarwith.'

'I thought as much.' Peter's face lights up and he nods. 'You've got a look of the Trebarwiths about you. How are you related to old Alice?'

'I'm her great-niece.'

'Didn't know she had one. But it's nice to meet you, Annie.' Peter wipes a chapped, red hand across his sweater and holds it out for me to shake. 'It's good to know you're one of us!'

One of us? I'm not part of this strange little community just because bits of shared DNA are buried in the clifftop cemetery. Mum certainly didn't feel that she was 'one of us'.

But I don't fancy debating the ins and outs of belonging with Peter, who's elbow-deep in flapping fish, so I say goodbye and head away from the quay to the newsagent's.

Jennifer is outside the shop straightening a rack of blow-up beach toys, though I don't know who in their right minds would buy them in January. She stops rearranging the brightly coloured plastic when she sees me.

'Are you here for Alice's magazine? I've kept it for her under the counter. Come with me.' Inside, she stoops with a loud 'oof' and pulls out a copy of *Bird Watching*. Funny, I never took Alice for a twitcher. 'How's Alice doing? I haven't seen her for a few days. Is she still feeling unwell?'

'She had a fall this morning so she's having a rest.' As soon as the words are out of my mouth, I regret telling Jennifer, especially when she purses her lips and folds her arms across her sturdy breasts.

'I keep telling her she's too old to be in that big house on her own. Poor Alice. She's had a lot to cope with, what with losing her husband like that and her brother in the Great Storm, and there was the baby of course.'

'The baby?'

Jennifer's eyes sparkle as she realises she's in possession of juicy gossip. 'Her little boy who died of measles back in the 1960s. She almost died of grief, that's what Mavis says. Mavis is in a home now. Gone a bit, you know' – Jennifer taps the side of her head and opens her eyes wide – 'mental.'

'That's terribly sad. About Alice,' I clarify when Jennifer looks uncertain. 'Very sad about Mavis too, I'm sure.'

'Yes, very sad. Poor Mavis,' says Jennifer, waving her arm dismissively. 'So you didn't know about the baby, then? That's strange. How exactly do you know Alice?'

'I'm her great-niece.'

'Fancy that,' says Jennifer, huge bosom heaving. 'I didn't know she had one. You must know Toby, and are you related to Samuel and Sheila?'

'My mum was their daughter.'

'Heavens! Not the mythical Joanna! Well, that's a turn-up for the books.' Jennifer looks as though she's about to combust with excitement and I decide that I don't like her very much.

'I'd really better get back to poor old Alice.' I shove the magazine into my bag and leave Jennifer standing in the middle of the shop, her mouth opening and closing like one of Peter's fish.

I don't want to leave Alice for too long but I take a detour on the way back and go past The Whistling Wave. I'm hoping to see Kayla because I'd rather not disappear without saying goodbye. But when

I look through the window the only person behind the bar is Roger, who's pulling a pint and chatting to customers. Maybe it's her day off. That's a shame.

'I didn't take you for a peeping Tom.' Kayla has sneaked up behind me. 'Or maybe you've got a thing for Roger. He's a darling – a lazy darling and he's three bangers short of a barbie but apart from that he's a really decent bloke.' She puts down the bucket of water and mop that she's carrying. 'Is everything all right?'

'I was hoping to see you before I leave tomorrow.'

'You're leaving so soon? That's a shame.'

'I need to get back to London but I wanted to say look me up if you're ever in the city. Here's my phone number and email address.' I pull a scrap of paper from my jeans pocket and hand it over. 'I can return the favour of showing you round.'

'Yeah, maybe.' Kayla shoves the paper into her apron pocket. 'I kind of hoped you might be staying for a while 'specially as you told me that Alice is family. You still haven't seen Cornwall at its best. You haven't been to Salt Bay beach yet and I thought we could try out the nightlife in Penzance.'

'Perhaps next time,' I lie, wondering what on earth nightclubs in Penzance are like. 'I can't stop for a drink because Alice had a fall this morning and I'm keeping an eye on her.'

Kayla shoves her mop into the pink plastic bucket and wrings out a stream of steaming water. 'Poor Alice, but it's good that you were around to look after her. She'll have to manage on her own from tomorrow.'

She says it lightly but there's a hint of reproach in her voice. Or maybe I'm imagining it and projecting my own guilt onto her. Jeez, I hate it when I get all psycho-babbly on myself but that's what families do to you. They make you feel guilty. All of the time. I've seen it often enough with friends who visit their parents every weekend or spend Christmas with argumentative siblings because they feel bad if they don't. Well, that's not for me and I'm leaving before I get sucked into family stuff even more. Alice is not my responsibility and tomorrow it'll be *London, here I come.*

'I'd better get on. This sign won't clean itself,' sighs Kayla, sloshing the mop across the pub sign and showering water over us. 'But it was lovely meeting you, Annie. Really. Look after yourself.'

'You too. And good luck with Ollie.'

'Huh, Ollie! I might shag Josh Pasco and his bonzer backside instead, just to show Ollie what he's missing.' She wields the mop around her head and hits the sign which swings violently back and forth. 'I'll email you and let you know what he's like.'

I really, really hope that Kayla won't send me Josh Pasco's out-of-ten shag score. There's something unsettling about the thought of them sleeping together, though I'm not sure why. She's young, free and single and so's he, as far as I'm aware, so it's none of my business if they hook up. In fact, she's welcome to the grumpy git and I reckon he'd only be a six anyway.

Chapter Eleven

Alice is pottering about when I get back and complaining that she can't sleep although she's tired. Despite going upstairs to get dressed, she's still wearing her grey dressing gown which drains all colour from her face, and she's shaky, though she insists rather predictably that she's 'fine'.

All the same, I insist she sits in front of the TV while I make her an omelette for lunch. Then I can do some vacuuming while she rests and make sure everything is shipshape before I leave. This is mostly to make me feel better because I feel guilty at the thought of abandoning her, especially since finding out that she lost a baby all those years ago. I can't help it, even though that's just the kind of overemotional thinking that will do nothing but bugger up my lovely, uncomplicated life.

I'm not leaving Alice in the lurch, I tell myself sternly, cracking three eggs into a glass bowl and searching through the cutlery drawer for a whisk. *I'm merely leaving her as she was before I arrived – elderly, unwell and prone to falling in a large house with lots of stairs.* For goodness' sake, that's not helping! I start beating hell out of the egg yolks, determined to distract myself from a ridiculous urge to 'do the right thing.'

Dr Rivers calls round again just after four o'clock, this time wearing navy cords and a pale blue shirt, but still carrying his fat, vintage bag.

'How's the patient?' he asks me, stepping over the vacuum cleaner that's blocking the sitting room doorway.

'Still with a full complement of her marbles and able to answer her own questions,' pipes up Alice.

'I wasn't implying otherwise, Alice. I wouldn't dare.' Dr Rivers rolls his eyes at me and opens his bag. 'Let's give you a quick check over.'

He listens to Alice's heart, takes her temperature and asks questions while I hover near the door, not sure if it's right for me to stay for this.

'Do sit down, Annabella,' murmurs Alice after a while. 'You'll wear a groove in the rug. You're just like your grandfather. He could never keep still either. Always had to be doing something.'

The examination takes five minutes and, when it's done, Dr Rivers sits opposite his patient with his elbows on his knees.

'Well, Alice, the good news is that you seem to have escaped this morning's fall fairly unscathed.'

Alice goes to speak but Dr Rivers holds up his hand.

'However, the bad news is that this can't go on for too much longer, you know that. Your condition is going to get worse and there's been some recent deterioration.' He puffs out his cheeks. 'I think it's time to start making plans about what you're going to do next.'

'I'm not leaving this house, Stephen, or Salt Bay. This is my home and it always will be.' Alice's breathing has quickened and there are bright spots of colour in her cheeks.

Dr Rivers shakes his head. 'I know, Alice, but you can't carry on living here alone for too much longer. Can she?' He glances at me for support. 'If your great-niece hadn't been here this morning what would you have done? What if next time you fall in the bath or down the stairs?' He takes Alice's hands in his. 'You're not going to get better, Alice. Your condition is progressive.'

'I'm very well aware of that.' Alice pulls her hands away and folds her arms. 'I can get Serena to come in for more hours each week and pay for carers.'

'The level of care and support you'll end up needing here will be expensive, and services are stretched, even if people are eligible for help. Just think about it,' he adds gently. 'Maybe talk to Annabella about what's best and perhaps I—'

'No,' says Alice firmly, pushing herself up and standing ramrod straight. Her white hair has fluffed up at the back where she's been resting against the sofa. 'I might have to sell this house if I move or go into full-time care – the Trebarwith family home. I just can't do it so I'll sort things out myself and find another way.'

Dr Rivers sighs and pats her shoulder. 'I've learned over the years never to underestimate the Trebarwiths, so I'm sure if there is another way, you'll find it.'

By the time I've shown Dr Rivers out, Alice has moved to a chair near the window. She's sitting in shadow sideways-on and reminds me of an 18th century silhouette portrait. Like a proud, elderly Jane Austen with a ray of pale, winter sunlight falling across her lap.

'What exactly is it you have, Alice?'

'A progressive neurological condition; that's how the doctors describe it. It's been coming on for some time.' Alice watches two children, wrapped up in coats and hats, who are scrabbling across the wet harbour sand and screaming with delight. 'At first I was just more tired and achey than usual but then I started getting stiff and shaky and, more recently, I've been falling down. It's a damn nuisance.'

'Why didn't you tell me?'

'I think you've had quite enough to take in, don't you? And I didn't want you to feel obliged to stay here.' She swivels round in her chair until she's facing me. 'My motivation in asking you here wasn't to cajole you into being my carer, Annabella, however it might seem. When I heard you didn't have a job at the moment I thought my business proposal might be mutually beneficial but, most of all, I wanted some time with you, to get to know you before – well, before it's too late. It's sad when people leave things too late. Anyway,' she adds, and pulls back her shoulders, 'it's not your problem and I'll manage as I always have.'

Of course she will. She'll be absolutely fine, and I can call her every now and again from Stratford to see how she's doing. She most definitely is not my responsibility just because we're related.

But then Alice sucker punches me by setting her mouth into a thin line and tilting her chin when she looks back out to sea. That's all; just a determined set of the jaw and a slight tilt of the chin, but she looks like Mum waiting at the window of our flat for the ambulance to take her to the hospice. Mum was vulnerable and scared but at least she had me there to help her. Alice has no one.

Oh bugger. I realise with a sick, sinking feeling that I can't leave Salt Bay, at least not for a while. Because however much I try to deny it, there's a strange pull between me and Alice and I can't leave her in the lurch. If this is how having family feels, I'm not sure I like it.

'Maybe I could stay for a couple of weeks or so while you sort something out that's more long term.' The words almost catch in my throat, even though 'doing the right thing' is supposed to make you feel warm and virtuous.

Alice glances at me. 'I don't want you to stay out of pity, Annabella. I do have some pride left.'

'It wouldn't be out of pity,' I say earnestly to cover up the fact that pity is a pretty major player in all of this. 'It makes sense because I don't have a job at the moment so I'm free to stay for a while. And it would be good to get to know you better.'

'Are you sure?'

'Absolutely,' I say before I can change my mind.

Alice smiles broadly for the first time since I arrived in Salt Bay and I'm surprised by how much younger she looks.

'That would be wonderful, if you're really sure. I can provide bed and board and the little bit I can pay you will cover your rent in London.'

Ah yes. It's all very well being kind to old folk but I haven't thought through the practicalities. I'm sure Alice's understanding of London rent levels bears no relation to the mind-blowing reality and my meagre savings will soon run out. Between work contracts in London, secretarial temping helps to keep the bills paid but that's not an option here where my work for the next few weeks will consist of keeping an elderly lady upright.

The first thing I need to do is speak to Amber. So I make an excuse about needing fresh air and head for the phone box near the village green, which is more private than Alice's landline. The green is deserted apart from Celine, who's running round in circles on the muddy grass.

Amber answers her mobile on the second ring. 'Hello? Who's that?' There's a racket going on in the background.

'It's Annie.'

'Annie who?'

'Annie from the flat.'

'Who?'

'Annie, the person you live with.'

There's a pause while Amber tries to remember the woman who's picked up her wet towels for the last eight months.

'Annie! Of course. Sorry, I can't hear you very well 'cos I'm with some friends in the uni bar.' Her friends break into an impromptu chorus of 'Annie, I'm Not Your Daddy' – Kid Creole and his Coconuts have nothing to worry about. 'Are you still in Coventry?'

'Cornwall.'

'Why have you gone from Coventry to Cornwall?'

'I never went to Coventry. I always went to Cornwall.'

'OK, whatever.'

The singing is getting louder and my attempts to be heard over the caterwauling attract Celine's attention. She stops trying to kick the seagulls resting on the grass and wanders over to press her nose against the salt-streaked glass.

'Something's come up which means I need to stay here for a couple of weeks or so. Do you know anyone who needs somewhere to stay, who could maybe have my room temporarily?'

Having overheard Amber speaking on the phone recently – it's hard not to listen in because she conducts all phone conversations at top volume – I feel pretty confident about her answer.

'As a matter of fact I do. Shush, everyone!' The background noise quietens down a smidgen. 'My friend Gracie, the one with green hair who lives in Tooting, is looking for somewhere to stay because her flatmate Chanelle has got a new boyfriend and they're a total nightmare. They keep doing it all over the place. Gracie caught them bumping uglies on the kitchen table last week, on top of the brie ciabatta she'd made for lunch, which is totally out of order. She didn't fancy eating it after that. And the other girl she shares with keeps following her round declaring her undying love. Gracie is like totally cool with lesbians but this girl is really pissing her off. So I know she'll jump at the chance of living with me. That's brilliant! She can move in this weekend.'

'I'm not moving out for good,' I say quickly while Amber pauses for breath. 'Just for a few weeks max; probably only a couple.'

'Yeah, of course. Gracie can live here while she's getting something more permanent sorted out. It'll be a good laugh having someone like her in the flat.' *More of a laugh than living with you* is the subtext.

'She'll need to cover the rent, I'm afraid.'

'Not a problem. Her dad's loaded so he'll stump up for it. What about all your stuff?'

'There isn't much, to be honest.' Moving from flat to flat as a child soon teaches you not to hoard possessions, not when everything you own has to fit into one battered suitcase and a couple of carrier bags. 'Can you put my stuff to one side and I'll nip up and collect some clothes and things in a day or two.'

'Will do. Gracie will think it's amazing being able to move out, like, straight away. Thanks, Annie, and have fun in Cheshire.'

'Cornwall.'

'Yeah, great.' There's a huge cheer in the background and the line goes dead.

Celine gives me an evil glare when I leave the phone box and rushes off to throttle any small animals she can lay her hands on. She's a perfect advert for remaining childless.

Alice comes into the hall when I clatter through the front door and kick off her borrowed shoes.

'Is everything all right?'

'Everything's fine. I rang my flatmate while I was out and a friend of hers might want to take over my room and the rent for a while, so that's good. But I'll need to nip back up to London this weekend to collect some clothes.'

'Of course, and thank you Annabella.' Alice holds out her blue-veined hands until I feel obliged to take hold of them. 'It will be wonderful to have family around me again.'

I smile faintly on hearing the F-word, already regretting my decision to stay and not quite sure why I haven't legged it from Salt Bay. Maybe I'm hormonally challenged or the break-up with Stuart has had a terrible effect on my sanity. Either way, I'm well and truly screwed.

Chapter Twelve

After a restless night, I find Alice in the kitchen scraping burnt toast over the sink and waiting for her tea to brew. She pours me a cup while I fetch our cornflakes and we sit at the table making small talk about the weather and Dr Rivers' impressive facial hair. I try to be upbeat and keep the conversation flowing but, truth be told, I'm feeling panicky, as if I've been kidnapped, which is daft because no one is forcing me to stay and kidnap would be pointless anyway because who would pay to get me back? I cheer myself up with the thought of my friends having a whip-round.

I'm imagining my friends handing over cash to a trench-coated Alice when the phone rings.

Alice frowns and finishes chewing her toast. 'Who would be calling me at this time of the morning?' She pulls herself up and slips her feet into her embroidered velvet slippers. 'Perhaps it's Stephen checking up on me.'

While Alice is talking on the phone in the sitting room, I finish my cornflakes and tell myself that the next few weeks of my life will pass quickly. Especially if I treat this as just another short-term contract and use my spare time to line up another London job. I'll have to search for work using The Whistling Wave's Wi-Fi, but spending time in the pub is no hardship, just so long as Josh Pasco isn't an alcoholic on the quiet. And looking at this situation positively, at least I won't bump into cheating Stuart down here, or matching-Myla Melinda.

'That's a coincidence.' Alice sits back down and prods at her soggy cereal with a spoon. 'That was Toby. He was surprised to hear about you but delighted too.'

'Who's Toby?' I vaguely remember Jennifer mentioning a Toby to me, shortly before she realised who I was and almost passed out with excitement.

'Toby is my second cousin twice removed which makes him your third cousin, I think. Something like that.'

Great, just what I've always wanted – more feckin' family. I struggle to keep my face neutral.

'Does he live in Cornwall?'

'Toby lives in London, in Islington, which I think is close to Stratford so you might know him,' says Alice, not grasping that the chances of me knowing some random bloke in the metropolis – albeit one apparently related to me – is about a zillion to one. 'He has a very important job helping to run an auction business selling paintings and antiques so I don't see much of him.' She pushes away her cereal, now congealed into a sodden lump. 'He calls me occasionally to make sure I'm still breathing and he was so excited to hear about you he's going to drive down later to meet you.'

'Wow, that will be great!' There's something about Cornwall that brings out the liar in me.

'The best part is, I suggested that he might be able to bring your clothes down in his car and he said that he could. He'll collect them from your flat if your flatmate can pack them up in time.'

'That's kind of him but I can nip up there.'

To be honest, I was looking forward to nipping up there but Alice is adamant that her idea is the best solution, and she's probably right.

The train takes hours, I'll feel duty-bound to pay the exorbitant fare myself and, once back in vibrant London, I'll probably change my mind and cancel my return to Salt Bay. Which is possibly why Alice suggested the plan to Toby in the first place. I steal a glance at my great-aunt and remember Dr Rivers' words: 'Never underestimate the Trebarwiths.' She takes a ladylike bite out of her cold toast and gives me a very unladylike wink.

When I call her, Amber says she'd be happy to pack a case for me so I give her a list of essentials. My raincoat (obviously), underwear, PJs, more jeans, a dress (just in case Kayla and I do get to a nightclub), warm tops, sturdy shoes, my pocket radio for a music fix, some toiletries and the photo of my mum in a polished wooden frame that's beside my bed.

I'm not overjoyed at the thought of Amber going through my underwear drawer but it can't be helped. She hangs G-string scraps of black lace on the radiators to dry, so my more capacious undies are likely to frighten the life out of her. Either that, or she'll Snapchat pictures of my comfiest knickers as a hilarious warning about ageing.

I'm not sure how to spend the morning once my packing is sorted and Alice has passed on Amber's mobile number to Toby. Thanks to my housework flurry yesterday the house is clean and tidy, and Alice is settled in the dining room doing paperwork.

'Bills to pay, Annabella. Lots of bills,' she murmurs when I poke my head round the door. She's writing cheques with a fountain pen and refuses my offer of help even though her hand is shaking and smudging blue ink across the paper.

When I wander back into the kitchen I notice a pair of green wellies tucked away down the side of the fridge. After upending them to check for spiders – Maura swears she found a false widow inside her trainers – I slip my feet inside and decide to have a go at tackling the garden. Is gardening even a thing in winter? I've no idea, having grown up with tiny backyards filled with communal dustbins, but how hard can it be? If it looks like a weed, pull it up; if it doesn't, leave it. Alan Titchmarsh, eat your heart out.

Unfortunately, Alice's garden doesn't so much need a spot of gardening as a full-scale rescue. Scrubby shrubs edging the lawn have grown together in a tangle and everything has been battered by vicious winds. It's hard to know where to start so I pull up a brown Triffid that looks weed-like and some dead grass curling round the base of a plant with tall, spiky fronds. As I crouch over, scrabbling about in the earth with the pale sun warming my back, I start to feel more positive about the whole staying-in-Cornwall-for-a-while thing. Maybe I can treat the next few weeks as a working holiday and learn some useful gardening skills along the way. Skills I can use to cultivate the balcony tubs at the flat which, last time I looked, contained bare soil, a crushed Coke can and the stub of a marijuana joint.

The sun is high in the sky and shadows thrown by the cliffs have long disappeared when I stagger to my feet two hours later, stretch my back and survey my handiwork. The garden isn't that different from when I started but there's a satisfying pile of weeds that I drop into the plastic bin by the back door. Gardening is good fun, I decide, putting my hands on my hips and smiling contentedly – apart from the backache and the ravenous appetite it induces. Fortunately, it's almost time for lunch.

Back in the kitchen, I catch sight of myself in the polished steel splashback and do a double-take. I look different, with glowing, flushed skin and bright eyes. I look outdoorsy and healthy, and it suits me. I steal a few more glances while I'm making sandwiches for myself and Alice, and refuse to calculate how many extra wrinkles I'll have in ten years' time thanks to my morning outside.

I'm planning to carry on with the gardening after lunch but an icy wind has picked up so I pass the time by clearing out the kitchen cupboards instead. I was going to wait until Serena arrived and rope her in to help me but she's cried off with a cold so I get stuck in on my own.

'Some of the food may be slightly out of date,' warns Alice, finding me a black bin liner. 'It's hard to get out of the village when the weather's very bad so I like to make sure I've always got enough in to keep me going.'

As it turns out, there's enough in Alice's cupboards to keep a rugby team going for a month. But they'd all die of food poisoning. The bin liner is soon half-filled with rusty tins of tuna and ham, bricks of ancient sugar, congealed spices from the Millennium and a bag of unidentifiable yellow powder that's gone mouldy. Once the food cupboards are empty, I wipe down the wallpaper-lined shelves and refill them with everything still in date.

Then I tackle the cupboards crammed full with mismatched crockery and the drawers almost overflowing with saucepans. I don't throw anything away but, by carefully rearranging the stacking system, the cupboards gradually become more ordered and tidy.

'That's wonderful,' declares Alice, coming to inspect the kitchen towards the end of the afternoon. She opens and closes the same cupboards several times as though she's expecting them to change back. Then she pulls two small steaks from the fridge.

'You deserve a treat for all your hard work today, Annabella, so let's have a special tea.'

Two hours later, full of fried steak and tomatoes, we're watching *Coronation Street* when a car pulls up outside.

'That must be Toby. He's early.' Alice tweaks aside the curtain. 'He's made very good time, and the big case he's getting out of his boot must be yours.'

The man pulling a huge case up the garden path is younger than I was expecting. I pictured Toby as a pudgy middle-aged man in a suit and tie but I'm way off beam. The man turning puce with the exertion of hauling my case is only a few years older than me and wearing cords, a tweed jacket and what looks like a cravat. Maybe that's to let everyone know he's arty. He's also got a brown hipster goatee and there's no hint of a paunch. I draw back behind the curtain so he won't see me ogling him. That wouldn't be a good start.

While Alice goes to let him in, I turn off the TV and arrange myself by the fireplace, unnerved by the double whammy of meeting two new relatives within a few days.

'Toby, how lovely to see you.' Alice's voice, floating in through the open sitting room door, is slightly obscured by a loud thud as my case hits the hall floor.

'Hello Alice. Looking gorgeous as ever.' There's no trace of a Cornish accent. In fact, Toby sounds rather posh which makes me even more jittery because posh people have that effect on me. It's very annoying. I rest my arm on the mantelpiece and try to look natural because that always works.

'You must be Annabella. How marvellous to meet you.' Toby breezes into the room with his hand outstretched, oozing confidence. 'I didn't realise that Alice had been hiding a relative. What else have you been hiding from me, Alice?' He gives a short laugh and raises his tidy eyebrows.

'It's Annie,' I say, moving forward and shaking his hand which is soft and cool. 'It's good to meet you too. And thank you so much for collecting my case. I hope it wasn't an inconvenience.'

'Not at all, though I think your flatmate – Amber, is it? – has filled it with bricks.' His hooded grey eyes flash with irritation but then he grins. 'I managed to get away from work at lunchtime as it's Friday so I was grateful that Amber was at home and had the case ready.'

'She's a student.'

'I thought as much. She asked me to tell you that she lost your list so she used her initiative about the clothes you might need.'

That sounds ominous. Knowing Amber's predilection for micro-minis and crop tops, she'll have packed my shortest dress and skimpiest T-shirts. Which means I'll have to prance round Cornwall like an ageing pole dancer until I die of hypothermia without ever seeing the Shard again. I suddenly ache with longing to see that amazing glass pyramid spearing the clouds above London Bridge station.

Toby's giving me an odd look so I beckon for him to sit down.

'I'm sure what she's packed will be fine, and thanks again for bringing it with you.'

'Don't mention it. We are family after all. But how strange that we've never met before, and Alice tells me you'd never met her either until a few days ago.'

'It's strange but marvellous.' Alice turns on the lamp and floods the room with more light. 'Toby, you can chat to Annabella while I get you some food. You must be exhausted after your long drive.'

'It was a killer but worth it for you, Alice.' Toby settles back against the chair and kicks off his tan brogues while I perch self-consciously on the arm of the sofa. 'So tell me all about you, Annie. Alice tells me that you live in London. I expect you've got a boyfriend up there you're keen to get back to, haven't you?'

His personal question knocks me off-guard and my face flushes.

'Not at the moment. I mean, there was someone but' – a vision of Stuart's head popping up over the back of his sofa floats into my mind – 'we recently decided to go our separate ways.'

'That's a shame.' Toby kicks absently at fluff on the Persian rug. 'Still, I'm sure a girl like you won't have to wait long for the next boyfriend.'

Is he flirting with me? It's hard to tell if Toby Trebarwith is implying I'm a drop-dead gorgeous man-magnet or a total slapper. His poker face is giving nothing away.

'And what about your job, Annie. What do you do?'

I shuffle nervously, finding it hard to shake the feeling that I'm being interviewed. 'I'm between jobs right now but I usually work as a PA.'

'Really? That's fascinating.'

'Not as fascinating as your job. Alice tells me you work for an antiques business.'

'That's right. I'm an associate partner at Fulbright and Linsom in Islington. We handle sales worth millions of pounds every year.' He smooths down the lapel of his jacket. 'It's hard work but interesting. You never know what you might discover when people bring things in to be auctioned.'

'What's the most surprising thing you've ever found?'

'Oh, I don't know.' Toby looks out of the window and exhales slowly. 'Probably a rare 18th century diamond necklace that the owner bought at a car boot sale from someone who believed the stones were paste.'

'Wow, that's amazing.' I'm desperate to ask how much it sold for but worry that might come across as vulgar.

Toby gives me a dazzling bleached smile. 'Amazing is the right word. It was champagne all round that day. But,' he drops the smile, 'what's money? Family is what matters which is why I take time out to come down from London and keep an eye on Alice.'

'How often do you get down to Salt Bay?'

'As often as I can manage.' Toby shifts in his chair, looking ill at ease for the first time since he arrived. 'It's quite a drive, you know.'

'I can imagine. It took hours on the train.'

'Public transport is appalling and I never bother with it now I've got the Beamer. Perhaps I could drive down again next weekend and give you a lift back to London. You'll never manage on the train with that heavy case.'

'That's kind of you but I'm sure I'll be fine, and I'm likely to be in Salt Bay for a few weeks anyway.'

I don't explain further because I'm not sure how much Toby knows about Alice's health and he doesn't ask any more questions. Instead, he steers the conversation towards London and we're debating the merits of Stratford versus Islington – obviously the Olympic Park trumps the Regent's Canal – when Alice pops her head round the door to say Toby's tea is ready.

He eats rare steak and oven chips in the kitchen, gamely admiring the tidy cupboards that Alice shows off, and telling us between mouthfuls about an important auction that's planned for next week. Detailed information about porcelain is interesting at first but, as someone who doesn't know her Ming from her Meissen, my concentration soon starts slipping and I desperately want to yawn.

The urge to yawn gets worse when he and Alice start discussing various people I've never heard of, until in the end I plead tiredness so I can leave the two of them to talk freely without me.

'Good night, Annie, it's been good to meet you,' says Toby, breaking off from discussing some man whose wife has had a tummy tuck. 'I'll see you in the morning and we'll have to make sure we stay in touch when you're back in London, seeing as we're long-lost family.' He sounds rather sarcastic but, when he smiles broadly and gets up to give me a hug, I put it down to my oversensitivity after having no family for so long.

My case is sitting in the hall and can stay there tonight because it's too heavy for me to drag upstairs. But, curious to see what Amber has packed, I unzip it and sit back on my heels as knickers and tights burst out and scatter across the floor. The girl has gone mad! Almost every piece of clothing I own is crammed in, along with shoes, books and my alarm clock. The only thing missing is a banner saying 'Don't hurry back'. Sighing, I root through the clothes mountain until my fingers close round the photo of my Mum. At least Amber packed the only thing I really need to make me feel more at home.

Chapter Thirteen

One thing that drives me nuts is people who are cheerful first thing in the morning. It takes half an hour for my brain to kick into gear and silence aids this process immeasurably. Alice seems to understand and doesn't talk too much at breakfast, but Toby belongs to the chirpy brigade.

'Good morning, Annie,' he booms when I stagger through the kitchen door, still semi-conscious. He's ditched his cords for navy chinos and a pale pink shirt with a button-down collar. 'It's a beautiful day out there and your timing is excellent.' He slides a spatula into a frying pan and plops a fried egg onto a plate already piled high with bacon, sausages, tomatoes, fried bread and baked beans. Then he puts the plate on the table and gestures for me to sit down. 'You can't beat a full English to get the day off to a good start. Bon appetit.'

Good grief! Wisps of steam are rising from the cholesterol-laced food mountain.

'Is that all for me?'

'Of course. I've already had mine and Alice declined and had toast. She's very good at looking after herself.' He glances at me sideways. 'Anyway, you look like the kind of girl who enjoys a good fry-up so I thought I'd go the whole hog.'

Again, it's hard to read Toby – he's either being very kind or implying that my arse is the size of a small country. But I give him the benefit of the doubt and pop a square of fried bread into my mouth. Warm fat oozes from the bread, coating my tongue and sliding down my throat.

I'm not much of a breakfast person, even in Salt Bay, but I do my best and polish off two-thirds.

'Is that all you're going to eat?' Toby sounds irritated, though he cheers up when I praise his culinary skills and launches into a long description of the lessons he's taken with some cordon bleu chef in Mayfair.

'He says I have a natural talent and should be running my own restaurant; maybe one day, when I've got the funding for it.' He takes my plate and scrapes the leftovers into the bin. 'Alice is going for a stroll this morning so I thought you and I could walk into the village.'

'Shouldn't we go with Alice, to make sure she's OK? And I'll do the washing up, by the way; it's the least I can do after you made me breakfast.'

Toby hands me Alice's rubber gloves without complaint and moves away from the deep enamel sink.

'Alice is very independent and enjoys walking on her own. Plus she's so slow these days, walking with her would drive us mad.' A bead of fat rolls lazily down the front of the Aga and Toby chases it with a piece of kitchen roll. 'What you have to realise, Annie, is that Alice managed fine until you got here and she'll be fine when you leave.'

'I suppose so.' I plunge my hands into the dirty water in the sink and start pulling out the used pans while Toby goes in search of his jacket and shoes. The washing up takes ages because it's so greasy but, at last, clean pots and plates are piled up on the draining board.

'You're doing a grand job,' says Alice, popping her head round the kitchen door and waving goodbye with her walking stick. 'Don't worry if I'm late back; I might walk as far as Zencor Head if my legs will take me.'

Zencor Head sounds high up but I advise her not to overdo it and hope for the best.

The morning air is chilly and carries a faint aroma of fish as Toby pulls the garden gate closed behind us and we head towards the village. His shiny black Puffa jacket squeaks with every swing of his arms.

'Did you grow up around here?'

Toby looks at me as if he'd forgotten I was there. 'Yeah, my parents lived in the next village.'

'Is that where they still live?'

'No, they died a few years ago. They were quite old when they had me.'

'I'm sorry. I know what it's like to be without parents.'

Toby nods curtly at an elderly man walking past and pulls sunglasses from his trouser pocket. The sunglasses are dead posh – the logo says Prada – but he still uses the bottom of his shirt to wipe the lenses.

'Alice said that your mum had died. So what about your dad, then? Is he still alive?'

'I'm not sure. I'm not in touch with him.'

'That's a shame. Where does he live?'

Memories of school friends asking me the same awkward questions stir in my mind. 'I'm not sure about that either. I've never met him.'

'Really,' says Toby without surprise, almost like he knew the answer before asking the question. 'Maybe he'll suddenly turn up out of the blue as well. More long-lost relatives – wouldn't that be lovely.'

Hmmm, I'm not getting good vibes from Toby, who appears to be skilled in the art of making passive-aggressive comments.

'Who's the vicar at Salt Bay church?' I ask, keen to change the subject.

'No idea. I've lost touch with what goes on around here. You're not a Christian, are you?'

'More a confused agnostic.'

'I thought as much.'

I'm not sure whether that's insulting or not and we walk in silence for a while until I blurt out, 'You didn't fancy staying here, then?'

'Good God, no. I escaped as fast as I could and now London's home. I expect you miss the city, don't you? The vibrancy and amazing people and fantastic urban landscapes. Without hordes of blessed seagulls shitting all over the place.' He sidesteps a pile of bird droppings but not before a creamy dollop has stuck to the side of his shiny shoe.

'London has a lot more crime, though.'

'I'd rather face burglars and muggers than the nosy lot round here.' Toby gestures for me to sit next to him on a low wall near the river. 'Talking of the locals, I wanted to get you on your own, Annie, to say you mustn't let Alice force you to give up your life in London by playing the illness card.'

'That's not what she's done and I'm not giving up anything. I wasn't sure that you knew about Alice's situation.'

'I'd guessed something was wrong and she told me properly last night after you'd gone to bed. But she's a stubborn old bird and perfectly able to look after herself.'

'Not according to Dr Rivers. Alice isn't too bad at the moment but he thinks she could deteriorate rapidly.'

'Old Rivers? Pah, you don't want to take much notice of him. He's an idiot; a small-town doctor who couldn't cut it in the big city.'

In the distance, two men are standing in the pretty little river and I crane my neck to see what they're doing.

'He's sure that Alice needs help in the house or she might have to move out before too long.'

'He's being overdramatic. Alice won't move out and she'll be able to get the help she needs locally without you having to give up everything.'

'To be honest, I don't have much to give up at the moment – no job and no partner.' I puff out my cheeks and push my hands into the pockets of the warm jacket that Amber packed. She also packed my denim jacket, my thin cotton jacket and a green jacket with a skull and crossbones on the back that I've never seen before.

'You won't find a job or a partner in this rundown place and Alice will be fine so there's no need to sacrifice yourself.'

'But what if she falls and' – I stumble over the word – 'dies?'

Toby takes off his sunglasses and frowns. 'I don't mean to sound harsh, Annie, but if Alice falls and dies at Tregavara House, so be it. That's what she would have wanted.'

Wow, that's a bit heartless! I must look taken aback because Toby smooths down his tidy goatee and has another go. 'What I mean is, Alice will never sell Tregavara House or leave Salt Bay so it's best that she's carried out of the village in a box one day. In the meantime, it's up to her to organise local help and it's selfish to expect you to look after her.'

'Maybe you and I could help with the cost of getting local carers in?' I'm willing to chip in with what I can because I feel I should. And Toby seems well-off if his brand new car, sunglasses and Gucci watch are anything to go by.

'I don't think that will be necessary,' blusters Toby, his face flushing. 'Alice might go on for years and she can afford all her own care, if that's what she wants.'

'Are you sure about that?'

'Absolutely! She's probably got thousands stuffed under her mattress. Anyway.' He stands up and brushes his trousers down. 'Have a think about what I said about going back to London, there's a good girl.'

Passive-aggressive and patronising too. My cousin is turning out to be quite the charmer.

'I'll think about it,' I promise, not convinced Toby has grasped how poorly Alice could become and not about to tell him I'm only staying because she reminded me of my mum. Shielding my eyes, I point towards the figures in the river who are hauling something out of the water and onto the bank.

'What are those men doing over there? It's too cold for paddling.'

'No idea. Let's walk past and take a look and then I'll show you the local sights, such as they are.'

'Kayla gave me a whistle-stop tour the other day but I'm happy to have another wander round.'

'Kayla?'

'The Australian girl who's here on an extended gap year.'

Toby frowns. 'Nope, don't know her. What the hell is an Aussie doing in this shithole, anyway?' Without warning, he stops as we get closer to the men in the sparkling water and his body stiffens. 'I don't bloody believe it,' he mutters, putting his head down and marching off with me running behind.

'Is that Toby?' calls one of the men, waving at us. 'Toby Trebarwith? Hey Toby, it's good to see you. Come and say hello.'

'Hello Jack.' Toby waves back reluctantly and wanders over to the men. They are both in thigh-high rubber waders. I don't recognise Jack, who is bald with round John Lennon glasses. But the other man, I realise, is a bare-chested Josh Pasco, looking like a Cornish pirate with a striped black and white T-shirt tied around his waist. Dark hair flops over his eyes as he shakes his head and looks at us in dismay. Wow, he's really pissed off to see me, or maybe it's Toby he's glaring at.

'What are you doing, Jack?' Toby ignores Josh, who is holding a huge net of dripping stones.

'Clearing the river bed. The storms we've had lately have washed lots of stone downstream that blocks up the channel and makes it more likely to flood. Poor Enid is frightened to death that she's going to drown in her bed so I got Josh here to give me a hand – it's a young man's work really.'

We all turn towards Josh and I try really hard not to stare at his smooth chest which is glistening with either sweat or droplets from the river. Either way, it's very distracting especially when the muscles in his shoulders ripple as he twists and drops his net onto the bank.

'Does the river ever flood?' Now everyone is looking at me. 'It's hardly a river really; more a large brook.'

Josh folds his arms across his very bare chest. 'It's not the mighty Thames but appearances can be deceptive.'

'If there's a lot of rain up on the moors, the river can swell to three times its normal size,' butts in Jack, looking me up and down. 'Is this lovely lady your girlfriend then, Toby?'

'No!' Toby and Josh declare at the same time, as though I'm a right minger.

'This is Annie, Alice's great-niece who I thought was going back to London.' Josh steadies himself in the fast-flowing current and pulls his waders higher up his thighs.

'My plans have changed.' And there's no reason why I should tell you about them, Josh Pasco.

'I thought as much. So you're the famous Annie, Joanna's daughter,' chuckles Jack. 'Your fame has spread around the village and beyond. I know all about you though I don't live in Salt Bay.'

Toby casually brushes the side of his nose and glances at me as if to say 'I told you so.'

'I'm Jack and this is Josh, who you seem to know already, and of course you boys know one another. Are you staying in Salt Bay for a while, Toby?'

'Until this afternoon, then I have to get back up to town to prepare for an important auction. It's worth hundreds of thousands of pounds and involves a great deal of work but my commission makes it all worthwhile. What about you, Josh? Still teaching teenagers to say their times-tables?'

His smile looks more like a sneer and Josh sneers back, not bothering to try and disguise it.

'I'm helping young people grow up to be decent, hardworking adults who care about their local community and the people in it, if that's what you mean.'

There's definitely bad blood between these two but Jack, stooping to pick up gleaming stones from the riverbed, seems blissfully unaware of the atmosphere.

'We'd better get on, Toby.' I pull at his sleeve, keen to drag him away. 'Especially if you have to head back to London later.'

'Yeah, I suppose so.' Toby and Josh are still staring and sneering. It's like a scene from the Cornish version of *The Sopranos*, with one hoodlum standing half-naked in a river and the other in expensive chinos and a shiny Puffa jacket. Toby walks backwards so they don't break eye contact until I grab hold of his arm and pull him round.

'Come on,' I hiss, dragging him along until we're out of earshot. 'What was that all about?'

'Do you know him?' sulks Toby, looking back over his shoulder.

'I've bumped into him a couple of times.'

'Unlucky! I'd try to avoid him in the future if I were you. I was a few years above him in school and he was like it even then.'

'Like what?'

'Violent,' whispers Toby close to my ear. 'He assaulted me a few years ago for no reason. Punched me in the face and deviated my septum.' He rubs his finger down the bridge of his long, straight nose. 'He's a fucking maniac.'

'That's terrible. Did you report him?'

'He's such a no-hoper I felt sorry for him, so I let it go.'

'That was fortunate for him because a criminal conviction would have scuppered his teaching career. But if he's so awful I'm surprised you speak to him at all.'

'I don't want to be petty,' sniffs Toby. He points ahead of us. 'Heavens, look at that seagull over there. It's eating a crisp packet.'

I know a deliberate change of subject when I hear one. So I don't ask any more though I'd love Toby to dish more dirt on Josh – and anyone else in Salt Bay who's bashed him in the face.

Toby's lost any enthusiasm for our walk and whizzes me round the village at breakneck speed before taking me back to Tregavara House. The views of a churning indigo sea stretching to the horizon are pretty awesome but Toby is mute and uninterested.

Back home, he goes upstairs to read a book, not even appearing when Alice gets back from her stroll, still upright and in one piece. Alice entices him down to have some lunch an hour later but he picks at his fish finger sandwich and says very little.

He doesn't mention meeting Josh and neither do I because I've got a funny feeling about the whole thing. Obviously I'd never condone violence but, having known my cousin for less than a day, I doubt that Toby was whiter than white before Josh took a swing at him.

All in all, I'm glad when Toby decides to head back to London just after four o'clock.

'You came a long way to check up on me. You're a good boy,' says Alice, patting his arm as though he's seven and giving him a cheese sandwich wrapped in greaseproof paper for the journey.

'I know, that's why I've always been your favourite.' Toby plants a kiss on her cheek and throws his Ferragamo duffle bag into the boot of his BMW. He wipes his mouth while Alice is shuffling back to the front door and gestures for me to come over. 'Don't forget what I said,' he murmurs. 'Get yourself back to London as quickly as you can, before this place and these people drain the life out of you.'

His car smells of expensive leather when he opens the door and gets in.

'I might be able to find you a job if you get stuck. You've got my mobile number so give me a call.'

As Toby zooms off, I'm tempted to run after him and beg for a lift back to London in his flash car; away from this place where everyone knows your business and the wind never stops blowing. But I made Alice a promise so I grit my teeth as Toby takes the bend in the road on two wheels and disappears into the distance.

Chapter Fourteen

I'm getting rid of trip hazards in the house and singing the 'Hallelujah Chorus' when Alice calls up the stairs the next morning, 'Annabella, there's someone here to see you.'

I've rolled the rug on the landing into a long sausage and I shove it under my bed before coming down. Alice will moan but it may as well have 'Trip Hazard' plastered across it in big letters. I've already moved a frayed mat from the back door, swept the garden path of stones and found a rubber mat that goes in the bath. Alice Gowan is not going to fall on my watch. Truth be told, it's good to feel useful again even though looking out for Alice has brought back bittersweet memories of caring for Mum.

When I get downstairs, Kayla is standing in the hall with a wide smile that reveals the slight gap between her top front teeth. 'G'day Annabella,' she sniggers.

'Hi there. How did you know that I'm still here?'

'Word gets around, and don't forget that I work in the pub. I know everything about everyone. Ev-er-y-thing!' She stresses each syllable and wrinkles her nose. 'More than I want to know sometimes. Anyway, talking of the pub, I'm not working for a few hours so I wondered if you'd like me to take you for a drive and show you something amazing.'

I don't have high hopes of Kayla's 'something amazing' but it would be lovely to escape this claustrophobic community for a while.

'Would that be OK?' I ask Alice, who is rearranging jackets on the coat stand in a blatant attempt to listen in.

'Of course,' she harrumphs. 'You're not a prisoner here.'

'Would you like to come too?' I ignore Kayla's wide eyes and her look of relief when Alice declines my invitation and encourages us to raid the fridge to make a picnic.

Ten minutes later, we bundle out of the front door with a hastily prepared lunch and Alice's warning about unstable cliff edges ringing in our ears. Outside, there's a tatty Ford Ka that can only be described as vomit-green.

'Is that yours?'

'Nah, I've borrowed it for a few hours from Roger's girlfriend.'

'Roger has a girlfriend?' There's no reason why he shouldn't have but I'm surprised nonetheless.

'Yeah, Short Sharon from Botallin.' Kayla tugs on the passenger door which opens with a rusty creak. 'Short Sharon has loads of dogs so I hope you're not allergic.'

The cloth seats are festooned in dog hairs and a rancid smell of kennel hits me when I get in and put my feet on the newspaper lining the floor. Winding down the window as far as it will go, I ferret in my handbag for an antihistamine tablet.

'Are we going far?'

'Just up onto the moors. You'll love it,' says Kayla confidently, pushing the car into first gear and setting off slowly. 'So your real name is Annabella then.'

'Afraid so. It's actually Annabella Sunshine Trebarwith.'

'You have got to be kidding me!' Kayla snorts. 'That is terrible. What was your mother thinking?'

'She was a bit of a hippy at the time and doing the rounds of music festivals so it could have been worse – Annabella Ban-The-Bomb Trebarwith would be even more embarrassing.' I pull fluff off the antihistamine pill I've found and pop it into my mouth. 'What's your middle name?'

'Dorothy. Kayla Dorothy Corrigan. What can I say? My mum's favourite film is *The Wizard of Oz*. I must have seen it, like, a hundred times growing up and my nightmares are still riddled with tin men and witches.' She laughs and pulls hard into the side of the road to let a tractor trundle past.

'Where are we actually going?'

'To a place on the moors that's magical,' says Kayla enigmatically, crunching the gears and pulling out into a spray of mud from the tractor's back wheel.

'Is it a Cornish Costa?'

'Even better than that. It's nature and everyone loves nature, right?'

'Right.' Though I can't remember the last time I opted to spend time communing with 'nature'. The Olympic Park probably doesn't count with its hum of traffic and people everywhere. Although it does have a river. And ducks.

We drive for ages, way above the village and along narrow, winding lanes, until Kayla pulls onto a grass verge and switches off the engine. We haven't passed another car for the last ten minutes.

'Come on, out you get.' She jumps out and strides off while I step out more gingerly and look around. We are in the middle of freaking nowhere. Around me there's scrubby ground, a few windblown dwarf trees and huge, grey stones scattered everywhere. The milk-white sky, scoured by thick clumps of cloud, looks enormous as it arcs to meet the sea at the horizon.

Kayla has reached a small hill dotted with golden-yellow gorse and is waving at me. To the left of the hill and close to where the land falls into the sea are the stark ruins of a building with large glassless windows and one tall, pale chimney.

'That's an old tin mine,' shouts Kayla, coming back to collect me. 'Like in *Poldark* on TV. There used to be loads of them all down this coast but all the tin's gone now or it's too tricky to get it out of the ground.'

'Apparently my great-great-great-great-grandfather made lots of money from tin.' It feels strange to be talking about a member of my family who's not Mum.

'That'll explain why you live in the poshest house in the village.' Kayla's trainer has come undone and she stoops to tie her laces. Straightening up, she gestures for me to follow her. 'Come on, there's something I want to show you.' She scampers off with her red hair flowing behind her, looking like Kate Bush in the 'Wuthering Heights' video.

When we get close to the tin mine, Kayla stops near a tower of huge stones that have been piled up on top of one another. They're so finely balanced a strong gust of wind might send the whole lot crashing down.

'Come and stand here with me.' Kayla jumps onto a flat stone slab and spreads her arms wide into the breeze. 'Come and listen.'

I join her on the stone and hold out my arms in case that's what's expected.

'I can hear the wind and some birds. And that plane.' I nod towards a light aircraft droning high overhead.

'Shush! Just wait and really listen.'

There's nothing and still nothing and then I hear it – a dull bang and a louder thud from underneath us. Deep in the belly of the earth, something is shifting. I glance at Kayla in alarm but she grins. 'Just wait.'

There it is again. A louder thud and a groan as if the rocks below us are sighing.

'What the hell is that?'

'Amazing, isn't it? The locals call it Karrek something or other, some old Cornish words that mean "the devil's rock". I think it's the old mine workings that have been flooded by the sea.'

'So that noise I can hear—'

'—is the tide rushing in through the tunnels where the miners used to work. Maybe some of them are still down there. Woo!' She waves her arms in front of me like a ghost.

'Is the ground up here safe?'

Kayla shrugs. 'I think so, and it's pretty cool, right? Nature is awesome.'

Kayla's right, it is awesome, but the thought of all that water rushing through the blackness and pounding the rocks beneath us is also disconcerting.

Kayla's clearly not spooked because she spreads out the picnic rug we found in the boot and plonks herself down. 'Let's have our lunch here.'

'Is it warm enough to have a picnic outside? Maybe we could eat in the car,' I say hopefully, but Kayla's having none of it.

'Eating outside in a place like this enhances the whole Cornwall experience. Cornwall is very mystical, you know, and full of folklore. Everyone believes in pixies.'

'Come off it, I can't imagine people like Josh Pasco believing in magic.'

'Ah yes, lovely Josh Pasco with his bonzer backside,' muses Kayla, taking the picnic bag from me and pulling out apples and cheese sandwiches.

Why the hell did I bring up Josh's name? I veer swiftly onto a safer subject.

'While we're eating, tell me more about your family. They must miss you.'

'I doubt it. Both of my sisters have sprogged so they're busy, and Mum and Dad have their hands full with grandchildren so they're happy for me to go off and do my own thing. Just so long as I check in now and again.' She bites into an apple and wipes juice from her chin. 'They all live in the Sydney suburbs. You'll have to come home with me one day and visit.' She leans back on her elbows as a wall of water thuds far beneath us and the rocks groan. 'How long will you be staying in Salt Bay?'

'For a few weeks while Alice is sorting out permanent help in the house.'

Kayla nods so I presume Alice's failing health is the talk of the pub.

'I'll be back in London by Spring and need to keep busy 'til then.'

'What do you think of Salt Bay?'

Kayla's fitted in well with the locals so I choose my words carefully. 'It's a pretty place but incredibly quiet and everyone seems subdued. There's no music which is weird and sad.'

Kayla thinks for a moment before handing me a doorstep-sandwich crammed with chunks of cheddar. 'You're right, there isn't any music though I hadn't really noticed. Roger won't have music in the pub because he's so grumpy. Was that you singing earlier when I called round for you? You've got a lovely voice.'

'Thanks,' I mumble, going red. 'I think music makes everything better.'

'Everything?' Kayla wrinkles her nose and brushes dog hair from the picnic rug. 'What about if your cat dies? Or you're clinically obese? Or a bloke you like calls you Carrie?'

I swallow a large piece of cheese before I've chewed it properly and wince. 'Not everything, obviously. But music was comforting when I was growing up and it still helps now when life gets difficult. Don't you think so?'

'I listen to Crowded House and Kylie when I'm feeling homesick. Does that count?'

'Absolutely. Music can ease homesickness, heartache, grief; the whole caboodle. I joined the choir at every school I went to which helped me to fit in. And when I was doing secretarial work in a primary school, I took over running the choir while the music teacher was off long-term sick. No one else wanted to do it but I loved it. It was great to see the children enjoying singing and even the naughty ones calmed down a little. It's a bit like therapy, you know? I always wanted to be a music therapist but didn't get the exam grades I needed. Moving from school to school in my teens didn't help and I needed to bring in a wage anyway as soon as—'

I stop mid-sentence, feeling embarrassed because Kayla is staring at me with a strange expression on her face. Are there crumbs round my mouth? I rub my palm across my lips to check.

'Therapy, you reckon,' says Kayla, putting down her half-eaten apple. 'Like what you'd provide for people who've had a trauma.'

'I guess so.'

'Like the people in Salt Bay whose relatives were killed in that kick-arse storm.'

'I… suppose…'

'Oh wow!' Kayla claps her hands excitedly. 'You should start up the Salt Bay choir again. That would cheer them all up and it would keep you busy.'

'I'm only here for a few more weeks, probably not even that long.'

And I have no urge to spend any more time with the locals than is absolutely necessary.

'It doesn't matter. Once the choir is up and running, we can sort out someone else to take it over. There's always loads of people who like doing that kind of stuff. This is going to be great! We can hold auditions and put up posters about it in the pub and in Jennifer's shop and in the villages nearby.'

'I'm not sure we'd need to hold auditions,' I protest faintly.

'Of course we'd need auditions. Like in *The X Factor*, because you don't want the choir to be crap. And what else are you going to do for weeks on end in Salt Bay? You'll go mad with boredom otherwise. I can help you with the organising.'

'I've never run a proper adult choir before and I'm sure it's harder than it looks.'

'Pah!' Kayla dismisses my fears with a wave of her hand. 'You know about music and choirs and it'll cheer everyone up and it'll be fun.'

'I'm not sure about fun. Lots of people in the original choir drowned, so wouldn't starting the choir up again be terribly insensitive?'

'Only if you go about it in a terribly insensitive way,' insists Kayla. 'We're trying to help people get over their grief and we'll make that clear. How much did music help you when your mum died?'

'Loads. I had a grief playlist that made me cry buckets – which was a good thing,' I add when Kayla looks unsure. 'Sad songs opened the floodgates and let out the emotions that were strangling me.' I gulp because remembering how raw my emotions were after Mum's death is making my throat tight.

Kayla rubs my arm and gives a sympathetic pout.

'It must have been horrid losing your mum. And yet music made it better and it can do the same for people in Salt Bay. I'm sure of it.

Please, Annie, let's give it a go and see how we get on. Or…' She pulls her scarf tighter and blows on her cold hands.

'Or what?'

'Or I'll tell everyone that your middle name is Sunshine.'

'That's blackmail,' I splutter, not sure whether to throw my sandwich at her or laugh.

'I know.' She grins and reaches for her apple. 'I'll do all the work. All you've got to do is convince everyone it's a good idea and turn up for the auditions. Bagsy being Simon Cowell!'

Chapter Fifteen

Kayla is as good as her word and posters start going up around the village over the next couple of days. She's used acid-yellow paper and a red marker pen so the posters are hard to miss. They scream out at me from Jennifer's shop, the pub, the notice board on the green and the telephone kiosk. And Kayla tells me people have taken them away from the pub to put in Trecaldwith and other villages nearby.

The posters invite anyone who likes singing to come along to auditions for the revived Salt Bay Choral Society at 7.30 pm this Friday in The Whistling Wave. Underneath in capital letters, it says: 'New choir set up in memory of those who died and as therapy for those who remember them'.

Eek, that manages to raise expectations while being insensitive at the same time, but Kayla is convinced it's fine when I corner her about it in the pub.

'You worry too much,' she insists, leaning against the bar looking bored. It's mid-week and only a few customers are in, huddled together in corners. 'The storm was a long time ago and people will understand what we're trying to do. We're trying to help.'

'I know but have you ever lost anyone close to you?'

As I suspected, Kayla shakes her head. 'Not really. My grandparents died but that was ages ago and I don't remember it. But I can imagine how awful it must feel.'

'I'm not sure you can, not unless you've been through it.' I would explain more – about the disbelief, anger and guilt that mush together into lingering, skewering sorrow – but a half-empty pub on a Wednesday night doesn't feel like the time or the place.

Kayla sticks out her bottom lip and drums her fingers on the bar.

'So are you pulling out? I'm not insensitive about what happened and lots of people have told me it's a great idea and what the village really needs.'

Maybe they're right, because they know the village far better than I do. Glancing round the deadly quiet pub, I make up my mind.

'OK, we'll give it a go but perhaps we should call the choir something different because the original name is linked with such a tragedy.'

'Annabella Sunshine Trebarwith.' Kayla puts a steadying hand on my shoulder. 'Tradition is like a big British thing, isn't it? Don't you have Black Rod in Parliament who still dresses up in tights to bang on a door or something? Black Rod!' she sniggers. 'Tradition decrees that our choir should be called the Salt Bay Choral Society, or the New Salt Bay Choral Society if that makes you feel any better, and then it'll be a proper tribute to what went before.'

'I guess so.'

'I know so,' states Kayla, and she sounds so confident I want to believe her. But it's hard to shake the feeling I'll be letting my family down if I upset the village where Trebarwiths have lived for generations.

As a test, I discuss our plans with Alice when I get back to Tregavara House. She says she's already spotted one of the posters and I'm reassured when she doesn't swoon or go nuclear on me. But she does suggest that I talk to local people most hit by the tragedy and get their blessing first.

'Two of the families moved away after the storm, wanting a fresh start away from the sea, and Mrs Hawkins died a long time ago.

But there are still people in and around Salt Bay who were directly affected. There's Cyril in the village.' Alice carefully writes down his address for me on a yellow Post-it. 'He lost two grandsons, poor man, and has become a bit of a recluse since his wife passed away last year. The other person to talk to is Ted Pawley's widow Marion who lives in Trecaldwith. I need to speak to her anyway so I'll mention your plan and tell you if she has a problem with it. Actually, she's the—'

'But do you give us your blessing, Alice?' I interrupt, keen to know how she feels. 'We won't start up the choir again if you'd rather we didn't. The last thing I want to do is upset you.'

Alice thinks for a moment, pen poised over the Post-it. 'Samuel always loved the choir and I think he would be pleased that his granddaughter wants to bring it back to life. You have my blessing.'

'Thank you, Alice.' I get a sudden urge to hug her but make do with patting her arm instead. My great-aunt doesn't come across as cuddly, and a half-hearted hug could be all kinds of awkward.

'Does this mean that you'll be staying in Salt Bay for a little longer?' she enquires, sliding the pen behind an ugly Victorian vase on the mantelpiece.

'Not really. Kayla reckons we can find someone to take over the choir when I go back to London, which will be soon. I'm only in Salt Bay while you're organising more help in the house.'

I emphasise that last bit because all Alice has done so far is put up a 'help required' advert in Jennifer's shop which – surprise, surprise – has elicited no response whatsoever.

Meanwhile, Amber is posting Facebook photos of her and Gracie in my flat with the hashtags #bestbuds and #togetherforever which doesn't bode well for turfing her out when I get back. I'm not one of

Amber's Facebook friends but if she didn't want me to stalk her she should have been more careful with her privacy settings.

'Did I overhear you saying that you're going to visit Cyril Barnley?' sniffs Jennifer, standing directly behind us in the tiny stationery section of her shop.

She's been following us round since we arrived so knows very well that we're on our way to see him. We only nipped in to pick up a Twix for Kayla who reckons blood sugar plummets to dangerous levels without regular infusions of chocolate.

'We thought we should check that Mr Barnley is OK with us reviving the choir,' I say, swinging round to face Jennifer and almost braining myself on the jauntily striped windbreaks she's carrying.

'Ooh, you don't want to do that!' Jennifer sucks her bottom lip between her teeth and puts the windbreaks down with a clatter.

'Which is exactly what I said!' exclaims Kayla, who's been dragged along under sufferance. Ripping the paper off her chocolate bar, she downs half a finger in one go and fishes about in her pocket for the money to pay for it.

'Why don't you think we should visit him?'

'There's no point. He won't let you in,' says Jennifer, taking the coins proffered by Kayla and dropping them into the till. 'Cyril's become a partial recluse since his wife died last year. He rarely goes out, he doesn't like strangers, and I doubt he'll like your idea of getting the choral society going again.' She settles down on her stool for a gossip. 'You know, of course, that his two grandsons were in the choir and were lost in the Great Storm, and then his daughter's marriage broke up under the strain and she moved away. She's gone Up North. It's tragic.'

'Which is why we ought to speak to him about the choir before we—'

'Blunder on,' interjects Jennifer, patting her new hairdo, which is ash-blonde and aggressively backcombed.

'I was going to say "carry on", but never mind. Do lots of people think reviving the choral society is a bad idea, then?'

'A few folk do. They say you're a newcomer who's poking her nose in where it's not wanted.'

Kayla squeaks behind me, desperate to comment but hindered by a mouthful of gooey caramel. 'Whereas others say it's good to keep the old traditions going and to bring some life back to the place.'

'What do you think?'

Jennifer folds her arms and ponders for a moment. 'I think you'll be lucky if you can get anyone round here to sing in tune, if the humming that goes on in my shop is anything to go by. Even if you are a talented and experienced choral conductor from London.'

I glare at Kayla, who's been doing what she describes as 'bigging me up' around the village, though I'd call it lying. She shoves the rest of the Twix into her mouth and pretends to look at the pen selection.

'However, you've got a link to the old choral society which pleases a lot of people,' adds Jennifer, 'so you might as well give it a try. And if you fall flat on your face, you do.'

Which is not the most ringing of endorsements, but hey ho. At least I've got an idea for getting us in with Mr Barnley.

'Jennifer, I'd like to get Mr Barnley – Cyril – onside so I'm not going against the wishes of someone directly affected by the tragedy. You know him well and you're good with people.' I ignore Kayla who gulps and starts coughing loudly. 'How would you suggest that we approach him?'

Delighted to be asked for advice, Jennifer ferrets under the counter and brings out a copy of *Cornwall Life*.

'You could always give him his magazine that I haven't delivered yet, and also make a point of mentioning that you're Samuel Trebarwith's granddaughter. He gets confused sometimes but he'll remember Samuel.'

'That's really helpful. Thank you.'

'You're welcome. It's good that you're taking local people's feelings into consideration. There's many that wouldn't.' She gives Kayla a filthy look and passes me the glossy magazine which has a beautiful picture on the cover of dark cliffs silhouetted against a ruby-red sky. I peep inside and see that the photo was taken in North Cornwall. Fair dues, the whole county is spectacularly wild and beautiful. If Cornwall was one of the Home Counties, I might even consider living in it.

Kayla stomps ahead of me when we come out of the shop.

'Crikey,' she says. 'Who rattled her cage, and did you see her wind-tunnel hairstyle? There's no way I'm letting myself go like that when I get old. I'm gonna be like Helen Mirren. But she had a good point about not bothering Mr Barnley – I've heard he's odd.'

I'm too busy peering at people's cottages to take much notice of Kayla's bad mood. Alice's Post-it says Cyril Barnley lives at Briar Cottage but it's not easy to find. Eventually I spot it, tucked away behind the grocery store in a tiny terraced row I've not noticed before. There's a bright blue planter outside the front door but the plant inside is withered and brown, and marketing brochures are hanging half in and half out of the letter box. I push them through and knock on the door.

'Maybe he's not in,' says Kayla when no one comes, trying to see through the frosted glass panel.

'He's a partial recluse; of course he's in.'

A dark shadow moves across the back of the hallway, and I call through the letter box, 'Mr Barnley, please can I have a quick word with you? My name's Annie and I've got your magazine from Jennifer. Samuel Trebarwith was my grandfather.'

After a few moments, the door opens a crack and I catch a glimpse of grey hair and a burgundy cardigan.

'Who did you say you were?'

'This is Kayla who works at the pub, and I'm Annie Trebarwith, Joanna Trebarwith's daughter.'

'Is that right.' Mr Barnley opens the door wider, pokes his head outside and surveys me, warily. 'You look a bit like the Trebarwiths but I've never seen you in Salt Bay before.'

'I've never been in Salt Bay before. I only met my great-aunt Alice for the first time a short while ago.'

Interest sparks in Mr Barnley's rheumy, faded eyes. 'And what do you want with me?'

'We'd like to talk to you about the Salt Bay Choral Society, if you wouldn't mind. We're thinking of re-starting the choir but wanted to ask you about it first.'

'You want my permission?'

'Something like that.'

Mr Barnley thinks for a moment and then pulls the door wide open. 'You'd best come in, then. Mind the cat.'

A scrawny ginger moggy with white ears hurtles out of the house and darts down the street, towards the sea.

'Should I try to catch it?'

'She'll be back soon enough when she wants food. Follow me, and don't touch anything.'

Kayla and I follow Mr Barnley along a tiny hallway and into an equally small living room that's dwarfed by an old television set in the corner. There's a pot of garish fake chrysanthemums on top of the TV and every other available surface is covered in mismatched photo frames. Some of the photos are black and white, others are in colour, but they all feature people who I presume are his family.

Mr Barnley sees me looking at them and picks up a photo of a pretty woman with two young boys sitting on her lap.

'That's my daughter Susan, and her sons Benjamin and Peter who were in the Choral Society. They had lovely voices, both of them, and were always singing so they joined the choir like me. But then the storm came and that was that.' He puts the photo frame back in its place. 'I hope you're not expecting tea because I don't have any milk.'

'We're fine, thanks,' says Kayla, licking chocolate crumbs from her bottom lip.

'Where are you from? You don't sound like you're from round here.'

'Australia. I've been in Salt Bay for a while and work in the pub, but I don't think we've ever met.'

'I can't be doing with the pub these days, not since Roger took it over and changed things round. Cecilia, my wife, used to enjoy a lime and lemonade in there but she's not here any more.' He pauses and wipes his eyes with a grubby handkerchief. 'What did you want to say to me, then? I haven't got all day.'

He's a curmudgeonly old soul but I like Mr Barnley, and the frayed collar of his creased shirt is breaking my heart. I'm not saying it's a wife's job to do the ironing and buy her husband's new shirts – I haven't slipped through a wormhole back to the 1950s. But there's something poignant about a dishevelled widower. They look so… lost.

Kayla is perching on the edge of Mr Barnley's tiny sofa and I take a seat next to her.

'We're hoping to relaunch the Salt Bay Choral Society. We think it would be good for the village. But first we want to check that relatives of choir members who died in the Great Storm wouldn't mind.'

'There aren't many people directly affected left in the village now. Susan lives in County Durham. She wanted me to move up there with her when Cecilia died but I didn't want to leave here. This is where Cecilia and I lived all our married life. Did you know Cecilia?' asks Mr Barnley, looking confused.

'Sadly, no,' I say gently. 'I've only recently come to Salt Bay.'

'And how's your grandmother?'

'I'm afraid she died.'

'That's a shame.' Mr Barnley shifts in his chair and squints at me. 'Did you say your mother is Joanna Trebarwith? You look very like her, apart from your eyes. What's she doing now?'

'She died too.' I'm beginning to feel like the Grim Reaper, reeling off a list of people who've passed away. I'm tempted to ask Mr Barnley for his memories of my mum, but Kayla nudges me in the ribs. 'We won't take up much more of your time, Mr Barnley, if you could let us know how you feel about us restarting the choir. We'd be very respectful about the men who were lost.'

'You can do what you like. I don't care much either way because it won't bring them back.' He rubs a thick finger across a photo of Benjamin and Peter on the sideboard next to him, and dust swirls into the air. Suddenly his demeanour changes and he looks agitated. 'I'm going to have my dinner now so you need to leave.' After pulling himself out of his chair, he leads me and Kayla through the dark hallway and pulls the front door open as far as a pile of unopened post and flyers will allow.

'Thank you, Mr Barnley, for seeing us and I hope talking about the choral society didn't upset you. I left your magazine on the sofa.'

'Yeah, thank you,' mumbles Kayla, standing on the front doorstep.

A thought strikes me when Mr Barnley turns to retreat back into his dark, lonely house. 'You said that you belonged to the old choral society. Why don't you come along to the new one? You'd be very welcome.'

'I don't get out much.' He tugs at the bottom of his cardigan, which is done up on the wrong buttons, and closes the door in our faces.

I'm half-expecting Kayla to grumble about rude old folk, seeing as she's in a mood today, but she's quiet all the way to the harbour. The sea's calm today, a gently undulating sheet reflecting the grey sky, and we sit on the harbour wall for a while, dangling our legs over the water.

'You were right,' she blurts out at last, kicking her heels against the smooth, cold stone.

'I'm always right.'

'Ha, no really, you were right to insist that we check with people like Mr Barnley about setting up the choir again. Poor old bugger, living in that house on his own with only his memories for company. I was choked up when he talked about his grandsons.' She gazes at the grey horizon and sniffs. 'But he seems all right with us going ahead which is good news. What about the widow that Alice phoned?'

'She was going to let me know if Mrs Pawley was against the idea, and she hasn't said anything.'

'So it's all systems go and the auditions can go ahead tomorrow. That's fantastic.' She gives a huge beaming grin and throws a stone, which plops beneath the waves. 'Don't look so worried, Annie. Just channel your inner Gareth Malone and this choir is going to be amazing.'

Chapter Sixteen

The auditions are being held in the back room of The Whistling Wave and I get there early on Friday evening to help get things organised. The small room smells of stale beer and has a sticky carpet but there's a battered piano in the corner and people can audition in private. Kayla has already placed a table at the end of the room along with paper and pencils, for us to make notes, presumably.

'This is so exciting', she gushes, breezing in and giving me a once-over. I've made an effort tonight, ditching my jeans in favour of a fitted, periwinkle-blue dress from Monsoon and putting on mascara and lipstick. 'You look nice. That dress matches your eyes and makes you look sexy. You'd better keep away from Roger.'

On cue, Roger shuffles in and sits at the table which I notice has three chairs. Kayla shrugs her shoulders and grins. 'He insisted on being a judge if we're using the pub.'

'We're not judges. This is an audition, not a competition,' I hiss, but Kayla is already at the door calling in the first victim.

A young nerdy-looking lad in torn jeans sidles in and stands awkwardly in front of us. He grunts hello at Kayla who announces, 'This is Tom from Trecaldwith,' before picking up her pencil and tapping it on the paper in front of her.

'How old are you, Tom?' I ask.

'Eighteen.'

'Do you enjoy singing?'

'I guess.' Tom blushes to the roots of his straggly, brown hair and looks at the floor.

'What are you going to sing for us?'

'"Halo" by Beyoncé.'

'Bold choice!' says Roger, sitting back and folding his arms. 'When you're ready.'

Tom pulls his mobile phone from his pocket, touches the screen and Beyoncé's voice floods out. He closes his eyes and starts to sing along, faintly and hesitantly at first. But his voice is sweet and clear and when he gets caught up in the music, he sings more strongly. His body sways slightly in time to the beat as he forgets the daily embarrassments of being an awkward teenager with too much testosterone and too little confidence. When Tom sings, he becomes sure and strong, which is why I love music and its transformative powers. You can keep your sex and drugs, give me rock 'n' roll any day.

When Tom finishes singing, he starts fidgeting.

'Was that all right?'

He's twisting his phone over and over in his hands and looks so anguished I want to leap up and give him a hug.

'That was lovely, Tom. Thank you so much. You'll be fantastic in the choir.'

'We'll let you know,' interrupts Kayla. 'Have you left your mobile number and email address on the list outside?'

Tom nods and I show him out of the room, whispering as I open the door, 'That was brilliant singing. You're definitely in.' He gives me a big grin, hoicks up his jeans over the top of his black pants and scurries out of the pub.

When I get back to the table, Kayla stops drawing a tick next to Tom's name on her sheet of paper and gives me a stern look.

'We can't tell people tonight if they're in the choir or not. We'll contact everyone over the weekend.'

'Or we could let everyone in who fancies joining the choir.'

'What, everyone?' snorts Kayla. 'We want this choir to be good, don't we?'

I thought the whole idea of resurrecting the choir was for the good of the local community. But perhaps Kayla has a point because the next few people who audition aren't as good as Tom. They're not awful but getting them to sing in tune could be challenging, and Roger keeps writing 'shite' on his piece of paper.

'Just two more people to go,' says Kayla, opening the door and beckoning the next person in. She stays where she is and flattens herself against the door frame so the man in blue jeans with bulky thighs has to brush against her to get into the room. Oh, for goodness' sake, it's Ollie. Kayla walks back to her seat with her hips swaying and starts sucking the end of her pencil in a frankly provocative manner.

Ollie stands before us in full Greek-god mode with straw-blonde hair falling across his forehead and upper-arm muscles bulging through his sweatshirt.

'So why are you here, Ollie?' Kayla's voice has gone all twenty-cigs-a-day husky.

'I'm always singing and I love it; always have done and always will. Everyone knows that.'

'Do they?' I glance at Kayla who stares steadfastly ahead. 'What are you going to sing for us?'

'I'm going to sing the Adele song, "Make You Feel My Love". Does that sound OK?'

'That sounds fucking fantastic,' drools Kayla, elbows on the table and chin in her hands.

Sadly, though Ollie loves his singing surely to God no one else does. He's incredibly flat, so much so that it's hard to fathom how something so ugly can come out of such a beautiful mouth.

When he finishes, there's a stunned silence before Kayla claps and jumps in ahead of Roger who's itching to give his opinion.

'That's amazing Ollie. I'll be in touch about the choir over the weekend so look out for a text or email from me. That's Kayla: K-A-Y-L-A. Or I might give you a call. Or we can meet up so I can let you know in person.'

'Uh, OK. That'll be good.' Ollie leaves the room, looking puzzled.

'He's in.' Kayla puts a large tick next to Ollie's name and draws a little heart while Roger licks the end of his pencil and writes 'absolute shite'.

'Tell me the truth; is he the main reason you suggested re-forming the choir?' I whisper so Roger won't hear.

'Absolutely not. Definitely not. No way. Not the main reason. I didn't even know he liked singing,' blusters Kayla, picking up her list and scanning down the names. 'Good grief, it's Jennifer next so get out your earplugs. She's the last one.'

Josh didn't come along with Ollie. That's great. Really great, because I was worried he might want to be in the choir. And then he'd be all snippy about my skills as a choir leader and I'd have to ban him for insubordination which would cause all sorts of problems. So the fact he doesn't want to be in the choir is fantastic news. I pull down my dress which is riding up over my thighs and wish I'd worn my jeans which are far more comfortable.

Kayla is only half-way to the door when it's flung open and Jennifer stomps in, looking flustered and cross. A young girl is scampering along behind her.

'I've been waiting for ages and have had to put up with Peter Seegrass and his friends who have had far too much to drink and are making inappropriate jokes. It's not acceptable.'

'We're very sorry, Jennifer. We've had more people auditioning than we expected.'

'Yes, well it's not very well organised,' she sniffs at me, riffling through her handbag for sheet music that she hands to the girl who has long, blonde plaits and can't be more than twelve.

'What are you going to sing?' asks Kayla, sounding totally uninterested now Ollie has left the building.

'Mozart's "Laudate dominum".'

'Blimey! Are you sure?' It's one of my favourite pieces of classical music but terribly hard to sing and only usually attempted by a professional.

'Of course.' Jennifer looks affronted that I've dared to question her musical judgement and barks at the girl who's sitting at the piano, 'Michaela, are you ready?' Michaela blinks rapidly and starts to play as Jennifer takes a deep breath and I prepare for Mozart to be mangled.

The funny thing is that Jennifer doesn't sound like Jennifer when she sings. Talking in the shop, she sounds like your average middle-aged Cornish woman. But when she starts singing, Jennifer has the voice of an angel. An angel floating on a cloud of marshmallows in a sky made of spun sugar.

'Bloody hell!' whispers Kayla, her mouth falling open, and Roger's pencil clatters to the floor as he sits bolt upright. I'm finding it hard not to cry every time Jennifer hits a high note with crystal-clear precision and we're not the only ones who are gobsmacked. The door opens a crack and a couple of men peep their heads round to listen to Salt Bay's answer to Susan Boyle giving Mozart some welly.

As the final note dies away, we all clap like mad and Jennifer smiles and bows like we're a proper audience.

'Where the hell did you learn to sing like that?' splutters Roger.

'At the Conservatoire de Paris in the early 1980s.'

'You're kidding.' Roger looks bemused. 'I didn't know that you learned singing abroad.'

'There's a lot you don't know about me and what I did before I came back to Cornwall, Roger. The world doesn't begin and end with Salt Bay, you know,' grumbles Jennifer, and I start to like her a little more. She snatches her music from the piano and crams it into her black Mrs Thatcher handbag. 'Let me know when and where the choir is meeting and I'll see if I can make it. Come on, Michaela. Your parents will think I've kidnapped you.' Michaela jumps to her feet and follows Jennifer without a word.

After everyone's gone and we've tidied up the room, Kayla and I find a cosy corner in the pub and look at our notes while swigging back vodkas. Roger has already handed over his written opinions which are short, to the point, and make Simon Cowell look like a pussycat.

We agree on most people, more or less, until we get to the thorny subject of Ollie. Folding my arms, I say sternly, 'You want the choir to be good and, on that basis, Ollie doesn't make the grade.'

'Are you deaf? He was brilliant!' Kayla splutters, spitting bubbles of vodka down her low-cut jumper. 'He was at least as good as Adele; probably better.'

'Only if you were listening with your ovaries rather than your ears.'

Kayla sketches an arrow through the love heart next to Ollie's name.

'Maybe I'm slightly biased but he'll look good in the choir if we stick him in the front row and we can ask him not to sing too loudly. Or he can mime.'

'Or we can let everyone in who wants to join the choir and then Ollie is guaranteed a place.'

'Huh.' Kayla stabs the paper a couple of times until her pencil lead snaps. 'I guess we could, but only if I'm the one who gets to tell Ollie that he's in.'

'It's a deal,' I laugh, sliding the list of mobile phone numbers across the table. Kayla and I have both got what we wanted. Now all we have to do is successfully resurrect a shattered choir and bring back some joy into this subdued little corner of Cornwall. No pressure, then.

At closing time, I'm walking home with my earphones in when I get a spooky feeling that someone's close behind me. All I can hear is Radiohead belting out 'Creep' but I know something's not right when the back of my neck starts prickling. It's happened before in edgy parts of London – Mum used to call it my spider sense – but I wasn't expecting it in sleepy Salt Bay.

When I flick off my music, there are heavy footsteps right behind me and I can hear a man breathing heavily as though he's been running. My first thought is that if I can survive Stratford Tube station at midnight I'll be safe in a Cornish backwater. My second thought is that the pepper spray Maura brought me from America is in my handbag and now might be the perfect time to try it out. I'm too spooked to turn round but I pick up speed as the man's long shadow falls across me.

Hurrying past the dimly lit village green, I start scrabbling in the bottom of my bag while the man keeps step. My fingers close round tissues, pens, keys, purse, notebook, but there's no spray and, with an icy rush of adrenaline, I remember decluttering my handbag yesterday and putting the spray in my suitcase. It seemed redundant in Salt Bay which is ironic now my spidey sense is on full alert.

Suddenly the man steps in front of me, blocking my way, and blood starts pounding in my ears. It's funny what goes through your mind at moments of crisis. Eye-gouging and crotch-kicking techniques would be useful right now. But all I can think, as the man towers above me and my fingers close round my keys, is that there's no way I'm being buried in Salt Bay and spending all eternity with Samuel Trebarwith on a wet and windy cliff top.

Just before I jab out with my keys and leg it, the broad-shouldered man tilts his head and light from a street lamp catches the contours of his face.

'Are you going to stop and talk to me?' he demands in a gruff Cornish accent. 'I called when you came out of the pub but you ignored me.'

'For goodness' sake, I didn't hear you because I was listening to music.' I take deep breaths to steady myself, not sure if I'm furious that the man who's following me is Josh Pasco or relieved that I didn't overreact and rake my keys across his face. He'd look even more like Poldark with a scar down his cheek.

'Are you all right?' He moves so close the soft wool of his jumper grazes my chin and I ignore a faint flicker of disappointment that he's fully dressed. 'I didn't mean to make you jump. Do you need to sit down?'

'Of course not. I'm absolutely fine. Why did you want to speak to me?'

I'd love a sit down, actually, because my legs are still like Bambi on ice but there's no way I'm letting on that Josh Pasco scared me. He'd probably blame it on murder rates in London and me being neurotic and we'd end up arguing. Again.

'I've heard about the auditions that were held in the pub and thought you might know something about them. I saw you leaving the pub when I parked my car.'

'I was running the auditions with Kayla and Roger.'

'Oh for f—' Josh screws up his eyes and sighs. 'I might have guessed a Trebarwith would be involved.'

'Involved in what, the choir? Did you want to join?'

'Do I look like I want to join the choir?'

'Not really.' Josh Pasco doesn't have the demeanour of a man who wants to be judged while singing Michael Bublé slightly out of key. 'Ollie was at the audition but he left a while ago.'

'I'm not looking for Ollie.'

I like enigmatic men; I really do. It gives them a beguiling air of mystery but it can also tip over into being frickin' annoying. And Josh Pasco has crossed that line.

'So tell me why you followed me?' I snap. 'I don't understand.'

'No, you don't, but that doesn't stop you leaping in where you're not wanted.' Josh scowls and rubs his hand across the dark stubble on his chin. 'Anyway, I thought you were leaving Salt Bay.'

'I am, soon.'

'So what's the point of reviving the choral society?' Light glints on his thick black hair. 'You city types are all the same. Like that idiot Toby, you bowl in here from London, turn things upside down and leave us to pick up the pieces.' His lip curls and he shoots me a daggers look. 'Who the hell do you lot think you are?'

Bastard!

Did I say that out loud? Hopefully not, because this man has a reputation for violence. Though that's only hearsay from Toby and I get the feeling he has an agenda of his own. For goodness' sake, this village with its swirling undercurrents is doing my head in.

Pulling myself up to my full height of five feet five inches – still only Josh Pasco nose-height – I try to push past him.

'Please get out of my way. I'm going home.'

A muscle in Josh's jaw is tensing and his eyes are narrowed as though he's about to go the whole Jack Nicholson in *The Shining*.

'You can't just walk away without sorting this out,' he growls, grabbing my arm and pulling me towards him.

There's a weird jolt when he touches me, like static electricity. Which would make sense if we were in the nylon-carpeted back room of The Whistling Wave but I'm standing on tarmac and I'm pretty sure Josh is ankle-deep in mud on the soggy green. It's all getting a little too *X-Files* for me.

'I'm leaving right now because you're frightening me.' All pretence has gone because I want to go home, back to Tregavara House where, I realise with one of those weird shifts of perspective, Alice makes me feel safe.

Josh squelches farther back onto the muddy green. 'I didn't mean to do that. I've been away for a few days on a school trip and only found out about the auditions when I got back an hour ago. It came as a shock.'

'I'm sorry you feel that way but you're overreacting,' I say as calmly as I can while my brain whirrs through the list of people who drowned in the Big Storm. There was no Pasco among them, I'm sure of it.

'Maybe.' Josh looks more sad than scary now. He shakes his head and holds his hands up in front of him, palms towards me. He has the most amazing long fingers, like a musician. 'I apologise for frightening you, I'm not that sort of bloke. But you don't know what you're doing and the memories you're stirring up.'

'I don't mean to upset people by setting up a choir. That's not my intention.'

'I don't suppose it is and my coming here was a mistake.' Josh turns without another word and almost canters towards his Mini which is the only car in the pub car park. As he reaches it, Roger turns out the lights spilling from the pub windows and Josh disappears into the darkness.

Chapter Seventeen

The argument with Josh has freaked me out but I can't discuss it with anyone. Kayla is working all day, I've stopped mentioning the choir to Alice because it makes her think I'll stay longer and Maura is up to her ears in soiled nappies. Eew, that's not a nice image. Which means there's only one person I can consult about all this weirdness: Salt Bay's biggest gossip, who knows everything about everyone.

Jennifer is chasing small boys out of her shop when I arrive the next morning, only ten minutes after she's opened up.

'Little horrors,' she hisses, shooing them outside. 'They wander round like butter wouldn't melt and steal sweets when they think I'm not looking. I've told their parents but they don't care because they're not true Cornish folk.'

'I'm sure it's not the case that all non-Cornish people approve of shoplifting.'

'Maybe not but lots do.' Jennifer ties the bow that's come undone at the neck of her cream blouse. 'Cornwall for Cornish folk is what I say.' Which sounds like a bid for Cornish independence.

'Of course, I don't mean you, Annie,' adds Jennifer, backpedalling like crazy. 'I'm sure you're not a shoplifter or indeed a criminal of any kind. You're a good Cornish girl and have every right to live here.'

Hoo-feckin-ray! Though I'm only half Cornish; don't forget that my dad is a cool, Nordic god who cycles round Copenhagen when not solving grisly murders.

'Anyway, what can I get you so early in the morning?' Jennifer sorts the *Daily Mails* into a nice, neat pile. 'Alice's magazine hasn't arrived yet.'

'I'm not here for that. I wanted…' Oops, I haven't thought this through properly. I peer round the shop for something cheap. '… chocolate. I'm horribly hormonal.' Too. Much. Information.

'What sort?' asks Jennifer, waving her arm at the vast array of chocolate bars on offer. I pick up the first one I see – Snickers, though I hate peanuts – and scrabble in my pocket for a two-pound coin.

While Jennifer is ringing up at the till, I say casually, 'The auditions went well last night.'

'Mine went exceedingly well though I can't say the same for some of the others I heard through the door while I was waiting. One word – Ollie.' She wrinkles her nose as if there's a bad smell. 'I don't know how people can be tone deaf and unaware of it when it's so offensive to a musical ear like mine. But at least he won't be in the choir with a voice like that.'

'Um, probably not.' I shove the Snickers into my pocket. 'I bumped into Josh Pasco after the auditions and he didn't seem too happy about it all.'

'That makes sense.' Jennifer slams the till shut and hands me my change. 'How's Alice doing these days? Has she found someone else to help her now her health is going downhill so quickly? It's sad to see such a proud woman in decline.'

Typical. The one time I want Jennifer to dish the dirt, she changes the subject.

'Alice is OK and still looking for a more permanent helper.' I pause and bite my lip before blurting out in a jumbled rush, 'So you think it makes sense for Josh to be unhappy about the choir?'

Jennifer looks at me blankly. 'Well it would do, wouldn't it, what with his dad running the old choir and drowning in the Great Storm when Josh was a teenager.'

'There's no Pasco on the list of drowned men.'

'There wouldn't be. Ted Pawley was Josh's stepdad but the lad worshipped him. He was cut up about it for ages and had to step up and take on responsibility for the whole family. A tragedy like that makes you grow up quickly and you never forget.'

Oh God, I should have listened to my misgivings about the choir. Just because Marion Pawley is OK with it doesn't mean that her children are. And it's just my chuffing luck that they happen to be Josh and Serena.

'Are you all right? You've gone horribly pale.' Jennifer leads me to the wooden stool behind the counter. 'Why don't you sit down? Are your hormonal problems' – she silently mouths the next word – 'menstrual?'

'Yes,' I lie, preferring that Jennifer thinks I'm having a heavy period rather than putting my foot in it big time with the Pasco-Pawley family.

Shivering up on the cliffs later, gazing at the coastline that jags and twists towards Land's End, I realise there's only one way out of this mess. And I'm not going to like it. My penance for being a blundering idiot is apologising to Josh face-to-face and explaining why I was planning to bring the choir back to life. He might be arrogant, boorish and annoying. In fact he is arrogant, boorish and annoying. But I've been insensitive and need to put things right.

While Alice is upstairs having a lie down after lunch, I riffle though the address book next to her phone and find a Pawley/Pasco family living at Bell's Hark Cottage, Seagull Lane, Trecaldwith. That must be them, although the address sounds more *Homes and Gardens* than Josh's rusty car would suggest.

Alice comes downstairs mid-afternoon while I'm putting my shoes on and I almost tell her where I'm going because isn't that what families do – tell each other stuff? But I don't feel a true Trebarwith, and though I've warmed to Alice that has nothing to do with her being my great-aunt. I'd like her even if she was some random woman who appeared out of the blue. Which, thinking about it, describes our relationship perfectly. So instead I tell her I'm going for a run – I might have got carried away and claimed I was in training for a marathon – and take the hourly minibus to Trecaldwith.

The bus trundles slowly along the coast, picking up locals along the way, and drops me at the edge of town. Houses on the outskirts are more modern than in Salt Bay and Trecaldwith School in the distance is an unremarkable glass and brick cube surrounded by playing fields. But the roads narrow the farther I walk into town and near the harbour they're cobblestoned and lined with centuries-old cottages. There's a tiny tourist information office set back from the quay, but it's closed so I take a chance and guess that Bell's Hark Cottage will be within spitting distance of the church.

I'm right! Bell's Hark Cottage is opposite the weathered church in a small terraced row of stone cottages, with several plant pots providing a splash of colour outside the front door. When I knock, the door is yanked open within seconds.

'Forgot your key again, pillock? Oops, sorry, I thought you were Josh.' Serena peers at me and pauses for breath. 'Why are you here? Is Mrs Gowan all right?'

'She's fine.' I'm touched by the concern on Serena's face though I have a sneaking suspicion she's more worried about losing her job if Alice drops off the perch. 'I wanted to have a quick word with your brother but it sounds like he's not in.'

Serena smirks. 'What do you want Josh for?'

'It's private.'

'I bet,' she murmurs, pulling the door wide open. 'You can come in and wait if you like. He'll be home any minute.'

She stands back as I step into the cottage and straight into the living room. An old-fashioned gas fire is blazing on one wall and there's a sofa with a cheerful coral-pink throw across it. Family photos are hanging on the magnolia walls and in the corner there's a pretty pink doll's house which has turrets and bow windows.

'Do you want to sit down?' Serena moves a magazine off the sofa and puts it on top of the school books piled up on the coffee table. 'Maths homework,' she grumbles. 'Like I care what a square root is. Do you want a cup of tea or something?' Before I can answer, an attractive woman with grey streaks in her dark hair bustles into the room. 'Mum, this is Mrs Gowan's niece Annie who I told you about.'

'How lovely to meet you. I'm Marion, Serena's mum.' She wipes her hands on her navy apron, leaving a white trail. 'I've been baking and don't want to cover you in flour.' She grasps my hand tightly and shakes it. 'We've heard such a lot about you.'

'Not really,' mumbles Serena, going pink and burying her head in her maths book.

'It's lovely to meet you too and I'm actually Alice's great-niece.'

'Alice told me all about you when she rang a couple of days ago. Oh—' Marion frowns. 'I hope you're not here with bad news about Alice.'

'She's fine,' interjects Serena. 'Annie's here to see Josh.'

'Is she, now?' Marion smiles and blows a strand of hair which has escaped her bun and flopped across her forehead. 'That must be him coming in now.'

Josh barrels into the room and drops a battered leather satchel onto the floor.

'I thought I'd never get home. There was an accident on the top road and—' He stops mid-flow when he spots me. 'What are you doing here?'

'Josh, don't be so inhospitable. And why is it so hot in here, Serena? Our gas bill will be enormous. Put another jumper on if you're chilly.' Marion clicks the fire off and gives her daughter a playful swipe across the back of her head. 'Annie's come to see you, Josh, so why don't you get her a cup of tea.'

What I really need is a stiff brandy with a vodka chaser for Dutch courage.

'I don't need a drink, thanks. Just a quick word with you, please, Josh.'

'Why don't you go into the kitchen anyway,' suggests Marion, ushering me and Josh towards a low doorway at the back of the room.

'Or your bedroom,' mutters Serena, sitting back on her heels with her arms folded and a huge grin on her face.

Josh ignores her, bends his head to get through the doorway and takes me through a narrow corridor that leads into a small, square kitchen. The air is thick with the smell of warm bread and there's a floured board on the worktop, above shaker-style cupboards painted soft dove-grey.

'You'd better sit down.' Josh closes the door and gestures towards a wooden chair with a padded cushion in bright blues and greens. 'Are you sure you don't want a cup of tea?'

'Definitely, completely, absolutely sure.' I perch awkwardly on the edge of the chair and swallow so loudly I'm sure he must have heard.

'Up to you but I'm going to have one.' Josh takes his time filling the kettle and switching it on before turning to face me. 'So why are you here?'

Blimey, Josh Pasco is a man of few words so there's no point in me beating about the bush. Let's get this over with.

'I don't want to intrude or take up your time but I want to apologise for not speaking to you about the choir. Alice spoke to your mum about it so I expect she thought you'd discuss it. And I didn't know Ted Pawley was your stepdad.' Josh's stiff body language is giving nothing away. 'So what I'm trying to say is that I'm sorry if I was an insensitive moron.'

'You're not a moron.' A faint flicker of a smile flits across Josh's face and he sits opposite me at the small oak table.

'Insensitive, though.'

He doesn't disagree so I plough on, determined to get it all off my chest. 'Kayla and I thought setting up the choir again would be a good idea because Salt Bay seems so silent and sad and music makes everything better. Like therapy. And I also wanted to do something to stop me from going mad while I'm here. Not that I have mental health issues. Though everyone has some mental health issues and if they say they don't, they're lying. There's no shame in it.'

Good grief, I'm so nervous I'm burbling. And Josh is frowning at me like I'm one of his difficult students.

'Anyway.' I pull myself together. 'I did try to check with local people who were directly affected by the tragedy and I should have made sure I checked with you too. But I didn't and for that I'm sorry.'

There! That feels better.

Clouds of steam start pouring from the kettle but Josh doesn't move. A wet fog is settling under the ceiling but he sits there silently until I can't stand it any longer.

'Please say something. You look stunned.'

'I've never heard a Trebarwith say sorry before,' he mutters, moving at last to switch off the kettle and open a window to let the steam out. Cold, salty air rushes in while Josh pours boiling water onto a teabag and brings his mug back to the table. He places the steaming cup between us and leans forward. 'What people like you don't realise is that, though the storm was a long time ago, people don't forget what happened.'

People like me? He really is insufferable but I try not to let my annoyance show.

'I realise that and it must have been awful for you all.'

'It was, at the time.' Josh is staring at the wall behind my head. A muscle is twitching in his jaw as though he's trying to hold in his emotions and, even though he's a right royal pain in the arse, I get a strong urge to stroke his face. I don't do it, obviously, because – well, just because. Instead, I shove my hands under my thighs so they can't get me into trouble.

'How long did your stepdad run the choir?'

'About four years.' Josh nods at a photo on the windowsill of a bearded man with rough, red cheeks and laughter lines round his eyes. 'He loved music – everything from Beethoven and The Rolling Stones to The New Seekers and Motörhead; he had eclectic tastes. Look.' Josh stands abruptly and starts pacing across the slate tiles. 'It was a shock when I heard about the choir being resurrected and I was away so didn't know your great-aunt had spoken to Mum about it. If she'd spoken to me, I'd have said it was a bad idea that rakes up too many memories and it shouldn't go ahead.'

'If you feel that strongly about it, we can forget the whole thing.' Giving up on the choir would have filled me with relief a few days ago, so I'm surprised by a pang of disappointment. And I don't rate my chances of survival once Kayla finds out I've scuppered Operation Shag Ollie.

Josh sits again at the table and regards me coolly over his mug of tea.

'Unfortunately it's not as easy as that because my mother thinks the choir should go ahead. In fact she's delighted because she sees it as a memorial to her husband.'

'Which it would be,' I insist. 'Mr Barnley in Salt Bay feels the same way and he lost two grandsons.'

'Cyril, really?' Josh murmurs almost to himself, 'Perhaps I am overreacting.'

'That's easy to do when you lose someone,' I say softly. 'My mum died three years ago of cancer so I know how it can mess with your head for ages…'

I tail off when Josh lifts his head and fading light from the window catches his high cheekbones, which are magnificent. He looks at me properly for the first time since arriving home and I notice that his chocolate-brown eyes are flecked with gold, like tiny streaks of sunshine. Oh dear, this is confusing. It's time to leave.

When I scramble to my feet, my chair scrapes noisily across the tiles.

'Anyway, I've said what I wanted to say so I'll get going.'

There's a scrabbling sound from outside and, when Josh pulls open the kitchen door, I catch a glimpse of Serena scurrying away.

'Younger sisters. They're worse than Year Eights with a post-lunch sugar rush.' Josh shakes his head and sighs. 'I'm afraid she was probably listening in.'

'Don't worry about it.' I hesitate at the kitchen door. 'Just to be clear, are you saying that you think I should go ahead with the choir or not? Only I got a bit confused.'

'I don't suppose what I think matters much either way and Mum wants it to go ahead. As long as it's done the right way.'

I'm not sure what he means by 'the right way' but I nod as though I do.

'I hear that Ollie, aka the Cornish Pavarotti, is one of your singers,' he deadpans.

'He's not the best singer I've ever heard but he's enthusiastic and loves music which counts for a lot. I presume it was him who told you about the auditions?'

'He left me a voicemail message while I was on the school trip but I didn't hear it until I got back.'

'Was it a good school trip?' I ask, hoping that small talk might ease the awkward atmosphere.

'Not bad. A week away and only one broken arm, one coach-vomit and a couple of missing children.' I presume he's joking but it's hard to tell. 'How are you getting back to Salt Bay?'

'On the bus.'

Josh glances at his watch. 'You'll have to wait for ages. I'll give you a lift.'

'No, please don't bother. I don't mind waiting and I'd rather not put you out.'

'You won't,' says Josh gruffly, fishing his car keys from his trouser pocket. 'I'm parked down the road.'

Serena has abandoned her maths homework and is glued to her mobile when we go back into the front room. Her thumbs are moving like lightning across the screen. Marion is sitting on the sofa, leafing through a picture book with a small girl curled up on her lap.

'All done? This is Freya, my gorgeous granddaughter. We were reading about Edith the elephant whose trunk has shrunk.' The girl giggles and leans her head against Marion's comforting bosom.

'Wow, you don't look old enough to be a grandmother,' I blurt out, taking in Freya's ebony plaits and pale, soulful eyes and wondering if Josh is Freya's father. There's so much I don't know about him. Maybe he's got a couple of kids and a wife tucked away that no one's told me about, though it's no business of mine if he's married or not.

'You can definitely come again,' chuckles Marion, moving Freya from her lap onto the sofa. 'My daughter Lucy, Freya's mum, is at work at the moment. It's a bit of a squash us all living here – Freya, Lucy, Josh, me and Serena – but we manage.'

No wife, then. Serena catches my eye and smirks as though she can read my mind.

'I'm going to run Annie back to Mrs Gowan's, Mum, so she won't have to wait for a bus.'

'OK my lovely, tea will be ready soon so don't be long,' says Marion in such a mumsy way I could cry.

'I'll only be half an hour.' When Josh kisses his mum on the cheek, Freya leaps off the sofa, throws her arms around his legs and he leans over to hug her. He doesn't come across as the sort of person who's good with small children – or adults, for that matter – but she obviously loves him. She clings to his knees until Marion laughs and pulls her away. It would make a fabulous photo – three generations of the same loving family; a proper family. I experience a sudden longing for something I've never had and never wanted before. Salt Bay is making me soft.

'Come again, Annie, maybe for tea next time.' Marion briefly touches my arm, leaving a faint smudge of flour. 'And good luck with the choir. It's an amazing idea and I'm sure it will benefit the village.'

'As long as it's run in the right way,' mutters Josh. Jeez, I wish he'd stop being so enigmatic and start saying exactly what he means.

'Josh has misgivings about the choir, as I'm sure he's told you.' When Marion winks at me and smiles, dimples appear in her flushed cheeks. She looks like the roly-poly mum from a children's book. 'Why don't you help Annie out with the first couple of rehearsals, Josh, and then you can make sure that it's being run in the *right way*.'

Josh's jaw drops in horror, though he can't be as shocked by the idea as I am. My newly found enthusiasm for setting up the damn choir begins to evaporate.

'I couldn't possibly ask Josh to do that,' I splutter.

'Nonsense,' soothes Marion. 'It would only be for a couple of rehearsals and it would put my mind at rest because Josh has a point. The new choir needs to be a fitting tribute to the men who died. Do it for your dad, Josh. He would be so proud of you getting involved.'

Josh breathes out so heavily he seems to deflate as Marion puts her arm round my shoulder.

'That's settled, then. Give my regards to your great-aunt and maybe we'll see you again soon.'

Josh doesn't speak on the way to his car or while he drives out of town and into the countryside. He's driving well today which is a relief. I was expecting him to motor along the winding lanes like Lewis Hamilton in a hurry, particularly after his mum's bombshell idea, but he stops at red lights and everything. A fine drizzle has started falling and the wipers make a rasping noise every time they scrape across the windscreen. It's putting my teeth on edge but it fills the silence.

We're only a mile or so from the village when Josh says, 'My mum has been very ill with heart problems.'

That's a bit left field but I go with it.

'I'm sorry to hear that. I wouldn't have realised, she looks well. And she seems lovely.'

'She's much better these days, just so long as she takes things easy. That's why I'm living with her.' Josh takes his eyes off the road and glances across at me. 'I was living in Penzance with a girlfriend but when Mum was ill she couldn't cope with looking after herself and Freya while Lucy worked shifts. And the bills were piling up so I moved back home a few months ago to help out.'

Don't ask, don't ask, don't ask! 'What happened to your girlfriend?' Oops, I asked.

'Felicity and I split up.'

'It must have been difficult moving back home.' I resist the urge to slag off Felicity who sounds like a grade one bitch for deserting someone whose mum was poorly. 'Look, you don't have to help out with the choir if you'd rather not.'

Josh's sigh is almost drowned out by the engine. 'I'll help out with the first two rehearsals if it makes Mum happy, but you're on your own after that.'

We drive on, through a faint mist that's caught between the folds of the valley and is smudging the lights of Salt Bay.

'Do you have any other family?' asks Josh after a while. 'What about your dad, or brothers and sisters?'

'Nope, no dad and no siblings.'

'Aunts and uncles? Anyone else apart from Mrs Gowan?'

'No one. It's just me.'

Josh pulls hard on the steering wheel to avoid a cat in the road whose eyes are shining in the headlights. 'I'm not sure if that's a blessing or a curse.'

It's a blessing, of course. No doubt about it. But I can't get the picture of Marion, Serena and Freya, all curled up together in the front room, out of my head. They seemed so at ease with one another.

When we reach The Whistling Wave, I start softly humming Mum's favourite tune. 'The Boy I Love is Up in the Gallery' is an old music hall song she used to sing when I couldn't sleep, and it's my go-to tune in awkward moments.

'Are you singing?' Josh couldn't sound more disapproving if I'd just farted in his precious car.

'Not really singing, just humming one of Mum's favourite songs. It makes me feel closer to her now she's gone.' That shuts him up.

At last we're on the narrow road that leads to the harbour and I can honestly say I've never been happier to see Tregavara House, whose lights mark the end of the village and the start of the black sea. Josh pulls up outside the house and leaves the engine running while I scrabble for my handbag on the back seat.

My fingers have just closed round the soft leather when he asks, 'When are you going back to London?'

'As soon as Alice has arranged some permanent help at home.'

'I expect you'll be glad to escape this provincial little life and get back to the big city.'

'I'll be glad to get home, if that's what you mean.' I push down on the chrome handle next to me but the passenger door doesn't move. I try again but the door won't budge.

'And what happens to the choir then?' asks Josh, leaning across me to give the door a shove. His body is heavy across my lap and he smells faintly of soap and cedar wood as the muscles across his shoulders strain against the cotton of his shirt.

'I'll sort something out. Don't worry, it won't be your problem.'

'Huh. The Trebarwiths always seem to be my problem.' He gives the door another almighty shove but it stays firmly shut.

What is Josh Pasco's beef with the Trebarwiths? His constant digs make me feel protective towards my family, even Toby whom I don't trust. But before I can leap to their defence, Josh removes his hot, heavy body from my lap and gets out of the car to try my door from the outside. It opens with a screech and Josh stands back to let me get out.

'Thank you for the lift.'

'Don't mention it.'

A lone seagull swoops round our heads and flies towards the cliffs while Josh folds himself back behind the wheel.

I'm halfway along the garden path, my breath white in the wintry air, when the car window winds down and Josh calls out, 'You do realise, don't you, that Toby is an utter shit?'

'That's funny,' I call back. 'He says exactly the same about you.'

Josh snorts and drives off, the rear bumper of his car scraping along the road when he bounces over a pothole.

'Who was that?' asks Alice disingenuously when I let myself into the house. She knows very well who it was because she was peering round the curtains when we pulled up.

'Josh Pasco, he gave me a lift home.'

'That was kind of him.'

'It was, though I think he's probably the grumpiest man I've ever met.'

Alice's laugh sounds faintly disapproving. 'Don't be too hard on him. He's had a lot to cope with.'

God knows I'd be grumpy if I had to live with my dependent family in Cornwall forever. But I'm tempted to tell Alice that Josh has taken against the whole Trebarwith family because Toby once annoyed him. She doesn't appear to know and it might make her think twice before sticking up for the grumpy bugger. But I don't bother because there's no point in upsetting an old lady who's got enough problems of her own.

When I go quiet, Alice pats my hand with her cold fingers. 'Don't worry, Annabella. Once you go back to London you'll probably never see Josh Pasco again.'

Wahey! I can't wait to be shot of his snarky comments, designer stubble and general glowering. Though I don't say any of that to Alice.

To be fair, he has some good points: many blokes would run a mile rather than move in with their sick mother, and his stubble is sexy. Very sexy actually. I shake my head to dislodge an image of Josh's strong jawline. But overall he's a pain and I'll be glad when the first two choir rehearsals are over and he's out of my hair.

Chapter Eighteen

The next few days are taken up with contacting new choir members and trying to find a permanent helper for Alice before my flat goes totally tits up. There have been a couple of replies to her ad in Jennifer's shop and both respondents call round for an informal interview.

One is a tall, spiky woman called Prudence who's in her mid-fifties and dressed head to toe in black. She runs her finger along the top of the radiator when she comes into the house and purses her lips sourly when she finds a smidgen of dust. Miserable old bat.

Alice gives her the benefit of the doubt and talks her through the daily support she's likely to need, including increasing personal care as time goes on.

'That won't be a problem,' sniffs Prudence, her beady eyes flitting round the sitting room. 'I'm experienced in giving effective, sanitary bed baths and my clients are always thoroughly cleansed. I don't tolerate dirt in the home or on the body.' She shudders at the thought and flicks imaginary dust from her squeaky-clean neck.

'Utterly terrifying,' is Alice's verdict when we finally get shot of Prudence in her funereal clothes. 'I'm not letting that woman anywhere near my private parts.'

Karen, the second candidate, is a middle-aged, dumpy woman who arrives late in a flowing floral skirt and chunky necklace. She seems more promising and is doing well until she starts patting Alice's hand and – the final nail in Karen's coffin – calling her 'my dear'.

'Patronising prig,' mutters Alice, slamming the front door shut and shuffling off unsteadily.

I suggest calling a few care agencies to see what they'd charge and offer to do it myself, to speed things along, but Alice is adamant that it's her care and she'll make the phone calls.

'I'm not sure I really need much care anyway,' she says airily, tightening the Velcro on her slippers. Which is rich seeing as I picked her up from another fall this morning. It was just a tiny tumble with no injuries, but it's a reminder that permanent support needs to be in place before I can escape back to London with a clear conscience.

In between doing choir stuff and keeping an eye on Alice, I'm mind-numbingly bored. I read a lot and walk a bit and listen to music on my phone, but there are only so many times I can saunter round the village without being tagged a total weirdo. So I end up spending time on the cliffs, looking at the view and dodging dive-bombing seagulls whose sole purpose in life appears to be shitting on my head.

Perched high above the village and the dishwater-grey sea, I think a lot about my mum and how Salt Bay must have stifled her. My London mum dressed in vibrant colours and revelled in new experiences and new people. Too many people, sometimes. Our flat was often full of strange, hippy types with their sweet, pot smell and laid-back attitudes.

There were times when Mum got overwhelmed and took to her bed, whispering, 'It's all too much, Pumpkin; all the colours and the sounds. I'm drowning and can't breathe.' That's when I knew a bad patch was coming and the flat would fall silent while the hangers-on drifted away and Mum slept for days on end, as though she was dead.

But eventually she'd emerge, looking pale but gradually lighting up until she shone brightly again – a butterfly emerging from a chrysalis. And the friends would come back, and the flat would be filled with laughter and music until the early hours. Which wasn't great when I was revising for exams, but Mum was happy and that was all that mattered.

Mum has become a taboo subject at Tregavara House since I slagged off my grandparents for abandoning her. Neither Alice nor I mention her, and my grandmother Sheila also seems to be on the taboo list and is no longer mentioned. Perhaps she fell out with Samuel and that's why she's buried in the churchyard rather than on the cliffs. But I don't want to find out. The less I know, the easier it will be to leave Alice when the time comes.

Alice does talk about the choir and mentions it one afternoon while I'm unpacking food.

'Where are you planning for the choir to meet?' she asks, picking up a tin of baked beans and balancing it on a tin of tomatoes in the food cupboard.

'I'm thinking in the pub initially. Roger says we can use the back room.'

'Or there's always the church.' Alice delves into the bag and brings out a cabbage. 'You could ask the vicar; she's a nice woman. Bit posh. The choir used to meet in the church and Samuel said the acoustics in there made singers sound better than they were.'

I haven't considered the church but it makes more sense than a busy pub and, acoustics-wise, we can do with all the help we can get.

Alice scrawls the vicar's phone number on a Post-it and sticks it on the kitchen table.

'There you are. Hilary looks after lots of parishes so it's best to catch her on the phone. Who will take over the choir when you go back to London?'

'I'm sure someone will come forward. If I get it up and running, these things usually take on a life of their own. And there's always Jennifer, who seems to have hidden musical talents.'

Alice looks doubtful and I mentally cross Jennifer off my 'could run the choir after I escape' list. There's no question that she could do it, but there wouldn't be a choir to run after she started barking orders at people and criticising them for being tone-deaf.

Fortunately I've already got a pianist lined up. Michaela, the young girl who played so well for Jennifer, was the obvious choice so I gave her a call and then spoke to her parents. They agreed that playing for us once a week wouldn't impact on her homework, and Michaela was delighted when she realised we'd pay her fifteen pounds per evening. If everyone in the choir puts two pounds into a kitty each week, we'll have enough to pay Michaela with some left over for juice and biscuits in the break.

The only thing that's missing is music so, several days before the choir's first ever rehearsal, I pay a visit to Penzance. The minibus wheezes out of Salt Bay and wends its way through tiny villages with pretty names until we reach the outskirts of the town. Only around 21,000 people live in Penzance – I looked it up on the web – but it feels like a huge metropolis after living out in the sticks. There's a Boots and a Costa, people rushing around, litter on the streets and dog poo on the pavements. It's almost like being at home, apart from the sea and the elegant, art deco Jubilee Pool jutting out into the ocean.

First of all, I make a beeline for the library, which is on the ground floor of a grand building set back behind black railings. A young man with horn-rimmed glasses too big for his face is tapping away at a computer on the information desk. He looks up and the glasses slide down his nose.

'Can I help you?' His hands are still hovering over the keyboard as if he's desperate to get back to what he was doing.

'I'm looking for your library's sheet music section. I'd like to hire some for my choir.'

'We don't have anything like that. You'd need to contact the Performing Arts Library.'

I should have checked before I came into Penzance, rather than assuming the local library would stock everything I need. When will I learn that I'm not in London now? The man behind the desk sees my shoulders drop and takes pity on me.

'You could always check out Cornwall Council's website and order the music you'd like,' he says kindly. 'We've got computers over there you can use.'

There's a long list of vocal scores online but the problem is I'm not sure what I'm looking for. Kayla suggested consulting Josh about the music but that would have involved having a normal conversation with him, which was never going to happen.

I run my eye down the musical scores and frown. There's everything available from Schubert and Bach to Mozart and Verdi, but heavyweight composers might be too much for a brand new choir. Particularly one with Ollie in it.

Luckily, the list includes some less ambitious scores from musicals, and another search online uncovers several choirs around the UK who hire out the scores they're not using. What a brilliant idea! We could even go for something more up to date maybe, from Enya or even The Clash. A vision of Jennifer belting out 'I Fought the Law' flits into my head and makes me giggle. It's hard to believe but Kayla's ridiculous notion of resurrecting the Salt Bay Choral Society is starting to come together.

Feeling more cheerful, I wander round the shops before heading back to Salt Bay, though it's window shopping only as I'm not earning at the moment. Gracie is covering my rent and bills and it's free bed and board at Alice's, so I'm not skint but I need to be careful. Alice offered me a weekly wage but I said no. Despite what Toby thinks, she doesn't appear to be loaded and my expenses here are minimal because there's bugger all to buy in the village.

I'm waiting at the bus stop when my mobile phone rings and Toby's name flashes up on the screen.

'Hello Annie,' he yells against a backdrop of revving engines and car horns. 'I'm in the middle of Piccadilly Circus and about to go into a meeting. Can you hear me? I wondered how things are going and if you're back in London.'

'Not yet. I've come into Penzance for the afternoon but I'll be heading back to Salt Bay as soon as the bus arrives.'

'Still putting your life on hold, are you?' Toby sounds annoyed, though it's hard to tell when he's shouting anyway. 'You must be going mad with boredom stuck in zombie land. Don't you miss London and your friends? A young girl like you should be out on the town.'

'Of course I miss London. But Alice is sorting out permanent help at the moment and I've said I'll stay until she has.'

'That was a rash promise. I bet she's not exactly rushing to get things organised.'

'Well…'

'I thought as much,' Toby groans. 'She'll take ages on purpose while you're stuck there wasting your time.'

'I'm sure she'll sort things out as soon as she can and I'm not wasting time, I'm helping Alice. And I'm starting up the Salt Bay Choral Society again so that's keeping my brain engaged.'

'What the hell are you doing that for?' splutters Toby as a battalion of tanks with broken exhaust pipes trundles past him. 'That choir was tedious enough the first time round. There's nothing worse than average singers performing traditional Cornish songs. Their concerts were interminable.'

'I'm hoping bringing back the choir will be good for the village and it should be fun. There's quite a lot of interest in it.'

'It sounds boring as feck to me and the locals won't thank you for it. Be careful, Annie. You're getting pulled into local life and what's the point of that if you're planning to leave? You are planning to leave, aren't you?'

'Of course.' Being told what to do by Toby is getting on my wick and he's being overdramatic. Though he's right to remind me that I mustn't get too involved. How ironic would it be if, having managed to stay fancy-free in London, I end up with ties to this place? Madrid maybe, New York or Paris, but Salt Bay?

'I'll definitely be leaving soon,' I say confidently.

'Hhmm.' Toby isn't convinced. 'I'll keep a lookout up here for any suitable jobs that might interest you. What is it you do again?'

'I'm a PA and do secretarial temping in between contracts. I've got lots of experience and good references.'

He sniffs loudly down the line. 'Secretarial work is rather more lowbrow than the calibre of vacancies I hear about but I'm well connected so I might be able to come up with something.'

'Thanks Toby, that would be brilliant.' My cousin is the most outrageous snob but I'm out of the job search loop down here and can do with all the help I can get. Quite why he's so keen to help me is a mystery and I wonder for a moment if I've misjudged him. Though I doubt there's a heart of gold beating beneath that supercilious exterior.

'I have to go,' yells Toby, 'or I'll be late for the important meeting I'm chairing. Take heart, Annie. You won't have to mix with that rum lot for much longer. I'll have you out of Cornwall and back to civilisation in no time. Talking of deadbeats, have you had the misfortune to bump into Josh Pasco again?'

'Only very briefly.' For some reason I don't feel like telling Toby about Josh helping out with the choir. Perhaps because he's only helping under duress and that might add to Toby's poor opinion of him. Not that I care.

'My advice stands to keep out of his way because he's trouble.'

'What did he do that was so awful?'

'I didn't catch that. What did you say? It's too noisy here to have a proper conversation and I've got to go. I'll be in touch.'

It's only after Toby has rung off that I realise he didn't once ask about Alice.

Chapter Nineteen

It turns out that Reverend Hilary Baxham is a very nice woman indeed, who not only gives us permission to rehearse in the church but also donates twenty-five pounds towards set-up costs. What an excellent Christian! She also promises to pray for me, which is an added bonus.

So rather than being squeezed into the tiny back room of The Whistling Wave, the members of Salt Bay Choral Society meet for the first time in the church. It's just as well the venue's changed because the choir has swelled to fifteen members, thanks to people signing up when they've had a few too many in the pub.

'To audition, I got them to sing something at me over the bar,' says Kayla, eyeing up Ollie who's shoving his hefty thighs into a pew near the front. 'They were all OK, except for Gordon who insisted on singing "Je t'aime" complete with orgasm noises. But it doesn't matter since we're letting anyone in now. You have got to be kidding me! I didn't realise Chloe was coming. She's not on the freakin' list.'

'Who's Chloe?'

'She comes into the pub sometimes and is so all over Ollie it's embarrassing to watch. She has no dignity.' Kayla scuttles off and sits behind Ollie, who's being gushed over by a pretty young woman.

A glance at my watch shows it's seven thirty and time for the first rehearsal of the new Salt Bay Choral Society to get underway. Josh hasn't turned up, which I'm mostly glad about when I stand on the worn stone steps leading to the altar and the church falls silent. Crikey, everyone is looking at me like I know what I'm doing. And I really don't. Kayla gives me a wide grin and does rabbit ears with her fingers behind Chloe's head.

I'm about to speak when the sound of the door latch echoes through the building and Josh steps into the church. He's all in black – skinny jeans, heavy army boots, chunky polo-neck jumper – but I can feel my face going red as he slips into a pew at the back and stretches out. Just what I need; a critic to tell me I'm not doing things 'the right way'.

Taking a deep breath, I gather myself together.

'Can everyone stand up please and we'll get started.' Oops, what's wrong with my voice? It's gone all wobbly. The younger members of the choir leap to their feet while the older ones groan and haul themselves up, holding on to the backs of pews.

'Welcome to all of you and thank you for coming along to the first meeting of the new Salt Bay Choral Society. I'm sure we're going to make some lovely music together.'

'Doubt it,' mutters Roger, who'd informed us he'd better come along and lend some support on account of everyone, bar Jennifer, being vocally challenged. Pretending not to hear him, I nod at Michaela, sitting poised at the piano.

'Let's do some warm-up exercises to start with. Can you all sing "the tram at the top of the towering turn" on the note that Michaela gives us.'

'I can but I'm not sure I want to,' grumbles Roger to laughter from the people around him. But Michaela plays a middle C and we all sing the tongue-twisting phrase together, more or less on the right note, and then sing it a tone higher as we start going up and then down the scale. It breaks the ice and, by the time everyone sits down again, people look flushed and happier.

'Before we sing any more, I expect you know one another but it would be helpful for me if you could all introduce yourselves. For those who haven't met me, I'm Annie and I'm the great-niece of Alice Gowan in the village.'

'Thought as much. Same big teeth,' pipes up a middle-aged bald man in the front row.

'I've also sung in choirs and I ran one for a while' – probably best not to mention it was for seven-year-olds – 'and I know that music has the power to move and heal people.'

The brass plaque to the lost men of the choral society is glinting on the wall and I suddenly feel out of my depth. Who the hell do I think I am, reckoning I can make a difference in this close-knit community where I don't belong? Kayla raises her eyebrows and gives me a sympathetic smile while I stand speechless in front of everyone.

I'm rescued by a stout woman with short grey hair and ruddy cheeks who jumps up and waves.

'Shall I start, then? As most of you know, my name is Florence and I live at Helligan's Farm.'

'How's Bob?' calls one woman from the back.

'Fine, thanks, Maureen. The wound has healed over and we're waiting for the scab to dry up and drop off.'

Ugh, that makes me feel sick. Maybe country folk have stronger stomachs than soft city types, though Jennifer looks appalled. Choir members take it in turns to give their names, some more confidently than others, and fortunately most keep their ailments to themselves, if not their opinions.

'The old choral society was just for men,' says a trim man in his fifties who introduces himself as Arthur. 'Wives weren't allowed to join.'

'That's very interesting but this isn't the old Salt Bay Choral Society,' butts in Jennifer. 'It's moved into the twenty-first century so women are allowed and you men will just have to lump it.' That shuts up Arthur who sits down with a scowl and starts muttering under his breath.

All in all, I've got a pretty good mix of singers; nine women and six men, ranging in age from teenagers like Tom whose pants are still showing, to Mary, an elegant woman in her late seventies whose hair falls in soft white waves. Maureen is particularly popular with everyone because she's brought cupcakes from her tea shop.

Once introductions are out of the way, I sort the women into altos and sopranos and the men into basses and tenors by getting everyone to sing together up and down the scale and sit down when a note is too low or high for them. Ollie reckons he can reach every note – though not necessarily in tune – so I put him with the tenors, who are thin on the ground. Ollie invites Josh to join him in the tenor section, but Josh declines and stays put.

'Now that's done, we're ready to start rehearsing,' says Kayla, handing out the sheet music that's arrived since I placed my online orders. She throws evil glares at Chloe, who's cuddling up close to Ollie and doesn't seem terribly interested in the singing.

'I can't be doing with reading musical notes.' Florence recoils from her sheet music as though it's hardcore porn.

'How many of you can read music?' I ask. Only eight hands go up, which could be a problem, but one we'll have to overcome. 'Reading music is an advantage but we can learn these pieces by heart. There's nothing too ambitious and some of them will be familiar to you.'

'"Amazing Grace"? I should think so,' pipes up Jennifer. 'I was expecting something a little more challenging.'

'This is just the start, Jennifer, to see how we get on.' I cross my fingers behind my back and hope Jennifer won't make a fuss. My stress levels are already through the roof with Josh still sitting at the back, staring at me and being no help whatsoever.

'"Amazing Grace" is a wonderful song and perfect for a new choir like us,' calls out Mary, giving me a thumbs up and Jennifer a serene smile that quashes any brewing tantrum. I think I might love Mary already.

At last we're ready to start, and the rest of the rehearsal goes well. The singing's not great but it'll improve – probably – and there's a semblance of four-part harmony by the end of an hour and a half. At least people seem to be enjoying themselves, even Roger, whose booming bass voice reminds me of Brian Blessed.

I've done my best to ignore Josh the whole time, but it's hard not to steal a glance every now and then. At first he was scanning round the church, looking bored. But when Kayla drops the copies of a traditional Cornish song she's handing round, he helps her pick them up and hand them round. He keeps a copy for himself, I notice, and follows the music when we're singing.

The most embarrassing part of the evening is singing solo in front of everyone when I'm demonstrating the harmonies. At first my voice is thin and quavery, but I have an epiphany when Ollie launches into 'Ave verum corpus' with gay abandon, not caring if he hits the right notes or not. It sounds awful – Jennifer puts her fingers in her ears at one point – but he's having a fabulous time and it makes people laugh, and I remember that's what this choir is all about. Bringing a touch of joy into this sad little village. After that, I sing out loud and proud, and don't care what anyone thinks. Even Josh.

At the end of the rehearsal, several people thank me when they're leaving the church. And most say they're planning to come back next week. Hopefully Bob's scab will have dropped off by then so we won't need an update.

'Phew, that went well.' Kayla picks up some sheet music that's fallen behind a pew and plonks it on top of the piano. 'Apart from Chloe, whose voice sounds like nails down a blackboard. She's a very screechy soprano.' Kayla is a proud alto. 'And he wasn't much help.' She tilts her head towards Josh, who's still at the back of the church, studying an ancient gravestone set into the floor.

'Don't forget his dad was conducting the last time the choral society met so I expect that's why he's being weird.' I'm so relieved at getting through the rehearsal without making an arse of myself, I'm willing to give Josh the benefit of the doubt.

'Maybe. Anyway, I'm going back to the pub to check if Ollie's there with Chloe. I'll see you later.' Kayla gives me a brief hug. 'Well done with the rehearsal. This choir is going to be amazing.'

Josh and I are the only people left in the church once Kayla's gone. Which means he probably wants to speak to me. He's probably made chuffing notes on my performance. Balls! I gather up the last of the music, shove it in my bag and march down the aisle.

'Did I run the rehearsal in the *right way*?'

Josh looks up from words chiselled into stone three hundred years ago. 'Not bad.'

'And what about the singing, how did that sound?'

'Not bad,' he intones again.

'Wow, I'm overwhelmed by your enthusiasm and positivity.'

Josh folds his arms across his lean frame. 'OK; the singing was quite good in places, though you've got your work cut out with Ollie, who can't sing for toffee, and Florence, who hasn't got a clue what's going on. Jennifer's singing is amazing and she knows it so she's drowning everyone else out, but Roger and Mary have good voices, and you too, actually.' He scuffs his feet across the flagstones, clearly ill at ease after paying a compliment to a Trebarwith. 'As for the way the rehearsal was run, it went pretty well, though you could do with a proper baton rather than waving a pencil at people.'

'I'm not sure I'm a baton sort of person.'

'Really? Surely you've used one before, seeing as you're a talented and experienced choral conductor from London?' Josh arches an eyebrow while I work out the best way to murder feckin' Kayla and her big mouth.

'Obviously I've used one before,' I scoff, heaping lie on top of lie, 'but I don't have one of my own.'

'Not a problem. I can bring one along next time.' Oh great! There's going to be a 'next time', so some ground rules are required, pronto.

'If you're here next week, I insist that you give us a hand rather than sitting back here' – I search for the right words to encapsulate his unnerving presence – 'giving me evils.'

Jeez, I have never used that phrase before in my whole life. The only people who use that phrase are adolescent girls. And Vicky Pollard. Not sophisticated twenty-nine-year-olds from London. I am a moron.

Josh gazes at me coolly and raises the other eyebrow. 'I didn't realise I was "giving you evils". I do apologise. And while I'm in an apologetic mood, I suppose I should say sorry again for alarming you near the pub after the auditions. I would have mentioned it when we last met but I was thrown when you ambushed me at home.'

'Hardly ambushed! I came round to speak to you, not shoot you.'

'Wrong choice of words,' murmurs Josh. 'I was thrown when you turned up at my home unannounced.'

'I didn't realise I was supposed to make an appointment,' I fire back. Well, this is going swimmingly. Taking a deep breath, I attempt to lower the temperature a notch. 'I hope the rehearsal didn't upset you. I expect it brought back memories of your dad.'

'Lots of memories. I remember him standing where you were, conducting the choir and joking with some of the younger men. It was only a small choir so losing seven men in one night was devastating. I knew them all.' He closes his eyes for a moment and swallows. 'And what about you? Your grandfather was one of the men who were lost.'

'I don't have any memories of him. It's hard to miss someone you've never met.'

'I remember him. He was tall and stern-looking and I was rather frightened of him as a child. But he loved music and he had a great voice. He often sang a solo when the choir gave public performances.'

'Did he?' It's hard to equate such a harsh, unforgiving man with someone who revelled in the joy and beauty of music.

'He'd come to our house sometimes to practise his solo with Dad, and I'd listen at the door with Mum.' Josh shrugs. 'But that was a long time ago.'

'How is your mum?'

'She's doing well.'

'And Freya?'

Josh's face softens and he smiles in spite of himself. 'She's decided she'd like to be an astronaut when she grows up so we're all having to pretend that we live on the moon.'

'That's sweet.'

'She's a very sweet child, and she liked you. She thought you were a princess because of your amazing blue eyes.'

There are muffled shouts outside from people passing by, but the air in here is very still.

'Anyway, that's what she thought,' says Josh in a rush. 'Um, how are your family?' He winces and a deep furrow appears between his eyebrows.

'Alice is doing pretty well, really.' Whatever you do, Annie, do not mention Toby! 'Considering her age and health problems…'

Josh steps closer to give me his sheet music that was rolled up in the back pocket of his jeans.

'And considering the fact that she's keeping a big house running…'

The paper is warm from being close to his body.

'And she's had no live-in help until now…'

He's staring at my mouth, which makes me feel ridiculously flustered. Why is he staring at my mouth like that?

'And Toby was OK, the last time we spoke.'

The spectre of my cousin steps between us as I wish I could take the words back. It's official; I truly am a moron.

Josh backs away as though I'm toxic. 'That's marvellous news. I'll sleep so much better now I know that Toby is OK.'

'Toby's not so bad.' Toby is a bossy, patronising prig, but he's my cousin and Josh's attacks on him are beginning to feel like attacks on me.

'Blood is thicker than water but you'll find out what he's like one day.' Josh pulls car keys from his front pocket and scrunches them tightly into his fist. 'I'll leave you to lock up the church and get back to your precious family.'

The heavy door bangs shut behind him and I'm left with only the ghosts of drowned fishermen to keep me company.

Chapter Twenty

The next few days pass more quickly as I get into the rhythm of life in Salt Bay. London feels distant, a mythical place where there's twenty-four-hour public transport, shops open in the evening, and wall-to-wall Wi-Fi. God, I miss Wi-Fi. I didn't realise how much I relied on my mobile, although life seems more serene without Twitter trolls and Facebook one-upmanship. I'm still nipping into the pub to stalk Amber online, obviously.

It's hard to admit but there are some things I like about Salt Bay. The weird heart palpitations I get on the Tube are gone and my body feels looser because I'm not tensing my shoulders all the time – only when I have a run-in with Josh, or Alice starts talking about the village like it's my permanent home. I'm also looking more healthy although there's no hairdresser for miles and the skin on my face is being scoured daily by harsh salt winds. My pale London pallor has been replaced by a glowing complexion and my longer hair has started curling softly on my shoulders. Maybe I should open a beauty parlour in Mayfair and charge women shedloads to stand in a wind tunnel and have their faces scrubbed with a Brillo pad.

But the thing I like most about Salt Bay is that looking after Alice reminds me of taking care of Mum and gives me a purpose I hadn't realised was lacking. I like looking after people and I'm good at it.

I'm even thinking about checking out care jobs when I get back to London.

Just before the weekend, Alice vets another couple of her potential carers and declares them 'hopeless', particularly the young girl with a tarnished silver stud in her nose. 'She has an actual hole in her nose! What happens to the phlegm when she has a cold? Does she leak? It's terribly unhygienic.'

When I insist, Alice finally sets up a meeting with a care agency and likes the woman who calls round, but the cost of a comprehensive care package almost gives her a heart attack on the spot. She does some sums and declares the agency option will work only if she does the decent thing and pops her clogs within a year or so. If she lingers any longer, both she and Tregavara House will be in trouble. I guess she doesn't have a mattress stuffed with fivers after all.

With such a lot going on, I'm able to put super-sarcastic Josh to the back of my mind, but I can't forget Cyril. Even Kayla admits she's concerned about him during one of our regular walks together on the cliffs.

'His luck's been shite,' she yells, trying to be heard above the waves pounding the rocks below us. The sea is ferocious today and strands of foam are swirling in the stiff breeze. 'First his grandsons die, followed by his wife, and then his only daughter buggers off to, where was it, County Deadham?'

'Durham,' I shout back, not sure why we're braving the elements when we could be drinking hot chocolate instead. We usually do when the weather's bad but Kayla's trying to lose weight off her skinny thighs.

She leads me into the clifftop cemetery and we sit with our backs to a gravestone, sheltered from the worst of the wind.

'But try not to worry about Mr Barnley,' she says. 'The folk round here keep an eye on him and you can't make him come to the choir.

Just accept he's the type of person who dies alone and no one notices for ages.'

Kayla is not the most reassuring of people, nor the most discreet if what she tells me about the pub regulars is anything to go by. That's why I've kept quiet about Josh, not that there's much to tell. She already knows he can be rude and grumpy.

A squall of freezing rain hits us and Kayla pulls up the hood on her bright yellow cagoule. 'Bugger this, shall we abandon our walk and head to the caff? I'll be good and have a calorie-free black coffee.'

Ten minutes later, we're sitting in a cosy corner of the tea shop with our wet cagoules draped across the back of our chairs. The bunting-draped windows have steamed up so much, people walking past look like ghosts.

'What? Don't judge me!' Kayla stirs in the Cornish cream on the top of her hot chocolate and licks the spoon. 'I need some energy for my lunchtime shift and Roger is so lazy I'll soon work this off.' She gulps down a fat-laced mouthful and stretches her legs out under the table with its gingham cloth. 'Are you feeling better about the choir now? I know you were worried that the locals wouldn't like it but I've had some great feedback in the pub.'

'I must admit I feel happier now the first rehearsal is over.'

'It was great, and you were right. It is good to have music in the village. Roger's even talking about getting some band to come in one evening to play live music for the customers. It's folk music' – she pretends to spit on the floor – 'but hey, small steps. The locals aren't ready for Kanye yet.'

'Live music of any kind will be brilliant.' Best to keep quiet about my extensive collection of folk music because I was ribbed about my musical tastes when I was growing up. While my school friends were fangirling over Blue and Busted, I was listening to Tony Bennett and The Carpenters. Karen Carpenter's smooth, rich voice still makes the hairs stand up on the back of my neck.

After we've demolished the hot chocolates, I walk Kayla to the pub before heading back towards Tregavara House. But I hesitate when I get to the tiny cobbled lane that leads to Mr Barnley's cottage. Unlike Mum and Alice, Mr Barnley is not my responsibility, but what if he thought being alone was the best option and now he's stuck? What if I'm stuck, too?

Shaking off such a self-indulgent notion, I knock on Mr Barnley's door and write a quick note when he doesn't answer. *Sorry not to see you at the first rehearsal of the choir. The next one is in the church on Wednesday at 7.30 pm. Maybe see you there? Annie.* Just before I pop it through the letterbox, I add a kiss after my name. He seems the sort of man who could do with some affection.

Much to my relief, everyone turns up for the next choir rehearsal, plus three new faces; Fiona, with unnaturally over-red hair, who's married to Arthur, and young couple Pippa and Charlie. They're so loved-up they wave sadly to one another when I separate them and sit Charlie with the tenors. He settles down beside Ollie with his back to the altar and pouts at his sweet fiancée.

The whole choir is facing the main body of the church this week because I raided the vestry for chairs and made a little semicircle with two rows. Josh gave a hand when he turned up early and helped Kayla to put music on each chair. He hardly said two words to me and then retreated to the back pew. But he beckons me over before the rehearsal begins.

'I've got this for you,' he says gruffly, handing over a long, thin wooden case with tarnished silver clasps. When I open it, my stomach sinks. There inside, resting on red satin, is a nut-brown baton that tapers from a bulb at one end to a rounded point at the other. Josh is looking at me closely, waiting for my reaction.

'Wow, that's gotta be better than a pencil,' I laugh, wishing he hadn't bothered. I don't want to use a baton – mostly because I feel like a conductor imposter, but also because Kayla will take the piss if I come over all Simon Rattle. 'Did you borrow it from school?'

'No, it was my dad's. He was presented with it by the choral society on his three-year anniversary as conductor.'

I gulp and run my hand over the polished wood. 'I'm not sure it's appropriate for me to use this when it's got such history.'

'The choral society has history and you're its conductor so' – Josh takes the baton from its case and hands it to me – 'knock yourself out. It's just on loan, obviously.'

'Obviously, and thank you,' I reply, gripping the baton tightly so I won't drop it. I can feel Josh's eyes on my back as I walk back to the choir, heels ringing on the worn flagstones.

Kayla spots the baton and sniggers but no one else takes a blind bit of notice. Not even when I tap it on the edge of my music stand, to call for quiet. Because that's what conductors do, I think.

While we're singing up and down scales to loosen our vocal cords, it registers that Cyril hasn't turned up. I put out an extra chair, just in case, but my note didn't convince him. Or maybe the kiss was a bad idea. Either way, it's disappointing but Kayla's right, he's not my responsibility.

Putting Cyril out of my mind, I throw myself into the rehearsal and only realise an hour has passed when Gerald starts tapping his watch and panting like a dog. We break for refreshments and I find myself standing next to Pippa in the queue for orange squash and biscuits.

'I love your ring,' I tell her. The diamond in Pippa's engagement ring has been dazzling me all evening. It's ginormous.

'It's not real,' she confides. 'It's cubic zirconia from Argos but no one can tell the difference.'

'Except a jeweller,' sniffs Jennifer, brushing past us to reach the digestives and deliberately waggling her fingers so her ring catches the light. Large square-cut diamonds glint and sparkle. Pippa mouths 'the real deal' at me and shrugs her shoulders.

'You'll have a proper diamond one day, from Tiffany's,' murmurs Charlie, slipping his arms around her waist. 'As soon as I've made my fortune, you can have any jewellery you like.' Gosh, what a lovely fiancé. For my next boyfriend, I want someone just like him.

'We haven't got much to spend on the wedding but it's going to be amazing,' gushes Pippa, her dark grey eyes sparkling more than Jennifer's kosher jewels. 'We want it to be special and wondered' – she looks at Charlie shyly – 'if the choir might sing for us during the service? We'd make a donation and invite you all to the evening do.'

'This choir? Are you sure?' I only ask because Jennifer has spent the last half hour singing vibrato to show off, Florence is refusing to sing at all because she can't read music, and Ollie is singing any note he feels like. But Pippa nods enthusiastically.

'That's not why we've joined,' adds Charlie quickly. 'We heard about the choir and thought it sounded great because we both used to sing at school, and then Pippa's mum suggested getting you to sing at the wedding. She knew people who belonged to the choir before… well, before the bad stuff happened, so she thought it would be fitting. Our wedding is in the summer. What do you reckon?'

I reckon I'll be back in London long before then, but why not? I say the choir would probably be delighted, and make a mental note to let the new choir leader know. Maybe I could even pay a flying visit for the wedding. Nooo, what am I thinking? Once I leave Salt Bay, that's it. Kaput. Finito. No more Cornwall. Ever.

I'm doing my best to ignore Josh but his brooding presence is hard to shake off. Even though he's talking to Roger and Gerald, every time I glance up he seems to be staring at me. It's very unsettling, particularly in light of his appearance this evening. He's got his pirate vibe going on big-time thanks to black skinny jeans, striped navy Breton jumper and thick dark hair that's more unruly than ever. It's sexy as hell, which is where I'll end up for having lewd thoughts in church.

I'm fanning myself with a copy of 'Amazing Grace' when Jennifer nudges me in the ribs.

'I'd never have believed it,' she hisses in my ear. 'Look who's just turned up.' She tilts her head towards the back of the church where Cyril's standing, looking shabby in an old brown jumper and baggy trousers. By the time I reach him, he's got his hand on the door latch and is about to flee.

'Cyril, we're so glad you came,' I say softly, putting my arm round his thin shoulders and guiding him away from the door.

'I thought I might pop in but then I thought better of it. There's too many people here.' His eyes dart around the church as he shuffles from foot to foot. His shoes are so scuffed it's hard to see what colour they used to be.

'Most of them are people you know who are pleased to see you. Please stay and we can find you a seat.'

Cyril grumbles gently but allows me to lead him to a chair next to Ollie, whose constant bonhomie will be comforting. Several of the men pat Cyril on the shoulder as they go back to their seats and lovely Mary grasps his hand and tells him how delighted she is to see him. There are some good, decent folk in Salt Bay and, for the first time, I really appreciate the sense of community here. Maybe belonging – to people and to places – isn't only about tricky ties and overwhelming responsibilities after all.

Sadly, kind community spirit isn't as apparent during the second half of the rehearsal when I ask for suggestions of more modern songs we might try singing in the future.

'What about that nice Gary Barlow, the one who's been on *X Factor*,' pipes up Maureen. 'Can't we sing one of his Take That tunes?'

'That's a good idea. I'll look into it,' I tell her, dismissing Roger's mutterings that Take That are for menopausal losers. But Arthur's comments are harder to ignore.

'For goodness' sake,' he booms, 'I thought this was a proper choir singing traditional choral works. Not some tin-pot community sing-song, especially with you being an experienced and talented choral leader from London. What are your qualifications for doing this, exactly?' Puffing his chest out, he leans forward with his hands on his thighs.

'I love music and I've sung in lots of choirs and—'

'Yes, yes,' butts in Arthur, who was probably a bully at school, 'that's all very well but what are your proper qualifications?' And he looks so fierce, I don't think warbling on about music being therapy and bringing people together is going to cut it. I'm about to be outed as an imposter.

'My dad led Salt Bay Choral Society for four years and he didn't have any musical qualifications.' Josh's voice is low and measured behind me. 'All he had was a love of music and a willingness to get involved, but the choir won the Kernow Choral Crown just the same. He even let me conduct during rehearsals sometimes when I was just a teenager.'

'Ted Pawley was a fine conductor, God rest his soul. He was good to my grandsons,' blurts out Cyril. His chin drops onto his chest and he shrinks back against the chair.

'That's true enough,' says Mary, leaning across to pat Cyril on the shoulder. 'Let the girl have a go.'

When the rest of the choir murmur in agreement, Arthur holds up his hands in surrender.

'Just my observation but if you're all happy with things as they are, there's no more to be said.'

Fiona shifts next to him, her mouth drooping at the corners.

Slightly shaken, I carry on with the rehearsal, very aware that the Cornish pirate who came to my rescue is now sitting directly behind me, watching my every move.

'Will you come again next week?' I ask Cyril when the rehearsal is over at last and people are gathering up their belongings.

'Might do. It depends.' He pauses and waits for Jennifer to sweep past in a fug of Diorissimo.

'We all hope you will join us again. I could ask someone to call in for you on their way here if you like.'

'That won't be necessary. I'll either be here or I won't.' He suddenly grabs my arm and pulls me closer. His clothes have the sour smell of being left too long in the washing machine. 'Don't let Arthur upset you,' he whispers. 'He was a jumped-up know-it-all, even as a child.'

Kayla sidles up while I'm watching Cyril shuffle away. There's a cigarette burn near the neckline of his jumper and his trousers are only staying up thanks to his belt. The grey bristles on his chin show he could do with a shave too. What a shame he has no one to care for him.

'Not. Your. Responsibility,' murmurs Kayla. 'See you in the pub.' She scuttles after Chloe who's linked arms with Ollie and is dragging him up the aisle.

Call it sixth sense, but I don't need to turn round to know that Josh is standing right behind me.

'Thank you.'

'For what?' he asks.

I've pulled my hair into a short ponytail and can feel his breath warming the back of my neck. 'For rescuing me from Arthur's third degree.'

'No problem.' He steps in front of me and our fingers brush when he hands over a pile of sheet music he's collected.

'And thank you for keeping your mum happy by coming to our first two rehearsals. Your duty is now done,' I say lightly, dropping the music into the tan leather briefcase that once belonged to my grandfather. Alice found it in the cellar and insists that I use it.

'I might need to come to a couple more just to keep Mum happy, if that's OK with you.'

Josh folds his arms and watches me while I take in the news that Marion Pawley is harder to please than expected. What does he expect me to say? 'Get lost, I don't need you,' probably. But I did need him this evening when Arthur was having a go at me, and he didn't let me down. So maybe having him at a few more rehearsals wouldn't be too awful.

Hang on a minute – ping! That's the sound of a Brilliant Idea flashing into my brain.

'If you're going to be around a bit longer, perhaps you could help out by conducting now and again, seeing as you've had some practice.'

Josh seems surprised by the suggestion but doesn't dismiss it out of hand.

'I'll think about it,' he says, as everything slots into place in my mind.

I have a problem: how can I head back to London without leaving the choir in the lurch? And now I have a solution: encourage Josh Pasco to follow in his father's footsteps and become the next conductor of Salt Bay Choral Society. That's how.

Chapter Twenty-One

Two days later I'm in the pub at lunchtime – drinking lemonade, I hasten to add – when Kayla calls across the bar.

'Hey Annie, what are you doing this weekend?' She finishes polishing the wine glass she's holding and stands on tiptoe to place it on a high shelf.

A medley of Take That songs is playing on a loop in my head and I blink rapidly to try and shift it. 'What did you have in mind?'

'You've never been to Salt Bay beach so I was thinking I could show you how to get down there.'

'That would be brilliant. It's not too scary, is it?'

'It is a tiny bit hairy but no worries, there's a sneaky little track that winds down the cliff and it's fine if you know what you're doing.'

'Which she does,' interrupts Roger. 'What with her being practically a local these days.'

Kayla beams with delight and gives Roger a huge hug. 'Aw, you're not so bad for a grumpy bastard Pom.'

'Gerroff,' growls Roger, going pink but looking pleased. 'You're daft as a brush.'

'I'm only working evening shifts this weekend so why don't we head down there tomorrow? I think the weather's going to be good. Hang on, let me check the tides.' She peers at the tide timetable which is tacked to the wall. 'It's low tide around noon so we could go mid-morning. You'll love it: Cornwall at its best and totally emmet-free.'

'Just you and me?'

'Just the two of us; we can have a girls' outing.'

Saturday dawns clear and unseasonably warm; one of those lovely bright February mornings when you pull out your spring clothes, only to pack them away the next day when the temperature plummets. But the weather holds so I risk cotton trousers, red jumper and thick blue sweatshirt on top for my trip to the beach. I throw caution to the winds and don't take a scarf.

Kayla and I have arranged to meet by the clifftop cemetery at eleven o'clock. Kayla's easy to spot with her flaming red hair as I get close to the rendezvous point, but she's not alone. Ollie is like a beacon with his blonde mop, and there's Chloe wearing more make-up for a beach walk than I would for a night out clubbing. There's also a young lad in surfer shorts, a woman I don't recognise, and Josh Pasco. My stomach does a weird little flip when Josh half raises his hand to wave at me and then folds his arms, as if thinking better of it.

'Hey Annie, there you are.' Kayla rushes over and gives me a hug. 'You know Ollie, Josh and Chloe, and this is Ben, Chloe's brother, who doesn't feel the cold. This is Felicity, Josh's friend, and that mad dog over there is Dodger, who belongs to Ben.' A black and brown collie is running round in circles, barking and nipping at wheeling seagulls, but I'm too busy staring at Felicity to pay him much attention. Felicity is gorgeous – model-tall and slim with golden-blonde hair that curls at the nape of her long, white neck.

'Hi Annie. We haven't met.' Felicity flashes me a dazzling Hollywood smile. 'I hear that you're related to Mrs Gowan. I've only met her once but she seemed lovely. I hope you don't mind me gatecrashing your first trip to the beach.'

'No, of course not.' I have to say that because she's being all friendly, but I remember what Josh told me about her. Is she here because they're back together? He's staring out to sea looking all Poldark-moody, with his arms crossed.

'Sorry to spring it on you,' hisses Kayla out of the corner of her mouth while Dodger is distracting the group. 'I thought it would be nice if Ollie came along so I invited him but Chloe heard and invited herself along. Bloody cheek! Then Bonzer Bum heard and said he'd come along too and he's brought Felicity with him. I didn't tell you 'cos I didn't want to put you off. I know you think Josh Pasco is a knobhead.'

I glance at Josh anxiously, praying he didn't hear. We seem to have forged a fragile peace so I don't want to upset him, particularly as I seem destined to bump into him all the damn time.

'It's fine, honestly. Don't worry about it.'

'Come on.' Ollie grabs Kayla's arm and pulls her perilously close to the cliff edge. 'I'll show you where the path down to the beach is, though I'm surprised no one's shown you it before. Follow me everyone.'

When people start disappearing over the cliff top, I shuffle forward and peer over. No feckin' way! A narrow track runs down the cliff, though it's less a path down to the beach and more a stony death-slide onto the jagged rocks below.

'Are you coming, Annie?' yells Ollie, who's leaping gazelle-like from tiny ledge to tinier ledge. 'Last one down's a sissy.'

'Of course.' I take a deep breath and gingerly lower myself onto the path, scuffing stones which clatter down, down, down and *woomph* into the sand. This is chuffing terrifying! The sun is scattering diamonds across the churning waves far below as I edge along and wonder what it feels like to die.

Almost at the bottom already, Chloe is squealing and hanging on to Ollie, with Kayla following disconsolately behind. And Dodger is already on the beach and careering across the sand. He runs in and out of the shallow waves, barking joyfully.

Josh, who's just ahead of me, turns round at a particularly hairy stage where the path narrows to little more than the width of my trainer.

'Are you OK?'

'Fine.' I try to smile nonchalantly but my face is tight as a drum.

'Just take it easy and don't rush. The first time is always the worst.' The first and last time in my case. Felicity is ahead of Josh and clambering elegantly down the cliff face like an experienced climber. I edge along at snail's pace, humming Mum's favourite music hall tune frantically, like a protective mantra.

It takes me three times as long as everyone else to reach the beach but at last my wobbly legs are on firm sand. 'Phew, made it.' I look back up at the crumbly brown cliff. Balls. I'll have to scramble back up there later, but I won't worry about that now.

Around me is a wide expanse of curved, golden sand, dotted with rocks and seaweed-fringed pools. Two tall rock stacks are standing a few metres out to sea, and plumes of foam are leaping into the air as the waves pound into them. Maybe it's my recent near-death experience but everything looks magical, and I half expect Cornish pixies in tiny Speedos to emerge from the water.

'OMG!' squeals Chloe as Dodger rushes over to us and shakes his whole body. Freezing droplets of seawater, like tiny beads of glass, fly in all directions. 'He's always doing that,' she complains, pressing herself against Ollie's chest. 'Bad dog!'

Ollie laughs. He doesn't put his arm round Chloe, though he doesn't move away either.

Kayla's mouth sets into a firm line. 'Perhaps you shouldn't have brought Dodger with you.'

'Why? You're not frightened of dogs, are you?' asks Chloe uber-sweetly.

'Hardly. Where I come from we've got spiders the size of dogs and every bit of wildlife wants to kill you.'

'That sounds terrible. No wonder you've moved here.'

'Actually, Australia is brilliant. Just a bit' – she searches for the right word – 'venomy.'

'I think it sounds amazing,' says Ollie.

'Yeah, terrible and amazing at the same time,' gushes Chloe, with her eyes on Ollie's face.

Josh raises an eyebrow. 'Why don't we show Annie the caves?'

'Must we?' Felicity peels off her shiny pink jacket to reveal a skin-tight jumper that hugs her impressive curves. She looks magnificent. 'I was going to sit in the sunshine. You could join me, Josh.'

Before Josh can answer, Chloe grabs hold of Ollie's arm and simpers, 'Caves sound really exciting, though you'll have to hold my hand because it's very dark in there.'

Kayla rolls her eyes and stomps off towards the cliffs on the far edge of the cove, with all of us following behind except for Felicity. When I look over my shoulder, she's throwing her jacket back on.

Wow! Just where the cliff meets the farthest curve of the bay, there's a huge archway in the rock and a high, wide cave beyond it. The sunlight only penetrates a few metres and then there's nothing but blackness.

Inside, the sand is wet and clumpy, and the temperature has dropped, making me shiver. The walls are worn smooth and damp when I put out my hand and brush them with my fingers.

'Awesome, isn't it?' Josh's voice is close to my ear and I can feel the warmth from his body. 'It was used by smugglers back in the 1700s who used to hide contraband here, to avoid paying tax.'

'One of the earliest tax avoidance schemes, then.'

Josh gives a deep laugh. 'Something like that. There are a couple of chambers higher up in the rock at the back of the cave that are usually above the water mark, even at high tide. We used to play in them when we were kids. I mistimed it once and spent several hours in there with the waves pounding the rocks close by. I'll never forget it and my mum almost killed me when I finally emerged at low tide.'

'I bet. She must have thought you'd drowned.'

Why did I say that? The poor woman had to cope with a real drowning not so long afterwards. I'm mentally kicking myself in the head when Felicity suddenly sidles up and cuddles in to Josh.

'I thought I'd take a look at the caves after all but it's really chilly in here.'

What's her game? She ditches Josh when he's at a low ebb and now she's back and all over him. There are squeals and frenzied barking from further inside the cave.

'Come on you lot,' yells Kayla from the darkness. 'Get your backsides into this cave.'

'Yes, ma'am!' Felicity does a mock salute and links her arm through Josh's. 'Have you brought a torch? I bet you've got one about your person.' She laughs and pushes her other hand into his jeans pocket, which is such an intimate gesture I feel like a gooseberry. 'Aha, I thought as much.' She pulls out a slender silver flashlight and waves it triumphantly.

'What can I say, once a boy scout… and I thought we might end up doing some caving.' Josh takes the torch, turns it on and points the beam ahead of us. Yellow light scatters across the dark walls, casting black shadows where it can't reach.

'You'd better lead the way, like you did the first time you brought me in here.' Felicity smiles up at him flirtatiously and I guess he smiles back. I can't tell because he has his back to me, but most men would smile if Felicity was flirting with them. Hell, I'd smile if Felicity was flirting with me. She has a very smiley face.

Josh and Felicity walk further into the cave with me close behind them. The strong smell of damp intensifies when the passage narrows and the sound of the sea outside becomes muffled. It's creepy in here but pretty amazing walking under a roof of rock with tons of cliff above you. The torch beam suddenly lights up Kayla, who's sitting on a boulder in the pitch black, cross-legged like a pixie. There's a dead-end wall of rock behind her, but she's completely alone.

'Ta-dah!' She raises her arms in the torchlight. 'And for my next trick...'

'Where's everybody gone?' I run my hand across the freezing cold rock that marks the end of the cave, almost expecting it to spring open.

'I told you Cornwall was magic. They've been spirited away.'

'No, really, where have they gone?'

Josh points his torch towards the back corner. 'Through there.' A small opening, only a metre wide, is lit up. 'There's a tunnel you can crawl through. It's hard work because it goes uphill but it opens out into a couple of small chambers. That's where the smugglers hid their booty.'

'Dodger went through it – that dog is mental – so the others followed. I didn't fancy it because I get a bit claustrophobic in really small spaces, only don't tell Chloe. I thought I'd wait for you instead and I'm in the dark because they took Ollie's torch with them.'

Josh hands Kayla his torch, bends down and shouts into the tunnel, 'Hey, Ollie! Shine a light down here because we're coming up.' After a few moments, a faint light spills out of the opening.

'Are you coming, Annie?' asks Felicity, kneeling down by Josh. I bend over and peer into the tunnel, which is about the height of a small child. Wouldn't it be awful if my hips got wedged as I crawled through? Rationally I know I'm not as wide as the tunnel, but all the same.

'Nah, you're OK. I'll stay and keep Kayla company.'

'If you're sure.' Felicity starts crawling through the opening, giving us all a brilliant view of her slender hips and pert bottom.

'We won't be long,' says Josh, getting onto his hands and knees and following Felicity until all I can see are his canvas trainers, and then he's gone.

'Woo-hoo!' Kayla puts the torch under her chin and opens her eyes wide. A halo of light shines around her ghostly white face. 'What do you think of Salt Bay's beach then?'

'It's beautiful, though I could have done without the death slide down the cliff.'

'It's terrifying, isn't it? I almost wet myself the first time I tried it.'

'You told me it wasn't too bad.'

'I lied,' says Kayla calmly, waving the torch around and bouncing light off the walls. 'I can't help it; it's genetic. My sister Marie told me giving birth only smarted a bit which was definitely a lie 'cos she reckons she hasn't peed straight since.'

Trying hard not to think of Marie's mangled nether regions, I lower my voice in case it echoes through the tunnel.

'How are things going with Ollie?'

'Not so great.' Though I can't see Kayla's face, I can hear her disappointment. 'I think he likes Chloe, though God knows why. I suppose she has got great tits.' She shines the torch on her less well-endowed chest and sighs. I reach out my hand and she tightens her fingers round mine before letting them go. 'But we Aussies always bounce back and, if all else fails, there's always a boob job. I think I'll go for double Ds. Talking of which, what do you think of Felicity, then?'

'She seems nice.'

'Nice? She's bloody gorgeous. Poor old Ben. His eyes have been on stalks since she arrived but she only has eyes for Josh, which is weird.'

'Why weird?'

'Someone said in the pub that they'd split up.'

'Maybe she regrets abandoning him in his hour of need and thinks she's made a mistake.'

'Maybe,' says Kayla, sounding puzzled. 'I don't know all the ins and outs, though it sounds like you do.'

'No, I'm just guessing.'

'Hhmmm.' Before Kayla can interrogate me further, furious barking comes from the tunnel and Dodger shoots out and barrels into the wall opposite. He blinks dazedly when Kayla shines the torch at him and gives a short, sharp bark at the tunnel opening when Ollie's head and shoulders appear. Ollie crawls out with Chloe so close behind him her head must have been almost touching his bum.

'Oh please,' mutters Kayla, as Ollie bends and shouts into the tunnel.

'Hey, the tide has turned. Come on you lot or we'll be swimming out of the cave.' He straightens up and shakes out his shoulders. 'Were you OK on your own in the dark, Kayla?'

'Yeah, fine.'

'At least he got your name right,' I whisper as Ben scrambles out of the tunnel, swiftly followed by Josh and Felicity, but Kayla grunts and stomps off into the darkness.

By the time we emerge blinking into the sunlight, the waves are licking at the entrance to the cave. The wind has picked up and is flicking sea spray across the shrinking sand, and almost half of the rock stacks are now under water. With the waves creeping ever closer, we relocate to the back of the beach, underneath the Path of Doom. Three huge boulders have formed a natural windbreak-cum-suntrap and we spread ourselves out across the sand.

Lying there, I pretend to gaze out to sea but really I'm watching Josh and Felicity, who have wandered off for a walk. Their heads are bent close together and they appear to be having an intense conversation. Not that it's any of my business. I'll be gone from Salt Bay within a few weeks. I hope that Josh and Felicity will be very happy and will have lots of perfect, smiley children. Sighing, I roll over onto my back, close my eyes and gradually slip into sleep.

'Wake up sleepy head or you're going to be underwater.' Chloe is shaking me, none too gently, and getting sand all over my head. Oh God, was I drooling? Stuart told me once that I drooled in my sleep and Ben is looking at me strangely. I surreptitiously feel the neckline of my sweatshirt but it's not wet, thank goodness.

'We need to climb back up before the tide comes fully in and the beach disappears,' explains Ollie, handing me my bag that I was using as a pillow. 'Follow me.'

He starts scrabbling up the cliff, closely followed by Chloe, Dodger and Ben. Tiny stones are dislodged from the track as they get higher and higher.

'Going up is easier than coming down, right?' I ask Kayla, strapping my bag across my body.

'Definitely. Absolutely.'

'Are you lying?'

'Yes. I told you, it's genetic,' yells Kayla, who's already three metres above me. 'Do you want me to come back down and help you?'

'Don't worry. I can give Annie a hand if she needs it.' Josh is busy collecting up the wrappers from the biscuits people had for lunch.

'Felicity, why don't you go up next to show Annie how to do it and I'll follow behind her.'

'I might fall on you.'

'That is a risk I'm willing to take,' says Josh, a muscle twitching in his cheek.

He shoves the wrappers into his trouser pocket and we start climbing: Felicity first, who's brilliant; Josh last, who knows what he's doing; and me, who once had a go on a climbing wall near Finsbury Park and had to be rescued by a hunky man in Lycra shorts. Thank God I'm not wearing Lycra now because Josh has a perfect view of my backside while I'm climbing the cliff ahead of him. Which could be a shock for a man used to Felicity's petite derrière.

Kayla's wrong. Going up the cliff isn't any worse than coming down, but it's no better, either. I'm sweating buckets by the time I reach what's probably the halfway point – there's no way I'm looking down to check – and my legs have gone all jelly-flubbery. And that's when my foot slides on loose stones and I feel myself sliding.

Chuffing hell! I grab frantically at a pretty weed with white flowers that's growing out of the cliff but it comes away in my hand. My slide starts to pick up speed and, with a squeak of horror, I twist round, sit down heavily and start hurtling down the cliff path on my backside.

'Woah!' Josh is a little way behind me on the track and is bracing himself as I get closer. 'Grab hold of my legs,' he yells, cupping his hands protectively over his privates.

Oh. My. God. We'll both fall off the cliff. My final act in this world will be to take out the person who's trying to save me. What a legacy.

I'm going so fast now there must be smoke rising from my arse. Just before impact, I close my eyes, reach out my arms in leg-hugging fashion, and pray that Mum is watching over me.

'Oof!' The collision brings me to a juddering halt and leaves me winded. When I open my eyes, my arms are wrapped tightly around Josh's thighs and my face is almost in his groin. Well, this is embarrassing, though any embarrassment is tempered by the whole not being dead thing.

'Are you all right, Annie?' yells Kayla.

'She's fine; just a bit shocked,' shouts Josh. Felicity has started scrambling down to us but he beckons for her to keep climbing. 'You lot carry on. We'll stay here for a few minutes to catch our breath and then we'll climb up.'

Josh puts his hands under my arms and tries to pull me to my feet but I can't move.

'Maybe I'll come down to your level. Um, you're going to have to let go of my legs.'

'Sorry.' I relax the locked muscles in my arms and Josh squats down beside me.

'You are fine, aren't you?'

'Yes, I think so. Just a few scrapes.'

'Where?' He grabs my wrists and turns my arms over, looking for any damage. 'Do you want me to have a look?'

Not likely. There's no way I'm baring my scraped bum on a Cornish cliff.

When I shake my head, Josh sits back on his heels. 'Do you think you can stand up yet?'

'Maybe we could sit here for a minute more. I'm feeling quite shaky.'

'Of course.' Josh sits down on the path with his back to the rock and waves at the others who have reached the top. I can see Felicity peering over the edge, looking worried.

Josh and I sit quietly for a while as seagulls fly past us screeching loudly. Having a human slide past at top speed must have been perturbing because they're louder than ever. A runny bird poo drops onto the path below us and splats in all directions.

'Thank you for saving me.'

'That's all right. I couldn't let you slide to your death or your great-aunt might have sacked Serena in revenge.'

There's that deadpan humour again that he keeps so well hidden. I smile at him but he's looking out across the water that's already submerged where we were sitting ten minutes earlier. I lean back against the cliff and take some long, deep breaths.

It's rather nice sitting here in companionable silence, which is why it's such a shame that a question is fizzing up inside me. I try clamping my mouth shut but it's no good; sliding down a cliff appears to loosen the tongue.

'I was surprised to see Felicity here. Didn't you tell me that you'd split up?'

For a moment I don't think Josh will answer but then he says quietly, 'We did, but she called and asked to see me today and wanted to come when she heard I was going to the beach.' He glances at me briefly and adjusts the collar of his jacket. 'When we went for a walk, she said she'd made a mistake and wants us to get back together.'

Ha! Just as I suspected. 'So what did you say?'

Josh turns away from the sea and his eyes lock on to mine. I get the weird feeling that he can see into my soul, though if Kayla or Maura said that I'd tell them they were talking rubbish. But he looks anguished in a soul-searchy kind of way.

He opens his mouth to speak but Felicity calls out from the cliff top, 'What are you two doing down there?'

Bugger off, Felicity, with your perfect body and hair; I want to hear what Josh has to say. But he's already getting to his feet and pulling me up. Tiny stones embedded in the back of my trousers fall away from the fabric and cascade over my feet.

'We'd better get you up to the top. Do you think you can manage it?'

'Is there another option?'

'You could try swimming round the headland.'

'Onwards and upwards it is, then.'

'That's the spirit.' Josh steps carefully round me and holds out his hand. 'Whatever you do, don't look down.'

His long, strong fingers close round mine and we start edging our way along the track. Every now and again we have to let go to scramble past a boulder but Josh always grabs my hand again afterwards and holds on tight. It makes me feel much better.

At last we reach the top. Hallelujah. Kayla rushes forward and flings her arms around me.

'I'm sorry,' she wails. 'I should have stayed to help you instead of rushing off on my own. You could have been killed if knob— um, Josh hadn't been there. Thank you, Josh.'

She unpeels herself from me and throws herself into Josh's arms. He pats her back awkwardly and gives Felicity a 'help me' look, but she ignores him and wanders over to me.

'I'm glad to see you're OK, Annie. You and Josh were down there for ages. What were you two talking about?'

'Nothing. Just about what a prat I am, and… and stuff like that.'

Felicity doesn't contest that I am a prat. She just stares at me with her yellow-brown eyes until I feel nervous and blush. It's not her fault – she's one of those women in whose company I turn into a total tit.

Ollie has gone to Josh's rescue and is pulling Kayla off him.

'Come on now, Kayla. There's no harm done.' He puts his arm round her and pats her shoulder gently. 'We'll come into the pub tonight and have a few to celebrate our survival.' He winks at me and laughs.

Dodger leads the way back to the village, still full of beans and chasing after seagulls. Felicity is walking with Josh which means I don't get a chance to thank him again so I fall back and walk with Kayla, who's subdued.

'Honestly, Kayla, there's no need to worry. I'm absolutely fine,' I reassure her.

'What? Oh, I'm over that now. It was quite funny really, seeing you sliding down on your arse and ramming Josh in the goolies.' She sniggers so hard a snot bubble pops out of her nose and she fishes in her pocket for a tissue.

Sighing, I resign myself to the fact that my mishap will be all over the village by teatime.

'So what's the problem? I thought you'd be happy that Ollie put his arm round you.'

'And?'

'And what?'

'And he patted my shoulder like a brother would pat his sister who's being annoyingly hysterical. You wouldn't pat someone if you wanted to snog their face off, would you? Well, would you?'

'Ummmm.' I sense there's no right answer to this question so I link my arm through Kayla's and try to change tack. 'You've seemed a bit subdued all morning. Is everything else all right?'

'It's silly really. It was telling Chloe' – she wrinkles her nose – 'it was telling her that Australia is brilliant. It made me miss the place.'

'I thought you were delighted to have escaped all those buff men surfing in their budgie smugglers.'

'Yeah, it was hell.' Kayla points at Dodger, who's winding himself round Felicity's legs. 'That animal could seriously do with some doggy discipline. Our dog at home would never get away with it.'

Felicity gives a little scream and grabs hold of Josh's arm to steady herself.

'I guess talking about Australia made me miss my family, who are godawful, so heaven knows why.'

'I'm sure they're not that bad.'

'I guess they're OK as families go but they're so different from me. You know how people in families get pigeonholed – the clever one, the pretty one, the anxious one. Well, I was the weird one.'

'You are a bit odd.'

Kayla punches me gently on the shoulder. 'Cheers. My sisters are quite a lot older than I am and did the whole school, uni, good jobs, marriage and babies thing. That wasn't what I wanted so I got tagged as weird. Which one were you in your family?'

I think back to life with Mum. 'I was the sensible one, I suppose, or the carer. The sensible carer.'

'That must have been a bit rough when you were a kid.'

'Not really.' Talking like this makes me feel disloyal to Mum. She never pigeonholed me or asked me to look after her. I took on that role by choice and was happy to do it.

'And now you're doing it for Alice – being the sensible carer, I mean. And you think it's your job to look after Mr Barnley, too,' says Kayla, stopping abruptly and shaking sand out of her shoe. 'It's funny how we run from old patterns but end up falling back into them. Freud would have a field day.'

Blimey, this is getting heavy. Freud might say that I run from family commitment because much of my childhood was spent caring for

Mum. But this is the same bloke who reckoned that all women have penis envy – and I really don't.

'Whatever,' sighs Kayla. 'Let's forget families and go and get, as you Brits so eloquently put it, shitfaced. I bet I can get us free drinks in the pub.'

'As enticing as that sounds, I'd better get back to Alice. She didn't look well when she got up this morning, though she'd never admit it.'

'Once a carer, always a carer,' murmurs Kayla as we rejoin the others who are waiting for us at the edge of the village. A small boat has just appeared between the harbour walls and is motoring into calmer water, surrounded by a flurry of swooping seagulls. It looks like something you see in a travel magazine or on a postcard.

Josh catches my eye while we're all saying our goodbyes and raises his eyebrows in an 'are you OK' kind of way. I would say something but Felicity is looking at me so I nod and smile which I hope conveys how grateful I am.

He and Felicity walk off together, looking like a couple from a celebrity magazine; him all tall, dark and brooding, and her all blonde, fluffy and pretty. Their children are going to be flipping gorgeous.

Chapter Twenty-Two

The house is deathly quiet when I kick off my trainers and hang my bag on the coat stand. It's funny how much this feels like home after less than a month here. Holiday syndrome, I guess, where you go on holiday and think you'll never settle in and two days later you want to stay on the beach drinking margaritas forever. Not that I want to stay here forever, obviously.

'Alice, are you here?'

Her walking shoes – flat, brown brogues – are placed tidily under the radiator and her handbag is on the table when I peep into the kitchen. But there's no sign of lunch; no washed pots on the drainer, no crumbs near the bread bin, though Alice always eats lunch at one o'clock on the dot. You can set your watch by her hunger pangs.

'Alice, where are you?' I call, starting to feel panicky. She really didn't look well this morning.

'There's no need to yell, Annabella.'

Phew, that's a relief. Alice, in an elegant blue and cream tea dress with her hair in a tidy bun, is in her favourite chair by the sitting room fireplace. She's sitting up straight with her hands on her lap.

'Did you have a good time on the beach?' she asks, hardly moving her head, though I'm not in her line of sight.

'It was great. The beach is beautiful and we went into an amazing cave.' There's no way Alice is hearing the whole story. Not from me, anyway.

'It is rather lovely. Sadly, I've not been fit enough to use the cliff path for some time. A tourist, a middle-aged man from Leicester, fell on it last summer and they had to call in the rescue team. He broke his leg in three places, apparently, and spent a week in hospital.'

Now she tells me. It seems I escaped lightly with a few scrapes and a bruised ego.

There's a book on Alice's lap but no plates or tea cups on the table next to her.

'Weren't you hungry at lunch time?'

'I was hungry, but' – Alice gives a short laugh – 'it's somewhat embarrassing but I don't seem to be able to move. I was achy this morning so I sat down for a while but I've stiffened up and I can't get out of the chair. I've given up trying and have been sitting here for ages. How ridiculous is that?' She laughs again but she looks scared.

'That's awful, Alice. Do you want me to call Dr Rivers?' Some carer I am, gallivanting about on the beach while Alice is a prisoner in her own chair.

Alice shakes her head slowly and grimaces.

'Please don't bother Stephen on a Saturday or he'll be insufferable about the state of my health. If you could help me out of the chair, I'll take some tablets and will feel much better.'

'Are you quite sure?'

'I wouldn't have said it if I wasn't.' Alice closes her eyes and breathes out slowly. 'Please, Annabella. I didn't mean to snap at you.'

Gently putting my hand under Alice's elbow, I pull her up slowly until I can get my arm around her back and lever her upwards. She sways slightly and groans but at last she's standing. Before taking any medication, she insists that I frogmarch her backwards and forwards across the room, to help get her joints moving again.

'This is so annoying,' she huffs, leaning on me heavily while we're pacing up and down. 'One minute I'm feeling all right and then a short while later my body won't do what my brain is telling it to do.'

'That must be incredibly frustrating.'

Alice's mouth sets into a determined line. 'A little, but there's no point in feeling sorry for myself. I need to sort myself out.'

'Talking of which, I'm going to take over the search for someone to look after you properly.'

'But—'

'No buts, Alice. I can't stay here forever and neither can you if we don't get something permanent arranged quickly. You haven't had much luck so it's time for me to have a go. I can post something online.'

For a moment, Alice's body sags in defeat. 'I suppose it is foolish of me to expect my situation to improve. Having an unerring sense of optimism can be rather ridiculous at times.' She glances at her left hand, which is trembling slightly, and sighs. But by the time I've tightened my grip around her waist, she's curled her hand into a fist and straightened her back. 'However, I do realise that more needs to be done so please, Annabella, go ahead and do whatever it is you do on the webby thing and we'll see if that's more successful.'

Alice takes some medication, has some food and a sleep, and claims she's feeling much better. She certainly seems to be moving more freely. But mid-afternoon, I'm surprised to find her in the hallway, with her outdoor shoes on and handbag over her arm.

'Where do you think you're going?' Good grief, I sound like the parents of my friends at school. They always envied me my cool mum who let me come and go without comment.

'Don't fuss, Annabella.' Alice glances at her reflection in the hall mirror and uses a finger to blot her lipstick. 'I promised a friend that I'd see her this afternoon and I don't want to let her down.'

'Which friend?'

'Penelope.' The hesitation was tiny, but definitely there. 'She's going to pick me up in her car from outside the phone box.'

Penelope has picked Alice up a couple of times recently but never comes to the house, which seems odd.

'Would you like me to walk to the phone box with you?'

'That's not necessary. I'm feeling better now and I'm sure you've got better things to do.' She puts on her hat and glances in the mirror again to adjust it. 'I'll see you later.'

As the front gate clangs shut behind Alice, I come over all Sherlock and feel an overwhelming urge to follow her.

Don't do it, Annie, says the calm, reasonable voice in my head while I'm slipping on my shoes and peeping outside to see how far she's gone. But since when have I listened to my calm, reasonable voice? Making sure that Alice is almost out of sight, I close the front door behind me as quietly as possible and start stalking my great-aunt.

It's incredibly hard following someone who walks at snail's pace. My technique involves a lot of loitering while pretending to admire people's gardens, and bending down to retie my shoes, which is painful when you've got a bruised bum. I bet Sherlock never had this problem. He worked everything out and left following people to Watson.

At last Alice reaches the phone box and goes inside it while I hide behind a ruddy great tree on the river bank. Celine is playing nearby in her garden and spots me but seems to accept a grown adult playing hide and seek as perfectly normal.

While I skulk, Alice makes a brief phone call and then sits on a bench that faces the fast-flowing water. She looks back a couple of times but moves her neck so painfully slowly I have plenty of time to flatten myself against the tree trunk.

Nothing happens for ages. And ages. And ages. Being a detective is pretty boring if the person you're following isn't a murderer. Bits of itchy bark keep falling off the tree and I'm scooping some out of my cleavage when a taxi drives along the road and stops next to Alice. The driver gets out to open the passenger door and Alice climbs slowly inside before the car heads out of the village. I'm not sure who the taxi driver is but he sure as hell isn't Penelope.

There must be a logical reason why Alice would lie to me and behave so furtively. Perhaps Penelope sent the taxi after being taken ill, but then surely she'd have cancelled the whole visit. Or maybe Alice has a fancy man and she's off to enjoy a little afternoon delight. Ewww. Alice is a good-looking woman and deserves some passion but disturbing images involving kinky sex and Zimmer frames are now whizzing round my head.

Alice gets back from 'Penelope's' soon after six o'clock and says she had a lovely time with her friend, though she's vague when pressed for details of how they spent the afternoon. I don't push it because what can I say? 'I stalked you to the phone box and hid behind a tree while you got into a taxi.' It wouldn't end well.

I also don't mention that Toby rang while Alice was out. He's taken to calling me on the landline every few days to check on my plans and my 'declining mental health' (his words).

During today's call, he hinted there could soon be a temporary job going at Fulbright and Linsom which might suit me, and he asked casually if I'd seen any more of Josh Pasco. When I said I had, he muttered something about Josh being an untrustworthy womaniser and a dickhead, which has been on my mind ever since. A dickhead maybe, though he's gone up in my estimation since his solid thighs saved me from certain death, but a womaniser? He's never hit on me, which is great, obviously. Though if he is a womaniser, that's like being ignored by the office lech – relief is tinged with wondering whether it's your face or personality that's so repulsive.

Putting Toby and Josh out of my mind, I spend the next couple of days concentrating on the search for Alice's live-in carer. Looking online and blitzing local carers' forums comes up with zilch so I re-write Alice's ad for local shops and get Jennifer on the case. And it's Jennifer who comes up trumps via the friend of a friend whose daughter Emily is looking to change her job.

'Emily's one of a kind,' explains Jennifer. 'She's young but she has an old soul and I think she'd suit Alice. You'll see what I mean.'

My first impression of Emily, when she arrives to meet Alice and me, is that she's eighteen going on eighty. Studious-looking and skinny, she's wearing an A-line skirt in green crimplene and a patterned blouse which could be her grandmother's. A long, mousey-brown plait snakes down her back, ending just above her skirt's elasticated waist. She's nothing like the sassy, fashionista teenagers I'm used to in London, who would eat poor Emily for breakfast.

She takes a seat opposite Alice, blinking nervously behind her thick-framed glasses and looking close to tears, and I like her. There's an aura of gentleness around her that hints she's from a nicer world; a world where no one nicks stuff or slags people off on Twitter.

'What do you do in your current job?' enquires Alice, while I pour Emily a cup of tea from the pot on the table next to her. Alice tends to spill the tea when she is shaky so I've taken to pouring it these days.

'Admin work, mainly. Lots of filing and typing and some answering the phone. And before that, while I was still in the sixth form, I worked in Tesco on the tills.'

'So you don't have any care experience?' Alice sounds disappointed so she must have picked up the good vibes from Emily, too.

'Yes, I do. I have loads.' Emily tilts her cup when she sits forward and a splash of tea soaks into her skirt. 'Mamm-wynn lived with us when I was growing up and I helped my mum look after her. I kept her company and when she got ill I helped with bed baths and taking her to doctor's appointments, and sorting out her medicines and lots of other stuff. I was often her only carer when Mum was at work.'

Alice smiles at me. 'Mamm-wynn is an old Cornish word for grandmother.' She turns back to Emily and passes her a tissue to blot her wet skirt. 'I presume your grandmother is no longer with us?'

Emily's eyes fill with tears and she scrubs her cheeks furiously with the tissue. 'Sorry, sorry. She died a year ago, but I still miss her.'

Alice pushes herself forward and pats the girl's hand. 'I'm sorry to hear that. You looked after your grandmother very well and I'm sure she appreciated that. You might actually have the experience I need but I don't think you realise that I'm looking for someone to live in, and I'm not sure a young girl like you would want to live here with an old lady like me.'

'Please, I'd love it,' gabbles Emily. 'Our house in Penzance is so small. I share a bedroom with my younger sister who's really annoying, and Patrick, my brother, has moved his girlfriend in, and my mum reckons my auntie will be moving in too now that my uncle has run off with Derek. And there's so much space here.' She gazes round Alice's elegant sitting room and out of the window towards the roiling sea. 'There's enough room to think and to breathe. Would I have my own bedroom?'

'Absolutely,' I say, charmed by the young girl's openness. 'You'd have a room looking out over the harbour and the cliffs.'

Emily's eyes light up and she glances at me shyly. 'I heard you come from London.' She says 'London' in hushed tones. 'Is your place up there as big as this?'

I picture my expensive Stratford shoebox. 'Not quite.'

Alice sinks back in her chair and steeples swollen fingers under her chin. 'You would have bed and board here but I'm afraid I couldn't pay much, Emily.'

'That wouldn't be a problem because I don't spend much. I'm a really hard worker, Mrs Gowan, and I don't go out clubbing or anything. I have hardly any friends.'

She says it with no trace of self-pity, simply an air of loneliness that folds around her like a cloak. Alice has got to give her the job. Turning her down would be akin to booting a helpless puppy off the harbour wall into deep water. A fluffy puppy with doe eyes that can't swim. Is telepathy a proper thing? I transmit my thoughts Alice's way, just in case. *Please let Emily be your new carer. Give her a chance.*

Alice catches my eye and nods, which is freaky. 'You're younger than I was anticipating, Emily, and it would be a leap into the dark for both of us, but I'm willing to give it a go if you are. I'd need to take up references, of course, before our new arrangement could be confirmed.'

'Of course.' Emily's face lights up when she smiles and her pale blue eyes, almost hidden behind her glasses, sparkle. 'Thank you so much, Mrs Gowan. You won't regret it. I'll look after you really well.'

'I'm sure you will, dear, and you'd better start calling me Alice.' She smooths down her snow-white hair. 'Who would be best to provide references?'

Emily bites her lip and frowns. 'My current employer, I suppose, and maybe Mrs Scholes, the deputy head at my school. Though I'm not sure she ever noticed me because I wasn't one of the clever girls.'

I can imagine Emily slipping under the radar.

We note down the reference details we need and Emily leaves after thanking Alice repeatedly and assuring her that she won't regret her decision.

'I don't believe I will,' murmurs Alice as we watch Emily almost skip down the garden path. Long strands of thick hair have escaped from her plait and are caught by the sea breeze. 'She seems the kind of girl I won't mind having around, someone who can keep an eye on my traitorous body and not blab about my business to everyone in the village.'

'What sort of business? Do you have deep, dark secrets then, Alice?'

'Of course not.' There's that slight hesitation again. 'I'd just rather that my business stayed my business.' She walks slowly upstairs, holding on to the bannister with both hands. 'I'm feeling tired after seeing Emily so I'll have a lie down.' She looks over her shoulder, 'Thank you for helping me find Emily but I will miss you when you leave, Annabella.'

When I hear Alice's bedroom door click shut, I head into the sitting room and perch on the thick stone window ledge. So that's it. As soon as Emily moves in, I'll be able to get back to London. Woo-hoo, that's great news, though I don't feel as relieved as I thought I would. I think I might miss Alice, too.

While Alice is napping, I nip to the pub with my laptop and email Emily's teacher with a reference request. And in spite of Emily's misgivings, she emails me back the same afternoon with a glowing report of her former pupil. Mrs Scholes describes Emily as 'serious, studious and caring' and paints a picture of a quiet, trustworthy girl who kept herself to herself. We'll have to wait for a reference from Emily's current employer – she promised to request one when handing in her notice – but the signs are looking good. It seems that Emily will be a perfect live-in carer for Alice.

Things are working out just the way I wanted, so I buy a huge bar of chocolate to celebrate and stuff my face with calories while trying to quash the ridiculous feeling that I'm being pushed out.

Chapter Twenty-Three

Knowing I'll be leaving Salt Bay very soon gives me a different perspective on the village. The cliffs don't seem as leg-achingly steep, the village as boring, or Jennifer as annoying, and my imminent departure brings into sharp focus the things I'm going to miss. Top of the list are Alice, Kayla (who's helped to keep me sane) and the choir, whose rehearsals are starting to be fun.

Then there are the views from Salt Bay. Nothing can beat standing on Waterloo Bridge at midnight, with old and new London lit up around you – St Paul's Cathedral and the London Eye, the Palace of Westminster and the Gherkin. It's awesome. But there's something profoundly soothing about the huge Cornish sky and the ever-changing sea and being able to see the horizon without a *mahoosive* office block in the way.

A couple of times I wonder whether I'll miss Josh – his soft Cornish accent, how his face lights up when he talks about Freya, his skinny jeans. But I nip those thoughts in the bud and focus instead on things I can't wait to leave behind.

That list includes: Cornish 'mizzle' (a potent drenching drizzle which can hang over the village for hours), the smell of Alice's vapour rub which permeates the house, and a complete dearth of celebrities. You never know who you might see in London. I once spotted Bill Nighy,

Jamie Oliver and a singer from The Saturdays during a shopping trip to the West End. But so far in Salt Bay, all I've spotted is one emmet who looked like Jennifer Saunders but wasn't.

I decide to keep my impending departure quiet at the next couple of choir rehearsals and none of the singers asks if and when I'm leaving – presumably expecting me to stay forever now I've experienced the endless delights of Salt Bay.

One reason for keeping schtum is Cyril, who's been shuffling into rehearsals at seven thirty on the dot and giving me a curt nod before finding a seat. I don't want to give him any reason to stop coming because the choir is doing him good. I'm sure of it. His shirt might still be frayed and creased, but he's clean-shaven these days and I was moved almost to tears when he arrived wearing a smart blue tie.

Another reason is Josh, because I want him to get his feet fully under the choral society table before I ask him to run it. Fortunately he hasn't asked about my departure, and I haven't enquired whether he and Felicity are back together again, either. To be honest, we've hardly spoken since I almost castrated him on the cliffs and he held my hand all the way to safety. He seems embarrassed and I'm all too aware that I'm a hopeless idiot compared to fragrant Felicity.

But Josh has taken up my suggestion of conducting occasionally – and he's a natural. His tall body sways as he moves his arm in time to the beat and the tension that usually bristles round him like an aura evaporates. Sometimes he seems almost serene when he gets caught up in the singing, which proves my point that music can be magic.

So I'm hopeful that Josh will agree to the whole taking-over-the-choir-forever plan, especially since he suggested that we give a public performance in a few weeks' time to mark the anniversary of the Great Storm. It's a great idea and a shame, in a way, that I won't be there on the day. I might even have met Florence's unfortunate husband Bob, who, according to her regular updates, is now suffering from piles. My singers are a strange bunch but I've grown rather fond of them.

Kayla knows I'll be leaving soon and is sworn to secrecy. But she almost lets the cat out of the bag when I tell her in the pub that Emily has confirmed when she'll be moving in. Which means that I'll be leaving Salt Bay for good in a fortnight's time.

'That's too soooon,' she wails, giving me an awkward hug while balancing two plates of steaming pasta. 'We're going to miss you so much. Who will I drink hot chocolate with when you're back in London?'

'Shush, Kayla. I haven't told the choir yet, or Josh.'

'Don't you think you should, seeing as you're expecting him to run the choir when you desert us?' A strand of spaghetti slithers off the plate and snakes onto the stone floor.

'I'm building up to it. First I want to make sure he's so involved in the choir, he can't possibly refuse.'

'Hhmm.' Kayla stoops to pick up the spaghetti, looking unconvinced.

'Or you could take over the choir, maybe?'

'Don't be ridiculous! There's no way I'm waving that poncy baton about and putting up with Arthur sighing every time we sing anything written later than the 1700s.' She has a point. Arthur has become the doyen of passive-aggressive protest recently. 'Anyway,' she raises her voice, 'I'm far too busy with my new man.'

'Still chasing Ollie?'

'Nah, I'm moving on, Annabella Sunshine,' she declares far more loudly than I'd like. 'I'm young, free and single, and I've got another man in my sights. A real man.' She winks at a young lad nursing a drink in the corner, who blushes furiously.

'Him?' I mouth at her, incredulously.

She shakes her head, red Pre-Raphaelite curls bouncing round her face. 'No, don't be silly, that's Kieran. He's just a kid. I'm not saying who my new man is because I'll jinx it, but I'll let you know. Anyway, must get on 'cos the pasta's getting cold. Can you dump this in the bin behind the bar for me?'

She drops the slimy spaghetti strand into my hand and sashays past me with an exaggerated hip wiggle and a wink. Yep, I'm really going to miss Kayla and her irrepressible Aussie-ness. She's at the very top of my Miss List.

The choir might be in the dark about my leaving plans but Serena corners me about them the next evening, while I'm reading in the kitchen. A thick sea-mist has blanketed the house and all's quiet, except for the mournful low tone of the foghorn keeping boats away from the treacherous rocks. It's perfect weather for my crime thriller and I've just reached a really juicy part when Serena walks in.

'So when exactly are you leaving, then?' She plonks herself into a chair and puts her elbows on the table.

Reluctantly dragging myself away from a homicidal psychopath, I focus on Serena, who's got her jacket on and is clutching her wages from Alice.

'Quite soon, once Emily's able to move in. Actually' – I'm going to have to start telling people soon – 'I'm going back to London in a fortnight.'

'Forever?'

'Yes, forever. That's where I live. But Emily will be here to look after Alice.'

'Hhmm, I don't know much about this Emily person but my friend's sister's cousin says she's weird.' She pouts and starts picking at a loose cuticle on her thumb. 'Mrs Gowan said she'll still keep me on, to do the bits round the house that I do now, but I s'pose that might change.'

'Not necessarily. I know Alice likes having you around.' I close the cover on my Kindle; the psychopath will have to wait. 'So how are your family?'

'Mum's annoying but everyone else is all right, I s'pose.' Serena's eyes narrow. 'Did you know that Josh is getting back together with Felicity? Mum's pleased because she felt guilty that she'd split them up, with her illness and everything.'

It's what I expected and my disappointment is purely because I can't shake the feeling that Felicity isn't good enough for him. But what do I know?

'Felicity seemed nice when I met her at the beach.'

'She's not too bad,' says Serena, condemning with faint praise as only a fifteen-year-old can.

There's a sharp rap on the back door, and my heart sinks when it swings open to reveal Josh. Standing there, with thick mist swirling behind him, he looks like the handsome hero of a Gothic novel, or a mass murderer. It's hard to tell which. My stomach does a weird flip.

'Are you ready, Ree?' he asks in his soft Cornish burr. 'Oh, hello Annie.' Stepping into the bright kitchen, he shakes out his damp fringe and closes the door behind him.

'Annie was just talking about you and Felicity,' says Serena, glancing at both of us.

'No, not really,' I stutter. 'Serena mentioned Felicity and I just said I'd met her at the beach and she seemed nice. As, indeed, was everyone at the beach that day. Chloe's a nice girl, and Ben seems a nice lad, and Kayla and Ollie are obviously nice people, we know that. And Dodger's a nice dog too. Though the cliffs certainly weren't' – how many feckin' times can I say 'nice' in five seconds? – 'pleasant that day.' I peter out and pat my face, which feels on fire.

'The cliffs are quite steep,' says Josh slowly.

'They are, and thanks again for your help with the, um, cliff thing.'

'Don't mention it.' His dark eyes lock on to mine and I can't look away. Blimey, I don't think I'm blinking, which isn't a good look. I once saw a woman being interviewed on TV who didn't blink and she looked bat-shit crazy.

Fortunately, Serena moves between us, breaking the spell.

'Annie's leaving Salt Bay for good in a fortnight,' she says. 'What do you think about that, Josh?' She half-smiles, like there's an in-joke and she's the only one who's in on it.

'I think if that's what Annie wants, it's the best thing,' answers Josh smoothly, without missing a beat. He shoves his hands into his jacket pockets and clears his throat. 'Come on, Serena, we need to keep an eye on Freya while Mum's out for a while. I presume you'll still be running the choir until you leave, Annie?'

'Absolutely, and we'll need to have a chat about that before I go.' Pushing my chair back, I get to my feet though I'm not sure why because now we're all standing in the kitchen, looking at one another and not moving. A melancholy blast from the foghorn fills the silence and then dies away to nothing. This is awkward.

'Oh, for f—' Serena stoops down as loose change tumbles out of her hand and clatters across the floor tiles. A fifty pence piece rolls under the table and I kneel down to chase after it. While I'm on my knees, a draught swirls round my shoulders and by the time I've given

Serena her money back, Josh has disappeared into the fog as though he was never there.

'Thanks. I'd better hurry or Josh will go mental.' Serena pauses at the back door and nods towards my Kindle. 'Enjoy your e-book. It's good when middle-aged people embrace new technology.'

Middle-aged? Cheeky cow. I might be twice her age but I'm au fait with Facebook, Twitter and Instagram, and I'd use Pinterest if I could be arsed. Maybe the choir could have its own Facebook page to attract new singers. I really couldn't bear it if the choir folds when I leave.

Wrenching the back door wide, I run into the garden in my socks. Jeez, this fog is a real Jack the Ripper pea-souper. Maybe reading about psychopaths wasn't such a good idea on a night like this. I can hardly see my hands in front of my face and, though it's high tide around now, there's no familiar crash of waves against the harbour wall. The fog is soaking up the sound like litmus paper.

'Josh, can I have a word with you?' My voice bounces back at me as I edge towards the garden gate, my foot occasionally missing the garden path and landing on soft earth. Suddenly two shapes loom out at me from the mist.

'Is that you, Annie? You scared the holy shit out of me!' squeals Serena.

'Language, Serena,' says Josh close to my ear. 'Is everything all right?'

'Yes, but I need to get something important sorted out with you right now.' Damp has seeped into the soles of my socks and is working its way up through the thick wool. I rub my hands briskly up and down my arms to generate some warmth.

'Get in the car, Serena, and I'll be with you in a minute.'

'Why can't I stay here with you two?' whines Serena.

'Because I've asked you to wait in the car and it's a long walk home.'

'That is so unfair. I wish I was an only child,' she splutters, disappearing into the fog.

'What did you want to sort out?' asks Josh, moving really close so I can see him better. Beads of moisture are sticking to his hair and I imagine him coming out of the shower, a fluffy white towel wrapped around his waist and drops of water glistening on his smooth, muscular chest. What the hell is wrong with me? Josh Pasco is back with Felicity and not my type anyway. Yes, he's good-looking in a tall, dark and grumpy way but he's far too complex to fit into my complication-free life. Plus he lives in Cornwall with his family. And I don't do Cornwall or family; not my own and certainly not someone else's.

The dull beep of a car horn jolts me back to my senses. The horn beeps again – Serena is really going for it.

'I'm leaving Salt Bay soon, as you know, and it's important to me that the choral society carries on. Important for the village, I think. You have doubts about it and I understand that, but it's good for the singers – people like Cyril who's all on his own and Florence whose husband has piles.'

'O-K,' says Josh, his face lost in the swirling mist.

'It struck me that the best person to take over leading the choir after I've gone would be you. You're a teacher and a natural at conducting, and it would be continuing your dad's legacy in a way. I – I hope you don't mind me asking. But you must have thought about it… you knew I was leaving.'

The car horn starts beeping continuously as if Serena is headbutting it.

'I've known from the start that you were leaving soon. You made that very clear. But you've seemed more settled recently so I thought you were staying for longer. My mistake.' He hesitates. 'I'm not sure about the choir.'

'But will you consider it? Please.'

I hold my breath while the foghorn and car horn honk in unison. If Josh says no and the choir folds, Cyril will die alone and be eaten by rats. And it will all be my fault for leaving.

'All right. No promises but I'll consider it.'

Phew! Maybe it's the relief but, without thinking, I lean forward and kiss Josh goodbye on the cheek. That's what we do in London and there's nothing sexual in it. I've cheek-kissed everyone from friends and business acquaintances to Maura's brother James who's fiercely, fabulously gay.

As my lips graze the faint stubble on Josh's cheek, the damp air is suffused with a warm tang of sandalwood and lime which smells gorgeous; a potent blend of masculinity and machismo with just a hint of metrosexuality. Blimey, I'm coming over all poetic about aftershave. I'm about to pull away when Josh turns his head and his lips touch mine. At first I think it's a mistake; something else to feel hot with embarrassment about later. But his warm lips press harder onto mine and he puts his arm round my waist and pulls me against him.

Wowzers, it's no mistake then. I start to kiss him back, partly because it would be rude not to, but mainly because it feels rather nice. His fingers slide through my hair when I put my arms round his neck and press my body tight against his. Tiny fireworks are going off all over my body because it quickly becomes apparent that Josh Pasco scores a ten when it comes to kissing. His kisses are surprisingly tender with just the right hint of urgency and when his hand moves down to the small of my back, I forget families and my wet socks and Cornwall and London, and I sink into the moment.

'Where the hell are you? I've been waiting for ages.'

Josh and I jump apart as Serena bursts out of the mist.

'What have you two been doing?' She peers at me while I adopt my best poker face and run a finger along my warm lips. 'I've been sitting in that car on my own for ages. I could have been abducted. Just wait 'til I tell Mum.'

'Stop making a fuss about nothing. I'm coming now.' Josh's voice sounds wobbly, though I might be imagining it because I'm feeling rather wobbly myself. What the hell just happened? When Serena stomps off, he whispers in my ear, 'That should never have happened. I apologise,' before he's engulfed by the fog.

The kitchen is just the same as when I left it: bright and cheery with cactus plants lined up on the windowsill and a pie for Alice's tea defrosting on the worktop. But something important has shifted. I sit down heavily at the table and put my head in my hands. I just snogged Josh Pasco and enjoyed it. A lot.

I'm no prude when it comes to snogging. Passionate kissing is fabulous, though my snog-a-thon with Seamus at the college disco gave me glandular fever, which was vile. But snogging in the past meant fun, anticipated kisses in dark corners while I was dressed up to the nines. Not being taken by surprise by a grumpy bastard while standing in a pea-souper in my socks.

Stuart floats into my mind and I realise that I haven't thought about him in ages. He's an adequate kisser, though rather self-obsessed. I caught him looking at himself in the mirror once while we were in a clinch, though he hotly denied it.

But snogging Josh wasn't 'snogging' at all. It was proper kissing with a sexy, grown-up man. And I want to do it again – which is a huge complication because I'm about to leave Salt Bay and Josh is obviously not keen on a re-match.

What does 'That shouldn't have happened, I apologise,' really mean anyway? Three possibilities spring to mind:

1. I'm back with Felicity, the love of my life, who's way out of your league.
2. I only kissed you because it was so foggy I couldn't see your face.
3. It was a reflex action when your lips brushed my cheek.

Numbers one and two make me feel sad as well as hideously unattractive so I plump for number three as my favourite. Maybe no one cheek-kisses goodbye round here so my sudden lunge caught him off guard. That's probably it, though it doesn't explain why the kiss lasted for ages or his tongue gently – crikey, I'd better pull myself together. Jumping up, I pull off my socks and head for the sink because nothing kills a sexy mood quicker than wringing out soggy wool over a pile of dirty plates.

'Has my fish pie defrosted enough to go into the oven?' Alice pops her head round the door and does a double-take when she sees what I'm doing. She shuffles into the room, shoulders slightly hunched, and roots through a drawer to find a baking tray. 'Is everything all right?'

'Everything's fine, except my socks got wet and I have a bit of a headache.'

'That's a shame. There are painkillers in the bathroom cabinet.' A wave of heat spreads through the kitchen when she puts the baking tray and pie into the oven. Then she straightens up and looks at me more closely. 'Did Serena get off OK in this weather? She told me Josh was collecting her.'

'He did but he's gone.' And soon he'll be gone for good which is what I wanted, though now I'm not so sure. Sadness floods over me and I make a big thing of hanging my socks on the back of a chair so Alice won't notice. She doesn't ask why they're wet but squeezes my shoulder when she passes me on her way to the cutlery drawer.

'It must be hard being on your own all the time, Annabella,' she says softly, placing a knife and fork on her tray.

That's exactly the kind of remark that can get you embroiled in a heavy discussion before you know it. Avoid, deny or deflect? I plump for deflection and start frantically chopping carrots on the wooden board next to the sink.

'Would you like some vegetables with your pie?' A chunk of carrot falls off the board and lands squarely between my toes. It feels cold and slimy.

'That would be lovely, thank you. I seem to remember that your mother hated carrots.'

'With a passion. When I gave them to her she'd hide them under her mashed potato.' Not for the first time since arriving in Salt Bay, it strikes me that my relationship with Mum was often the wrong way round.

'That sounds like the Joanna I knew.' Alice puts the salt and pepper pots next to the cutlery on her tray. 'I wish I'd known your mother as a grown-up and you as a child.'

Just for a moment, I let myself dwell on how life might have been with a family. With a feisty great-aunt on my side, supporting me through Mum's more difficult times. With happy summer holidays on Salt Bay beach, rather than the occasional afternoon at a city swimming pool.

'Me too, Alice. Me too.'

Chapter Twenty-Four

All trace of fog has disappeared when I pull back my bedroom curtains the next morning. It's early but the sun is rising in a china-blue sky and two fishing boats are motoring into harbour, leaving a foamy trail in their wake. All is right with the world – but I feel like crap.

I tossed and turned all night thanks to weird dreams featuring Josh with a huge trout pout. And now every time I think of Josh – and I'm thinking about him a lot – my lips feel tingly. The last time they felt this way was when I kissed a friend's kitten – well, it was really cute – and had to mainline antihistamine to halt an allergic reaction.

Other bits of me feel tingly, too, when I think of Josh and The Kiss. But I can't put everything down to lust because there's something more. I can hardly believe my own stupidity but Josh Pasco, grumpy Cornish pirate, has got under my skin. And so has Alice and the Salt Bay Choral Society. I haven't even been looking for another job recently. Bugger. Toby was right all along.

Sighing loudly, I open my window, grab my mobile phone and lean out as far as I can without falling into the garden. Tregavara House might be a black hole but I've discovered that waving my arm out of the window gives me an intermittent mobile phone signal. It's not strong enough to call anyone; I tried with Maura until being constantly cut off almost drove us demented. But the signal is strong enough for texts and emails to come piling in, and maybe Josh has been in touch.

My phone beeps several times while I'm at full stretch, my pyjama sleeve flapping in the breeze, and I wave at a couple of fishermen who are pointing at me. They appear to be laughing, which is harsh when I could be about to fling myself onto the garden path for all they know.

Once the beeping stops, I sit on the splintery floorboards and scan through my text messages. There are none from Josh but one from Toby says '*check your email*'.

Toby's email was sent late last night and reads:

> Dear Annie,
>
> I've come up trumps and have a job for you. Our administrator Abigail has decided that she's depressed and urgently needs to 'find herself'. Personally, this is why I would never hire women because they're far too emotional. But anyway, she's taking a six-month sabbatical and we're looking for a temp to take her place. I've talked you up to the CEO and the job is yours if you can be here to start on Monday morning. It's an excellent opportunity and I'm sure you'll be up to the job if you can type and do filing.
>
> Alice will be perfectly fine on her own for a few days until that other girl starts. Please confirm by return and get yourself out of Salt Bay a.s.a.p.
>
> Toby

I reread the email several times. My savings are dwindling and I could do with a guaranteed job, but how can I start in just three days' time? Throwing on some clothes, I slip out of the quiet house and walk away from the sea. It's not long past dawn and, away from the harbour, the village is still largely sleeping.

Maura won't be sleeping, not with alarm-clock Harry permanently set to go off at stupid o'clock. She describes it as uncanny – and a few other choice words – how his little head pops up and he starts wailing every morning on the dot of half past five. She'll have been awake with him for ages.

As I expected, Maura's mobile only rings a few times before it's answered.

'Gghmmfff.'

'Maura, is that you? God, I didn't wake you up did I?'

'Annie? Of course not. I've been awake since the dawn of time, thanks to my darling son, but you're the first person I've spoken to this morning.' She yawns loudly. 'Where are you and why are you calling me when you could be sleeping? Are you mad?'

'I'm in the only phone box for miles around and I need to talk. Is now a good time?'

'Harry's fed, I've changed his disgusting nappy and he's in his rocker chair dozing, so shoot. What's happening in Cornwall, you lucky cow.'

'I've been offered a new job, starting in Islington next week.'

'Woo-hoo. The wanderer returns. That's great news and Islington is very right on, don't you know.'

'I guess so.' I trace a capital 'A' with my finger in the condensation on the phone box glass.

'You guess so? What's really going on?'

'I don't know. I feel weird about leaving Alice.'

'I thought you said you'd found a carer for her. Someone to live in.'

'I have and Emily's lovely but she doesn't start for another two weeks and she's not – well, she's not family.' I feed more coins into the call box. 'Plus I feel bad about leaving the choir because they're nice people and I enjoy singing with them. I've asked Josh to take over running the choir and he's said he'll think about it.'

There's a squeak from Harry in the background and Maura lowers her voice. 'Is this the Josh you've mentioned a couple of times? The one you can't stand.'

'That's the one. And he kissed me so it's got even more confusing. And then there's the practical issue of getting all my stuff back up to London, and getting Gracie out of the flat, and—'

'Whoah! Hold your horses, Trebarwith. Let me get this straight.' Maura is no longer speaking quietly. 'Are you telling me that Josh, the bloke who you told me more than once was a total dickhead, kissed you? The one who looks like a cross between Poldark with his shirt off and Richard Armitage?'

'How do you know what he looks like?'

'I tracked him down on the Internet, of course. When a friend keeps talking about a bloke she says she can't stand, you Google him. That's the law. He was in a local newspaper pic of a football team, and I was impressed. Very dark and brooding. Cracking legs. So was the kiss a corker?'

'It was lovely.'

'That's great.'

'But then he said he was sorry it happened.'

'Not so great.'

'And now I'm confused because coming back to London is best and what I wanted, but for some stupid reason I keep thinking about the people here and how much I'm going to miss them.'

'Oh Annie.' Maura chuckles. 'It's finally happened. You've got attached to people and let them in. Welcome to the real world. You've been running away from getting close to people for so long, but you can't escape forever.'

'But I'm a free spirit,' I splutter, realising as the words leave my mouth that they make me sound like a wanker.

'You were a free spirit, Annie, but now you've got family and roots and a boyfriend who looks eminently shaggable and might be "the one". I'm dead jealous. Anyway, why should you escape the daily annoyances and frustrations of being shackled to people forever?'

'Paul still not doing night feeds, then?' I ignore the boyfriend jibe.

'Nope. He says I'm more genetically primed to cope with disturbed sleep than he is. Let's hope I'm not genetically primed to brain him with a frying pan while he's snoring. Oh great, here we go.' The adorable squeaks coming down the line have turned into a blood-curdling yell.

'The kraken awakes,' yawns Maura, 'I'd better go. Keep in touch and let me know what you're doing.'

Maura's right, I admit to myself while I'm stomping back to Tregavara House. I'm stomping because I'm cross. Really furious that my plan to visit Alice for a day or two and then get the hell out has gone hideously wrong.

It's Alice's fault for needing me. And the choir's for being good fun. And Kayla's for being such an excellent friend. And Josh's for being so unexpectedly, annoyingly sexy. But most of all it's mine for letting my guard down. I'm an idiot.

By the time I get home, I've calmed down so I sit on the harbour wall and have a long think about things. A skinny black cat wanders along, gobbling up pieces of discarded fish, while I go over my options. It's simple really – on one hand there's cosmopolitan London, a new job and my old, uncomplicated life; while on the other, there's back-of-beyond Cornwall, family responsibilities and lots of complications. The old Annie would say it's a total no-brainer, but Salt Bay has changed me.

The cat bats its head against my legs and stretches out on the smooth, cold stone while the pros and cons of leaving or staying ping round my brain. At last I come to a (probably) final decision. I'll stay at least another fortnight until Emily has moved in. That will give me longer with Alice and more time for Gracie to find another flat.

It will also give me a chance to make sure the choir will survive without me. Toby's job sounds dead boring anyway and something else will come up; it always does. Maybe I can tackle Josh about what happened in the garden, too. Jeez, I've got to stop thinking about him because it makes me hyperventilate. I deliberately slow my breathing down and, stepping carefully over the cat, make my way back to the house.

It's almost nine o'clock and I can hear the bath running upstairs and Alice singing softly on the landing. She'll be pleased that I'm staying at least until Emily moves in.

While I'm waiting for her to come downstairs, I lay the table for breakfast. It's become a ritual that we sit together over cereal and toast and tell one another our plans for the day. This morning I make a special effort and find a clean cloth, pour orange juice into a glass jug and lay out plates. For a finishing touch, I pick some greenery from the garden and put it into a jam jar in the centre. The table looks lovely. I truly am a domestic goddess.

I'm pouring Rice Krispies into my bowl when the phone starts ringing in the sitting room. The box jolts and Krispies scatter across the worktop and disappear down the gap next to the Aga. Who's calling this early? Fingers crossed it's not Toby ringing about his job offer.

'Hello madam.' Yay, it's definitely not Toby. 'My name's Melody and I'm calling about today's appointment.' Melody sounds very young and as if she's reading from a script. 'I'm afraid Dr Fulton is unwell and therefore unable to see Mrs Trebarwith this afternoon as planned. We apologise for the inconvenience.'

That's weird. I went to a hospital check-up with Alice last week but she hasn't mentioned this one.

'I'll let Alice know and ask her to call to rearrange. Thank you for ringing.' I'm about to end the call when something strikes me. 'By the way, she's Mrs Gowan, not Trebarwith.'

'You what?' There's the sound of fast typing. 'The appointment is for Mrs Trebarwith.'

'She was a Trebarwith but now she's Gowan, Alice Gowan.'

Cue more frantic typing. God, this girl's a bit dozy.

'The computer definitely says that Dr Fulton was due to see Mrs Trebarwith at three o'clock. Mrs Sheila Trebarwith.'

'Sheila?'

'Yes. S-H-E-I-L-A.' I can hear the sigh in Melody's voice as she spells out the name.

'You're telling me that Mrs Sheila Trebarwith has an appointment this afternoon?'

'No, as I said, the appointment has been cancelled.' Melody says this painfully slowly in her sing-song voice because she's obviously talking to a total moron. 'Do you understand what I've just told you?'

I'm not sure that I do but Melody is super-keen to end the call so there's no time for more questions. I'm not sure what I'd ask anyway: 'Tell me Melody, are you cancelling an appointment with the deceased Mrs Sheila Trebarwith?'

'Who was that on the phone?' Alice appears in the doorway, her face glowing from the bath and her damp hair flat against her scalp. I'm still standing with the receiver in my hand although Melody rang off five minutes ago.

'It was someone ringing about this afternoon's hospital appointment.'

'Really?' says Alice, her eyes growing wide. She plumps up the cushions on the sofa. 'What did she say?'

'She said that the appointment has been cancelled.'

'Never mind. I can reschedule it. Shall we go and have breakfast?' Alice takes the phone and places it back in its cradle.

'She also said that the appointment was for Mrs Sheila Trebarwith.'

'Oh.' Alice stops dead in her tracks and sucks in air through her teeth. 'That's awkward.'

'And surprising.' I'm trying really hard to keep my voice level but my stomach is turning somersaults. 'Tell me Alice, was the appointment for my grandmother?'

Alice exhales slowly and sinks onto the sofa. 'Yes, it was.'

'You never said that my grandmother was still alive.'

'You never asked.' Alice sits quietly for a moment, biting her lip and struggling with a decision. Then she speaks quickly, her words tumbling into each other. 'Sheila is living a few miles away in a home for people with dementia.'

What the feckin' – *what?* Alice and I have discussed all kinds of crap over the last few weeks – who's leaving *Coronation Street*, is taupe really a colour, Boris Johnson: villain or hero. But did she mention that my grandmother is still breathing? Nope, not a peep.

'And you didn't think to tell me this?'

'Yes, I thought about it and almost told you many times.' Alice pulls herself up slowly. 'But you don't seem to want to know about your family. You've shut us out, Annabella. So I thought I'd tell you when you were ready.'

'When would that have been?'

'I don't know. Maybe never. I can see how much your childhood has affected you. It can't have been easy, just you and your mother.' Alice touches my shoulder but I shake off her hand.

'So when you went to visit "Penelope"?' I put 'Penelope' in air quotes even though people who do that are knobs.

'I was really visiting Sheila.'

'And you never thought of taking me with you.'

'Absolutely not.' For the first time since we've met, Alice is angry. Her jaw tightens and bright spots flare in her cheeks. 'How long were you ever going to stick around, Annabella? It would have been cruel for you to see Sheila once, maybe twice, and then to disappear, like your mother did. Sheila couldn't cope with that again. She's a very vulnerable woman.'

Bringing my mum into this deception stings, and my voice gets louder. 'Just like my mother was vulnerable when Sheila and Samuel threw her out, because she was pregnant with me.'

Hot guilt bubbles up inside. I'm the reason that this family is fractured. It's all my fault.

'Your mother was no saint, Annabella.' Alice sighs heavily, all the fight gone out of her as quickly as it arrived.

'Because she dared to have sex when she wasn't married?'

'We've all done that,' murmurs Alice. 'Look, I admit that Sheila and Samuel didn't behave well when Joanna broke the news of her pregnancy. Salt Bay is a small place and times were different then. They were terribly shocked. Oh, Annabella.' She wipes a veiny hand across her pale, thin mouth. 'I didn't want to get into all of this but I suppose you have a right to know. All right.' She sits on the arm of the sofa and wraps her arms round her waist. 'Samuel was an old-fashioned man. Words were said in the heat of the moment and Joanna took herself off to London.

But it broke Sheila's heart and she contacted your mother just before you were born and asked her to come home.'

'That's not true. Mum told me she was thrown out and her family never had anything more to do with her.' When I was a child, I'd hug her and promise that I'd never abandon her. We'd be together forever; two Trebarwiths against the world.

'I'm afraid it is true. Joanna refused to come back or to have anything more to do with her parents. She always was headstrong and troubled, even as a child.'

'It can't be true, because Sheila would have kept on trying. She wouldn't have given up on her daughter.' My bottom lip is wobbling because my mum would never have given up on me. I'm sure of that.

'Your mother kept moving house and Sheila lost track of where she was. This was in the days before you could find people on the web thing, when people could easily disappear, even if they had a distinctive surname.'

I do remember Mum telling people her surname was 'Smith', particularly when she was unwell and convinced we weren't safe. But what's wrong with wanting to be anonymous in a big city? It doesn't mean that what my mum told me about the Trebarwiths was a lie.

Alice is looking at me intently, her dark brown eyes glinting in pale light from the window.

'Samuel was too proud to keep on trying to find Joanna. He was a stubborn man and told Sheila to leave her be. But after he died so tragically, Sheila was hopeful that Joanna would finally come home, with you. But she never did.'

'She would have if she'd heard about her dad's death. She obviously didn't know.'

'It was headline news, Annabella. She must have known,' says Alice sadly. 'Come and eat breakfast and we can talk some more.'

But I don't want to talk. Alice has deceived me about Sheila and now she's accusing Mum of being a heartless liar. Everything's a jumble in my head. The lid has been wrenched off a big box of secrets and bad things are tumbling out with no way for me to shove them back in. This is why I hate fucking families. All they do is ruin your life.

'I need to get some air,' I gulp, brushing past Alice and rushing out of the house.

Chapter Twenty-Five

Walking out seemed a good idea at the time; a symbolic gesture as well as a chance to breathe. A metaphorical two fingers up to Alice's version of the truth. But it wasn't well thought through. In the last half hour, clouds have bubbled up and covered the sun and a stiff breeze is whipping off the sea. Meanwhile, I'm standing at the front gate with bare feet. Who grabs her jacket as she storms out of a house but forgets her shoes? A total eejit, that's who.

I could sneak back in for my trainers but I don't want to see Alice until I've had time to think about what she said. Not that I believe all that stuff about my mum. She was abandoned by the terrible Trebarwiths, just like she said. Why else would she have deprived herself of having a family? Why would she have deprived me?

My feet are freezing on the cold path so I start walking towards the village. Spots of rain start falling from a steel sky as I trudge along. Does it ever stop raining in Cornwall? Stupid Cornwall, stupid families… and stupid pavements! I've never noticed it before but the tarmac is scattered with super-sharp pieces of gravel, like teeny landmines. Another shard pierces my skin but I grit my teeth and keep on walking. At least physical pain is easier to cope with than the emotional maelstrom in my head.

After a while, I realise I'm walking towards the pub. The Whistling Wave must be my autopilot sanctuary: when the world's going to hell, I need Kayla and a ginormous glass of gin. And maybe Josh will call in later and give me a hug. How I'd love his strong arms around me, pulling me tight against his muscular chest, and his lips… oh no, my breathing has gone weird again. I must stop thinking about Josh Flaming Pasco because it makes things worse.

When I get to the pub, I nip round the back so no one will see me. Luckily, the door to the kitchen is propped open with a beer barrel and I slip inside. Plates of clingfilm-wrapped 'nibbles' are lined up next to the industrial-size fridge – cheese and pineapple chunks on sticks, mini sausages, tiny puff pastry cases overflowing with pink stuff. At the sink, Kayla is washing glasses and whistling along tunelessly to the radio.

'Jeez!' She jumps and soapy water splashes over her orange Crocs. 'You'll frighten someone to death sneaking up on people like that. What's with the shoe-less look? Is that what people do in London? In February?' She peers at me more closely. 'Not meaning to be rude or anything, but you look terrible. What's going on? Alice hasn't carked, has she?'

I balance against the crockery cupboard and rub the soles of my frozen feet on my jeans.

'No one's died but there has been a resurrection of sorts.'

'Nope.' Kayla wipes her hands on the tea towel slung over her shoulder. 'You're going to have to give me more of a clue if you're talking about resurrection. Crikey!' Her eyes open wide. 'You're not going all religious on me, are you?'

I shake my head. 'I just found out some news about Sheila Trebarwith, my grandmother.'

'The one who chucked your mum out and died a few years ago.'

'That's the one, only it turns out she's not dead.'

'Cool! Is she one of the undead, like a vampire? Is Salt Bay full of zombies? I've had my suspicions about Cyril for a while.'

'I'm not joking, Kayla. Sheila isn't dead.'

'Don't be daft, of course she is.' The tea towel falls to the floor and Kayla scoops it up. 'She's buried on the cliff.'

'Her husband is, and I presumed she was buried in the churchyard. But Alice told me this morning that she's actually living near here in a home for people with dementia. When Alice was visiting Penelope, she was really visiting Sheila.'

'Feck me sideways!' exclaims Kayla, her jaw dropping. 'And Alice didn't mention this before because…?'

'Because it would upset Sheila if I visited her and then went back to London.'

'Good point,' says Kayla, starting to nod but turning it into a shake of the head when I glower at her.

'No, Kayla, not a good point. Alice has been lying to me about my family from the start. This is why I don't do family. It's all lies and subterfuge.'

'Well, not exactly lying, more…' Kayla glances at me and shrugs. 'Yes, you're right. Families – pah! I spit on them all, or I would if it wasn't terribly unhygienic in a kitchen. Look, Annie Sunshine.' She puts down the tea towel, comes over and puts her arm round my shoulder. 'I can understand that the lying and the not being dead was a shock But maybe it's a good thing to find out you still have a grandparent who's alive. Are you going to see her?'

'Alice has made it very clear that wouldn't be a good idea. Toby found me a job starting on Monday but I'd decided to stay here longer, but now I don't know what to do.' I relax against Kayla and stifle a sneeze when her long, red curls tickle my nose. 'Also, something else happened this week with Josh, who—'

'Hey Kayla, how long does it take you to get a few more glasses?' Roger sticks his head into the kitchen from the bar area. His face is red and there are damp patches under the arms of his blue T-shirt. 'Hello Annie, I didn't realise you were in here. Kayla, chat later and get yourself back round here. We're going to be mega busy later and need to get things ready now.' He notices my bare feet and frowns. 'You shouldn't have bare feet in here. If you cut yourself, there's no point in suing me.'

Kayla grabs a handful of dripping glasses from the draining board and raises her eyebrows as she follows Roger into the bar.

'Sorry, Annie, we're hosting Kieran's eighteenth birthday party at lunchtime so it's all hands on deck. It's half-term and he and his mates are already here helping us to set things up. Speak later about the zombies thing? I'll call round after my shift.'

Will Young is singing about joy on the radio but I switch him off after Kayla's gone and the kitchen goes quiet, except for a low hum from the fridge. Usually, Will's voice cheers me up when I'm down and soothes me when I'm stressed, but today it's just not happening. The Trebarwiths have murdered my love of music. It's like *Game of Thrones* with musical scores.

I drag a high stool towards the window and sit watching as people come and go from the pub. Some are carrying helium balloons and birthday banners and one man arrives wearing a face mask of Prince William. He does a royal wave to some approaching friends and flips them the middle finger when they get closer. Her Majesty would not be amused.

I've reached that awful self-pitying stage where other people's happiness only magnifies my own misery. So I slip off the stool and head for the bar to find out what time Kayla's shift ends.

Oops. As I come round a corner in the narrow passageway, I spot Kayla getting up close and personal with a punter. Chuffing hell! I'm all for good customer service but Kayla is taking the concept to extremes. Standing on tiptoe, she's snogging the life out of some bloke while birthday boy Kieran, the bashful kid I met recently in the pub, looks on aghast. Kayla has her hands clamped to the man's face and is pressed up against his tight, muscular body. Hold on a second. For the love of all that's holy, the man kissing Kayla is Josh.

I draw back round the corner, heart hammering. He must be the new man she was secretive about. The real man. Wow, she's certainly changed her tune. One minute Josh is a knobhead and the next she has her tongue down his throat.

The worst thing – well, almost the worst – is that Toby's right. Josh Pasco really is an unprincipled womaniser who uses his good looks and sexy vibe to get off with all and sundry. Felicity, Kayla and who knows how many others have fallen for his grumpy charms? I was almost added to his list.

What a perfectly horrible day this is turning out to be! I run through the kitchen, bare feet slapping on the tiles, and don't stop running when I get to the pavement. I hardly notice the sharp gravel.

Alice is clattering about in the kitchen when I get back so I close the front door quietly, creep upstairs to my room and lie on the bed, staring at the ceiling. Fat tears spill out of my eyes, roll into my ears and trickle down my neck.

High above me, a large spider is weaving an intricate web that stretches from the light fitting to the cornicing. Normally I'd throw a hissy fit because I hate spiders but right now I can't be arsed. A squadron of spiders with hairy legs could march in here and start line dancing and I wouldn't give a monkey's.

After a while I pull myself together and write a brief email to Toby. *Thanks for the job offer. Happy to accept. See you at work on Monday. All the best, Annie.* Then I hang out of the window and press 'send'. There, that's done.

Pulling out my huge suitcase from under the bed, I pack the clothes and belongings Amber sent for me. The case is too heavy for me to manage but I'm sure Toby will bring it back to London the next time he's visiting Alice. Next I share out essentials – a few work clothes, make-up and toiletries, the photo of my poor, maligned mum – between my rucksack and a canvas bag and lug them down the stairs.

Alice hears the commotion and comes from the kitchen into the hall. 'What's this, Annabella? Are you leaving so soon?'

I ignore the tremor in her hand when she takes off her apron and folds it on top of the radiator. The next few minutes are going to be awful but I can't stay here any longer.

'I'm sorry, Alice, but I need to go. I've had a job offer from Toby and it starts on Monday. Look.'

I thrust my phone under Alice's nose so she'll know I'm not lying.

She glances at Toby's email. 'I see.'

'If I go now I can get a seat on the lunchtime London train.'

Alice nods. 'That makes sense.'

'I'm sorry it's all a bit rushed but if I get back to London today I've got the weekend to get ready for my new job. And Emily will be moving in soon so I'm no longer needed.'

'Of course.' Alice's smile doesn't reach her eyes. I so don't want her eyes to look sad. 'Before you go, let me apologise for not telling you about Sheila. I see now that I should have, and I didn't mean to tarnish your memories of your mother.'

'It's all right, Alice.' The fight has gone out of me too and I can't face talking about Mum any more. 'I can't stay here forever and you'll be OK until Emily moves in, won't you?'

'Of course. I'll be fine.'

'Please could you get this back to Josh.' I hand over the polished wood box with Ted Pawley's baton nestling inside it. 'Tell him – just tell him I had to leave.'

'If that's what you want. How will you get to the station?'

'I'll walk to the phone box and call a taxi.'

'And there's nothing I can do to persuade you to stay a little longer?'

'I really need to get back to the life I had before I came to Salt Bay.'

'In that case, thank you for all your help and it's been lovely getting to know my great-niece.' Alice smells of violets and face powder when she leans forward and kisses me on the cheek. 'I'll miss you, Annabella. Please come back and see me. We don't need to talk about your mother if you'd rather not.'

Her eyes look bright and I nod, too full of emotion to speak. Grabbing my bags, I rush to the front door and, when I look back, she's standing at the foot of the stairs.

'Bye,' I blurt out. 'Look after yourself, Alice.'

The taxi driver slings my bags into his boot and drives slowly out of Salt Bay. As the car climbs high above the village, I look out of the grubby back window. Was it only a few weeks ago that I stumbled down this hill and Josh almost ran me over? The village is spread out behind me – the vast, never-still ocean, huddled cottages, and I can just make out Tregavara House standing sentry where the land meets the sea. It all looks beautiful.

I think of Alice in the house on her own. Jeez, am I doing the right thing? Curling my hands into tight fists, I take slow, deep breaths. Of course I am. It was only ever a short-term arrangement, and staying longer is out of the question now Alice has slagged off my mum, Kayla and Josh are getting it on, and I've discovered that Sheila's alive.

It was dangerous, too, chips in my niggly inner voice, *because you were getting sucked in. And what is there to stay for anyway? You'll soon be forgotten. Emily can look after Alice, Josh can run the choir and they'll both make a better job of it than you. And why did you think that Josh would be interested in you, with your squidgy thighs and boring brown hair?* Don't you just hate your inner voice when it's being a right bitch?

The taxi driver does a double-take in his rear-view mirror when I blow my nose.

'Are you all right, love?' he calls over his shoulder.

'Fine, thanks,' I gulp, gazing pointedly out of the window. Please mate, don't be sympathetic or I'll end up sobbing and snotting all over your taxi. It won't be pretty. He takes the hint and turns on his radio, flooding the car with music. I know that song. It's The Communards' classic 'Don't Leave Me This Way'. I sigh and put my fingers in my ears. Sometimes music can be cruel.

Chapter Twenty-Six

By the time we reach Penzance station, I've composed myself and – hooray – the one o'clock train to London Paddington is running as scheduled. That's the first good news of the day. And there's time to buy a sandwich and nip to the ladies' for a safety wee, so I can avoid using the train toilet later – my pelvic floor muscles refuse to relax when the door could slide across at any moment to reveal my lily-white arse.

With a couple of minutes to spare, I board the train and nab a window seat near the luggage rack. Opposite me, a pinch-faced woman with black hair and pale, translucent skin settles down with her knitting and a tub of salad. Her needles click as she knits one, purls one.

The train is warm, clean and comfy but I'm miserable as we pull out of Penzance. And my low mood persists while we trundle through Cornwall, stopping at small stations with pretty names; St Erth, Camborne, Redruth. This journey is going to take forever. After we've gone through Liskeard, I try to get some sleep. But whenever I settle down for a snooze, all I can see are Josh and Kayla locked in a steamy embrace while Alice looks on with sad, sad eyes. After a while I give up and resign myself to the fact that I might never sleep again.

As the miles crawl by, I email Kayla to apologise for leaving and ask her to persuade Josh to take over as the choir's conductor. Leaving the choir without saying goodbye makes me feel awful and, to be honest, I'm starting to feel foolish for bolting. But life was too complicated with Alice accusing my mum of being a heartless liar, and grandmothers appearing out of the blue, and Josh turning out to be the man Toby said he was. Anyone in that position would have done a runner. Beyoncé, Dame Judi Dench, the Queen. Absolutely anyone. Wouldn't they? I'm tempted to ask the woman opposite what she thinks but that would be crazy, so I finish off my email to Kayla and press 'send'. I don't mention seeing her with her tongue down Josh's throat. What's the point?

The stations we're passing through get bigger and busier as we approach the capital and my spirits rise when we reach the outskirts of London. I'm almost home! Closer to the city centre, we trundle past the backs of terraced houses, blackened by pollution. Grubby forgotten washing flutters from lines strung up between flats, and graffiti is plastered across high, red-brick walls. In the distance I can see lofty buildings dominating the skyline. God, it's good to be back.

At last, almost five and a half hours after leaving Penzance, our train edges slowly into Paddington station and I haul my bags onto the platform. Jeez, it's like stepping out of a bubble into the first day of the Harrods sale. A wall of sound hits me, with commuters pushing past, jabbering into their mobile phones and tutting when I can't find my Oyster card.

The tide of rush-hour commuters sweeps me into the Tube station and onto the District Line platform which is totally rammed. The train arrives with a belch of hot air from the tunnel and we all pile in, almost on top of one another. I can tell from the filthy looks that my bags are getting in people's way but no one complains, because that's not what Londoners do. I soak up the smells and the clattering of the train on the tracks and notice that my heart palpitations are back already.

At Notting Hill Gate, I switch to the Central Line and before long I'm walking through Westfield shopping centre in Stratford. Annabella Sunshine Trebarwith is back in her 'manor'.

Jennifer would hate the shopping centre's opening hours. She shuts up shop at half past five and will be gossiping right now in The Whistling Wave. Possibly with me as the topic of conversation. I'll probably never see Jennifer again, which makes me more sad than I would have expected. And chances are I've seen the last of Alice, Kayla, Cyril and Josh. But it's for the best, I tell myself firmly, ignoring the heavy feeling in my chest. The Trebarwith family and Salt Bay were an experiment that didn't work out; a different life that's come to an end. Now everything can get back to normal. Hallelujah!

Lights are shining from apartment windows when I head away from Westfield towards home. My flat is near the area that was regenerated for the London Olympics. Olympians at the peak of physical fitness strolled through these streets, close to the flat where I now slob around in my PJs. Which is pretty cool, though dispiriting on days when I don't have the energy to move off the sofa.

With my waistline in mind, I climb the stairs to the third floor of our block and give a deep sigh as I push my front door key into the lock. I'm finally home.

'Annie, what the hell are you doing back?' Amber is sitting on the sofa in her bra and pants and is a vibrant shade of orange. 'I've just fake-tanned and wasn't expecting anyone.' She grabs the thin dressing gown next to her and pulls it across her lap. 'Why are you here?'

'I texted from the train and said I was on my way home.' I drop my bags, roll my aching shoulders and take a good look round. The flat looks like closing time at The Whistling Wave. Dirty glasses and empty wine bottles cover the kitchen worktops, a foil tray of congealed curry is in the sink, and the floor is littered with strips of coloured paper from party poppers. That's the problem with having an open plan flat – you can't close a door on the mess.

'I can't get texts right now,' says Amber, moving her leg and smudging orange across the cream sofa. 'I dropped my mobile down the toilet last night and now it's not working, which is well annoying. You'd think they'd, like, make them waterproof or something 'cos everyone texts on the toilet. Anyway, my mum said to put it in a bag of rice, like that's going to help.' She snorts and points at a box of Uncle Ben's on the windowsill. 'But I thought I'd better try or Mum won't buy me another one. She got well lippy because I've only had this one for a month. The last one got nicked at Cinderella's, you know… the club,' she adds helpfully, just in case I'm under the mistaken impression that one of her friends is named after a fairytale.

'Though dropping the phone wasn't my fault,' pouts Amber. 'I'm sure they're making mobiles more slippery on purpose so you have to keep replacing them. It's a conspiracy.' She frowns and smooths out some streaks on her legs. 'Um, when are you going back to Cheshire, then?'

'I'm not.'

'Oh – my – God!' Amber's eyes open wide in her tangerine face. 'You're back for good?'

'Afraid so.'

'But what about Gracie? She lives here now and you can't just throw her out and make her homeless. There are laws about that.'

'I'm not planning on making Gracie homeless. I know I've come back a fortnight earlier than I said so I'll sleep on the sofa until Gracie can find somewhere else and move out. That was always the plan when she moved in.'

'I suppose, though it might take a while,' mutters Amber.

'That's OK. She doesn't have to rush. Well, not too much. Though it would be good to have my room back quite soon.'

I eye the streaked, lumpy sofa apprehensively.

'I'm sure she'll do her best. But it's not terribly convenient.' Amber stands up, shoves her arms into her dressing gown and strops past me into her bedroom. When she slams her door, the vibration makes the empty bottles and glasses rattle. Welcome home, Annie!

The next couple of days are pretty dire. The sofa is more uncomfortable than it looks and, though there are no screeching seagulls to wake me up, people streaming towards Stratford station do exactly the same thing. Still half-asleep and disorientated, I listen out for the dull boom of waves hitting hard stone and the sound of Alice pottering in the kitchen and feel a stab of disappointment when I hear sirens and car horns instead.

Gracie is not amused by my sudden appearance and either ignores me or grunts in my general direction. In the evening, she and Amber sit in one another's bedrooms playing music or watching the Kardashians until well gone midnight. And the bathroom looks like the stockroom at Boots.

Bottles and potions litter every surface and I find a pot of anti-wrinkle cream wedged behind the false nails. They're both teenagers for goodness' sake! I, on the other hand, am getting on a bit so I nick a few splodges for the skin around my eyes which has been knackered by all that Cornish weather.

All in all, I'm not feeling my best when I arrive at Fulbright and Linsom on Monday morning to start my new job. Getting into the shower was almost impossible with Amber and Gracie bagging it first, and my clothes are creased because the iron is broken. Gracie grunted that she dropped it while she was drunk, and pointed out a scorch mark on the carpet. She's proving to be rather tiresome.

Putting all that to one side, I plaster on a smile and push open the heavy front door of my new employer. Tucked away behind the market with McDonald's cartons blowing across the doorstep, Fulbright and Linsom is less grand from the outside than I expected. But inside it's awesome. Huge gilt-framed oil paintings of country landscapes hang from the picture rail and there's an enormous walnut desk with gold edges across the back wall. Behind it is a well-preserved woman in a fitted dress whose perm is tight and yellow-blonde. The name badge above her left breast says 'Madeleine'.

'May I help you?' Her voice is so posh it's intimidating. She sounds like a female version of Simon Callow.

'I'm here to see Toby.' Madeleine stares at my creased shirt and raises an eyebrow. 'He's arranged for me to work here, from today.'

'You're the temp?' She gives a tinkly laugh, as though it's the most ridiculous thing she's ever heard. 'I'll let Mr Trebarwith know that you're here at' – she glances at an ornate gilt clock on the wall '– nine twenty-two.'

'Mr Trebarwith said I didn't need to be here until nine thirty,' I say sweetly, hoping that she can read my mind. What a total cow.

'Annie, there you are.' Toby breezes into reception wearing raspberry-red trousers and a matching V-neck jumper. He's drenched in aftershave and I try not to breathe in when he leans over to kiss me on the cheek. Oops, that didn't work – a suffocating scent of musk flies up my nose and starts tickling the top bit near my eyes. Damn my stupid allergies! I start sneezing over and over while Toby winces and pulls a crisp white handkerchief from his pocket.

'You'd better have this.' He takes a step back as my sneezing reaches a crescendo. 'I see you've met our magnificent Madeleine.'

Madeleine gives me a smug smile while I dab at my streaming eyes with the hanky. I'm leaving black mascara trails all over it and it's probably made of the finest linen.

'Come with me and I'll show you where you'll be working,' says Toby, backing off when my sneezing stops and I try to give the hanky back. I don't blame him. Crumpling it into a sodden ball, I shove it into my bag for washing later.

Toby takes me along a brightly lit corridor which has glass doors leading into offices larger than my flat. In the most enormous one of all is a bald man with the physique of a beach ball who calls out good morning to Toby when we pass by. Toby returns the greeting and, once we're out of earshot, murmurs, 'That's Rafe Johnston-Fulbright. He's a partner here, though who knows for how long. He's clinically obese so there might be opportunities for advancement in the future, if you get my drift.' He clutches at his chest and grins broadly.

At the end of the corridor, he flings open a featureless wooden door and stands back so I can go in first. 'Here's your office for the next six months.'

Toby says office, I say cupboard. The tiny space has no windows, a cheap-looking desk and chair, a phone and a noisy fan which is recirculating stale air. Someone has tacked a couple of fine art posters to the wall in a vain attempt to beautify the space. No wonder poor Abigail needed to 'find herself' – find herself a new job, if she's got any sense.

Toby moves a pile of tattered papers from the chair onto the floor and beckons for me to sit down. 'The job is very straightforward and involves answering the phones when Madeleine is already on a call, typing up letters from our audio tapes and filing. Money for old rope, really.' He points at a tower of manila folders that's about to topple over. 'The filing cabinets are in the basement. You'll soon get used to it and Madeleine will be happy to help if you get stuck.'

Hhmm, I'm not so sure about that.

'So, tell me.' Toby perches on the edge of the desk. 'How does it feel to have escaped Salt Bay?'

'OK.'

'Just OK?' Toby looks puzzled. 'Surely it's wonderful to be back in London, the greatest city on Earth.'

'Of course, it's lovely to be back here and I'm very grateful for this job. Thank you again for arranging it. I guess I just got used to being in Cornwall.'

'Then you got out just in time,' asserts Toby, standing up and stretching his legs. 'I knew you were getting too involved when you said you were resurrecting the choral society. Why on earth would you want to be involved with a bunch of local yokels who think they can sing? Still, you're back in London now so no harm done.' He glances around my new work empire. 'Why don't you get used to your office and then you can get started on the typing and filing. Rafe will expect you to be up to speed pretty quickly.'

He's almost at the door when I ask, 'Why didn't you tell me about Sheila?'

'Who?' Toby swings round, looking puzzled.

'Sheila, my grandmother who's in the dementia home.'

'Oh her! To be totally honest, I forgot about the old girl. I haven't seen Sheila for years, not since she went ga-ga, and I tend to forget she's still alive. Did you go to see her?'

'I didn't know she existed until I found out by accident on Friday.'

'Really?' Toby's eyes narrow and he crosses his arms. 'That's strange, and rather distressing for you that Alice kept it a secret. You must be very upset with her.'

'Not really, I was fine about it,' I lie, not wanting to criticise Alice in front of him. 'Just surprised, that's all.'

'I did warn you that the Trebarwiths are a strange lot, excluding you and me of course. Talking of Alice, how was she doing when you left?'

'Fairly well I think, and Emily will be moving in soon which will help to ensure she can stay at Tregavara House.'

'Great, really great,' says Toby, distractedly, straightening one of the posters on the wall. 'And what about Josh Pasco? Have you seen him recently?'

Seen him. Kissed him. Discovered he's a love rat.

'Our paths haven't crossed.'

'Just as well. Anyway, I'd better get on.'

He's half-way down the corridor when I call after him, 'Why did Josh punch you?'

'What?'

'You told me that he punched you and I wondered why.'

Toby walks back to me and lowers his voice. 'I don't like to speak ill of people but he behaved appallingly with a woman I know.'

'What did he do?' It's like picking at a scab – you know it will sting, but you just can't help yourself.

Toby pushes me into my cupboard and closes the door. 'He got a young woman pregnant and then wanted nothing more to do with her.'

Ooh, that is bad. 'Did she have the baby?' Pick, pick, pick…

'Yes, she did.'

'Does he ever see his son or daughter?'

'No,' says Toby, an angry flush creeping up his neck.

He sniffs loudly while I remember how fondly Josh spoke about Freya. For all his faults, he doesn't seem the sort of man who'd walk away from his own child.

'Are you quite sure about all of this or is it just a rumour?'

'A rumour?' huffs Toby. 'I don't deal in rumours. Believe me, it's completely true. But I've said too much and it was a long time ago.'

'Alice didn't tell me about any of this.'

'Like she didn't tell you about Sheila.'

It's a good point. Cornwall is full of secrets and lies. But I get the feeling that Toby is possibly the biggest liar of all. I know we're related and he got me this job, but the man is starting to creep me out. And I get the feeling he'll one day expect something in return for fixing me up with employment.

Toby leans towards me, almost whispering now. 'Hardly anyone knows the truth about all this. So it's probably best if you don't mention what I've just told you to anyone in Salt Bay. It's best forgotten.'

'Of course, and I don't plan on going back to Salt Bay any time soon.'

'Just as well.' Toby opens my door and waves at Rafe who's come out of his office and is gesturing for Toby to join him. 'I'll catch up with you later. Ask Madeleine if you need anything.'

The first few days in my new job whizz by as I get to grips with the antiquated filing system. Fulbright and Linsom has yet to fully enter the digital age and the company is far from green. There are at least two forests-worth of paper in the filing cabinets lined up in the gloomy basement and more papers are being added to the stack every day.

I sneak a look into some of the folders while I'm going about the filing and marvel at the jaw-dropping financial info. It's amazing how much people will pay for old stuff. Twenty thousand pounds for a vase here; fifty thousand pounds for a painting there; and all the while, Fulbright and Linsom is taking a hefty commission from each sale. Toby must be earning a packet.

Madeleine, as expected, isn't terribly helpful but the job is easy to pick up and surprisingly interesting as I learn about different artists and their work. It's not what I want to do forever but temping here is fine while I get some proper PA work lined up.

On Wednesday evening I've arranged to have a meal out with Maura so I take the Tube to the restaurant in King's Cross where we're meeting. I've been sitting at a table by the window for ten minutes, nursing a glass of Pinot Grigio, when she bustles in, looking flushed.

'Am I late?' She checks her watch and plonks herself down opposite me. 'Paul was late back from work, as usual, so I had to get ready in a rush. Have I got regurgitated rusk down my boobs? Harry was spitting it everywhere.' She scours her cleavage for cereal stains. 'Right, where's the wine? This is my first night out in ages and I intend to get totally wasted.'

When I push her glass of Pinot Grigio across the table, she gulps down half in one go and licks her lips. She's looking great with her blonde hair in a chic chignon and her trendy red-framed glasses on. When she came into the restaurant I noticed she was wearing odd shoes – one black court shoe and one navy blue – but I don't mention it.

'So how's life with the gorgeous Harry, then?'

'Knackering. Awful. Fabulous. Here, look what he's doing now.' Maura pulls out her phone and shows me a video of Harry smiling and clapping his hands. I've only been away a few weeks but he's doubled in size.

'Anyway, enough baby talk.' Maura switches her phone to silent and drops it into her handbag. 'It's lovely to see you and I want to hear all about your adventures in Cornwall so I can live vicariously through you. I especially want to hear more about Sheila rising from the grave – that was totally sick.'

I tell her all about Cornwall while we tuck into spaghetti carbonara and polish off a bottle of house white. Well, I have about a quarter of a bottle and Maura necks the rest. I'm starting to feel as if I'm melting into the chair, while Maura is getting increasingly loud.

'The choir sounds brilliant, Annie. You are clever.' Maura pours a lake of double cream over her tiramisu and runs her finger up the jug to catch the drips. 'You could always set one up around here.'

'There's no point. There are loads of choirs in London already and this one was special.' Salt Bay Choral Society should be meeting tonight and suddenly I wish I was there, welcoming Cyril, encouraging Ollie to sing in tune and giggling at Jennifer's appalled expression during Florence's update on Bob. I cross my fingers that Josh has agreed to keep it running. I've been too scared to text Kayla in case he's refused.

'Are you all right?' Maura is trying to look at me closely but her eyes aren't focusing too well.

'I was just thinking.'

'About your lovely, sexy new boyfriend?' A young couple behind her turn round and grin at me.

'No,' I hiss, gesturing for Maura to lower her voice. 'He's obviously not my boyfriend, unless kissing the face off your friend is some kind of Cornish foreplay. And anyway, since I saw him with Kayla, I've discovered more bad stuff about him.'

Maura pauses with her spoon halfway to her mouth. 'Ooh, what?'

'He got a girl pregnant and then abandoned her and the baby.'

'Says who?'

'Says Toby.'

Maura drops the spoon into her bowl and frowns. 'Do you think he's telling you the truth? No offence but he sounds like a bit of a douchebag.'

I choose my words carefully because Toby might be a slimeball but he's a Trebarwith slimeball and I can't help feeling a tug of familial loyalty. 'I have no idea what the real story is because Toby has his own agenda, though I'm not sure what it is.'

'Hhmmm.' Maura is disappointed by my inability to slag off the 'douchebag'. 'It's a shame because Josh is hot.'

'Looks aren't everything, Maura.'

'Maybe not, but it helps if the bloke you're banging is fit. Talking of which, did you notice the last time you were round at our place that Paul is getting jowly? I think he's letting himself go. That's what happens when couples have children. It all goes to pot.' She scoops an obscene amount of sponge onto her spoon and shovels it into her mouth.

'Paul is lovely, and you're just going through a difficult patch at the moment. That's what happens when you have a baby and stop having sex and stuff. I'm sure things will get easier as Harry gets older.'

Maura nods disconsolately while she chews and swallows. 'So tell me what you miss about Cornwall. So far you've only told me the bad bits – the undead granny, the cheating boyfriend, the appalling weather, the lack of phone signal' – she shudders – 'but there must be some good bits about Salt Bay and discovering a long-lost family.'

'There's an amazingly beautiful beach. It's like something out of a Seychelles ad, and it's empty. Just loads of clean, yellow sand, seaweed and rock pools. Harry would love it. And there's a brilliant cave where smugglers used to hide their contraband.'

Maura takes another slug of wine. 'Contraband? Fancy.' She's slurring her words slightly and drips of carbonara sauce have splattered all down the front of her dress.

'The air was fresh too with no pollution, and the fish was straight off the boat and tasted divine, and the weather was amazing sometimes, even when it was pants. I was up on the cliffs one day and the sky was black with storm clouds and the sea was thundering against the rocks, and all of a sudden the sun broke through and lit a sparkly path across the water, as if it was leading the way to heaven.'

I pause, feeling embarrassed, but Maura gestures for me to carry on. 'I also grew really fond of the people in the choir, especially an old boy called Cyril. And Alice, of course, because she's lovely. I suppose it was nice to have family for a while and to feel as if I mattered to someone. But then Alice started slagging off my mum and I remembered that I'm better off on my own.'

'Yeah, that was a bit of a downer.' Maura reaches across the table and grabs my hands. 'It's true that you don't have anyone in the whole wide world but you'll always matter to me 'cos you're my lovely, lonely friend. And I promise I'll come and visit when you're old with dementia and I'll never pretend that you don't exist.'

Gee, thanks Maura. She's only trying to be nice, though, so I squeeze her hands and concentrate on my good fortune. It's lovely to be sitting here with her, in the middle of an exciting city that never sleeps. With shops on every corner and museums and parks and fantastic buildings and 4G Internet. Everything is easy and simple and just as it should be. If only I could stop worrying about Alice, and thinking about Josh, and wondering if Salt Bay Choral Society still exists.

Chapter Twenty-Seven

I've survived a whole fortnight at Fulbright and Linsom when an email from Kayla pings into my inbox. Checking my Hotmail during work hours is against one of Rafe's many rules so I scoot over on my wheely chair and kick the door shut. It feels even more like a coffin in here now.

Kayla's email reads: Hey stranger, how's life in the big, bad city? I'm in London overnight on Friday so let's hook up. It'll have to be short and sweet – how about 6 p.m.? Anywhere near Victoria station will be fine. Love K x

I reread it a few times, biting my lip. It's the first time we've been in touch since exchanging brief emails just after I left Salt Bay. I didn't mention seeing her with Josh; Kayla sounded put out I'd left Cornwall without telling her and, just like that, our relationship subtly shifted. Before my hasty departure it was fun and easy, but now there are secrets and resentments between us.

I could say I'm busy on Friday evening and put Salt Bay behind me but I'm keen to know how Alice is doing. Although I've called her to check she's all right, our conversation was stilted and left me feeling more worried and guilty than ever. Kayla can also fill me in on what's happening with my choir, though I guess it's not 'my choir' any more. Even so, I can't stop thinking about it and almost accosted a man in Starbucks yesterday because he looked like Tom from the back. It was the purple pants peeping above the top of his low-slung jeans that did it.

Quickly, before I can change my mind, I send a reply saying that I'd love to meet up and suggest a bar I know round the corner from Victoria station.

After the email has gone, I sit back and look around my office. I'm getting used to the cramped space, lack of natural light and the smell from the office next door that belongs to finance director Malcolm. I'm sure Malcolm showers every day and has a very fragrant body odour – I've never got close enough to sniff him – but his lunchtime diet appears to consist entirely of pongy egg sandwiches, and the smell wafts.

Even Madeleine doesn't seem so bad these days and we've settled on an uneasy truce, mainly because she has a sweet tooth and I'm not above bribing people with chocolate cake to like me.

Toby has been out of the office for much of the last fortnight because a couple of big auctions are coming up. Everyone is rushing round getting things ready and I've been roped in to help out, which is far more fun than typing, filing and picking up Madeleine's overspill calls.

Friday is particularly hectic which means I'm late leaving work and end up rushing to the Tube station in my tight-fitting dress. Thanks to Rafe, I've had to raise my game when it comes to work clothes, even though I work in a cupboard and never see clients. The man might look affable and roly-poly but he's a stickler for the rules which include no jeans, no cords, no sweatshirts – and absolutely no tattoos. I don't have any but Madeleine never reveals her arms, which is suspicious. Hitching my dress higher up my thighs so I can take longer strides, I weave my way through the pavement throng towards the Tube and hope I'll make it to the bar before Kayla.

It's the height of rush hour at Angel station and the place is heaving with people squashed onto the escalator taking us deep into the bowels of the earth. I'm surprised by how disorientating it is being swept along with the crowd, and how annoyed I get these days when people stand too close to me.

I got soft in Salt Bay and forgot there's no such thing as personal space when travelling in London. With well over eight million people living here, things are bound to get up close and personal. And that's OK. It's the price we pay for living in the greatest city in the world. So I push down my annoyance, close my eyes as I'm being crammed into a stranger's damp armpit, and imagine I'm on the beach at Salt Bay with seagulls wheeling above me and waves crashing onto golden sand. Imagining the smell of seaweed and ozone almost blots out the acrid whiff of commuter sweat.

At last I reach the bar and grab a window seat to watch people scuttling past. Telling the difference between tourists and Londoners is easy. Tourists tend to loiter along with their cameras before stopping abruptly, while Londoners rush past mouthing obscenities when tourists get in their way. Which they do. All the blessed time. There's that bubble of annoyance again which has been a constant companion since my return from Cornwall. It's like having perpetual PMT. Salt Bay has taken the sheen off my home city. Where once I saw mainly glitz and glamour, now I notice the noise, the crush and the dirt. Everywhere is so grubby. Taking a deep breath, I settle back in my chair and try to relax.

Suddenly, there's a flash of red on the opposite side of the road and I spot Kayla with her hair tied back in a ponytail. Chuffing hell! Kayla has brought Josh with her. While I stare out of the window in horror, the two of them clasp hands and leg it across the road between a stream of cars and taxis. Josh looks fashionably casual in jeans and a battered leather jacket, and his thick black hair flicks into his eyes as he dodges round the back of a bus. I feel sick.

When the two of them burst into the bar, flushed from their sprint across the road, Kayla sees me at once and waves frantically.

'Hey Annie!' Heads turn as the pretty, flame-haired Aussie makes her way between the tables. 'It's so good to see you.' She plants a huge smacker on my cheek while Josh hangs back. He's had a haircut and looks tidier than usual but there's a dark shadow of stubble across his strong jaw that looks sexy as hell. What is wrong with me? I force myself to think of Stuart's clean-shaven jaw and immaculate clothing. That's the sort of man I go for. Clean-cut. Metrosexual. Uncomplicated and cheerful. London-based. It's true that he turned out to be a cheating git, but you can't have everything.

Thinking about Stuart isn't working so I picture Josh and Kayla kissing passionately and remember how quickly he moved on from kissing me. That definitely does the trick! I glower at Josh when he sits down and gives me a slight nod across the table. He seems ill at ease and stands up immediately, pushing his chair back across the concrete floor with a scraping sound that puts my teeth on edge.

'Can I get both you ladies a drink? I could do with a pint.'

Once we've given him our orders, Kayla watches Josh weave past people to the bar and then drags her chair round next to me.

'It's so weird seeing you here rather than in Salt Bay, and you look super sophisticated in that dress. You'd never have managed the death slide to the beach in that.'

'Ha, perish the thought! It's lovely to see you too, Kayla, but what are you doing in London?'

'Helping Josh. He's supervising a load of science nerds from his school who went to a talk about the Francis Crick Institute this morning and to the Science Museum this arvo. It was really fascinating but, believe me, you do not want to know how much bacteria is living inside you. It's gross.' A huge cheer goes up as a glass shatters on the hard floor and Kayla shuffles closer so I can hear. 'I stepped in to help with the trip 'cos the science teacher coming with Josh ruptured his Achilles tendon last week. I've helped with trips before so I've already been checked out by the school.'

'How long are you up here?' I have to shout above the wailing of an ambulance rushing past on blue lights.

'Only two nights. We got here late yesterday and had to settle the kids in. They're seventeen and a nightmare with rampaging hormones so we're having to make sure there's no boy-girl bed hopping.'

'How's Alice doing?' I ask quickly, keen to move on from bed hopping.

'Not so bad. I've been keeping an eye on her since you left and Emily is about to move in. I bumped into her the other day while she was wandering round the village and we had a chat. She's quite' – Kayla frowns – 'old-fashioned, but she seems great. Oh, that was quick.'

Kayla moves her bag off the table to make room for the tray of drinks Josh is carrying, while I ignore a flash of disquiet that Emily is about to take my place. It was never 'my place', just as Salt Bay with its windswept beach and fledgling choir was never going to be my home.

'The prices here are crazy. Roger would have a heart attack,' grumbles Josh, thrusting the change into his jacket pocket and handing out the drinks; a white wine for me, gin and tonic for Kayla and a pint of bitter for him.

'Josh isn't a huge fan of London,' grins Kayla, winking at me.

'Why did you come up with the students, then? There must have been another teacher who'd do it.'

Josh takes a sip of his beer and wipes foam from his lip. 'To be honest, none of us were clamouring to come up here and leave the fresh air of Cornwall behind.'

'And the rain.'

'Does it never rain in London, then?' asks Josh snippily, his dark eyes glinting in the bar's halogen lights. 'I suppose you get nothing but wall-to-wall sunshine three hundred and sixty-five days of the year.'

'Ha ha, hardly.' Kayla flashes me a 'what's his problem?' look. 'Though to be fair, it's done nothing but chuck it down since you left us, Annie. Cornwall is crying out for you to come back.'

'What about the choir?' I ask, sidestepping any further conversation about me returning.

'The choir's doing great, thanks to Josh.' Kayla has a slurp of gin and pats Josh on the back, making his leather jacket creak. 'He's been a star and has taken over running it since you had to leave. Jennifer insisted it should be her at first, but she's coming round thanks to Josh's charm and overall fabulousness.'

The thought of Josh being charming makes me choke on my Chardonnay but I'm incredibly relieved that he's running the choir, and grateful too.

'That's very good of you, Josh. Is the concert still going ahead?'

'That's the plan, though there's lots of work to do.' Josh sits back, looking bored or sulky or tired. He's almost impossible to read.

'And how are your family doing?' I'm determined to be an adult and make conversation even if he is having a strop.

'Fine, thank you.' Josh hugs his beer close to his chest. 'Alice is keeping Serena on a couple of times a week even after Emily moves in.'

'That's good news and I know Serena will be pleased.'

Josh merely shrugs but I battle on.

'Where are your students while you and Kayla are here with me?'

'At a hotel round the corner. They're under strict orders to sit and watch TV until we get back, and there's a student teacher with us who's keeping an eye on them. We're taking them to see a show so we can't stay long.'

He glances at his watch while I wonder if he and Kayla have booked one or two rooms in their Victoria hotel. I knock back the last of my wine and wish I'd ordered a larger glass.

After a while I give up trying to talk to Josh and he sits quietly while Kayla and I catch up on life in Salt Bay and London. He's causing quite a stir in the bar, which is packed with twenty-something women, but he doesn't seem to notice, not even when two spray-tanned girls in micro-minis walk past a few times and shoot me daggers looks. They must be mad if they think we look like a happy couple.

'So what about your love life?' I ask Kayla when Josh disappears to the loo at last. If she is still romantically entwined with Josh, I'm in two minds about mentioning the abandoned baby, especially since the information came from Toby, who's not the most reliable source.

Kayla's face lights up as if she's about to burst with happiness.

'It's brilliant! He says we're made for each other and he was an idiot not to realise it before.' Wow, that feels weird. As though someone has clouted me in the stomach.

'I think I might want to spend the rest of my life with Ollie,' adds Kayla dreamily.

'With Josh, you mean.'

Kayla runs her hands through her hair and laughs. 'No, with Ollie. Why the hell would I want to spend my life with old grumpy pants? Though he's not so bad when you get to know him. Why on earth would you think I was getting it on with Josh?'

'Because I saw you and him all over each other in the pub,' I stutter, feeling hot and clammy. Nothing is making sense but I think I might have made a mistake. A big one.

Kayla wrinkles her nose. 'When? What are you talking about?'

'The day I left Salt Bay and went back to London, after I found out about Sheila still being alive. I nipped into the pub to find you and saw you and Josh kissing. Proper kissing.'

'Oh, that.' Kayla raises her voice when a group of men in suits behind her start laughing loudly. 'I didn't realise you saw that. It was a ruse.'

'A what?' I yell so she can hear me.

'A ruse.' The men behind her have quietened down and she leans forward until our heads are almost touching. 'Don't speak too loudly. I don't want the whole pub to know about my wiles.'

She's lost me completely. 'Your what?'

'My wiles. Feminine wiles. I adore Ollie and he felt the same way only he hadn't realised it. Chloe didn't help, sniffing around and messing with his mind. She's such a cow. So I helped him make up his mind with some assistance from Josh.'

I'm still staring at her.

'Jeez, keep up Annie. Don't you have any wiles of your own? I wanted to make Ollie jealous so I kissed Josh in front of Kieran.'

'Who's Kieran? That young kid going moony over you in the pub? What's he got to do with it?'

'Everything. That kid is Ollie's cousin and worships the ground he walks on. I knew he'd report back that I was kissing Josh, which he did. And it totally did the trick. Ollie asked me out right away. He said he realised what he might lose if he didn't make a move quickly. See? Feminine wiles. You should get some.' Kayla folds her arms, looking mightily pleased with herself.

'But surely Ollie asked Josh about the whole kissing thing and realised he'd been… *rused*?'

Kayla snorts with laughter. 'Oh Annie, do you know men at all? They don't talk to one another about personal things. They'll chat away for ages about cars and *Peaky Blinders* and the size of their boats. But discussing issues of the heart and appearing vulnerable in front of another alpha male? You've gotta be kidding. They'd rather sit through a chick-flick. Anyway, just to make sure, I got Josh on board. That's why I'm helping him out in London, to repay the favour.'

'So he knew about the ruse.'

She grins and starts ripping chunks off a beer mat. 'Not at first. He thought I'd gone mad when I pounced on him. But after Kieran scuttled off and I explained what I was doing, he said it was about time Ollie made his mind up and settled down. I used to think Josh was a knobhead but he's a lot nicer than he first appears.'

'So Ollie still thinks that you and Josh were together for a while.'

'Nah. After Ollie had been ensnared by my overall fabulousness, I told him Kieran got the wrong end of the stick and Josh and I were just friends. Ollie was relieved and now everything is wonderful.' She starts swaying with a dreamy expression on her face.

'Just to be totally sure, you're not and never have been in any sort of romantic relationship with Josh.'

Kayla shakes her head. 'Why?' Suddenly, she starts gasping and shifting in her chair. 'Bloody hell!' she yells. 'You want to have Josh Pasco's babies.'

Jeez, there's no need to tell the whole bar!

'Shush!'

Kayla has knocked over her glass and I dab at the dregs of her G&T with a clean tissue.

'Of course I don't want his babies. You're being ridiculous.'

'Ha! You've fallen under the Pasco spell,' stage-whispers Kayla. 'I can't quite see it myself. He's too dark and brooding for me even though his backside is top notch. But why didn't you tell me you had the hots for JP?'

'I'm not sure how I feel about Josh and I don't think he likes me that much. It's pointless anyway because I live in London and he lives in the back of bleeding beyond. No offence. Why didn't you tell me about your ruse?'

'Honestly? I thought you might not approve. You're quite prudish sometimes and I don't know what you're thinking most of the time because you're very…' She pauses. 'Self-contained and independent. You don't trust people, Annie, and you're scared to let them into your safe city life.'

Psychoanalysed and summed up by a love-struck Aussie in a noisy London bar. Nice.

'So what are you going to do about it?' demands Kayla.

'About what?'

She gives an exaggerated sigh and slumps theatrically across the table. 'About Josh, you drongo. Now you know that I'm not abusing his body. Although…' She runs her tongue along her lips.

'Stop it, Kayla,' I hiss because Josh is making his way back towards us. My head is reeling with what I've just learned and now I have to make small talk with him. Awkward doesn't even begin to describe it – and then Kayla makes it worse.

'Hey Joshie, welcome back. Where are the toilets? I suddenly have an overwhelming urge to pee.' She gives me an exaggerated wink and bustles off, leaving us alone together while I mentally cross her off my Christmas card list.

Josh takes a seat and starts drumming his fingers on the table.

'So Josh, did you ever get back together with Felicity?' That was the last thing I meant to ask but the first thing that came out of my mouth. I look at Josh, aghast, but he just shakes his head and keeps on drumming.

'Why not? She's gorgeous. She's tall and slim and pretty with fabulous shiny hair. Not like mine that goes frizzy in the rain.' Stop talking, Annie! I clamp my lips tightly shut to stop the words tumbling out.

'I didn't want to get back together with Felicity,' says Josh in his rich, dark-chocolate voice, putting his hands into his lap.

We sit in silence for a few moments before we both start talking over one another.

'You go first,' I insist. 'I was only going to bore you about my new job.'

'The job that Toby arranged for you, by all accounts.' His words are loaded with sarcasm and put my back up.

'That's right. Because Toby's family and that's what families do, help one another. Like the Waltons or – or the Mafia.' I wish I could take back the Mafia reference as soon as the words are out of my mouth but it's too late. The Trebarwiths have now become the Corleones of south-east Cornwall.

'I was sorry to say goodbye to the choir,' I blurt out to cover my embarrassment.

'Even though you didn't,' remarks Josh, gazing at me coolly.

'What do you mean?'

'You didn't actually say goodbye to them, or to any of us.' He sits up straighter, looking flushed. 'The thing that happened in the garden when I picked up Serena – I apologised at the time and said it shouldn't have happened, so you getting upset and rushing off the next day was a huge overreaction because you needn't have worried that I'd pounce on you again. Although you're very attractive, you're not irresistible and I would have managed to control myself. Somehow.'

He raises an eyebrow and sits back with his arms folded and the muscle in his jaw working overtime. The arrogance of the man is breathtaking, thinking that I left Salt Bay early just because he kissed me. But mixed in with my indignation is a treacherous little thought that whirls round my brain: Josh Pasco thinks I'm attractive. Very attractive. I'm appalled when I realise I've pulled back my shoulders, which lifts my boobs and pushes them forward – it must be a reflex action when a handsome man pays me a compliment. I'm so sorry, Germaine; I am a terrible feminist.

'I didn't leave Salt Bay early because of what happened in the garden,' I say as levelly as possible. 'I left because I found out that my grandmother, the one who abandoned my mother when she was pregnant, is still alive and my great-aunt was keeping it a secret.' Which does sound rather Mafia-like but that can't be helped.

'Why would she keep that a secret, for goodness' sake?' splutters Josh. 'Good grief, you Trebarwiths make out you're all holier than thou but you'd give Jeremy Kyle a run for his money. It's all secrets and lies.'

'What exactly is your problem with the Trebarwiths?' I shoot back, not caring that people around us have stopped talking. 'You had a run-in with Toby a few years ago. I get that, but isn't it about time you got over it and stopped blaming the whole lot of us?' I'm tempted to throw in the abandoned-baby rumour to judge his reaction but too many people are earwigging.

Josh glances round at our audience and bites his lip before saying in a low voice, 'I don't blame the lot of you, though I do think it was pretty shabby to leave Salt Bay without saying goodbye.'

For a moment he looks hurt and the urge to stroke my fingers across his strong, handsome face is back. I've always been a sucker for vulnerability – in Mum, in Alice, in Stuart, who told me the first time we met that he cried when his cat died. But Josh swallows and his expression hardens.

'The choir were upset that you disappeared without a word so close to the concert, and before we'd properly sorted out a replacement for you,' he says. 'Cyril, in particular, was very disappointed.'

The thought of having disappointed poor bereaved Cyril makes me want to cry and I pinch my thigh hard to stop myself. I can picture them all in that ancient church, slagging me off for leaving and – far worse – thinking that I don't care about them.

'I'm sorry,' I mumble into my empty glass. 'What Alice told me was a shock and I had to get away. It was nothing to do with what happened in the garden, and you made it very clear at the time that you regretted it.'

'Only because anything between us would be pointless with you about to leave Salt Bay. I'd been keeping my distance on purpose.'

'So you didn't kiss me by mistake.' My mouth appears to be in full 'speak before engaging your brain' mode.

'What on earth are you going on about? Do you really think that I kissed you by accident?' The corner of Josh's full mouth twitches and tiny crow's feet fan out around his eyes. 'I think you're probably the strangest woman I've ever met,' he says, pulling in his chair closer to the table.

The sound around me becomes muffled as Josh leans towards me, his dark eyes focused on my mouth.

'As well as the most annoying,' he murmurs.

Chuffing hell, I think he might be about to kiss me again, so I let his last remark slide.

'Are you finished with these?' A gigantic man in a neon-yellow T-shirt barges between us and grabs hold of our empty glasses with hands like two slabs of meat. 'Happy Hour finishes in five minutes so get your refills now,' he intones lifelessly, a vision of boredom. The glasses clank together when he lumbers off, trailing a scent of fried food, and Josh pulls back from the table. The spell is broken, and I'm not sure now that Josh was going to kiss me anyway.

'Woah, did that bloke take away my G&T?' demands Kayla, who's just appeared wiping her wet hands on her trousers. 'There was a bit left in the bottom and I need all the alcohol I can get if I'm spending the evening supervising teenagers. Talking of which, have you seen the time, Josh?' She pulls back her sleeve and shoves her watch into his face. 'The curtain goes up in forty-five minutes. We're taking the kids to see *Wicked*,' she explains, slinging her bag over her shoulder. 'I've learned all the songs so I can sing along. It'll be good practice for the choir. Is everything all right with you two?'

'Fine.' Josh gets to his feet and zips up his leather jacket while I scramble up from the table. There's something I must say to him before they leave.

'Please tell Cyril and the rest of the choir I'm sorry for leaving so abruptly, and thank you for keeping the choir going. I really appreciate it and I'm sure your dad would be proud of you.'

Josh stares over my shoulder at the cars and taxis gridlocked outside. 'Will you come back for the concert?'

I'm tempted, I really am, but Josh hit the nail on the head in Alice's garden – what's the point when my life is here in London? What's the point of getting involved, and hurt?

'I don't think so.'

Josh nods as though that was the answer he expected. 'Come on then, Kayla, or we'll be late for the show. Goodbye Annie; look after yourself.'

Kayla flings herself into my arms and hugs me tight. 'Ooh, I wish we had longer. Please come back and see us in Salt Bay before too long. The place isn't the same without you and half the locals are mad as a meat-axe.'

After checking that Josh is heading for the door, she whispers in my ear, 'How did things go with Mr Hotness?' and hugs me tighter when I shake my head.

'I can speak to him about it if you like.' But she looks relieved when I tell that her that she's never to mention anything about it to anyone. On pain of death.

Tearing herself away, she gives me a smacking kiss on the cheek and races after Josh, who's waiting on the pavement.

'Enjoy the show and don't sing along too loudly!' I shout. At least I think that's what I say. My head is spinning with all that has happened in the last half hour or so and I can't think clearly. All I want to do is chase after Josh, fling my arms round his neck and see if he still smells of cedar wood. Which in one tiny way would be lovely, but in every other gigantic way would be a Very Bad Idea. He's tied to his family in Cornwall three hundred miles away – and I can't be tied to mine.

So I wave at Kayla through the window and grin like a loon while Josh crosses the road without a backward glance and is swallowed up in a crush of people rushing past.

Chapter Twenty-Eight

There's a box waiting for me when I get home from work a few days after meeting up with Kayla and Josh. The battered shoebox has been placed in the middle of the coffee table and I recognise it immediately. It belonged to Mum. Sighing, I make myself a cup of coffee, sit on the lumpy sofa and rub my head which has been aching for hours.

I was rubbish at work today because I kept thinking about Salt Bay; or, to be more accurate, about Josh in the bar. Was he about to kiss me again? I'm not sure, but I really wanted him to. Partly – I can't help it – because I fancy the pants off him, but mostly because of that flash of hurt vulnerability I've noticed in him before. It strips away his moody layers and gets to the sensitive man underneath. A man who's given up everything to support his family – whereas I've done a runner from mine.

'It would never work,' I say out loud to myself. 'How could I possibly live in Salt Bay and give up everything I have here?' I glance round the muddled, empty flat and the ready meal for one peeping out of my carrier bag. Even if I could, one thing I can never give up is being a Trebarwith and that would always come between us. 'Don't worry, Germaine, I'm not about to change my whole life for a man,' I murmur, picking up the note on top of the shoebox that Gracie's scrawled on a used envelope. It reads: *Found this under your bed during my clear-out. Do you still want it?*

The note raises a couple of worrying questions.

1. When is Gracie going to move out? No time soon, judging by the way she's ferreting under my bed as if she owns the place. She keeps promising she's looking for somewhere else to live but there's no evidence of flat-hunting. No newspaper adverts or Internet searching or viewing appointments. At least she's now sleeping on the sofa and I've got my bed back, but I need to be more firm about a moving out deadline.
2. What exactly is she clearing out? If it's her stuff, that's fine; the bedroom is still jam-packed with her possessions with mine shoved into a corner. But it's not so good if she's ousting my stuff in a stealthy takeover bid.

When Amber and Gracie get home, I'll have a word and hope Gracie doesn't get hysterical. She threw a wobbly when asked to clean fake-tan stains off the bath, so bringing up her moving-out date will probably herald an evening of door slamming. Oh, the joys of living with hormonal teenagers.

I turn my attention back to the box, which is crammed to the brim with bits of paper, old bills and receipts. Mum kept strange things. She'd throw out important information like school reports and NHS numbers, but hang on to bills from way back. The first piece of paper I pull out proves my point. It's an electricity bill for our tiny Crouch End flat, from June 1998. I haven't thought about that flat for ages. It was one of the few we lived in that had outside space for me to play, and I was so sad when we moved out after a few months. We had to move because Mum was convinced the neighbours were spying on us.

I've not looked at the box since Mum died and I cleared out her things. At the time I was too cut up to deal with her paperwork so I shoved the box out of sight and forgot all about it.

Perhaps now is the right time to go through it and get rid of stuff. Maybe a clear-out will help me to get back on track and back to how I used to be – before Alice and Salt Bay, before Josh.

Yep, I'm going in. Taking a deep breath, I start flicking through the curling bills and scraps of paper. Jeez, Mum kept a load of crap. There are receipts for who-knows-what stretching back over twenty years, several ancient red bills and a bailiff's letter I never knew about.

Buried among the dross, I'm touched to find a drawing in thick crayon with 'Sept 1993' pencilled in the corner. Both stick-people in the picture have green hair but the one with bright blue splodges for eyes must be me. I run my finger across the chunky writing underneath – 'Mummy and me' – and try to remember how it felt to be young and unaware of life's challenges. The 'throw away' pile on the coffee table is getting higher but I put my drawing into a new 'keep' pile.

Towards the bottom of the box there's a ripped-open envelope with a letter inside on thick Basildon Bond paper. The writing is large and looping like mine.

Dearest Joanna. I'm not sure where you are so I've asked people who know you to forward this letter on. I hope and pray that it will eventually reach you. I want to ask you to please come home. The house is so quiet and empty without you. Your father is a proud man, but he regrets what was said and I'm sure he will come round if you come home with your baby.

It's signed 'Your loving mother.'

I'm not sure how long I sit staring at the letter. Mum was lying when she said her family had cut her off completely. This letter is proof of that, and everything I thought was true has shifted.

Carefully placing the letter on the 'keep' pile, I delve further into the box and pull out a tattered newspaper cutting that was hidden underneath the envelope. It's yellowing and faded with age but the headline jumps out in thick, black letters: *Seven drown in Cornish fishing tragedy*. The story is only a few paragraphs long and gives only brief details about the storm that hit Salt Bay, but Samuel is named among the dead.

Mum knew! She knew that Sheila wanted her to come home; she knew that her dad had drowned and her mum was all alone. Yet she still didn't tell me. Or go home. Alice was right all along.

Now the initial shock is wearing off, I feel a rush of hot anger. I've never been properly angry with Mum before, not even when she showed me up at the school gates with her strange behaviour. Instinctively, I knew she was fragile and couldn't help it. But now there's so much I want to ask Mum but I can't because I found out too late.

I want to know why she kept all this a secret from me and why she never went home, and another question is niggling at the edges of my mind. Why did she deprive me of belonging to a proper family and sentence me to a life of flat-hopping around the seedier parts of London?

Sentence is too strong a word. I shake my head to dislodge the mutinous thought but it won't budge, even though I wouldn't have changed growing up in this city. The flats might have been rubbish but Mum and I had some good times together, dodging the Saturday crowds on Oxford Street, paddling in the Serpentine, riding to the end of Underground lines and exploring where we found ourselves. Thinking about our happy times together always makes me smile.

But there could have been lazy holidays by the sea as well, and ice creams on Salt Bay's magical beach. And grandparents, Alice, a family. They were things I never wanted because I thought they didn't want me, but I was wrong.

Picking up my grandmother's letter, I smooth out the creases in the blue paper and feel unutterably sad. The fallout from my mother's decisions have reverberated down the decades, leaving a lonely widow waiting in vain for a daughter who never came home. And me, twenty-nine years old and completely alone, living in a cramped flat with people who don't want me here. I'm not a free spirit. I'm unloved and lonely.

Why does it feel as if an elephant has parked its wrinkly backside on my chest? This must be what a panic attack feels like. It's getting harder and harder to breathe and a strange whooshing sound in my head is blocking out shouts from the street below. I read somewhere that a panic attack won't kill you but, knowing my luck, I'll be the one person who drops dead. I'll end up a footnote in a text book for medical students: Annabella Sunshine Trebarwith, the woman who panicked herself to death.

Reaching shakily for my cup of coffee, I take a huge gulp but it's stone cold and that's the final straw.

Hurling the cup at the wall, I start to cry. Not in a genteel way, that's not my style. My crying consists of snotty, gulping, ugly sobs that fill the flat while muddy-brown liquid runs down the wall and pools on the carpet.

The last time I cried like this was after Mum's funeral, while her hippy friends put down their spliffs, patted me awkwardly on the shoulder and burbled on about nirvana. The neighbours will think I'm being murdered but I don't care.

After snotting and gulping my way through half a box of tissues, I feel spent and strangely calm. Coffee has soaked into the grey carpet, but I don't care if the landlord makes me pay for it to be cleaned. Nothing really matters. I fetch a wet cloth and I'm half-heartedly attempting to clean it up when Amber and Gracie bowl in through the front door, arm in arm and laughing.

They stop dead at the sight of me, hair all over the place, with red, swollen eyes and on my knees, scrubbing coffee from the wall.

'Is everything OK?' squeaks Amber, giving Gracie a 'she's gone mental' glance. 'Did you spill your drink? Don't worry about it.' She scurries across the room and starts placing broken china onto the coffee table. 'There's no need to get upset. I'm sure it can be cleaned up and we can buy another cup just the same, can't we Gracie?'

Gracie nods, her eyes huge.

'We'll help you clear it up, won't we?'

Another mute nod from Gracie.

'And then I'll make you another coffee and everything will seem better.'

Amber is sweet and helps me to clear up the mess and we move a chair on top of the stained carpet. Out of sight, out of mind and all that. A new cup of steaming coffee is presented to me by Gracie, who backs away quickly while I take it out onto the balcony and look across the lights of Stratford.

I take a sip and wince as the thick treacly liquid hits the back of my throat. Gracie must have stirred in half a dozen teaspoons of sugar but at least she cared enough to make me a drink. I give her a small wave through the open balcony door and she smiles back. Maybe I'll give her a bit more leeway about moving out.

Cars are streaming out of the Westfield centre and people are walking home from work. Things around me are normal but I feel weird after my huge crying jag. Everything seems to have slowed down, including my thinking, which is crystal clear now the panic attack has faded.

Mum was eccentric, a one-off and – I admit properly to myself for the first time – often very unwell. She made some strange decisions and kept the truth from me but it wasn't all her fault. Hopping about from flat to flat meant she never saw the same GP twice and didn't get the help she needed. She rarely went to the doctors anyway because she didn't trust them. That's why she ignored the lump in her breast for so long.

But now Mum's gone and I know the truth. Where does that leave me?

Chapter Twenty-Nine

By the next morning, I've decided the best thing to do is talk things over with Toby. All I've had from Kayla recently is a text with a smiley face, saying she got back to Cornwall safely. And Maura is out of action, dealing with what she delicately referred to as Harry's 'runny tummy', before launching into a detailed description of his nappy contents. Let's just say that I won't be eating curry for some time.

Toby is a strange choice of confidante but he's family, he knows the people involved and maybe he knows more about what happened thirty years ago than he's letting on. I don't need to tell him about Mum's more bizarre behaviour.

His office is empty when I poke my head round the door first thing. I haven't been in here before and it's pretty impressive; not overly large but light with a huge sash window and sunbeams flooding in across his sparkling, glass-topped desk.

My desk is piled high with papers, pens and tissues. Toby's desk is the least cluttered I've ever seen and a thing of beauty. All that's on it is a chunky gold pen, a wireless mouse and a ginormous silver-backed computer screen. Above me, a gold ceiling fan is turning noiselessly, wafting the leaves of a glossy plant in a corner of the room. Everything is calm and peaceful.

I want Toby's feng-shui office. I want it with all my heart. If I was working in here I'd be more organised, more disciplined, more driven.

Hell, I could rule the world from this gorgeous place. Checking no one is around, I sink into Toby's high-backed leather chair and twirl round. Glass shelves behind me are packed with hardback books about fine art and there's a small gilt plaque on one shelf with *Toby Trebarwith* picked out in black, like a proper VIP.

Outside the window, everything looks cold and grubby and grey. But inside it's an oasis of squeaky-clean calm.

Swinging back round, I notice that Toby's computer screen is switched on and there's a beautiful picture on screen; a painting of a woman and her child standing in the wind with a steel-grey sea behind them. The woman has her hair up and is wearing a long dress, and the baby – I can't tell if it's a boy or girl – is in a flowing old-fashioned christening robe. In the left-hand corner, almost out of the painting, is an ancient church tower built of grey stone.

The painting is so detailed it could almost be a photograph and it seems familiar. The wild background, the rich colours, the luminosity of the woman's face; they remind me of the painting in Alice's sitting room, of the woman who looks like me with her oval face and high cheekbones.

There's a line of text underneath the painting: 'Cornish Christening. Painted by Ludo Van Teel in 1863. Sold at auction in Geneva, January 2016, for £75,000.' Hang on a minute, I read that wrong. It was sold for £755,000. Over three-quarters of a million pounds. What the…?

'What are you doing in here, young lady?' Malcolm sweeps into the office carrying a pile of folders.

'I'm waiting to speak to Toby,' I stutter, trying not to sound guilty which is a sure-fire way of sounding like you've just murdered someone.

'Are you now?' Malcolm brushes past me to check what I'm looking at on the computer screen and I take a sniff. Nope, he doesn't smell of eggy sandwiches. Malcolm doesn't really smell of anything. Just clean.

'I see you're admiring Ludo Van Teel, a much overlooked artist who's recently been discovered by collectors.'

'I love this picture. Where was it painted?'

'We don't know for sure; somewhere in Cornwall.' Malcolm puts his folders onto the desk, fastens a button on his straining pink shirt and moves too close to me. His face looks pinched and I'm sure he's trying to hold his stomach in. 'The artist is Dutch but spent two years in Cornwall in the mid 1800s, I believe. He loved the rugged coastline and mainly painted landscapes but he made money doing commissions for people, usually portraits. It's a travesty his genius was never recognised during his lifetime.'

He caresses the painting with his middle finger, leaving a greasy streak across the screen.

'Are there lots of undiscovered paintings by him?' I ask, an idea half-forming in my mind.

'Probably.' Malcolm is staring at the painting with a soppy expression on his face. 'Toby reckons he's on to one, the sly dog. He won't say where but he says he'll have his hands on it before too long. Why?'

'No reason. I don't really know anything about art,' I say sweetly, while my brain whirrs at ninety miles per hour. What if Alice's painting is a Ludo Van Teel? She could be sitting on a goldmine without realising it. And if that's the case, why hasn't Toby mentioned it?

Talk of the devil.

'Are you having a party without me?' Toby appears carrying a Starbucks coffee in one hand and his mobile in the other.

'Hardly. We'll hold off on the celebrations until after the auctions, old chap,' guffaws Malcolm. His comb-over has been dislodged by the breeze from the ceiling fan and he pushes his hair back into place. 'I found this little lady waiting for you and just nipped in for a chat.'

Little lady! Eeew.

'Is that right?' Toby puts his coffee down on top of the folders and scoots round to switch off his computer screen.

'We were discussing Ludo Van Teel,' says Malcolm as the screen goes black. 'And I was telling – what's your name?'

'Annie.'

'I was telling Annie here that you think you might have one squirrelled away somewhere.'

'Ha. Possibly. Probably not,' blusters Toby. He puts two fingers down the back of his shirt collar and eases it away from his neck. 'Lovely to see you, Malcolm, but I'd better be getting on.'

'Of course.' Malcolm passes Toby his coffee, gathers up his folders and bumbles to the door. 'Annie, if there's anything else you'd like to know about Ludo Van Teel don't hesitate to ask. My door is always open to you.'

Ugh, creepy.

Toby watches him go, wipes the top of his desk with a tissue and drops it into his bin. Even the bin is beautiful, with swirling loops of silver wire interlocking in an intricate pattern. The one in my office is a blue plastic tub with the price tag still on it.

'Why did you want to see me?' Toby sinks into his chair and sizes me up over the top of his cardboard cup.

'It doesn't matter. Um, that painting on your computer screen, it looks quite similar to the one in Alice's sitting room.'

Toby's face is a picture. He looks utterly appalled.

'Alice's painting? You have to be joking. That's merely a pale imitation of a bona fide Ludo Van Teel. Don't take this the wrong way, Annie, but you're a complete amateur and know nothing about an artist's distinctive brush strokes and personality that comes through on the canvas, whereas I'm an expert with a degree in fine art.'

That's me told but I can't let it go.

'Where have you seen the Ludo Van Teel you might be getting your hands on, the one that Malcolm mentioned?'

Toby pulls his lips into such a thin line they almost disappear. 'Malcolm, frankly, is talking out of his backside. There was a possible sighting of a Van Teel in Gloucestershire but it proved not to be the real deal.' He switches his screen back on and starts clicking with the mouse. 'If there's nothing urgent you need to talk about…'

'Nothing that can't wait.'

I back out of Toby's lovely office and scurry back to my cupboard to do some Googling. There's something funny going on here.

'Funny? Downright dodgy if you ask me,' snorts Maura.

Ignoring her warnings of tummy bugs, I turned up on her doorstep half an hour ago, straight from work. I need to speak to someone who'll say it like it is, and that's one of Maura's defining characteristics. So far she's been sympathetic about my grandmother's bombshell letter and the newspaper cutting, especially when I opened up about how Mum behaved when I was growing up. Maura's been bandying words about like 'bipolar' as if she's a mental health expert or something.

But she's being far less sympathetic about Toby.

'Toby definitely wants to get his hands on Alice's painting,' she asserts, putting her hands on her hips and looking cross. 'And he was in line to inherit it before you appeared on the scene. He definitely wanted to get you out of Salt Bay before Alice altered her will and left it to you.' Motherhood has only enhanced Maura's ability to cut straight to the chase.

'That's what I thought,' I mutter, bouncing Harry on my knee. 'There's been something off about Toby from the start. At first I thought he might be jealous of my relationship with Alice and I wouldn't have blamed him for that because I did appear out of the blue. But if this painting really is a Van Teel—'

'It would explain why he lined up a new job to get you out of Cornwall and away from the bosom of your long lost but recently found again great-aunt Alice. What a conniving slimebag! I'm not sure whether to be appalled or impressed.' She grabs a bib and mops dribble from Harry's bright red chin. He's teething big-time, poor lad. 'All that stuff he told you about your boyfriend is probably a pack of lies too,' she adds, catching a string of dribble that's about to gloop onto Harry's knee.

'He's not my boyfriend.'

'Shame. You should have pounced on Juicy Josh while you had the chance.' Harry starts wailing and Maura scoops him into her arms.

'What are you going to do about the painting? It could be worth an absolute fortune.'

'I don't want to inherit it. I've got no claims on the painting after being absent from Alice's life for twenty-nine years.'

'I know that, you dork.' Maura starts rocking Harry vigorously back and forth. 'But are you going to tell Alice about what's hanging on her wall?'

'I think I have to. The picture is a family heirloom so she might want to leave it to Toby in her will whatever. But if her illness progresses and Emily can't cope, Alice might want to sell the painting to pay for loads of professional care. It could make all the difference between her having to go into a home or being able to stay forever at Tregavara House.'

Maura nods before lifting Harry's bottom up to her nose and sniffing.

'For pity's sake, this child is a pooing machine, and Paul has given up nappy changing because he says it makes him gag. Bloody wimp!' She grabs a new nappy from her changing bag. 'I don't suppose Harry's lovely Auntie Annie would like to…?' She waves the nappy in my face.

'Nah, Maura, you're all right. I wouldn't know what to do.' I know, I'm a wimp and a bad friend but I have some sympathy with Paul's weak stomach.

While Maura and Harry are out of the room, I consider my options. If Toby isn't lying and Alice's painting really is a cheap knock-off, I could ignore the whole thing. Though I've become a bit of a Van Teel expert recently (thanks, Google) and her painting does show striking similarities to his other work – the colours, the background, the almost photographic quality of the picture.

I've also discovered that Van Teel spent a summer in Penzance so perhaps a local man, with money made from tin mining, commissioned him to capture forever the beauty of his young Trebarwith wife. It's not completely out of the question.

Another option is letting Alice know of my suspicions via a letter or phone call but that seems rather brutal for an elderly woman not in the best of health. 'Hey Alice, Toby might be trying to fleece you out of a painting that's worth a mint. Hope all's well with you. Bye.' I can't do that.

Or I could take a trip to Salt Bay and speak to Alice face-to-face. It's a long way to go but it would give me a chance to apologise to her for doubting her version of events with Mum. And maybe we could have the proper talk about Mum and Sheila and the rest of my family that I've been trying so hard to avoid – though butterflies are dancing in my stomach at the thought of it. I could catch up with Kayla as well and, if I time it right, go to the choir's inaugural concert to lend support. I guess I'd have to see Josh, too. The butterflies start doing a paso doble, but I've made up my mind by the time Maura comes back. She plonks Harry onto my lap and he bats at my face with his tiny hands, smelling of milk and talcum powder.

'What are you going to do then about your slimeball cousin and the mysterious painting? Ooh, it sounds like an Agatha Christie plot.'

'I'm going back to Salt Bay to have a word with Alice about it.'

'Yay!' yells Maura, making Harry jump. 'You know it makes sense.'

I nod, though nothing in my life seems to make sense any more.

Chapter Thirty

So here I am, back in Cornwall after vowing I'd never return. Is it only four weeks since I was last at Penzance station? So much has happened since then. I tick off events in my mind: started a job, tick; found proof that my mother's a liar, tick; had my heart pummelled by a tall, dark and vulnerable man, tick; went mental and chucked a hot beverage at a wall, tick. With a rueful smile, I pull out the handle on my suitcase and start trundling across the car park.

It's quite nice to be back. The air is fresher here than in London and there are pretty, white crests topping the silver sea. Across the bay, St Michael's Mount is rising out of the waves like a fairytale island and looks amazing. It's like a set from *Game of Thrones*, with glowering clouds dipping down to brush the mount's castle walls. I half expect a fiery dragon to swoop into view but only seagulls are riding the air currents above me, like surfers catching a wave.

The train fare was daylight robbery – I could be sitting on a beach in Benidorm for about the same price. And there's no way I'm forking out for a taxi. So I hop on the bus and sit near the back, next to people with bulging carrier bags at their feet and children on their laps. A toddler in front of me starts wailing and his mum placates him with a bag of jelly sweets as the bus swings out of the tiny bus station and into the traffic.

It's Saturday afternoon and shoppers are bustling through the centre of town. For a while I play a game of 'spot the tourist' but it's way too easy because tourists dress for the beach, whatever the weather. Even in a force eight gale with hailstones raining down, I'd bet money on them wearing tiny shorts, skimpy tops and a determined expression. I feel like a local in my jeans and jumper.

The bus is hot and steamy and the steady thrum of the engine is almost hypnotic as we drive on into the countryside. Wipers scrape intermittently across the windscreen because it's spitting with rain and everything outside my window looks soaking wet. Kayla did say it had been chucking it down since I left. I rub a viewing circle in the misted-up glass and peer outside. Wow, the countryside looks like it's on acid. The fields are a vivid emerald-green, far brighter than the Olympic Park grass or the scrubby ground between my flat and the Westfield centre.

Only in Cornwall for twenty minutes and I'm already waxing lyrical over flippin' grass. Closing my eyes, I plan out the next few days in my head before I can get back to London and normality. Though even London doesn't feel normal these days.

I've booked Monday off work so that'll give me plenty of time. I'll catch up with Alice today, maybe meet up with Kayla, go to the choir concert on Sunday evening, and head for home the day after. I'll avoid Josh as much as possible – not because I don't want to see him but because I do. And that's far more dangerous when we live in such different worlds.

Alice isn't expecting me – I didn't ring in case I bottled it and stayed in London – but hopefully she'll be pleased to see me. I'm surprised by how much I'm looking forward to seeing her now most secrets are out in the open.

The bus trundles down the hill towards Salt Bay and drops me off at the edge of the village, where the valley narrows as it nears the sea. I can tell that something's wrong as soon as I start wheeling my case along the road. Loads of cars are parked higgledy-piggledy on the grass verges and there's a strange vibration in the air; a deep thrumming which I can feel rather than hear. It's too constant to be the ebb and flow of the sea, but I've no idea what else it could be.

The mystery's solved when I round a bend near the village green and come to an abrupt halt. The gentle river that meanders down the valley and through Salt Bay is a roaring, swollen torrent of brown water. Plants and branches are being swept along and are catching in young trees on the bank that are bending under the onslaught.

The water has breached the opposite bank and men in canary-yellow wellies are moving furniture out of Mrs Johnson's cottage which is under threat of being swamped. She's lovely, Mrs Johnson, and I hope she's OK. One of the men is Charlie from the choir, who waves at me with a chair under his arm. The furniture is being moved to higher ground and probably to the pub where there's room to store it. Good old Roger. He might be contrary but I bet he's good in a community crisis.

For a while I stand and watch because I've never seen anything like it. The torrent is gathering power as it rushes headlong towards the harbour and is roaring like a wild animal. The wall of water seems malevolent, an evil force intent on destroying everything in its path. Shivering, I hurry on towards Tregavara House, keen to check on Alice.

Further downstream, the waters are swollen but contained between the muddy banks and Tregavara House is untouched. That's a relief. I had visions of it bobbing out to sea with Alice's sad face pressed against an upstairs window. But the house has been safe for centuries so chances are it never floods. Even when Salt Bay's gentle stream gets a right cob on and turns into a raging monster.

Being face-to-face with nature in the raw is starting to freak me out and I hammer on the front door, keen to get inside. Alice and I can sit by the window with a cup of tea and watch water cascading into the harbour. Or if she'd rather play it safe, we can head for the pub until things have calmed down. Either way, it will be good to see her again. Only it's not Alice who opens the door.

'Well, well, fancy seeing you here.' Toby has swapped his expensive work clothes for expensive casuals and looks less than delighted to find me on the doorstep of the Trebarwith family home.

My first reaction on finding Toby on the doorstep is guilt. It's not as if I'm planning on dropping him in it about the painting. I was hardly going to mention him at all. But I feel caught out.

Toby raises his eyebrows while I gather myself together and manage to blurt out, 'What are you doing here?'

'I could ask you the same,' snipes Toby, frowning at the rushing water.

'I'm here to see Alice and have a chat about my mum.'

'To tell her some cock and bull story about her painting, no doubt.' Toby steps outside and pulls the door shut behind him. 'Come with me. Alice is sleeping so let's talk somewhere where we won't wake her.' Like he's expecting a shouting match or fisticuffs.

He pulls me away from the water and strides towards the back of the garden which slopes up towards the cliffs. His body language screams 'annoyed', and I have to run to keep up.

'Why are you here, Toby?' I ask, jogging along beside him and raising my voice to be heard above the din from the water.

'I decided to pay Alice a visit and drove down last night.'

'When I saw you yesterday, you didn't mention it.'

Toby stops where the garden ends and the rock face begins and turns to face me. It's gloomy back here, with the cliffs towering above us. 'I thought you'd had enough of the Trebarwith family and Salt Bay so I kept my visit quiet.'

'So your visit is nothing to do with me asking you about the painting and then taking time off?'

Toby folds his arms across his purple cashmere jumper and shakes his head.

'I didn't know you were taking time off, and the painting is not a Van Teel, Annie, as I keep telling you. It's a good painting done by an accomplished artist and that's all. Don't you think I'd have mentioned it to Alice otherwise?'

If people maintain eye contact they're not lying, apparently, but I'm way too distracted by the raging water to watch Toby's face. I'm sure the roaring is getting worse.

'Do you think we should be doing something about the stream? It's flooding further up the village.'

'Don't panic. It does flood sometimes when there's been a lot of rainfall up on the moors. This was a stupid place to build a village. But it never floods badly this far down because there's drainage straight into the sea. I moved my car in case the road gets splashed but the house will be fine.'

'I don't know, Toby. Maybe we should move Alice out, to be on the safe side.'

'There's no point in waking her and she needs to catch up on her sleep after a bad night. Whatever you may think of my motives, Annie, I care about Alice and have cared about her for the past thirty-odd years.' The implication being that I've only been in her life for the last few weeks. He's got a point.

Oops, that can't be good. Water has started swirling over the bank, across the road and under Alice's garden gate. The brown tide is already eddying round the plants in her garden and, as I watch wide-eyed, the water level rises like a scene from a horror film and starts lapping at her front door. I grab Toby's arm, too shocked to speak, and gesticulate at what's happening.

'Bloody hell.' Toby's gone pale. 'It's never done that before. We'd better ring for help.' He takes out his phone and keys in his code to unlock it.

'Have you got a signal?'

Toby stares at his screen, then waves the phone in the air. 'No. Have you?'

'I've never got a signal round here.'

It strikes me that perhaps Toby's right and this wasn't the best place to build a village, though I don't suppose the founders of Salt Bay had mobile phone masts in mind when they put down roots.

'So what do we do?' gulps Toby.

Muddy water is creeping up the rough stone of Tregavara House and swirling strongly round the corners of the building. Who knows how high the flood waters will go and how much battering such an ancient house can take? I link my arm through Toby's.

'We have to get Alice out now.'

Together we rush towards the house, yelling for help from the men further up the valley. I'm not sure they can hear us but there's no time to lose. Jeez, the water is freezing and up to my knees by the time I reach the front door and push it open. Water has seeped in under the door and is rising, splashing higher and higher up the walls. The radiator is half submerged and Alice's shoes float past me while ripples soak into the carpet on the stairs. Toby has splashed in behind me.

'Is Alice up there?'

He nods, his face frozen in fear.

'Come on then. We've got to get her out.'

I wade to the stairs and run up to the landing, my shoes squelching water with every step. All I can think, as I rush towards Alice's bedroom, is that we're well and truly stuffed because I don't know how to swim and Alice is too old to breaststroke through a flood.

If I'd spent summer holidays in Salt Bay when I was growing up, I'd have learned to swim in the sea. Alice would have taught me, or Sheila. Either way, my chances of surviving the next few minutes would be higher, especially as Toby's nowhere to be seen when I look behind me.

Alice is sitting up in bed, sleepy and confused, when I barge into her room. A fluffy pink blanket is covering her legs and her hair has flattened where she's been lying.

'Annabella, is that you?' Her eyes light up at the sight of me but then she looks alarmed. 'Why are you here and what's that noise?'

'No time to talk, Alice,' I snap, striding towards her. 'The river is flooding into the house and we need to get you out.'

'Righty-o.' You can tell Alice has lived through a war. With no argument, she swings her legs off the bed, grabs the photo of her husband from the bedside table, and pushes her feet into her slippers.

'Let's go. Where's Toby?'

'I'm not sure but he's fine.' Putting my arm round Alice's waist, I drag her to her feet and she totters against me. She's wobbly at the best of times and still disorientated after waking to find me in her room.

'Put your arm round my shoulder and let me do most of the work,' I instruct her, half-carrying her to the top of the stairs.

Alice stiffens when she sees the dirty water swirling over the bottom stairs and murmurs, close to my ear, 'Oh my! I'm not sure I can do this, dear.'

'Of course you can. We can do this together.'

We stumble down the first couple of stairs and it becomes apparent that Alice's mobility has worsened since I was last here. Her legs are hardly moving and she keeps yelping in pain.

On the third stair down from the landing, she stands up straighter and pushes herself away from me.

'Come on Alice, we can do this.'

Alice's lined face softens into a sad smile. 'I don't think so, and I'm just holding you up.'

A surge of water rushes along the hallway and the old house shifts and groans at the indignity.

'I'm an old woman, not a young thing like you, and I'd rather go down with this marvellous house.' She sinks onto the stair, clasping her precious photo to her chest.

Fantastic! We need to get down the stairs pronto while there's still time to wade our way out, and Alice chooses this moment to sacrifice herself. My horror film has turned into a weepie, with the elderly heroine opting to die alone and save her young companion from a watery grave. God, I hate manipulative weepy movies. Give me Jason Bourne and a car chase any day.

'No way, Alice.' I stoop down to her level, nose to nose. 'We Trebarwiths have to stick together, so get your arse in gear and your feckin' legs down those stairs.'

Alice opens and closes her mouth a couple of times like a fish. But she stays silent and doesn't resist when I pull her to her feet and start frogmarching her down into the flood.

When we reach the water, I have to force myself to keep going. Hell's bells, it hasn't got any warmer. The coldness hits Alice like a blow and she flinches against me when we reach the bottom of the stairs and start pushing against the rising tide surging into the house.

'Toby!' I yell, using my free arm to carve a way through the water and its surface scum of plants ripped from the valley. My foot catches on something hidden beneath the surface and I stumble. My shoulders sink under the water but I manage to right myself, still holding on to Alice who's clinging round my neck. The water has risen past my waist, Alice's face is a grim mask of fear, and I still can't bloody well swim.

I push on past the sitting room, steadfastly staring ahead because seeing Alice's elegant room sunken and wrecked would be too much to bear. We're hardly making any progress because it's hard moving against the force of the water and my legs are so numb I can't tell if my feet are on solid ground. This is how Samuel must have felt, just before he succumbed to the waves. Soaked, exhausted, and thoroughly peed off that his time was up.

But I can't die yet. Not when there's so much left on my bucket list. I haven't mastered cooking without setting off the smoke alarm yet, or taking regular exercise without hating it. And I want to become magnificently serene, and to French-kiss Richard Armitage while he's wearing his Guy of Gisbourne black leather, obviously. Plus there's all the finding out about where I come from and maybe, just maybe, settling down one day with – well, with someone. Having a home and a family isn't so bad. In fact, right now I think I'd quite like it. But what a shame if that all counts for nothing because Trebarwiths are cursed to drown.

Suddenly, there's lots of shouting and splashing and two men push their way through the front door.

'Toby, thank God.'

But it's not Toby. Charlie and Josh are moving through the flood, twisting from side to side and using the force of the water to propel themselves forwards. Charlie reaches us first and grabs hold of Alice, who clings on to me, refusing to let go.

'It's all right,' shouts Charlie, 'I've got you, Mrs Gowan.'

'What about Annabella?' she yells, digging her nails into my neck. 'I'm not leaving her behind.' Which is really kind, even though she's a dead weight and dragging me under the water.

'No one's getting left behind. Josh will look after Annie,' promises Charlie, unpeeling Alice, who immediately flings her arms round his shoulders. The heavy photo frame she's holding clonks into the back of his head and he winces.

'My poor house,' cries Alice with a final look round the ruined hallway before Charlie starts wading with her in his arms towards the garden. Josh steps to one side to let him go past, before pushing on through the flood towards me.

I've lost feeling everywhere and my life should be flashing in front of my eyes right now. But all I can think as Josh gets closer is that he looks totally hot. Ridiculous I know, but his soaking-wet cotton jacket is clinging to the muscles in his chest and upper arms, and damp strands of dark hair are plastered to his forehead in a very appealing way. There's something rather Richard about him. Plus he's being terribly heroic.

'Are you all right?' he asks when he reaches me. The mini tidal wave that's built up ahead of him splashes over my shoulders and across my chin.

'I can't swim,' I reply, teeth chattering as Alice's hat bounces off the wall and starts sailing up the stairs. I've always liked that hat. It's the one that makes her look like Miss Marple.

'That doesn't surprise me, bloody townies,' mutters Josh but he doesn't say it unkindly. Putting his hands round my waist, he pulls me close into his body and his peppermint-breath warms my frozen face. 'Come on then, Annabella Sunshine Trebarwith, let's get you out of this hellhole.'

'Sunshine?' I squeak.

'Never tell Kayla anything you want to keep a secret.' He grins down at me and I forget for a moment that hypothermia is setting in and I may well end up with organ failure.

Together we start pushing our way through the flood. The water seems to have stopped rising but it's an obstacle course underfoot, with plants wrapping themselves round my legs and all sorts of detritus hidden beneath the surface. When I stumble for the second time, Josh sweeps me into his arms without a word and keeps moving forwards.

I have to admit that I like being carried by Josh. Being rescued like a damsel in distress smacks against any remaining feminist leanings. But sod it. I am in distress and it's lovely to be rescued for once. Being independent isn't all it's cracked up to be when a gigantic feckin' flood is trying to finish you off.

At last we're out of the house and into the garden, only the garden no longer exists. In its place is a vast lake with islands of plants poking above the water line. A fire engine and two ambulances are parked close to the water's edge, their blue lights reflecting and scattering in the floodwater lake.

'Oh my God, what about Toby?' I twist in Josh's arms as he wades towards dry land. Ahead of us, Alice and Charlie are being led towards an ambulance.

'Don't worry about him,' says Josh gruffly, carefully setting me down on my feet. 'He's the one who told us you and Alice were inside. He's over there.' He tilts his head at a bedraggled Toby, who's sitting on the steps of the fire engine with a thick blanket round his shoulders. 'Did he get wet trying to rescue you and Alice?'

'No, he was too busy rescuing that.' I nod towards the large, gilt-framed painting next to him. It looks wildly out of place, propped up against the fire engine's wheel arch. But the canvas looks dry from here.

'You're kidding me,' snorts Josh, his dark eyes flashing.

'Afraid not.'

Without another word, Josh spins round and marches towards Toby. Ooh, this cannot end well. I scurry after him as best I can, seeing as I've still got almost no feeling in my legs.

'What the hell were you thinking?'

Toby spots Josh bearing down on him and cowers against the fire engine.

'Annie and Alice could have drowned while you were rescuing a painting. What is wrong with you, you moron?'

Toby springs to his feet so he and Josh are eyeball to eyeball, and the blanket falls to the floor.

'What's so important about the painting anyway?' demands Josh, staring at the woman in the picture who stares right back. He looks quickly at me and then back at the painting. He can see the resemblance too.

I push my way between Josh and Toby to avoid any fighting, though right now I feel like giving my lying cousin a swift kick in the privates. 'It's a Van Teel,' I say calmly.

Toby shrugs and doesn't deny it. But he refuses to look me in the eye and, if I didn't know better, I'd say that he was feeling a tad guilty.

'A Van what?' Josh's sopping jacket and jeans are dripping over Toby's feet.

'A Van Teel. Toby has discovered that Ludo Van Teel is the artist and this could be a very valuable painting, though I'm not sure he was going to tell Alice that.'

'I bet be wasn't,' hisses Josh through gritted teeth. 'Always thinking only of yourself, hey, Toby?'

'You have no idea how much this painting is worth,' retorts Toby, moving in front of the canvas to protect it. 'What do you earn, twenty-five grand a year? You'd have done exactly the same as me if you'd known. And Annie and Alice got out fine anyway.'

'Only just. That's the difference between you and me. Whatever this painting is worth, I'd put people above money every time.'

'Yeah, maybe if it's Annie.'

'What do you mean by that?'

The two of them start doing that weird squaring up dance that men do; chests out, chins jutting, fists clenched. Good grief, I think they are going to fight. I'm contemplating throwing myself back into Josh's arms to stop them when a paramedic hurries up to us.

'Come on you two and have a quick check up in the ambulance to see if you've got hypothermia.' She smiles broadly as if the prospect of hypothermia is rather pleasant. 'Did either of you swallow any water? Heaven knows what's in it. Let's find you some blankets to start with. Follow me.' She links her arm through mine and leads us away from Toby.

'I can't believe it,' I say as Josh and I sit next to one another in the back of the ambulance, wrapped in foil blankets like oven-ready turkeys. We've been prodded and poked by the ambulance crew who have declared that we'll survive. Alice, Charlie and Toby are OK too, though Alice has been taken to hospital as a precaution, and I've thanked Josh so many times that he's begged me to stop.

'I know the painting could be worth three-quarters of a million but—'

'*How* much?' asks Josh, still shivering. We've both taken off almost all our clothes and are slowly warming up thanks to lots of blankets and paramedic Andrea whacking the heating in the ambulance up to high.

'One Ludo Van Teel painting sold recently for £755,000.'

'Good grief, that's crazy money.' His foil blanket crackles when he shakes his head.

'Are you reconsidering your actions in rescuing me and Alice rather than fine art?' I ask, aware that beneath my blankets I'm dressed in only my bra and pants. And they don't match.

'I'd have missed you and your annoying ways if you'd drowned. Though I'm not sure why you're back in Salt Bay when you hate it so much.'

'I don't hate it. In fact I quite missed it – the windswept cliffs, the never-ending rain, the difficult people.'

Josh grins and my legs shake even more.

'I'm back because I found out that the painting is valuable and I wanted to tell Alice.'

'She doesn't know?' When I shake my head, Josh gives a hollow laugh. 'And I bet Toby wasn't going to tell her either. He's even more of a self-centred shit than I thought.'

'Hhhmmm.' Before I can change my mind, I say in a rush, 'He told me that you got a girl pregnant and then abandoned her and the baby, and when he challenged you about it, that's when you hit him.'

'You're kidding.' Josh twists round in his seat, revealing the thighs of a rugby player. 'Did you believe him?'

'No, not really – I wasn't sure,' I say miserably, any relief at not drowning now receding swiftly. 'But only at first when I thought you were rude and grumpy, but not now…' I tail off.

Josh leans forward, speaking so quietly I can hardly hear him. 'Do you want to know the real story? Yes, I hit Toby because a pregnant girl was abandoned. But he was the one doing the abandoning, not me.'

'So who was the – oh.' Suddenly it all makes perfect, horrible sense. 'Your niece Freya is Toby's daughter. She's a Trebarwith.'

'Yes, poor little mite.' Josh glances round to make sure that Andrea can't hear. 'Lucy was only seventeen and swept off her feet by Toby in his flash car. And when he wanted to keep their relationship a secret it only made the whole thing more romantic in Lucy's eyes. But when she got pregnant, he couldn't escape fast enough and the Trebarwiths closed ranks.'

'Who knows that Toby is Freya's dad?'

'Hardly anyone. I guessed because I'd seen her and Toby together but she made me promise never to let on. So I haven't until now. But I confronted Toby and he laughed and said it wasn't his problem and he wasn't going to be tied to this deadbeat place by some stupid kid.' The muscles in Josh's jaw tighten.

'And that's when you hit him?'

Josh nods miserably. 'I don't make a habit of hitting people, but he pushed me too far.'

'Have you ever chased him for maintenance?'

'Nope. Lucy doesn't want anything more to do with Toby or the Trebarwiths and I have to stick with what she wants. She's been through enough already and couldn't face a paternity fight and everyone knowing her business.'

Which means that while Toby has escaped scot-free, Lucy is working all hours to support her child and Josh is working hard to help her. It all seems very unfair.

'Does your mum know?'

Josh nods.

'And yet she still lets Serena work for Alice.'

'My mum is more forgiving than me and says Alice probably doesn't know anything about it. Toby's snooty parents were horrified that their son's glittering career might be derailed by a brief fling with a lowly Pawley so Mum reckons they kept it to themselves. Freya, one of the sweetest little girls on the planet, was just a dirty secret as far as they were concerned.'

'Alice doesn't know.' I'm sure of it. Even though I met my great-aunt for the first time just a few short weeks ago, it's plain to see that she's a woman of principle who would, at the very least, apologise for Toby's behaviour. I feel as though I'm speaking on her behalf when I say, 'I'm terribly sorry about the trouble you've had with the Trebarwith family.'

'With your family, you mean. And you believed what Toby told you about me.'

'No I didn't, not really. Toby's a liar.'

'Yes he is and I've always known it. But I can't believe you thought even for a moment that I was capable of behaving like him. What a very low opinion you've had of me from the start.' And he sounds so terribly disappointed, I start to wish I had drowned.

'How are you two feeling now?' says Andrea cheerfully, flinging open the back door of the ambulance and climbing inside. 'Phew, it's toasty in here.' She mimes wiping sweat from her forehead, totally oblivious to the frosty atmosphere. 'Here you go.' She hands a Sainsbury's carrier bag to me and one to Josh. 'Your neighbours have rallied round and found some clothes for you. They're not the height of fashion, but will do until you get home. Oh, Annie.' She grins. 'Some big bloke called Roger said you can stay at his place tonight. It's nice to be in demand.'

'Thank you for all your help. It's much appreciated.' Josh stands up, pulls his blankets tight and squeezes past Andrea to get out of the ambulance. 'I'll head off now to find Charlie and get dressed and sort out a lift home.'

'You're not both staying at Roger's place then, love? That's a shame,' says Andrea chirpily, giving me a wink as Josh disappears into the distance.

I smile faintly and slip an orange polyester blouse over my head. Being cheerful must help paramedics to cope with an incredibly difficult job but I wish Andrea would rein it in a bit. It's not that I'm not grateful to be safe and warming up on dry land, but it's been a rubbish day: almost drowned in a flood, tick; confirmed that my cousin is a nasty piece of work, tick; disappointed the man that I rather inconveniently think I may be falling in love with, tick, tick, tick.

Chapter Thirty-One

'Big bloke' Roger is as good as his word, bless him, and finds me a bed for the night in a box room at The Whistling Wave. A bit of mountaineering is involved in getting to the bed because the room is jam-packed with Mrs Johnson's furniture, but it's worth it as I sink into the fat mattress, all drowsy after a hot bath. At first all I see on closing my eyes are me and Alice clinging together and sinking under murky water, like Leonardo in *Titanic*. But I'm exhausted after the day's traumas and slide quickly into a deep, dreamless sleep.

I have absolutely no idea where I am when I wake the next morning in a strange bed, but the dramatic events of yesterday soon come flooding back. Though 'flooding' probably isn't the best word in the circumstances. Rolling across the mattress, I stretch out like a starfish and take stock: Alice is in hospital, Tregavara House is under water, Toby is a lying toe-rag, and Josh… heroic Josh, whose brow furrows into a cute line between his eyebrows when he's concentrating…

'Pack it in, Annie,' I say out loud, throwing back the duvet and contemplating whether my best route to the bathroom is over Mrs Johnson's occasional tables or TV cabinet. Definitely the tables because the finely balanced cabinet looks dead dodgy. After making it to the bathroom with no broken bones, I stand under the shower for ages letting the hot water stream down my body and pool round my feet. And

I wonder how, after being so careful not to need anyone or anything, I've ended up in a no man's land – I don't fully belong in Salt Bay or London either. What a mess!

It's little wonder that Josh thinks badly of the Trebarwith family with its secrets and lies and appalling behaviour. God knows I'm pretty gutted that I share DNA with treacherous Toby, though I've grown very fond of Alice. I stretch my neck back and water pours over my face like cleansing rain.

Ten minutes later I've made up my mind. I'll tell Alice that she's loaded and thank Charlie for being such a hero yesterday. Then I'll head back to London and hope that eventually these inconvenient feelings about Josh and my family roots will fade.

Back in the bedroom, I delve into the carrier bag of clothes for something to wear. My suitcase was left on the doorstep of Tregavara House when Toby pulled me into the garden and I haven't seen it since. It's probably halfway to France by now. At the bottom of the bag there's a pair of donated pants. They're white – I give them a quick sniff – clean and almost come up to my boobs, but they'll do. There's a pleated brown skirt that almost fits, and the orange blouse will do another day.

As I'm leaving the bedroom, I catch sight of myself in Mrs Johnson's mirror and wince. Today, Gok, my look can best be described as elderly fashion victim meets make-up-free trauma survivor. Yuk. But at least I'm alive and well, though I'm not so sure about Alice. It's only half past eight so too early to call the hospital and check on her. Poor Alice and her wrecked home. What will happen to her now?

Downstairs, Roger grunts a greeting and stops sliding wine glasses into the wooden rack above the bar. 'Do you want some breakfast? Kayla's not back from her sleepover at Sarah's but I can rustle up cornflakes.'

He disappears into the kitchen and reappears a few minutes later with the cornflakes box and a milk carton on a tray, and he keeps an eye on me while I'm crunching my way through half a bowlful. I'm not hungry and have just pushed the cereal to one side when Kayla hurtles into the pub looking like she's shoved her fingers into an electric socket.

'Flaming heck,' she yells, bright red cheeks matching the hair frizzed out round her face. 'Are you all right? Nothing happens in Salt Bay for ages until I go to Penzance for one night and then all hell is let loose.' She puffs over and engulfs me in a bear hug. 'I met Jennifer down the road and she told me you were back and almost drowned. What the hell happened and why didn't you tell me you were coming, and oh my God' – she pulls back and puts her hands on her hips – 'what on earth are you wearing? You look like an ancient bag lady.'

Giggling, I gesture for her to sit down. 'Don't worry Kayla, I'm fine. I was paying a flying visit to see Aunt Alice and got caught in the flood. Everyone's safe but my clothes smell like the bottom of a pond so I've borrowed the blouse from Jennifer and the skirt's been lent to me by someone called Margery Hailsham, according to Roger.' I finger the tight pleats fanning out round my stomach that are giving me a fetching pregnancy look.

'Huh,' snorts Kayla, 'Margery is at least ninety!'

'That figures,' I laugh, before whispering, 'You should see the pants I'm wearing. A homeless family could use them as a tent.'

'Only Tregavara House and Enid Johnson's cottage were flooded out,' calls Roger from the bar. 'The water's gone down now but it's a bit of a mess out there. Some of the men have made the properties secure. I don't suppose we'd get looters round here but you can never be too careful, 'specially at this time of year with emmets starting to appear.'

'Thank you, Roger, you've all been absolutely brilliant.'

Roger harrumphs but looks pleased.

'Now tell me exactly what happened and how you managed to get out,' demands Kayla. 'Jennifer said the flood was up to the ceiling and you had to swim underwater with Alice holding on to your legs.'

'Hardly, seeing as I can't swim.'

'I can see that would be a disadvantage. Tell me what really happened then while I was missing all the excitement in boring old Penzance.'

So I go through the whole thing again, keeping it as light as possible and not mentioning the painting. But I still end up shaking when I describe the water getting higher and my legs going numb. Kayla gently strokes my arm and doesn't say anything. But when I get to the bit about Josh and Charlie appearing like the aquatic cavalry, she gasps, 'That is amazing.'

'It was totally amazing.'

'And terribly romantic.' She nudges my arm and winks.

'Only if being immersed in filthy, freezing water turns you on.' I don't mention Josh's muscles and overall hotness because it would only encourage Kayla, who can't ever know the full story.

'Hey Kayla,' yells Roger from the kitchen. 'I was very kind and gave you the night off but that didn't include the morning. Now you've seen that Annie isn't dead, can you finish your chinwag and start doing some of the work you get paid for.'

Kayla scrunches up her nose and flicks a V-sign towards the kitchen. 'We can catch up properly later but it all sounds very exciting. Now get yourself into my bedroom and choose some clothes. You can't go out looking like that or you'll be arrested by the style police. And give my best wishes to Alice when you see her.'

After she's gone into the kitchen, I sit with my eyes closed for a few moments and focus on my breathing. In, out, in, out, just like they advise in the meditation apps, but I'm too agitated to sit still for long. Instead, I use the pub landline to call the hospital and check on Alice.

'She's doing quite well,' says a nurse on Alice's ward. He sounds busy and distracted. 'But in light of her other medical issues, the doctors want to keep her in for a day or two to keep an eye on her.'

'But she is going to be all right, isn't she?'

'She's an elderly lady and she's had a nasty shock but you can visit this afternoon if you like and see how she is for yourself. We're hopeful she should be able to go home later in the week.' Wherever home might be.

After the call, I go through Kayla's wardrobe to find myself a new outfit suitable for hospital visiting. Flicking past the hoodies and T-shirts in vivid shades – Kayla's far braver than me when it comes to colour – I choose a pair of soft grey trousers and a navy-blue sweatshirt which kind of fit. My feet are bigger than Kayla's but Roger, top bloke, has managed to dry out my shoes on a radiator. And though there's a faint waft of river water about them, it does feel good to be wearing something that's mine.

While Kayla and Roger are busy in the kitchen, I slip out of the pub and wander down the road. Early spring sunshine is trying to burn through high cloud and a few people are out and about, talking about the traumas of yesterday. The stream is more full than usual but the waters have retreated to within its muddy banks which are strewn with plant debris. I follow the debris trail towards Tregavara House with a sense of dread but the house is still standing and looks the same, apart from the swampy garden and a tide mark just below the ground-floor windows.

'Don't worry, old house,' I mutter, blinking hard to ward off the tears that are prickling. 'You'll dry out and Alice will soon be back.'

Jeez, now I'm talking to a house. It's either delayed shock, or there's something seriously wrong with my mental health. Maybe that's why I've not felt right for weeks. Anxiety and dissatisfaction are always with me these days and I've started craving the great outdoors. I want to see grass and trees and wide-open spaces rather than bricks and concrete. During my lunch breaks, I've been going for walks along the Regent's Canal towpath, just to see some water and greenery. I've even started agreeing with people who say that the Barbican is ugly.

'It's not fair,' I mutter, scuffing up gravel on the path. There I was, minding my own business and getting along just fine on my own, with no family complications and no responsibilities. And now I can't stop worrying about Alice or thinking about Josh or talking to inanimate objects. Thank you so much, Cornwall. I kick at a stone, which sails over Alice's garden gate and plops into a massive puddle in her garden. Ripples spread out around the palm tree.

The splash distracts a couple of men with clipboards who are checking the harbour wall for damage and they give me a weird look. They must think I'm the local nutter. Putting my head down, I hurry back towards the pub so I can help Roger and Kayla get the place ready for opening time. It's the least I can do after they've both been so kind.

Then I'll head to the hospital and see what help Alice needs before I leave Salt Bay. And I'd better have a word with Emily, because she can hardly move into a waterlogged house. And what has Toby done with Alice's valuable painting? I wouldn't put it past him to flog it on the quiet.

So much to do, and so many complications.

Chapter Thirty-Two

I get horribly lost in the hospital. Heaven knows how when I'm used to finding my way round a massive city but, by the time I puff into Alice's ward, I'm hot, bothered, and ten minutes later than I meant to be.

It didn't help that the handles on my carrier bag gave up the ghost as I came through the hospital entrance and dumped everything on the floor. Scrabbling round picking up old-lady nighties, big pants and tins of talcum powder isn't the best way to keep to schedule. The talc and pants are now shoved into my bag out of sight, the nighties – donated by Margery – are piled over one arm, and under the other I've got various magazines to help Alice pass the time.

At first I can't see Alice in the ward but then I spot her sitting propped up against her pillows. She's talking to another patient shuffling past the foot of her bed so I wait and watch her, shocked at how much she's changed seemingly overnight. At home, Alice is a fabulous advert for the older woman. She's bright and sassy and gets on with life in spite of her health problems. But here she looks out of place and old and frail, as though her spark has been extinguished. Obviously she's had a huge shock and anyone her age would take time to recover from being manhandled through a flood. But, I realise with overwhelming sadness, this is how Alice will become if she ever has to leave Tregavara House. It just can't happen. Whatever it takes, Alice has to go home to Salt Bay and stay there.

'Annie.' Alice's face lights up and she opens her arms wide. 'How fortunate for me that you happened to be visiting yesterday.'

Dumping nighties and magazines on her bed, I lean over and give her a huge hug. A wave of emotion sweeps over me and, much to my embarrassment, I begin to weep. Alice rocks me like a child and whispers in my ear, 'My dear girl, you were so brave coming to rescue me. Your mother and grandparents would be proud of you.' Which just sets me off even more. Finding long-lost family is turning me into a right old cry baby.

'Ahem.'

When I look up tearfully from Alice's bosom, Toby is towering over us. His face is obscured by the biggest bouquet of exotic flowers I've ever seen but I can tell it's him by the red trousers and tan leather loafers on sock-less feet. He carefully places the flowers on top of the *People's Friend* and *Woman's Weekly* and air-kisses Alice on both cheeks.

'It's good to see you looking well, Alice.'

Alice settles back in the bed and the cellophane-wrapped flowers rustle. 'I'm fine, thank you Toby, and not sure why they're insisting on keeping me in. It's such a nuisance. Thank you for the beautiful flowers; that's very kind of you. Now why don't the two of you sit down and tell me what's happening back at home.'

Toby and I draw up chairs on opposite sides of Alice's bed and sit eyeballing one another. He's got a nerve turning up with flowers after abandoning me and Alice to drown. It's lucky that Josh – nope. I dig my nails into my palms until it hurts. I'm not going to think about Josh any more because it makes me sad.

'So tell me, what state is my house in?' asks Alice, closing her eyes as though she doesn't really want to know.

'I went and had a look at it today. The house is fine and the water's gone down but it's going to take a while for the old place to dry out.'

I gently squeeze Alice's bony hand and she squeezes me back. 'What are you going to do until you can move back in?'

Alice opens her eyes. 'My friend Penelope rang the ward this morning and said I can move in with her for a while. The real Penelope,' she adds when I look sceptical. 'So I won't be homeless and Tregavara House can be fixed. No one was hurt which is the main thing and I still have my photo of David.' She smiles at the photo on her bedside table. 'But I must have lost so many other possessions. I have insurance, of course, but some things can't be replaced.'

'There's one piece of good news. Toby managed to save the painting in your sitting room; the one of the lady on the cliffs with the sea behind her.'

'Did you? That's marvellous, you clever thing.' Alice beams at Toby. 'I couldn't bear to think of it being damaged when it's been a part of Tregavara House for so many decades. That's the best news I've had all day.'

Toby gives a faint smile and starts fidgeting.

'Toby also has something to tell you about the painting, don't you Toby?'

'I suppose I do.' Toby puffs a few times like women I've seen giving birth on TV. 'I've done some research recently and I believe that the painting might be by an artist called Ludo Van Teel. If it is, it could be quite valuable.' He glances at me across the hospital bed. 'Very valuable in fact. It could be worth around, um, half a million pounds.'

'Or even more.'

'Yes, or even more,' says Toby, resignedly.

'Gosh, that is a lot of money,' gasps Alice, her face more pale than ever. 'I – I'm not sure what to say. To think that a painting worth that much money has been hanging in the sitting room my entire life and none of the family knew it.' She slowly shakes her head and breathes out heavily. 'Good heavens, Toby, it'll take time for that news to sink in. But it's so clever of you to find that out. You've always been such a good boy to me.'

She pats Toby's arm and at least he has the good grace to look embarrassed.

The subject of the painting is dropped, much to Toby's relief, and for the next half an hour we talk mostly about the flood. Alice wants to go over and over what happened as though talking about it will help to make things better, whereas I'd rather forget the whole sorry event. But I let her lead the conversation and she begins to look more like Normal Alice after a while.

After telling us for the fourth time that Charlie is her hero, Alice starts yawning and Toby and I leave so she can take a nap. She needs to conserve her strength because Jennifer is visiting later – and though beneath her bluster Jennifer is quite kind and caring, her bluster can still be rather draining.

Toby and I kiss Alice's dry, papery cheek and walk out of the ward together. He's carrying the huge bouquet because Alice reckons the hospital discourages flowers at the bedside. Something to do with hygiene rules. And we're almost at the lift when he thrusts the blooms at me.

'You'd better have these. You deserve them,' he grunts. 'What I did' – he swallows hard – 'perhaps it wasn't the best thing in the circumstances. I'm not saying that I regret saving the painting but maybe I should have helped you to get Alice safely out of the house first. I'm sorry.' Staring straight ahead, he presses the button to summon the lift.

Taking the flowers, I breathe in their heady scent. There are lilies, small buds that look like pale pink orchids, and other exotic, brightly coloured flowers I don't recognise. They must have cost a fortune.

'Thank you for your apology, and I guess everything worked out all right in the end. We're both OK and I'm glad the painting's not ruined. Whether it's worth a fortune or not, it's still a beautiful picture.'

'It is, isn't it?' murmurs Toby, staring at his feet. 'It would have been a shame to lose it.'

The lift is taking ages to arrive. But at least the delay gives me a chance to tackle the elephant that's still very much in the room.

I move closer to Toby so that no one can overhear us. 'I spoke to Josh about the pregnancy thing you mentioned and he said the proper story is that you got his sister Lucy pregnant and you've had nothing to do with her or her daughter Freya since.'

'Did he.' Toby jabs repeatedly at the button until the lift arrives and the doors slide open. It's crammed with hospital visitors but we push our way in and stand silently side by side while the lift descends.

When the doors open on the ground floor, Toby hurries out and I run to catch him up while he strides ahead. He sidesteps round a woman in a wheelchair and scoots towards the car park, only stopping and turning to face me when he reaches his BMW.

'I would offer you a lift back to Salt Bay, Annie, but I'm heading straight back to London. Unless you want to come back with me too?'

It's as if Lucy and her baby were never mentioned.

'I don't think so, thank you. I'll stay here until Monday so I can make sure that Alice is all right. Rafe isn't expecting me back at work until the day after.'

Toby presses his key fob and the car springs to life with beeps and flashing lights. 'You can let me know how she's doing on Tuesday, then, and I'll come down again when I can.'

'Where's the painting by the way?' I ask, eyeing up the car boot.

'I sent it up to London this morning by special courier. Don't worry.' He holds out his hands palm up and shrugs his shoulders; all innocence and bonhomie. 'I won't do anything with the painting without talking to Alice first.'

He slides into his posh car and lowers his window when I'm walking away.

'What's she like?' he calls after me.

'Who?'

'Freya, I think you said her name was.'

So my words did hit home. I walk back to the car and rest my arm on the roof, being careful not to scratch the paintwork with my watch.

'I've only met her once but she was very sweet, with big pale eyes and dark hair. I didn't notice it at the time because why would I, but she looks a lot like a Trebarwith.'

Anguish flits across Toby's face but it's gone almost immediately. 'I'll see you at work on Tuesday, Annie. Don't be late.'

He revs the engine and zooms off, forcing a young couple holding hands to jump out of his way.

'Prat!' yells the young lad, flipping a finger at the disappearing car.

Yes, Toby is a prize prat. He's arrogant and avaricious and a terrible driver. But underneath the rich, responsibility-free facade, there are glimpses of a lonely man who's been damaged by bad choices. And, just for a moment, I can't help feeling sorry for him.

Chapter Thirty-Three

Unlike some people, mentioning no names (Maura), I've always been pretty good at making decisions. I weigh things up, come down on one side or the other and that's that. Quick, rational and without regret. But deciding whether or not to go to tonight's first ever concert by the new Salt Bay Choral Society is proving tricky.

On the one hand, it's simple. I'm proud of the choir and seeing all the singers again and hearing them sing would be wonderful. But I'm not involved with the choir now so the evening will be bittersweet, plus there's the risk of another awkward encounter with Josh. I'm not sure I can cope with Ollie and Kayla exchanging lovey-dovey looks across the sheet music either. She's done nothing but talk about him since I got back from the hospital.

'Why wouldn't you want to go to the concert?' pouts Kayla, peering myopically into the mirror while she concentrates on getting her eyeliner just right. 'Everyone will be pleased to see you and the concert's only happening because you brought the choir back to life. You're Salt Bay's very own Doctor Frankenstein.' She flicks up the liner at the outer corner of her eye and smiles in satisfaction.

'Much as I like being compared to a bonkers scientist and would enjoy seeing everyone, I'm not feeling a hundred percent at the moment.' Well, I can hardly say I'm avoiding the concert because I'm in love with Josh Pasco and gutted because he hates my family and will never leave Cornwall. As far as Kayla's concerned, my feelings for Josh were merely a passing fancy.

Kayla swings round from the full-length mirror propped up against her wall. She's wearing black from head to toe and even her make-up has a goth vibe going on.

'Do you think you might have swallowed some of the flood water? Back home, we get warned about bacteria in rivers. Did any dead animals float past you?'

'Eew, no. Just lots of sticks and plants.'

'If you start chundering, you'd better see a doctor quick. A friend of mine went swimming in a Queensland river, picked up a bug and lost almost a quarter of her body weight in a week. It worked out all right in the end 'cos she wanted to lose a few pounds, but trust me' – Kayla grimaces – 'it wasn't pretty at the time.'

'It sounds awful but I'm sure I don't have any kind of bug. It's probably just the shock catching up with me.'

'Maybe.' Kayla's not convinced. 'But do try and come tonight if you can, Annie. You gave the choir a brilliant start and we've been working hard with Josh over the last few weeks. We don't sound half as shite as we did, honestly. Oh, and did I tell you that I'm in love and he actually loves me back?' She claps excitedly, dropping her eyeliner which splatters black bits across the carpet. 'Ollie says that I was right under his nose all this time, and now he's realised how wonderful I am he's never going to let me go.'

'Yes, you did mention it once or twice, and I think it's utterly fantastic!' Throwing my arms round her gives me time to get my 'happy face' on and I laugh when she does a shuffle-dance in the narrow gap between her chest of drawers and the end of the bed.

'Please come tonight, Annie, please. It's your choir after all.' Kayla grabs my hands and pulls me up to dance with her. There's no music but her excitement is so infectious we do some 'Gangnam Style' moves anyway. And we both look so ridiculous, arms and legs flailing as we jump about like eejits, we end up collapsed on her bed, red-faced and laughing hysterically. It's ages since I've had a good belly laugh like this.

'So will you come?' Kayla flutters her eyelashes at me across the duvet and sticks out her bottom lip. 'Pretty please? It won't be the same without you, and I'll be less nervous if you're there.'

How can I refuse? Kayla's been a good friend and, however awkward the situation is with Josh, I can't abandon the choir for a second time.

Salt Bay Church is almost full when I slip inside five minutes before the concert's due to start. For one awful moment the only free seats I can see are in the front row. But then I spot a space in the back pew and a young Asian woman shuffles along sharpish while I squeeze in on the end. She's being nice, though I can't shake the feeling she took one look at my arse in Kayla's tight jeans and realised more room was needed.

Some of the people round me are Salt Bay locals but others are unfamiliar and must have come from villages nearby. Friends and relatives of the singers, perhaps, or people touched by the tragic end of the last choral society. Either way, I'm chuffed that the church is full and Reverend Baxham looks delighted. I bet she never gets a full house for her Sunday services.

The choir are sitting in front of the altar on wooden chairs and look great. They're smartly dressed in black and white, with the men in suits and the women in trousers or long skirts. Cyril's in the back row so he must have kept coming to rehearsals, which is brilliant. He keeps smiling at a plump woman a few pews ahead of me and I cross my fingers that it's his daughter, visiting from Up North to hear him sing. A few chairs along from Cyril is Kayla, who waves at me and nudges Fiona, who grins and waves too. They're such good, kind people and I've missed them all.

If only Alice could be here to enjoy this evening. Thinking of her lying homeless and alone in a hospital bed makes me panicky about going back to London tomorrow. Friends and neighbours will help her with the Tregavara House clear-up, I'm sure of that. But they have their own responsibilities and they're not – oh God, I'm going to say it – they're not family.

Perhaps I could stay in Salt Bay a little longer and give her a hand, but how would that work when I'm bound to bump into Josh all the time, and Ollie and Kayla are getting it on? Being happy for them is all very well from a distance, but seeing them so loved-up at close quarters will eventually turn me into an embittered old bat. It's inevitable.

As if thinking about Josh conjures him up, he walks in front of the choir and sits in the front row. Wow! He scrubs up very nicely. The tailored suit he's wearing fits his tall frame perfectly and his crisp white shirt, open at the neck, accentuates his dark complexion. He's brushed his unruly hair back off his forehead and there's only a hint of stubble on his strong jaw. He looks like a lovely Cornish James Bond.

Reverend Baxham claps her hands together and a hush falls over the audience.

'Ladies and gentlemen, thank you for supporting the first ever concert by the new Salt Bay Choral Society, especially after the excitement of yesterday. Speaking of which, it's very good to see Enid here.'

There's a ripple of applause as Enid half-stands and gives a regal wave.

'I'm sure you'll all join me in sending our best wishes to Alice and hoping she'll soon be back in Salt Bay where she belongs.'

'Hear, hear,' calls a ruddy-faced man a few rows in front of me and several other people murmur in agreement. It's heartening to see how much Alice is loved in this village.

With a quick thumbs up to the choir, the vicar steps to one side. 'Without further ado, let me hand over to our conductor this evening, Mr Josh Pasco.'

Josh stands quickly and turns to face everyone. I'd rather stick pins in my eyes than speak in front of an audience, but Josh exudes calm and confidence.

'Thank you, Hilary.' His deep Cornish burr rolls round the ancient stone. 'Tonight the new Salt Bay Choral Society is going to sing some traditional Cornish favourites and some newer songs too, with the support of Michaela on the piano.' Everyone's eyes turn towards Michaela, who goes bright red and dips her head so her long, blonde hair swings in front of her face.

'As Hilary said, this is our first concert so it won't be terribly long but I think you'll be surprised by your friends' and neighbours' musical talent. In a good way,' he adds, with a smile. 'Tonight's concert is in memory of the men who belonged to this choir when it gave its last performance fifteen years ago.' For the first time, he falters slightly, making me want to rush up the aisle and put my arms round him. 'It's also in memory of others from Salt Bay who are sadly no longer with us. There was no charge to come in this evening but there will be a collection afterwards for the RNLI and we hope you'll give generously.'

He suddenly looks straight at me. 'Annie Trebarwith, the woman who revived the choir, is here tonight and she'll be conducting the first half of the evening.'

No way! Is this how he's getting his revenge? Making me look an arse in front of local people? I shrink back in my seat but the woman next to me nudges me in the ribs until I jump to my feet. Everyone turns to look at me and my face burns when they start to applaud.

When Josh beckons me to come forward, my neighbour gives me a shove into the aisle. I'm starting to actively dislike her. People carry on applauding while I walk towards the choir, horribly aware that I'm wearing jeans. And though a few members of the audience whisper behind their hands, most smile at me, including Josh's mum Marion, who's in the second row. The fact that she's here makes me even more nervous.

'What are you doing?' I hiss at Josh when I get to the front and he hands me his stepdad's baton.

'This is your choir and you should lead it,' he mumbles out of the corner of his mouth. 'Here's the programme, and they're all songs you rehearsed with them. Good luck.' He slides into a seat behind me and Kayla gives me a thumbs up.

A hush falls over the church as I consider legging it up the aisle and out of the village. I could go back to London and never mention Salt Bay again, just like my mum. No more family, no more complications.

'Come on, girl,' murmurs Cyril. His white shirt is clean and beautifully ironed. 'You can do it.'

I raise the baton and the choir stand up. Some of the older members have dodgy hips so it takes a while, and Roger swears loudly after accidentally knocking his chair over. But they look like a proper choir when they're all on their feet; smart, attentive and ready to sing. Please let this be good! I send up a quick prayer to the ghosts of the original choir and nod at Michaela.

The first notes of 'Panis angelicus' echo round the church. The choir come in at the right time, which is a definite improvement, and after a few bars I start to relax. Sure, there are a few bum notes here and there and Jennifer's vibrato voice drowns out some of the singers, including Ollie, thank goodness. But their earnest faces and heartfelt voices make me feel tearful and I'm not the only one. Mrs James, who lives in the village, is crying quietly and her husband looks choked. They're old enough to remember the men who sang here fifteen years ago, before setting out to sea for the last time.

My mind wanders while the choir are singing a cheerful sea shanty about driving men through with swords. It's very much like we last rehearsed it and a touch ropey in places but that adds to the authentic feel of it. Chances are this very same song was performed here long ago by Samuel Trebarwith and his friends, with Josh's stepdad conducting. Living, breathing men with hopes, fears and family. But all that remains of them now is a brass plaque, hidden in deep shadow on a church wall. I hope they'd approve of me starting up the choir again. And for the first time since arriving in Salt Bay, I hope that Samuel would be proud of me.

The star turn of the first half is Jennifer, who takes centre stage just before the interval and sings a pretty song from *The Pirates of Penzance*. Diamond chunks in her ears sparkle under the lights and her silk skirt ripples like black water while her voice soars. As she sings, she clasps her hands together under her bosom and closes her eyes, which looks rather affected for an amateur concert in a tiny Cornish village. But the clarity of Jennifer's beautiful soprano voice means she can get away with it.

As her final, triumphant note dies away, everyone claps enthusiastically, including me, while Jennifer does a sweeping curtsey, revealing her magnificent cleavage. We've reached the interval at last and the first half was OK. Better than OK, actually – it was terrifying and exhilarating and I loved it. The choir did me proud.

Some enterprising person has brought along two plastic cold-boxes crammed with ice creams and people descend on them during the interval. Josh and his mum are talking so I try to attract Kayla's attention, to see if she fancies a strawberry Cornetto, but she's in a lip-lock with Ollie, right in front of the altar. She's shameless.

'Hey, Annie. How are you?' says Ollie, coming up for air. 'How's your great-aunt doing?'

'OK, thanks. Kayla, can I have a word?' I drag her into the vestry and out through a heavy wooden door into the back of the churchyard. The vestry lights throw white beams across the jumbled gravestones. 'Did you know Josh was going to ambush me like that?'

'Not really.' Kayla massages her overworked lips as Mr James saunters past sucking on a Solero. 'It was dead romantic though.'

'Potentially making me look a tit in front of the whole village?'

'But you didn't, did you? And admit it, you loved it. I could tell you were having fun.'

'Once I stopped shaking, but yes.' I smile in spite of myself. 'It was lovely to be a part of the choir again and a part of such a special concert. You all sounded brilliant.'

'Even Ollie?'

'Even Ollie. I couldn't hear him much, to be honest.'

'He's mostly miming,' admits Kayla, scuffing her feet against the gnarled trunk of a tree whose roots are spreading across the graveyard like veins. 'So what exactly are you going to do about sexy Josh Pasco? It's obvious that he's totally into you. I saw the way he was looking at you while you were conducting.'

'I'm going to do absolutely nothing. He's no fan of the Trebarwiths, we live hundreds of miles apart, and I'm not sure he does like me that much anyway.'

'You're kidding me, right? He waded through bacteria-riddled waters to rescue you from certain death.'

'Which he'd have done for anyone in trouble.'

'You're hopeless and beyond help,' sighs Kayla, waving at Ollie who's gesturing to us to go back into the church. 'We're just coming,' she shouts. 'Don't start without us.'

We only just make it back to our seats before the second half begins with Michaela's note-perfect recital of some of Beethoven's 'Moonlight' sonata. She's incredibly talented and the music sounds lovely, echoing round the church. But she could be playing 'Chopsticks' for all I care. I can't concentrate, and what little concentration I have disappears completely when her recital ends and Josh starts conducting the choir. I can't stop staring at his broad back as he sways gently, feeling the music and marking out the beat.

The rest of the concert passes in a blur of choral singing and audience applause. Hold on. I drag my eyes away from Josh and concentrate on the choir. What are they singing now? The first few chords sound familiar but hard to place, and then I know. It's Mum's favourite song, the one she sang to me, and her mum sang to her when she was growing up: 'The Boy I Love is Up in the Gallery.'

An elderly lady near me starts singing along under her breath and swaying slightly to the music. The song is slower than I remember and a bittersweet feeling fizzes up from my toes when the choir sings, 'But I haven't got a penny so we'll live on love and kisses, And be just as happy as the birds on the tree.' That was me and Mum; no money but lots of love and we were happy, mostly. Tears are dripping off my chin and a woman nearby passes me a tissue without a word. Salt Bay Choral Society singing that song in this church is perfect and squares the circle. It brings Mum home.

Chapter Thirty-Four

I need to know if the choir singing Mum's special song was a coincidence or not but getting Josh on his own after the concert is proving impossible. Members of the audience keep talking to him and saying lovely things about the concert. And they congratulate me, too.

'I wasn't sure if this was a good idea.' Mr James has nabbed another Solero from somewhere and it's dripping over the worn flagstones. 'I thought you were poking your nose in where it wasn't wanted but I have to admit that was very touching.'

'It was a lovely tribute to my Ted and I'm proud of both you and Josh,' says Marion, coming up and putting her arm round my waist. 'I have to go because Lucy and Serena are going out but I wanted to say how good it is to see you again, Annie. I hope we'll see you again soon.' She waves at Josh, who's talking to people in the corner, and bustles out of the church.

'You came back then.' Cyril appears at my shoulder with the plump lady behind him. 'This is my daughter Susan who I told you about.'

Susan steps forward and shakes my hand. 'It was marvellous to see Dad out and about again and singing, too. I'd never have thought it. Thank you for getting him involved, it wasn't good for him stuck in that tiny cottage all day and night. I was worried about him but he's too stubborn to move up and live near me.'

'I can hear you, you know,' says Cyril grumpily, though he doesn't look particularly cross. He shuffles up close. 'I know I can be a crotchety old bugger so thank you for not giving up on me,' he murmurs just loudly enough for me to hear. 'I'll see you at the next rehearsal.'

I need to leave the church after that to have a little cry, which is why I'm now waiting outside for Josh like a groupie at a Justin Bieber gig. Though I might have to rethink my hiding place. Hiding in the shadow of the church tower is obviously not working because people keep waving at me. It doesn't help that a huge moon has risen in the inky sky, lighting up the graveyard with a cool, silvery light that makes skulking rather difficult. And for once, there's not a Cornish cloud in sight. Typical.

I slink further back into the shadows when Pippa and Charlie wander past. They chat excitedly about the concert while I press up tight against the rough stone wall. This is ridiculous. Nabbing Josh in full view would be far more sensible, but I need a private word with him. Hopefully I'll get the chance before I'm arrested for suspicious loitering.

At last, the few remaining members of the choir burst through the church door into the stone porch, laughing and joking. Josh is among them, in shirtsleeves with his jacket slung over his shoulder, and I kick myself for thinking I could get him on his own. This is all a big waste of time but now it's too late to move without being spotted.

'Right then,' says Ollie, linking his arm through Kayla's and pulling her out of the porch. The others follow them along the path. 'Are we all retiring to The Whistling Wave for a well-earned pint? Roger, the drinks are on you, mate.'

'Dream on,' grumbles Roger while I try to stay out of sight, already hot with embarrassment at the thought of being discovered skulking. 'Just 'cos I run a pub doesn't mean I'm made of money.'

'Not if my wages are anything to go by,' shouts Kayla indignantly and everyone cheers when Josh offers to buy the first round. I can add 'generous' to the list of Josh's attributes that are fast outweighing his bad points.

Kayla is closest to me when the group gets nearer and looks so happy, snuggled up to Ollie with her head dipping towards his shoulder. Suddenly she stops dead and gives the side of her head a cartoonish slap. 'Duh! I'm really sorry, Josh, but I think I might have left a window open in the vestry. What am I like?'

Roger groans and carries on walking but Josh turns on his heel towards the church and pulls a large key from his trouser pocket. 'Don't worry, I'll go and check. It won't take a minute.'

'We can come with you,' says Ollie cheerfully.

'No we can't,' insists Kayla. 'I'm desperate for a drink so let's walk on and meet Josh in the Wave, Ollie. Josh won't mind, and that lovely refreshing beer won't drink itself.' The prospect of a pint proves too much for Ollie, who shrugs and allows himself to be led off towards the pub.

'Over to you, Sunshine,' murmurs Kayla out of the corner of her mouth as she passes by. She's got bat-like radar, that one, or she can see in the dark. Either way, she's separated Josh from the rest of the herd and now it's up to me to pounce, if only I didn't feel sick with nerves.

For the next few minutes I shuffle anxiously from foot to foot until the church door slams and Josh walks along the path. He resembles a vampire with moonlight glinting on his black hair and his jacket flowing behind him like a cloak. A dangerous, sexy vampire. Stepping out of the shadows, I stand directly in front of him.

'Josh, can I have a quick word please?'

'Jeez, Annie.' The heavy key falls from his hand and clatters onto the path. 'Not content with almost drowning me, are you trying to give me a heart attack now?'

'I didn't mean to alarm you.'

'Then can I suggest you don't leap out at people in deserted graveyards.' He shakes his head as he picks up the key and drops it into his trouser pocket. 'Are you here to have a go at me for making you conduct the first half? The choir was your idea so it was only right that you took part in the concert. You only had the songs that you knew.'

'I'd have appreciated some warning but no, I don't want to talk about that. I want to know if the last song the choir sang was a coincidence.'

'What are you talking about?' His voice carries in the cool air.

'Was it a coincidence that the choir sang that old music hall song at the end? Only it was my mum's special song.'

Josh smiles. 'Yes, I know.'

'How do you know?'

'You were humming it in the car when I took you back to Alice's one time and you mentioned it was your mum's favourite.'

'But it's ages old and I don't think I said what it was.'

'You didn't.' Josh steps closer. 'But fortunately Miss Arnott's drama club at school was staging an old-time music hall so I recognised it. The song's quite distinctive.' When he takes another step towards me, a fresh tang of cedar wood and lime mingles with the graveyard aroma of damp moss.

'It was lovely of the choir to sing it.'

'Roger was absolutely delighted to be singing about being in love with a bloke.' The corner of Josh's mouth twitches. 'He said he wasn't homophobic but he'd never been that way inclined.'

I grin at the thought of Roger's discomfort. 'Why did you get them to sing that song?'

'For your mum. She had a connection to the choir through her dad, so it seemed appropriate.'

'Even though both of them were dreaded Trebarwiths?'

Josh shrugs and his white shirt gleams in the moonlight. 'I wasn't thinking much about that at the time.' He opens his mouth as though to say more but shakes his head.

'Well, it sounded lovely and I appreciate it, especially as you weren't sure I'd be at the concert to hear it.'

'I didn't think you were ever coming back but it made me feel closer… um,' he trails off, sucking his lower lip between his teeth.

'Made you feel closer to what?'

Josh lets out a weary sigh and his chin drops to his chest. 'To you. Yes, I admit it. I like you, Annie. A lot. God knows why because you're far too London-y.'

'Is that even a word?'

'Probably not. But you're like a breath of fresh air around here. I felt as though I was stagnating, living with my family and back where I grew up, but I'd accepted it and I was OK and then you arrived and churned everything up. But then you were gone again, without a word, back to your real life. And I don't even know for sure what you think of me, after the lies you were fed by Toby. Oh, this is pointless.' He tries to push past me but I place my hand on his arm. Heat radiating through the thin cotton warms my fingers.

'I think quite a lot of you actually,' I whisper, my mouth too dry to get the words out properly.

'Really? Even though I've been so rude about your family? I've been angry for so long,' he says wearily, pulling his arm away from me and dropping his jacket on top of a gravestone. 'It eats me up that Toby is off living his life with no responsibilities while I'm eking out a living with my family and clearing up his mess. Not that we'd want to be without Freya. We love her, but it's hard sometimes.'

'I'm sure it is, and of course you're angry when you're supporting your family and Toby is living it up in London and being such a – such a free spirit.' Which is what I want to be. Oh, come off it, Annie. It's what I wanted to be once; before Alice and the Salt Bay Choral Society, and this difficult, interesting, vulnerable man got under my skin and hinted at a different kind of life. A life with responsibilities and roots, and love that lasts.

I shiver and Josh drapes his jacket over my shoulders, the soft black fabric settling around me like a hug.

He takes a deep breath and says softly, 'When I started having feelings for you – which were terribly inconvenient, I might add – I couldn't get past the fact that you're a Trebarwith and related to Toby. But he left you to drown in the flood while he rescued a damn painting. I couldn't get that out of my mind and the more I've thought about it, the more I've realised that family means nothing to Toby so why should it matter to me? You, he and Alice share a surname but that's all. I've been angry at the wrong people. I'm sorry.'

A bat swoops low over us and up towards the top of the church tower.

'And when I started having feelings for you – which were equally inconvenient, I might add – I couldn't get past the fact that you're tied to Cornwall and I was frightened to think that might happen to me. I know it's ridiculous to be scared of my family but I've never had a proper one before. It was always just me and Mum and we never let anyone else in.'

Josh grabs hold of my hand and holds it against his face. 'I know, but do you think you might take a chance and let me in? I know I can be grouchy and I keep everything locked up inside, and Lord knows you can be incredibly irritating and thoughtless and—'

There's only one way to shut him up. Moving forward until our hips are touching, I stand on tiptoe and press my lips against his. He flinches in surprise but then his arms go round me and we're kissing as if our lives depend on it, among the gravestones of the dead.

'Wait, wait.' I push the palm of my hand into the middle of his chest, breathing heavily.

'What now?' His pupils are so dilated his eyes look black.

'I have trust issues, apparently.'

'Me too,' says Josh drily, giving a sexy smile. 'How about we work on them together?'

We kiss again for ages and it's even better than the first time in Alice's garden. I've never felt like this about anyone and I want the kiss to go on forever but Josh pulls away.

'Oh God,' he says, with a pained expression. 'I suppose I'll spend half my life on the train now, visiting you in London.'

'Would you come to London for me?'

He shudders but grins. 'Yes, I would, because I guess it's not such an awful place if you're in it. For some strange reason, Annabella Sunshine Trebarwith, I want to be wherever you are.' And he smiles down at me with such warmth, my breath catches in my throat.

Slipping my arms round his neck, I press against him and rest my cheek against his. 'That's terribly kind of you but I think I might stay in Salt Bay for a while, to help Alice get back on her feet, and so I can get to know my family.'

'What about your job?'

'There'll be other jobs.'

'What will Toby think?'

'I don't care. We share a surname and that's all.'

A slow smile spreads across Josh's handsome face. 'What changed your mind?'

'You and Alice, the choir, horribly wet Cornwall, all of it. And realising that belonging to people and to places isn't as scary as I thought it was.'

There's more I could say, about having roots and mattering to people who matter to me, but I don't get a chance because Josh's hands are in my hair and he's kissing me like nothing else matters in the whole wide world.

Chapter Thirty-Five

Six weeks later

Josh pulls hard on the wheel and manoeuvres his Mini into a tight parking space near an ancient oak tree with a thick trunk. The leaves are throwing dappled shade across the bonnet and will help to keep the inside cool until we get back. It's still May but Cornwall is having a heatwave and emmets are out in force.

I open my window a crack to help keep the temperature down, though I don't suppose we'll be long. Alice reckons about thirty minutes at the most. Thirty long minutes. I pick a piece of fluff from my smart jeans and wonder whether a skirt might have been more appropriate this morning. A long skirt. And a hat because I couldn't possibly feel more nervous if I was about to have a cuppa with the Queen.

Alice has picked up on my anxious vibes and been quiet all the way to Polrugan, apart from giving Josh directions. Or maybe she's also secretly dreading what we're about to do. That would explain why she wanted to wait a few weeks to do this, until she felt properly up to it. Even though she's recovered remarkably well for an elderly woman with health problems, she seems more fragile these days and I worry about the long-term effects of losing her home. Tregavara House is drying out nicely in the sea breeze but it'll be a while before she can move back in.

Leaning forward, I pat Alice reassuringly on the shoulder and attempt to sound jaunty. 'Here we are at last. Stay where you are and Josh can help you out.'

'Your wish is my command,' says Josh, looking over his shoulder and giving me a wink. 'Stay put, Alice, I won't be a sec.' It's sweet how protective he's been towards Alice since the flood, and he offered to be our taxi service this morning and pick Alice up from Penelope's.

Yes, the elusive Penelope does exist! I've met her several times now Alice has moved into her spare room, and I like her a lot. I expected her to be posh and snooty; a human version of Lady Penelope from *Thunderbirds*. But surprise, surprise, it turns out that judging people purely on their name isn't a terribly good idea. In the flesh, Penelope is short and cuddly with a frizz of grey curls and her untidy house smells of warm bread and an elderly spaniel called Dickens. He's permanently spread-eagled on the living room rug and can hardly be bothered to lift his head to greet visitors. Living for a while with Penelope and Dickens is just what Alice needs to get back on her feet.

'Give me your hand,' commands Josh, opening the passenger door and stooping down to Alice's level. 'And be careful when you're getting out. I've lost count of the number of people who've brained themselves in this car, including me.'

He gives Alice the slow smile that's becoming so familiar and my stomach does a flip. When his friends and family remark that he's smiling far more these days, he says it's because of me. And every time he says it, I kiss him so he's taken to saying it a lot. Especially when we're lying so close in his double bed I can hear his heart beating.

Fortunately his mum has been brilliant about me moving into their cottage until the work at Tregavara House is finished, and I'm slowly getting used to being part of a big family. The lack of personal space takes some getting used to and Serena playing Justin Timberlake at top volume is doing my head in. But the way they all look out for one another and the easy ribbing between them has come as a pleasant surprise. It's what being part of a proper family is all about, I suppose.

After helping Alice, Josh folds the seat forward and holds my hand to help me clamber out of the Mini. His next car is so going to have four doors. And electric windows. And a roof that doesn't leak when it rains.

'Are you sure that you're all right about this, Annabella?' asks Alice, leaning on the walking stick I've persuaded her to start using permanently. The wooden stick is stained lime-green and has parrots painted on it, but Alice was never going to choose something boring.

'Of course, I'm fine. After almost thirty years it's about time I met my grandmother.'

Josh is standing behind me and gently squeezes my shoulder to give me courage. He knows how I'm really feeling because we talked about it as the pale dawn light filtered through his curtains. He knows about the anxiety, anger and guilt that are jumbled up in my head and overshadowing my excitement at finally meeting Sheila – the evil woman I thought was dead who turned out not to be evil at all. Or dead, for that matter.

Alice frowns at me. 'And you're all right with us not telling Sheila who you are.'

'Yes, I understand. Please don't worry.'

'She doesn't always know me these days and I can't remember the last time she mentioned your mother. When I've tried to remind her about Joanna she gets distressed, though I'm not sure whether that's because she remembers, or because she can't. It wouldn't be fair.'

'I know, Alice. We'll play this however you think is best.'

'Talking of which,' interrupts Josh, 'I'll wait here for you two and meet Sheila another day. Meeting a grandmother for the first time is special and just for Trebarwiths. You don't need a Pasco sticking his nose in.' Sliding his arm round my waist, he pulls me in close and murmurs, 'Is that OK? Like we decided this morning?'

When I nod, he puts his hand under my chin and gently tilts my face before kissing me on the mouth. Josh always closes his eyes when he kisses me, even brief out-in-public kisses. I know this because I've been opening my eyes a fraction to check; not because I'm some sort of kissing-police weirdo but because Stuart always kept his eyes wide open and look how that turned out. The cheating swine was probably checking there wasn't someone more fanciable nearby.

But everything feels more 'right' with Josh, from kissing to, well, other things, and Alice says we're made for one another. Mind you, she approves of anything that keeps me in Cornwall so she'll be cock-a-hoop about the local job interviews I've got lined up. The first is for an accountancy firm needing secretarial support which sounds solid if boring, but I've set my heart on the second interview. That's for a role as PA to the chief exec of a charity providing music sessions for people with disabilities. I can do everything on the job spec so fingers crossed, and I might mention that Josh and I are running Salt Bay Choral Society together. I could always tell the chief exec how the choir and its music helped bring me and Josh together, though that's probably what Amber would call 'TMI' – too much information.

'Are you ready then?' Alice brings my thoughts back to what I have to do first. She hooks her arm through mine and we walk slowly along the gravel path to Celandine House. The care home looks imposing from the road, with high stone walls and a tall metal gate painted shiny black. But the building itself is softer with curves and bay windows and a bright blue front door with a ramp leading up to it. There are palm trees in huge terracotta pots on either side of the ramp and their long fronds are swishing in the breeze. We're further inland here but the air still tastes of salt.

Alice rings the doorbell while I glance at Josh, who's leaning against his car near the dent that's a permanent reminder of how we met. Isn't it funny how something seemingly insignificant can change the course of your life so completely? All it took was one small stone, one bad mood and one surprisingly accurate throw. Josh smiles reassuringly at me and puts his thumb up while I feel grateful for my good fortune.

Alice rings the bell again and, after a minute or two, the door is opened by a stout woman with pink apple-cheeks and the vaguest hint of a moustache. She gives a wide grin and beckons for us to come inside.

'How are you now, Mrs Gowan? And how is your poor house doing? I read about it in the paper.'

'It's a bit of a mess but everything can be mended, thank you Maria. Annabella is overseeing the clean-up and I should be able to move back in before too long.' Alice pauses to write our names and the time in the visitors' book on the hall table. 'How is Sheila today?'

'Oh you know, much the same,' says Maria, eyeing me curiously. 'She was in one of her anxious states yesterday and very confused but she's calmer today and she ate a decent breakfast. The last time I saw her she was in the Garden Room.'

While Alice and Maria are chatting about Sheila, I take a good look round. The hallway is elegant and high-ceilinged with white plaster cornicing and a picture rail. But there's no disguising we're in a care home. Charts and checklists on the walls are a giveaway, including a laminated sheet informing visitors that the latest CQC inspection awarded a 'good' rating. All the rooms leading off the hall have fire doors and there's a faint acrid smell of urine overlaid with pine disinfectant. Staff are busying about in bottle-green tabards and an elderly man wanders past with his coat on although it's hot indoors. He's wearing a natty fedora hat which he tips at me before he disappears round a corner.

'Follow me, Annabella.' Alice bids goodbye to Maria and leads me through the hall, past a lift and into a bright room with lemon-painted walls. Comfy chairs with brown cushions are lined up around the edges of the room and there are double-glazed French doors in the end wall, leading into a small garden.

Residents are sitting on benches outside enjoying the sunshine but Alice makes a beeline for the far corner of the room where a woman is sitting hunched over and alone. A multicoloured crochet blanket is draped over her knees in spite of warm air from outside wafting through the open French windows.

'Sheila, how are you? It's Alice here to see you.' Alice bends to kiss the woman on the cheek before smoothing white hair from the woman's forehead. So this is Sheila. This is my grandmother. However many times I say it in my head, it doesn't seem real. Sheila smiles up at Alice, like you'd smile at a kind stranger who's just wandered in, while I hang back.

'Come and sit down, dear.' Alice sinks heavily into a chair and points at the chair on the other side of my grandmother. 'Sheila, this is my friend, Annabella. And how are you doing?' She rubs Sheila's knee through the blanket. 'Are you keeping well?'

'Very well, thank you.' Sheila looks at Alice and tilts her head to one side as though trying to place her.

'Do you remember me, Sheila? You came to live with us at Tregavara House when you married my brother, Samuel.'

A flash of recognition flares in Sheila's hazel eyes but is almost immediately extinguished.

'How is Samuel?' she asks politely.

'Samuel is fine,' says Alice quietly while I wonder whether forgetting your husband and child is preferable to the pain of remembering you've lost them.

'Who is this?' Sheila stares directly at me, ignoring two women in tabards who hurry past towards the sound of a bell ringing deep in the heart of the house.

'This is my friend who's going to be staying with me at Tregavara House.'

'My name is Annabella and it's lovely to meet you at last.' Sheila's hands are resting in her lap. I put my hand on hers and our eyes meet properly for the first time. She looks like my mum, or at least how Mum would have looked if she'd had the chance to age. They share the same snub nose and fine hair, and the almond-shaped eyes that Alice doesn't have but I do. I suppose this is how I'll look in fifty-five years' time. Sheila pulls her hand away and leans her head back against the chair as though she's tired.

I'm not sure what one says to a long-lost grandmother so I keep quiet while Alice chats. But though Sheila listens and smiles when Alice talks to her, she seems to be somewhere else in her head, somewhere she can't be reached. News about the aftermath of the flood is greeted without a flicker and she doesn't react when Alice explains that I'll be staying with her when the house is repaired, and Emily will be moving in too.

We did think of telling Emily there was no longer a job for her, now that I'm moving back in. But we've grown rather fond of kind, other-worldly Emily so she'll look after Alice as planned while I go out to work. I'm not sure I have the patience to be a full-time carer so it makes sense. Until then Emily's been chucked in the deep end with a temporary job at The Whistling Wave. Roger took some persuading that 'odd Emily' could manage behind the bar, and he'll be on my case if she messes up. But she needs to fill the gap until she moves into Tregavara House and maybe dealing with Roger's punters will build up her confidence and be good for her.

It's definitely good for Kayla, who's heading off on an extended holiday Down Under with Ollie in tow.

'I intend to show him off to my family and especially to my sisters, the Smug Marrieds,' she told me with a wink, chucking another tiny bikini into her suitcase. 'They settled for boring, stick-thin accountants while I've got my very own rugby god with thighs to die for. Let's see if they think I'm the weird one now.' I'm going to miss her.

Ouch! Sheila has grabbed my arm and is digging her fingers into my skin, and I'd guess it's some time since she had her nails trimmed.

'Are you all right, Sheila?' asks Alice, concerned about the change in her sister-in-law who's pulled herself up straight in her chair. Her eyes are different; more focused and alert. It's as though someone has flicked a switch and she's back.

Ignoring Alice, Sheila lets go of my arm – thank goodness – but grasps hold of my hand instead and raises it to her face. She holds my palm against the wrinkled skin on her cheek and breathes heavily. Her grip is remarkably strong for an old lady.

Sheila's lips are moving though it's hard to make out the words because she's speaking so quietly. But then I understand.

'Joanna,' whispers Sheila, looking at me intently. 'My darling Joanna. You came back to me. You came home.'

Alice makes a strangled sound and I realise that she's crying. I'm blubbing too and big fat tears plop off our chins while Sheila beams at me in delight. But the moment is passing, Sheila's memories are beginning to fade and her eyes become unfocused as she retreats back into her own world. I hope with all my heart that it's a wonderful world where she's standing with her daughter on the beach in Salt Bay, while seagulls wheel above them and a salty wind blows through their hair.

And now it's my world too. I look at lovely Alice who's dabbing at her face with a handkerchief and think of the kind, strong man waiting for me outside. Next week Salt Bay Choral Society will begin rehearsals for Charlie and Pippa's wedding, and Josh and I will wander hand in hand to Tregavara House afterwards to check on my family home. This is what belonging feels like and there's nowhere else I'd rather be.

'Yes,' I say, stroking the back of Sheila's hand. 'I came back to you. I came home.'

A Letter From Liz

Well, the book's written and this is the extra-special part for me where I get the chance to thank you for reading it. I really hope you've enjoyed getting to know Annie and following her struggle to settle in Cornwall with Alice. And with Josh, of course, who (you might have gathered) looks rather like a mixture of Aidan Turner and Richard Armitage. That's how I see him anyway. If he's different in your head, that's fine. Just so long as he's gorgeous.

If you did enjoy reading *Annie's Holiday by the Sea,* I'd be incredibly grateful if you could spend just a few minutes posting a review. I can't wait to hear what you think, and your views might help persuade new readers to spend time in Salt Bay. It's only a small village but the more visitors the merrier!

If you'd like to get in touch, you can also contact me through Facebook, Twitter or Instagram where I'm often loitering. I know I should be writing but I'm far too easily distracted by social media. In my defence, a writer's life can be lonely so it's great to catch up with old friends and make new ones – and whose day isn't improved by GIFs of cats in party hats?

I've had that much fun in Salt Bay I don't want to leave. So, I'm writing a new book about what Annie, Josh and the Salt Bay Choral Society get up to next. I can't give too much away but I promise it'll be

Christmassy with lots more surprises for Annie as she adjusts to life in the wilds of wonderful Cornwall. If you use the link below and sign up to my mailing list, I can let you know when it's published later this year.

Until then, thank you again and happy reading!

www.bookouture.com/liz-eeles/

: @lizeelesauthor

: lizeelesauthor/

: lizeelesauthor

Acknowledgements

Annie's Holiday by the Sea would never have been written or published without the support of some very special people.

My heartfelt thanks to the talented team at Bookouture for making my writing dreams come true, and to fairy godmother Kirsty Greenwood who first brought me and Bookouture together. I've been pinching myself ever since. It's been my good fortune to work with editors Emily Ruston and Abigail Fenton during the exciting (and slightly scary for a debut author) publication process, and my book is all the better for their astute advice and encouragement.

I'm indebted to my lovely family and friends for their unwavering support. In particular, northern goddess Sue Becker who went above and beyond as First Reader/Chief Cheerleader. And my wonderful mum and dad, Margaret and Ivor Eeles, who first sparked my love of Cornwall when they took me and my brothers there for family holidays. I have joyful memories of sitting on Perranuthnoe Beach in my plastic mac, making sandcastles – which proves that Cornwall is always magical, even in the rain.

Huge thanks also to the choirs I've belonged to over the years for giving me the opportunity to help make marvellous music.

Finally, I'd be lost without my husband Tim who gave me the time and chance to pursue my writing dreams. In return I introduced him to the genre of romantic comedy, which wasn't quite as genteel as he'd imagined. To Sam and Ellie, who make everything worthwhile, I'd just like to say: hey kids, your stressy mum has written a proper book!

Made in the USA
Middletown, DE
17 February 2020

84938256R00188